# The Uprising

T.H. Hernandez

T.H. Hernandez
http://thhernandez.com

This is a work of fiction. Names, characters, places, and incidents are a product of the author's imagination. Locales and public names are sometimes used for atmospheric purposes. Any resemblance to actual people, living or dead, or to businesses, companies, events, institutions, or locales is completely coincidental.

Cover Art © 2016 by Mark Sgarbossa (www.popgroovy.com)
Interior Graphics © 2016 by Suzanne C. Walker (http://pajamapress.com)
Edited by Barbara Trageser and E.J. Hernandez

Ordering Information:
Quantity sales. Special discounts are available on quantity purchases by corporations, schools, associations, and others. For details, send an email to the above account with the subject line of "Bulk Discount."

The Ruins / T.H. Hernandez. -- 1st ed.

Library of Congress Cataloging-in-Publication Data is available

ISBN 978-0-9908688-6-6

*To Mom and Dad, for everything.*

# Contents

# Book 1 – The Union

## 100 Years After the Second U.S. Civil War

*"When you walk in purpose, you collide with destiny."*

—RALPH BUCHANAN

# Gloominess

*Evan*

fter two weeks in the Northwestern Province, I loathe the color gray. Everything is colorless, from the clouds to the rain. Even the buildings have a sickly gray cast to them without the bright rays of the sun to liven them up.

I turn from the window with a heavy sigh and take a seat on the exam table to wait for Dr. Martinez.

My mood is as gray and gloomy as everything else up here, although I have no one to blame but myself. By now, Cyrus suspects Bryce and I have been intimate. I'm sure he's figured out that's what I was trying to tell him, the thing he said he didn't need to know.

I've tried talking to him a dozen times, but he refuses. He's sullen and withdrawn the way he was in the Ruins over the summer when he found out Bryce was looking for me.

A thread of uneasiness pulls at the delicate fabric of my friendships, and I'm not sure what to do about it. Not being able to discuss it with Cyrus isn't helping. The way he's pulled away from me is like a knife in my gut to go along with the gunshot wound in my shoulder.

The door to my exam room opens and Dr. Martinez enters, crossing the room with a warm smile. "Good morning, Miss Taylor, how are you doing?"

"Okay, I guess. Can I get out of here now?"

"You're not enjoying our 'liquid sunshine'?"

"That's what you call it?"

He chuckles and lifts my shirt to examine where a bullet tore through my shoulder less than a month ago. He runs his hands lightly over the skin before pressing harder.

I suck in a breath and jerk away from his touch.

So far he hasn't commented on my Uprising tattoo. No one has tattoos in the Union. They're considered unnatural and unclean, in direct conflict with the Union way of life. But when you join the Uprising, the first thing they do is mark you as one of theirs.

"It's healing nicely. I do good work." Dr. Martinez moves around the table to face me, all humor fading. "I'm concerned with the level of pain you're experiencing. I can insert another implant, but there might be more side effects."

"Like what?"

"Drowsiness, nausea, and brain fog are the most common, but they should fade in a few days as your system adjusts."

For a couple of days after he inserted the first one I couldn't think straight and fell asleep in the middle of dinner. I need a clear head if we're going to be making plans to stop the Uprising.

"I'm okay."

"I beg to differ. You couldn't even handle a gentle probing of the area surrounding the wound."

"You call that gentle?"

He glances at me out of the top of his eyes before tapping something into his tablet. "The threaded bullet I dug out of you shattered your shoulder. I put it back together, but you still need time to heal. Your body is too stressed to recover properly when you're in this much pain."

I roll my eyes. "Fine."

He reaches out to shake my hand. "Amy will be in shortly to inject the implant." His mouth tightens into a line. "I really hope I don't see you again."

"Same here. And thanks...for everything."

## *Cyrus*

Hot showers, beds that conform to my body, soft clothes, public transportation — there's a shitload of stuff to love about the Union, but by far my favorite is the beach. I never tire of watching the ocean, struggling to understand it, the way it seems to go on forever. Standing here, feeling the coarse sand beneath my feet and the cool mist on exposed skin, helps me think.

Like an idiot, I figured nothing else mattered as long as Evan and I were together, but every damn thing matters. It's not safe to stay here, and it's not safe to return to the Ruins. Not that she'd even agree to that. Hell, I don't know what she wants. We barely talk and I know that's mostly on me. I can't pretend her sleeping with that douche doesn't piss me off. I want to punch something every time I see him, which is pretty much every fucking day.

"Figured I'd find you here," Rainey's raspy voice comes from behind me.

I grit my teeth and turn to face her. "Hey."

"It's beautiful, isn't it?"

"Yeah. Never thought I'd see the ocean, now I can't seem to leave."

She's quiet for a few moments, staring out at the crashing waves. I've stared at them for plenty of hours myself, now I stare at her. She's pretty, in a rough sort of way. The scar running from her ear to her jaw only enhances her looks. But she's not someone you'd ever want to mess with.

"Quit staring at me."

I turn back to the water. "Sorry."

"Colin went with her. You know, in case you were wondering."

"Not really." I wasn't, only because I chose not to think about it. But if it'd been Bryce, I'd have needed to pound something.

"Are you going to punish her forever?"

Dragging my gaze away from the surf, I glare at her. "You don't know what you're talking about."

Her eyebrows go up. "Really? You two were this sappy sweet, gag-inducing couple until her ex showed up. Now you're always in a foul mood, and you barely talk to the girl you supposedly gave up everything to follow."

"Fine, I don't like the guy, never have. Why the hell is he here again?"

"We need everyone if we have any hope of doing what you're planning. We can't send him packing because he got naked and horizontal with your girl."

If Rainey wasn't a girl, I'd have no problem decking her, but she is, so I walk down to the water to get away from her.

Whatever went on between Evan and the douchebag was before she joined the Uprising, but it's more than that. It's everything. She had no idea what she was getting herself into and no plan to get out. She nearly got herself killed.

She's impulsive and reckless, and I don't know if I can deal with that.

The one thing that sucks about the beach is the sand. It gets everywhere and the salty air coats my skin with a sticky film.

When I get back to the room, I shower before throwing on a fresh pair of jeans. I towel off my hair with one hand and open the bathroom door with the other.

Simon glances up from packing. "Hey, we're leaving. Rainey came by when you were in the shower. Everyone's meeting downstairs in five minutes."

"Okay."

I pull on a T-shirt and cram what little I have, the stuff Evan's dad bought me, into my duffel bag and follow Simon.

My eyes are immediately drawn to her leaning against the wall on the opposite side of the lobby. Her head rests on a support pillar while she talks to Rainey. The tightness in her features tells me she's still in pain. Pain inflicted by a bullet the night I tried to get her out of the Uprising camp.

It's another reminder of how close I came to losing her and how dangerous her impulsiveness is. I should go home, head back out to the Ruins, so I don't have to watch another person I love die.

But I can't, not until I know she's safe.

Even if it kills me.

I cross the long marble floor, never taking my eyes off her until she turns toward me, her gaze connecting with mine. She stands a little straighter and lifts her head.

Rainey's words from the beach about forgiving her push their way into my brain. At least until the elevator dings behind me and the douchebag's voice carries across the lobby. My shoulders tense, and I reach down to snag Evan's bag before he can, slinging it over my shoulder, and head outside.

The cold air bites through my thin shirt, but I packed my jacket. I'm leading the way with no clue where I'm going, but it's not like I'm going to admit that. Under the pretense of fishing out my jacket, I step to the side, letting the others pass.

Block after block, we make our way past tall buildings, watching us through mirrored window eyes. I miss the openness of the Ruins.

Colin turns a corner and leads us down an alley to a set of stairs. We hike up two flights and exit the stairwell onto a packed platform with a glass barrier overlooking the Union on one side and a brick wall on the other. Two elevated rails run down the middle, disappearing into the distance in either direction.

Despite the abundance of sweaty bodies, the air is fresh up here, like a mixture of ocean breezes and wildflowers. The wide platform is scattered with large potted pine trees, although that scent doesn't make it into the mix for some reason. Above the din of hundreds of voices, I can make out birds, but there aren't any here. The Union tries too hard to seem like it's a part of nature.

A body brushes past, bumping into me. "Sorry," a harried girl calls over her shoulder before stopping briefly to size me up. Her lips twist up in a quick appreciative smile before she turns and rushes off.

She's the kind of girl I would have chased before Evan. Now...I have no clue what the hell I want.

"Here," Colin says, shoving something in my hand.

I glance down at a cardboard rectangle with the number forty-seven stamped on it.

"Your boarding pass," he says.

I stuff it in my back pocket and head over to the windows overlooking the Union. The beach is twenty-five miles away, and I can see the darker shadow of ocean sitting beneath a cloud-covered sky. Between here and the coast, buildings and parks move down and away from me like giant steps.

Looking up at it from the sand, it seems less imposing than it does from the Ruins. Out there, the Union is nothing but a solid wall more than a hundred stories tall. You'd never guess what's on the other side.

The voices grow louder, and I turn to see a long white train pulling into the station, gliding along one of the rails. It's shiny and clean, cutting a smooth path like a bird through the air, hissing as it pulls to a stop.

The others step forward to queue up, and I follow as Rainey herds Evan to the back of line, about a dozen people behind me. I give a brief thought to joining them, but I'm not sure what I'd say if I did. Instead, I board behind Bryce and follow him to the back of the car.

He takes a seat, scooting over to the window, his gaze cutting my way before shifting beyond me. I'm tempted to sit next to him just to keep Evan from sitting there, but I'd probably end up decking him in the first five minutes, so I keep going, finding another pair of empty seats.

I slide over, too, although I don't know why, it's not like Evan will sit with me. She tried talking to me, but I was too pissed after I saw Bryce in the hotel lobby that morning. I couldn't even look at her without blowing up. The longer we've gone without talking about it, the harder it is to say anything at all.

Evan glances at Bryce, then me, before lifting her chin in that little defiant way she has and keeps going.

Simon plops down next to me, and Rainey sits with Bryce. *Traitor.*

"Ever been on a train before?" Simon asks.

"Nope."

"They're cool. They go super fast."

He's not kidding. The train pulls away from the station without so much as a jerk and quickly picks up speed. Soon shit's flying by outside the window so fast, my stomach rolls.

"You're gettin' kinda green," Simon says. "It's weird at first, but ya gotta look farther out instead of the stuff close to us. Then it's not so bad."

I take in a deep breath and focus on the coastline. He's right, it doesn't affect me as much.

Sighing, I lean my head back against the seat and wonder, again, what the hell I'm even doing here.

# Doubts

*Evan*

The soft hum of the ventilation system and low murmur of voices invade my dreams, dragging me back to consciousness. Sitting up, I try to shake the painkiller-induced grogginess enveloping me. My tongue is parched, like a sponge left in the sun too long. Something wet brushes against my cheek. My right lapel. Lovely. Apparently I drooled all over myself. This day just keeps getting better and better.

The train rolls to a stop and I nudge a still-sleeping Colin. His eyes flutter open. "Oh, hey EvTay." He narrows his eyes, his lips pulling into a smirk as he points to the corner of my mouth. "You've got a little spit there."

I wipe my jaw on my coat sleeve and stand, stretching while I wait for the passengers blocking the aisle to move. Loopiness aside, I feel better, and reach for my bag as I pass Cyrus.

He snatches it before I can get a hand on it and slings it over his shoulder, shooting a quick glance over at Bryce.

I roll my eyes. He may be mad at me, but he's not going to let Bryce win whatever pissing match they're engaged in.

Bryce leads the way through the terminal and out to the sidewalk where brilliant sunshine bounces off gleaming stucco buildings sporting crimson tile roofs. Gnarled limbs of wisteria wrap up trellises, draping blossoms of lavender and white. Soft petals float to the clay tiles below like snowflakes dancing around our ankles. Even though I didn't live here long, it's like coming home after spending so much time in the soggy northwest.

We traipse single-file through the borough like some sort of deranged parade, to the nearest commuter terminal. The plan is to head straight to the beach and check in with Jack and Lisa.

When we get off the commuter train, I pull Colin aside. "Hey, I'll meet you guys down there. I'm going to stop by Eddie's first."

"I don't know, Ev, we agreed to stay together."

"It's a short detour. I'll be fine."

He walks up to the others, and a heated discussion breaks out between Colin, Cyrus, and Bryce. Wild gesturing leads to stiff shoulders and a few gazes narrowed in my direction before Bryce stalks off and Colin returns to my side.

"We're gonna walk you to Eddie's, but Eddie has to escort you down to the beach after," Colin says.

"Fine."

I text Eddie that we're on our way and follow my friends the two blocks to his apartment. My dad throws open the massive front door before anyone has a chance to knock. Pushing past everyone else, he wraps me in a bear hug, lifting me off the ground.

"It's good to see you," he says, voice choked.

Liam and Quinn rush outside as Eddie sets me down. Quinn bypasses me and jumps straight into Bryce's arms while Liam grabs his hand. "Did you shoot any bad guys today?"

"Again with this?" I ask Liam.

I catch the grim set to Cyrus's mouth out of the corner of my eye. Yeah, so he's never met my younger half-siblings, and it's pretty clear Bryce has not only met them, but that they love him. I steal another glance Cyrus's way, noting the tenseness in his jaw and shoulders, but there's not much I can do about it. This is just another reminder that Bryce and I share a different history than the one I share with him.

The kids have both changed so much over the past few months. Quinn is taller and her words are more sure. Liam, too, but the changes in him are more subtle.

Eager to ease some of the tension, I throw my arms wide. "What? No one cares their big sister is home?"

They abandon Bryce to hug me.

"These are my friends," I say, hoping that's still true for all of them. "This is Rainey, Simon, and Cyrus. And this is my brother, Liam, and my sister, Quinn."

Liam studies the three of them, hazel eyes narrowed, his gaze landing on Rainey's scar. "What happened to your face?"

"Liam!" I yell.

People in the Union don't usually have scars since they're so easily fixed, although a few wear them like badges of honor, permanent reminders of a stupid prank someone dared them to do.

"It's okay," Rainey says. I gotta admit, I'm curious about the scar myself. "I got into a fight and fell through a window."

"Cool," Liam says, voice laced with awe.

Quinn is staring at Cyrus, but if he notices, he doesn't let on. She approaches him with slow steps, as if he's a butterfly on a flower in the park. Stopping at his feet, she stares up at him, blinking her pretty blue eyes. He grins, and it's the first smile I've seen on him in weeks. How I've missed that smile. When he squats down to her level, she reaches out and touches his whiskers. His smile grows, making my heart stumble in my chest. I'd give anything for that expression directed at me.

A lilting voice coming from behind me draws my attention. I turn and see a stunning woman on the front porch wiping her hands on one of Eddie's orange kitchen towels.

She makes her way to Bryce, throwing her arms around him. "Good to see you, baby brother."

*What. The. Hell?*

She releases Bryce and walks over to Eddie, glancing up at him with pale gray eyes. His hand slides around her waist as if it belongs there.

"Evan this is Talia. Talia, this is my daughter, Evan."

She reaches out her light brown hand to shake mine. "It's truly a pleasure to meet you, Evan. I've heard so much about you." Her voice sounds the way honey tastes.

"How..." I say when I find my voice, then stop, realizing I'm being rude. "It's nice to meet you."

"When you texted you all were on your way, I made lunch," Talia says, ignoring my inappropriateness. "Come inside and eat."

I know I've been a little sponge-brained lately, but I can't be the only one having an existential crisis over my dad dating Bryce's sister. Can I?

After my friends head down to the beach and Talia takes the kids to get ice cream, quiet settles over the apartment like a feather floating to the floor. Leaning against the back of the couch, I stare at my biological father, struggling to wrap my head around his new girlfriend.

"How? When?" I ask, gesturing toward the door where Talia just exited.

He scrubs a hand across his face. "I met her when we were trying to figure out what happened to you."

"So you decided to start dating my ex-boyfriend's sister? Isn't she a little young?"

He cuts his eyes to me and moves his lips as if he's rolling a marble around in his mouth. "I don't think my love life is really yours to judge. That said, she's ten years older than Bryce and only seven years younger than me."

This is all so insane. But then what in my life isn't these days?

"Well this is gonna make family holidays awkward."

"Contrary to what you may think, I'm not trying to ruin your life."

"No," I mutter, "there's a madman running around doing that for you."

"Speaking of…I've been in touch with Captain Jackson, and you still need to stay off the grid. You'll all be safer if they believe you're still out in the Ruins."

"Yeah, we figured as much. Does he know anything more?"

Eddie nods. "The memo was tracked to a guy by the name of Walker."

I think I always knew he was behind the memo, but hearing his name doesn't help. "So can't Max arrest him?"

"He hasn't been able to locate him."

Of course not, because that would be too easy. I toy with telling Eddie about Walker's involvement in the Uprising, but I don't think that information will make him feel any better.

Eddie walks around to the front of the couch and sits, patting the seat next to him. "How are you feeling?"

I move to join him. "Okay. The doctor had another implant put in. It's making it hard to think, but it helps with the pain. And then…" I pause wondering if I want to say more. Maybe it's the drugs, but I decide to go for it. "Cyrus is pretty pissed at me. About Bryce, I mean. I didn't tell him Bryce was in the northwest, and I think he's figured out what went on with us, but he won't discuss it. I wanted to explain, but he said it didn't matter. And now…I think he might be done with me. That hurts a lot more than my shoulder, and the drugs don't fix that." Wow, I upchucked a load there.

Eddie sits back, his arms coming out to rest on the back cushion. "I got to know Cyrus while we were up north waiting for you to wake up. He's got a good head on his shoulders, and he cares for you very much."

"He won't even talk to me though. How can I fix things?"

"I don't know if this is something you fix like a pair of torn jeans. You need to work through it. I don't know what all went down with you two, but I can tell you if that boy was done with you, he wouldn't still be here."

A small flicker of hope tickles my belly. That makes sense. This isn't his fight with the Uprising, it's mine. I remind myself of all the things he said to me in the hospital before Bryce showed up.

"I think…no, I know he's mad at me, and I'd be hurt and angry, too, if I was in his shoes." I stare at my hands twisting in my lap. "I mean, I heard about this girl he was hooking up with up there, but I didn't have to see her. She wasn't there every day." With a sigh, I lift my gaze to my dad's. "I don't know how we can get past this. Part of me thinks there's so much to do, maybe it doesn't matter right now…but I need things to be right between us. I'm lost without him."

Eddie shakes his head. "You're not, honey, trust me, but I know he means a great deal to you. Recognizing your role in all of this is the first step in figuring it out."

"So you're not going to tell me what to do?"

He gives me a wry grin. "Even if I had the answer, this is something you need to figure out on your own."

"Yeah, you're probably right."

His eyes widen in mock surprise. "What? You actually think I'm right about something? I should record this or no one will believe me."

I roll my eyes.

He smiles. "You've grown up so much in the past year. I've always been proud of you, but you are becoming a responsible young woman. Someone your sister will grow up wanting to emulate."

We've both come a long way over the years. He was never around when I was younger, so my stepdad, Joe, was the father I went to for advice. Once Eddie showed up ready to be a parent, I was too angry to let him step into that role. It's taken a lot for us to get to this place in our relationship.

Somewhere over these past few years, I guess we both grew up.

## Cyrus

Seagulls screech above the ocean roar, and the briny air slams into me like a wall. Everyone else took a transport out to the campground, but I needed the walk. Unis spend far too much time not using their bodies. What the hell do they do with all that pent-up energy?

I take a seat on a stone bench on the boardwalk and untie my shoes, slipping them off along with my socks, and toss them in my bag.

It's much warmer here than up north thanks to the sun. Sun I thought might not exist at the coast. I hoist my duffel over my shoulder and grab Evan's bag, making the trek across the sand to the others, gathered beside a large tent.

I peek in, because I can't help myself, and it's nicer on the inside than most homes in the Ruins. A huge light with dangling crystals hangs from the ceiling, casting rainbows on the white canvas walls. A polished wooden counter stretches the length of the tent, and several people with nothing better to do laugh with the guy standing behind it.

A pretty blonde next to a douchebag-looking dude stands close to Bryce. The girl eyes me and smiles, showing me a row of straight gleaming teeth. The guy tips his chin at me, only furthering my assumption of his douchy-ness.

He reaches out to shake. "Jack."

I nod, my hands full of duffel bags, and he drops his arm back to his side.

"Cyrus," I say.

The girl's smile broadens. "I'm Lisa." I swear her words bounce.

"I've heard a lot about you," I say with another nod. "Both of you."

Jack turns and heads toward a couple of tents, gripping Lisa's hand in his. She keeps turning and glancing at me over her shoulder, making me wonder exactly what she's heard about me.

We stop in front of a large tent. "You guys are in here," Jack says.

Simon pushes his way forward, going inside. "I'll take this one," he says, tossing his bag onto one of two cots.

I follow him in and set mine on the other and heft Evan's bag, wondering where she's staying.

Rainey slides up next to me and grabs the beige canvas duffel from me. "I got it."

Lisa yelps from outside the tent. "Evan's on her way. I'll go get her."

I duck back outside just in time to see her traipsing off through loose sand, her gait like a sloppy drunk. My gaze follows her until she becomes a small dot on the boardwalk, but even from here I can make out her squeals as she greets Evan.

With a sigh, I turn and head back into my tent to settle in.

# Settling In

## Cyrus

different atmosphere takes over as we eat dinner, one less tense than earlier. Maybe adding Jack and Lisa to the mix changed things. Or maybe it's me avoiding Bryce. Whatever it is, it's welcomed.

The air cools as sunset approaches, but it's still comfortable enough to sit outside. Evan sits between Colin and Lisa, far away from the jackass across from me. I cut him a few glares, and he glares right back. Guess he doesn't like me either.

"Hey can you pass the rolls?" Simon asks around a mouthful of salmon.

Rainey reaches in front of me to grab the rolls and shoves them over to Simon.

I bite into my first burger, and juicy, charbroiled meat hits my tongue. *Damn.* I might've just found something in the Union better than hot showers. Shit this is good. For a few minutes, I don't think about my girlfriend sleeping with dickhead and instead focus on the best food I've ever eaten.

After dinner, we head over to an isolated concrete ring on the beach with a roaring fire. I drop down to the sand and lean back against a log, closing my eyes, letting the warmth of the flames lick my face.

Colin tells the others what he and Evan were up to since they parted ways. I've already heard all this from Evan so my attention wanders. Other fires burn up and down the beach, each with their own campers gathered around. Snapping sparks chase after the smoke climbing up into the night.

Evan's voice draws me back to our group and the conversation at hand. "So, anyway, we joined the Uprising. I thought we could learn about their plans from within, but they don't really tell the recruits anything."

Her statement only reinforces her habit of doing shit without first thinking it through. Listening to Rainey fill in some details, I discover in addition to not having a plan to get out, they didn't even know how to join up without raising suspicions. If I didn't already know it before, now I'm sure there's no way I can leave her on her own.

"So what about you?" Colin asks, and it takes me a second to realize he's talking to me. "How'd you end up as our camp commander?"

I take a deep breath and launch into my story. "After parting ways at the footbridge, we hiked northeast for a week before hiring a ride. We rode for another week, walked some more, and eventually ended up at a town near the border where we could lay low for a while. Not long after we settled in, I hooked up with a group of people from the Northern Territories. They liked to drink and talk and were soon sharing stories about the Uprising."

I skip over the part where I met Simon and decided to find Evan. "Over the summer, my brother thought joining the Uprising might be the best way to find out what they were up to. Based on what I learned from my new friends, the only way to learn anything valuable was to be a leader. Armed with a little insider information, I aced training camp. That, coupled with the fact that I had no family or other attachments and a convincing story of my hatred for the Union, I was fast tracked for leadership, making assistant commander in record time."

I spend some time explaining about the Uprising, the role of the Mexican cartels, and how I was transferred to another camp when I was promoted to commander. "I definitely gained useful intel, but the things I had to do and oversee made me wonder if I could stick it out. Turns out a buddy of mine was a leader at the new camp, a guy named Mateo. He's a hired gun without any loyalty to the Uprising, and what was going on didn't sit right with him either."

I lean forward, resting my forearms on my knees. "He came to me with a proposal on my first day to end the Hole, a disturbing practice of isolating children underground to force compliance. We switched from punishing recruits to rewarding desired behavior, and Mateo began replacing the sentries' bone-drilling ammunition with blanks. Neither of us could understand the logic behind shooting scared kids who just wanted to go home."

"Wow," Lisa says, turning toward me with an expression of awe.

I'm not sure how to process that or what to say.

Thankfully Colin saves me. "What about you?" he asks Lisa. "What've you two been up to?

Jack leans back and stretches his arm across the log. "We kept doing what we were doing before you left. We met with my dad every couple days, but he wasn't coming up with much either. I was getting frustrated."

"Someone care to fill in us latecomers?" Rainey says.

"Oh, sorry," Lisa says. "Jack's dad's a detective, too. I guess I figured Bryce told you all this by now."

"Some, but not all. Okay, I think I got it now. Go on," Rainey says with a wave of her hand.

"We spent months searching for any lead we could follow, even ones that led to dead ends, but there was nothing, which was weird. Nothing could be that clean without very careful planning. But then I stopped looking for a connection and instead started observing everything, and we began to see stuff."

"What kinda stuff?" Colin asks, leaning forward to peer around Evan.

"We'd been trying to find Walker or anyone connected to him but kept coming up empty. So I switched it up and looked for anything that seemed off, putting aside for a moment Walker was the target."

"Huh?" Evan says, her eyebrows drawing together.

"Let's say you're looking for a guy with blue shoes. You watch for blue shoes, but you see guys with shoes in every color except blue. And that's strange because surely at least one person is going to be wearing blue shoes, right? The fact that no one's wearing blue shoes is a sign something's wrong. So you stop looking for blue shoes and just observe people. Before long, you realize the guy you've been looking for is there, but he's not wearing blue shoes, he's wearing a shirt that says 'Blu Shoos,' you know, like the band."

"Wait, so are you looking for shoes or not?" Evan asks, and I'm with her on this, I don't get it.

"Go back to sleep, EvTay," Colin says.

"No, I think I get it," Rainey says. "So once you stopped looking for something in particular, and started generally observing, what did you find?"

Jack smiles. "We discovered a lot, actually. Low-level government officials making little mistakes that on the surface didn't look like much, but when added up, formed a pattern. Things like unsent requisitions, misplaced approvals for supplies, sloppy work, stuff that wouldn't be noticed by anyone not looking for it."

Now he has my full attention, and I lean forward, locking eyes with him. "What kinds of requisitions and approvals?"

Jack nods, probably sensing I'm putting the pieces together. "For things no one would ever connect to a movement. Dairy products, toiletries, everyday stuff. It flies under the radar because it's so mundane."

"But it's moving Union money out into the Uprising where it's needed," I say as it all falls into place.

"Precisely," Jack says. "And it all fits with what you and Bryce discovered back east."

I suppress a growl. Being reminded that Bryce was alone with her is enough to make me want to beat the shit out of him.

Bryce leans forward and rests his forearms on his knees. "Evan and I met with her uncle while we were there."

My hands ball into fists. I don't even want him to say her name.

"He mentioned similar stuff going on along with a high turnover rate among junior staff members, people he wasn't directly involved with. Then I staked out Peter Benton's place."

He turns toward Rainey and explains, "The mayor of the borough back there. We've been watching him off and on for the past year." He returns his attention to the fire. "I noticed a stream of people coming and going and eventually discovered they were getting forged Union credentials. After Evan left, I stuck around the Eastern Province and continued my investigation."

My head swivels to Evan, who's busy chewing her bottom lip. Why *did* she leave? She never told me and I never asked. Based on the way Bryce looks at her like a wounded puppy, my money's on him fucking up. Not sure if I should be happy about that or pissed.

"We were scheduled to meet with her uncle the following week," Bryce continues. "I kept the appointment and filled him in on what I knew. In the meantime, he'd been doing some digging around of his own, but he didn't have anything concrete. We agreed to meet weekly and compare notes."

He stands and grabs a couple pieces of wood off the pile next to the ring, and tosses them on. Sparks swarm and hover before fading. "Over several weeks, I discovered a pattern of couriers arriving and leaving Benton's place. The same teams of couriers showed up a couple of days in a row then disappeared for a week, before returning. It didn't take long to connect the dots that they were from the Ruins and getting credentials to bring people into the Union."

As much as I hate the asshole, I can't deny he's smart.

"I noticed this guy on my one of my early stakeouts," Bryce says, jerking a thumb toward Simon as he resumes his seat in the sand. "I cornered him outside the apartment and got him to talk to me."

"How'd you do that?" Evan asks.

Simon shrugs. "He can be persuasive."

Evan cuts her eyes to Bryce, who throws her a cheesy grin. *Asshat.*

"Simon told me he was working independently of the other couriers, and that he usually helps people from the Northern Territories but also a handful of people from the Ruins."

With that, I push up and wander over to the other side of the fire. I stare at the flames for several minutes while they talk.

Whatever went on between Bryce and Evan appears to be over, but I can't seem to get past it. I can't close my eyes without picturing them together.

There's nothing more I need to hear tonight, and without another word, I turn and head back to my tent.

# Getting Past It

*Evan*

**L**ying in bed, tears stubbornly fall regardless of how angrily I wipe them away. No matter what Eddie said, I can't shake the feeling Cyrus is done with me.

I push all thoughts of Cyrus aside and force myself to focus on the conversation around the fire earlier tonight. My eyelids get heavy before I can sort it all out, and soon, messy jumbled dreams that come in fits and starts take center stage.

A loud scream tears me from scenes of war and death, and I bolt up, realizing I'm the one screaming.

"Hey, you okay?" Rainey mumbles next to me.

"Yeah, sorry. Go back to sleep."

Our tent is one of the "honeymoon" tents with a king sized bed instead of cots. I guess Colin wasn't too hip on sharing a bed with Bryce, so Rainey and I got the fancy digs.

Sleep is no longer an option, so I roll out of bed and dress in a pair of lounge pants and a giant sweatshirt I took from Eddie's closet. I slip outside and make my way down to the water's edge.

The hard, cold sand beneath my feet makes me shiver, and a huge wave crashes ashore, spraying me with saltwater, sending me scurrying to the mess tent. I pull my hands inside the sleeves of the sweatshirt and wrap them around a mug of coffee, taking it to an outside table.

"Mornin' EvTay," Colin says a few minutes later, dropping next to me with his own coffee.

"Hey, Col."

We sit in quiet contemplation until the others make a gradual migration from tent to table, surrounding us with bodies and superficial chatter. With my head still too foggy to participate, I'm content to nurse my coffee in silence from the end of the table, staring at a line of ants climbing the sea wall behind me.

"We need to talk," Lisa announces, drawing my attention away from the parade of insects. A slight scowl mars her usually cheerful face as her gaze sweeps our group. She pushes back and dumps her tray on the conveyor belt before leading us across the sand to a fishing pier, jutting a quarter-mile into the ocean.

We climb creaky steps, joining a handful of avid fishermen, the only others crazy enough to be out here on a cold, gray morning. Clouds hang heavy in the sky, and soft waves tumble ashore in a hypnotic shush. Only the screech of the seagulls disrupts the tranquility.

I lean on the weathered railing and stare south at a scattering of surfers paddling out to catch a ride back in. As flat as the surf is, they'll be waiting awhile.

"Have you ever done that?" Rainey asks, nodding toward the surfers.

"No. I grew up in the east. Some people surf there, but not like here. Here, it's almost a religion."

"Alright," Lisa says from behind me, clapping her hands. "We need a plan."

Rainey and I turn to face her. The others are lined up along the railing, those from the Union on my left and those from the Ruins on my right. Segregation at its finest.

"Do we even have enough information to be making any plans worth pursuing?" I ask.

Lisa shakes her head. "No, but we need a plan to move forward from here."

"We need weapons," Cyrus says.

Rainey nods. "We definitely need weapons, but we also need to find out more about the people they're bringing in from the Ruins and the overall plan of attack. Cyrus and I only learned what was required as commanders to operate our own camps. We don't have the big picture."

"Cyrus knew about the drug cartels," Lisa says.

"Only what Mateo told me."

"If he's a hired gun, why can't we hire him?" Lisa asks.

Cyrus runs a hand through his hair. "That's actually a good idea."

She beams, her brown eyes shining, and he smiles back. I feel a little stab of envy that he'll smile for her but won't even talk to me.

"Bryce and I can head back east and get more info on who's coming in and why," Jack says. "I have a bad feeling about all this, like they're trying to sneak operatives in. With the weapons smuggling we discovered, they could be building a stealth army."

Rainey taps her finger on her chin. "If we get Mateo and whatever he knows about the Uprising, if Bryce and Jack get a list of everyone coming in, and we get our hands on some weapons, we might actually be able to do something."

"Cool," Colin says. "We have three immediate objectives and eight of us. Let's team up and get it done."

"I'll work on getting weapons," Cyrus says.

"From where?" I ask, forgetting for a moment we're not speaking, but thoughts of him returning to the Ruins knot my stomach.

"I think our best option is Mexico."

Cold fear climbs through me — that's even worse than the Ruins.

Before I can try to talk him out of it, Rainey says, "I'll go with you. I speak fluent Spanish." She glances at Cyrus, excitement blossoming on both of their faces.

"You're both crazy." Mounting panic makes my voice rise. "You can't go down there."

"No, they're right," Jack says. "Mexico is the best place to get our hands on what we need. Something small, powerful, accurate, easy to use and conceal. We need more than guns, though, we need a way to take out larger targets, depending on what we find."

As much as I hate the idea, I have to admit, as former Uprising commanders, Rainey and Cyrus are the best positioned to not only know what's needed, but blend in with that guerrilla subculture.

"That just leaves finding Mateo. Colin and I can handle that," I say.

Cyrus pushes off the railing and closes the distance between us in a matter of seconds. The suddenness of it startles me, and I step back. It's the biggest reaction he's had to anything in days. My gaze rises to meet his, and I recognize the fear threaded through his eyes before he assembles the unreadable expression of his I've come to know and loathe.

"No." His tone is quiet, but his clenching jaw means he's working hard to keep it under control.

"It makes the most sense. Like you and Rainey going to Mexico. Colin and I know that Uprising camp."

He reaches a hand up toward his head before dropping it to his side. "You were shot less than a month ago. *Shot.* You're supposed to be taking it easy."

"How would you even know that? You've barely said two words to me in more than a week."

He closes his eyes, his fists balling at his sides, and lets out a slow breath. When he opens his eyes again, he stares over my shoulder, as if he can't even stand to look at me. "You're a deserter. Both of you. They don't chase deserters, but if anyone recognizes you, they *will* shoot you, no questions asked."

"I'll go," Lisa says.

"Lisa, I don't think—" Jack starts.

"I can do this," she says, uncharacteristically cutting him off. "I was out there with you guys looking for Evan. Plus Simon can come with me. He knows the Ruins."

"I'm up for it," Simon says.

Colin scowls. "What about me?"

"You need to remain here with Evan," Jack says. "No one's left alone."

"What?" Colin yells. "Why do I have to be stuck babysitting her? Why can't she stay with Eddie?"

"Because," Lisa says. "She listens to you."

"Hey! Stop talking about me like I'm not even here." My gaze travels around my friends, and one by one, they glance away.

Anger burns through my chest and frustrated tears threaten to betray me. Before I start crying, I turn and head back across the pier.

"Nice going, Colin," Lisa says behind me, her footsteps picking up speed as she rushes to catch up. She falls in step next to me as I hit the soft sand. "Colin shouldn't have said that."

I carve a path closer to the water. "But it's true, isn't it? No one wants to be stuck with me. I'm a liability."

"Ev…" She pauses for a long while, and when she speaks again, her words are slow, as if carefully chosen. "We came close to losing you twice now. Sometimes you don't think before you act, and it doesn't always work out the way you want it to."

Willow's little body lying bleeding on the forest floor fills my mind. Shit, I wouldn't want to be teamed with me either.

"I know he was gruff, but Cyrus means well."

My head snaps up. Why is she talking about him as if she knows him and I don't?

"He loves you," she says softly.

I narrow my eyes. She's crazy. He barely tolerates me, and there's something bordering on angry hatred just below the surface. It's my fault, though. I slept with Bryce.

"He hates me," I mumble.

Lisa sighs. "I've seen the way he looks at you, Ev. Like if I cut you, I swear he'd be the one bleeding."

"He might feel protective of me, but it doesn't mean he's still in love with me." I turn to stare at the waves. The surf moves in, reaching up cold fingers to nudge my toes. My feet sink down into the sand as the water rushes out below them, making me feel as if I'm the one moving.

"We need you at a hundred percent. You're the glue holding us together."

My head whips around and I gape at her. "What?"

She gives me a slow smile. "You're the common denominator in our little band of rebels. If it wasn't for you, we wouldn't all be here. Well except Simon, he's only here for Rainey."

"That doesn't make me glue, especially if no one wants to be stuck with me."

"Yes, you're stubborn, opinionated, and even a little bossy at times, but you're brave. Remember how you jumped into a raging creek to save Bryce? You didn't even think about it."

"Right. I'm impulsive, I think we've established that."

"That's not what I said. I said it doesn't always work out the way you want. But, when you do take the time to plan first, you come up with good ideas. Bryce said you figured out how to get into your uncle's place, and Colin told me how you planned the escape when those guys kidnapped him. So, you just need to do more planning and less blind reacting."

Her words spin around in my head for a minute and I realize she's right. With a sigh, I nod. "Okay."

"Good. Now…let's go see Eddie and get some money. We're going to need a lot of it."

My eyes open and fading twinkling lights come into focus, dimly illuminating the white walls of our tent. How the hell did I get here? The snoring body next to me doesn't sound like Rainey. I turn my head to see Colin splayed out beside me.

The last thing I remember was sitting around the bonfire listening to everyone else talk about their plans. Colin must have carried me in here after I fell asleep. The fact that he could drag me to bed without me having any recollection of it is scary as hell. Cyrus is right, I have no business going out to the Ruins.

I try to clear the static from my brain and remember what was discussed last night before I dozed off. Rainey and Cyrus were leaving early this morning. They're renting a sailboat to head down to Mexico.

Colin lets out a ripping snore, and I fling my pillow at his head.

"What?" he grumbles, opening one eye to look at me before closing it again.

"Oh, were you sleeping? Sorry."

He flips me off, which only makes me laugh.

"Are you still mad at me?"

He sighs and rolls over, propping his head up on his forearms. "No. I'm sorry. I shouldn't have said what I did. I was frustrated."

"I'm sorry, too, for being such a pain. And thanks for bringing me in here last night. Scary I slept through it."

"Wasn't me. I was gonna wake your ass up and make you walk. Cyrus carried you."

Cyrus carried me? That simple, yet thoughtful gesture blends with what Lisa said. Maybe he *doesn't* hate me. But *I* hate the way things are between us right now, and I know there's a very real chance he won't come back.

Suddenly, I need to see him before he leaves and dash over to the tent he shares with Simon.

Simon's out cold, but Cyrus's cot is empty and his duffel bag is gone.

Heart pounding, I turn and race down to the water, hoping to catch them before they sail off.

But they're gone.

He left without saying goodbye.

I slump down to the sand and pull my legs to my chest, wrapping my arms around them.

Things are so awful between us now. He has to come back.

I need to tell him how much I love him.

# Awful

## Cyrus

The unevenly paved Mexico streets are as jacked up as any out in the Ruins. Rainey and I make our way past colorful buildings with chipping paint and rusted railings surrounding precarious balconies. But at least the ground isn't moving.

"You're looking a little less ripe, there, Cyrus," Rainey says with her raspy voice.

I cut my eyes to her, but don't respond. I've never been as sick in my life as I was on that boat. All I want to do is get to a hotel and lie down. Aside from the sea sickness, we had an uneventful trip. No one paid any attention to us when we docked, and we've walked for several hours now without being accosted.

Since we're posing as a couple, when we approach the center of town, I reach down and take Rainey's hand. It's even smaller than Evan's and feels foreign resting in mine.

Rainey lifts her gaze to mine and smirks. Yeah, she's about as thrilled with this ruse as I am. We enter the lobby of a stained green two-story hotel with crooked, worn shutters. A stone floor lists to one side as we make our way to the registration desk where a guy with a thick mustache and a bright orange button up shirt greets us. He says something in Spanish with enthusiasm, smiling so hard his cheeks nearly touch his ears.

Rainey responds, indicating me and continues on in a rapid fire conversation. She hands him a few bills and he gives her a key.

I follow her back outside, carrying our bags. One duffel is filled with a handful of clothes and toiletries and the others are stuffed with more bags to carry guns and ammo back to the Union. Money is sewn in hidden pockets in our fatigues, a knife is strapped to my ankle, and a gun sits in the waistband of my jeans.

Rainey heads down an alley only wide enough for us to fit through single-file. Behind the hotel is a staircase that wobbles with each step. Great. She stops at a door at the end of a narrow balcony with only a suspect railing to keep us from tumbling down the rocks to the beach a hundred feet below.

We enter a dark room smelling of vomit and dirty socks. A queen-sized bed is against the wall and a beat-up upholstered chair and ottoman sit in the corner.

"Only one bed?"

"We're supposed to be a couple visiting from the Northern Territories," she says. "I couldn't very well ask for two beds."

Rainey is about half my size, but there's no way I'm letting her sleep anywhere but the bed.

"Okay, I'll take the chair."

She snorts. "You don't have to do that. Your virtue is safe with me. Plus, you're not exactly my type."

My head swings her way. "Wrong plumbing?"

"Ego much? Wow, just because I don't want to get all sweaty and horizontal with you, I must not be into guys. Is it really that rare for a hetero girl not to fling herself at you?"

I roll my eyes, not in the mood for this, but if we're going to share a bed, might as well get this conversation over with. "No. It was the way you said it. I don't know, forget I said anything."

"You're not bad to look at or anything, I just prefer my guys to be…less pathetically in love with someone else."

"Point made. I'm gonna lie down until my stomach stops heaving. Join me or don't."

I flop on the bed and close my eyes, still feeling the gentle, and then not-so-gentle, rocking of the waves until I doze off.

## Evan

I'm still in a funk over the way Cyrus and I left things at breakfast, and end up only picking at my food. After everyone is done eating, Colin and I pack our stuff and accompany the others to the train station.

The A-Train station bustles with hurried passengers rushing to buy tickets and saying last-minute goodbyes.

Lisa slides up to the automated ticket machine and buys two tickets to the Northwestern Province, where she and Simon will enter the Ruins near where Colin and I did. Colin loaded a map on their tablets with the location of the training camp where we last saw Mateo. With any luck, he's still there.

Jack and Lisa wander off to say goodbye, while the rest of us study the illuminated display tracking the current whereabouts of every A-Train in the Union.

Colin traces his finger along the route of the northbound train. "It'll be here in twenty minutes, and the one Jack and Bryce will take is up here, about a half-hour out."

Simon grins and nods. "That's cool."

"How have you been getting around this whole time if you don't know how the A-Trains work?" I ask.

"Cargo trains."

"Dude, those are slowwww," Colin says.

Simon grins again. "Yup. I slept a lot."

"Why have you never gotten yourself credentials?" I ask him.

He rubs his thumb and forefinger together. "No money."

Colin lifts a brow. "You don't get paid for what you do?"

"Yeah, but the credentials I deal in are pricey. Like five Gs."

My mouth drops open. Cyrus has one of those credentials. His name and fingerprint are in the Union database as if he was born here. He paid with the only thing he had of any value, his mother's engagement ring dating back to before the war. That ring must have been worth a lot more than five thousand dollars, though, and he gave it up to be with me.

I have to find a way to make things right between us when he gets back.

He has to come back.

Lisa and Jack rejoin us when the train glides into the station. Lisa's long blond hair is pulled into a single braid, her dark eyes overflowing with confidence. Gone is the fearful girl, sobbing in the hospital after Colin was shot. The girl standing before me is poised without even a hint of uneasiness on her girl-next-door face.

She gives Jack one last hug before throwing her arms around Colin. Jack watches with a wary eye, but for once, I'm not worried about Colin's feelings for Lisa. He might still love her, but their relationship has evolved now that he's fallen for Ally. Lisa sniffs a few times when Colin backs away, her eyes sparkling with sudden tears.

I pull her into a tight hug. "You got this, Lis, but if you're not back in two weeks, I'll come find you."

"I'll be back. Don't worry."

After letting me go and wiping a runaway tear, she grabs Simon's sleeve and tugs him into line. The rest of us huddle together until the train departs the station and disappears. Jack wanders down to the end of the platform and rests his elbows on the railing, staring out at the Union below us.

Bryce takes my hand and pulls me aside. "How's the shoulder?"

"Still there."

"Any chance you'll spend the next two weeks taking it easy?"

"I don't know."

He sighs and turns me to face him, wrapping me in a hug. I surprise myself by letting him, resting my head on his chest. Some of the tension that's taken up residence in me over the past couple of weeks begins to ease. A hug from a friend is such a simple thing, and yet it has the power to heal. It's as if he's telling me he forgives me. His warm lips press against my hairline, but it feels more platonic than romantic. I'm not sure if his feelings toward me have changed, or if he's just respecting the fact that mine toward him have.

"Are we good?" I ask.

"Yeah. We're good." He reaches up and strokes my hair. "I love you, Evansville, but I know you don't feel the same. For now, while we do what we need to do, I'll pretend that's okay."

I sigh and pull out of his arms before wandering over to the railing to look out toward the beach. A low-lying cloud cover obscures the water. "Can I ask you something?"

"Sure." He moves beside me and we stare out at the yawning Union, stretching to life after a night of slumber.

"The morning on the train...when you told me you loved me...Why? You barely knew me."

He takes his time answering. "I grew up in a house of make-believe. With my dad an undercover cop, he spent so much time pretending to be someone he wasn't. Not around us, but he couldn't tell us what he was doing. So we only got to see a slice of who our dad was. My mom spent all her time pretending our lives were normal and that she wasn't worried about my dad every time he left. My sisters felt it was their responsibility to keep up the charade for my sake."

I drag my gaze away from the city below me and turn to the boy next to me with fresh eyes.

His jaw tenses and he seems to be searching for the right words to continue. "Then I went undercover and started to pretend I was someone I wasn't. I pretended to like a girl I couldn't stand. She pretended the world revolved around her." He turns toward me, his soft gray eyes locking on to mine. "You were the most genuine, honest person I'd ever met. So maybe I wasn't in love with you, but I was deeply infatuated with you, and I thought it was love."

I stare at his profile, and there's something different about his posture, or maybe I'm seeing him differently, but for the first time, I feel as if I'm catching a glimpse of the real Michael Bryce Cooper.

Before I can respond, the train glides into the station. Bryce gives my hand a squeeze and joins Jack in line. I watch him go, feeling like I just gorged myself on a smorgasbord of emotions.

With a quick wave, Bryce and Jack disappear inside the sleek white tube.

Colin tosses an arm over my shoulders. "So, what do we do now?"

I glance at him out of the corner of my eye and realize I have absolutely no idea.

## Cyrus

A fly buzzing my head pulls me from a sound sleep. I swat it and sit up, scrubbing my hands across my face. Since Rainey's not back yet, I guess I should go look for her.

Hanging on to the handrail with white-knuckled force, I make my way down the rickety stairs and back to the lobby. Ceiling fans move air and bring in ocean breezes. To the right of the front desk is a doorway leading to a dimly-lit pub, emitting a mixture of clinking glasses, the low murmur of conversation, and some sort of tinny music. A square bar squats in the center of the room with dried palm fronds draped across the top.

Rainey is on the other side of the bar and lifts her head when I enter. She plasters a smile on her face and waves with enthusiasm. "Hey, honey, over here."

I resist the urge to roll my eyes as I make my way over and take the stool next to her. I lean in and press my lips lightly to her temple.

She nods at the bartender and points to her glass. He returns moments later with two pint glasses filled with a rich golden brew, foam sliding down the frosty sides.

"Gracias," she says.

With a nod, he shuffles off to help a rowdy table of guys.

"So, what's the lay of the land?" I ask.

"They speak English here, so be careful what you say," she whispers.

"Got it." I take a sip of beer, savoring the hoppy flavor with a hint of lime. "What's the plan for the rest of the day?"

"Hang out. Blend in. Tomorrow we can start asking around, but I want to get a feel for the town first. Been talking to the bartender. He may know some people."

I nod and take another swig.

"So, tell me what's going on with you and the crazy redhead."

"We're not having this conversation, Rainey."

"Sure we are. You're acting like a giant ass, you know."

I turn to her, eyes narrowed. "She didn't even go out there for me. You know that right?"

"When I first met her, she said she was out there to find the guy she fell in love with."

"That was bullshit. She wasn't gonna tell you she was there to join the Uprising. I gave up everything to be with her, but it was just dumb luck she tripped over me in that camp."

"Are you for real? She's a Uni." Rainey pauses, and glances around the bar before lowering her voice. "Where would she have looked for you even if she'd wanted to? You're asking too much of her."

"She's reckless and impulsive. She got that girl killed."

"Now you're making excuses. I talked to Colin. He said that girl was dead either way, and based on what he told me, I agree with him. Look, if you don't love her, set her free, because she's clearly hurting. But I think you do, so I stand by my original statement. You're acting like a giant ass."

I finish my beer and signal the bartender for another, refusing to engage further.

"Okay, I guess we're done talking about this."

"We always were."

## Evan

Colin and I checked into a low-rent hotel on the twenty-third level. Not quite the bottom, but nowhere near the top. Nice and obscure. Even though the order to "eliminate" us as a threat to the Uprising has been canceled, we still can't be parading around the Union. We'll stay off the grid, pay with cash, and use key cards to access our room instead of the PrintPad system. The Union's commitment to privacy, allowing citizens to remain as anonymous as they want, is fast becoming my favorite part of life here.

We decided for safety's sake to share a room. It's small, but big enough to hold two twin beds, a short dresser, and a table with a couple of chairs. I drop my bag on the bed closest to the door and check out the closet-sized bathroom with a tiny shower. While it's far less spacious and more sparsely furnished than the rooms we had up in the northwest, it's clean, smells okay, and is within walking distance to several restaurants and a commuter station. Plus, we only need to hole up here for a couple of weeks before heading back to the campground to reunite with the others.

"I still don't get why we couldn't stay at the beach," I say.

"That's because you slept on a king-sized pillow pretending to be a bed. I was stuck on a stiff cot."

"Got it."

Colin sits on his bed, back against the headboard, long legs stretched out in front of him. "So, what's the plan? I know you're not going to listen to me, despite what Lisa thinks."

"I don't know yet, but we have to do something. I can't sit around worrying about everyone else the whole time."

"Didn't think you would." He pulls out his tablet and launches an app. "What do we have so far?"

I tick off a very short list. "We know the attack will probably be on two fronts — from the Ruins and from within the Union. Bryce and Jack are trying to find out the identities of the planted soldiers. Lisa and Simon are out getting Mateo, who we hope will be able to tell us more about the Uprising. But we're still missing a huge piece of the puzzle. The one that tells us everything, from every angle."

We discuss our list for over an hour before Colin tosses his tablet onto the bed. "I need a break. Let's go get some coffee."

After locking up, we walk to a café not far from our hotel. It's noisy and crowded, which seems odd for a Wednesday afternoon. Glancing around, most of the patrons appear to be our age or younger. They must have come here after getting out of school. We take our drinks to a champagne-colored velvet couch along the wall, but with all the noise in here, it's impossible to have any kind of a conversation.

Colin jerks his head. "Let's go outside."

We find an empty table on the patio, but once we're in the quiet outdoors, neither one of us seems to have anything to say.

"So what did Bryce want?" Colin finally asks.

"I'm not sure. He asked about my shoulder and hugged me. It was weird. He said he still loves me, but knows I don't feel the same."

We sit in silence for a while, me mulling over my conversation with Bryce, Colin thinking about whatever it is Colin thinks about when he's not talking. I know where I stand with Bryce. It would be so easy to be with him, but I'm not in love with him. The boy I *am* in love with is pissed off at me. Boy problems are the least of my worries now, so I focus on coming up with a plan for the next two weeks. By the time I finish my coffee, a thought slowly starts to take shape.

"Hey, Col, I have an idea. You're not going to like it, but I think I know what we can do." He lifts an eyebrow and waits for me to go on. "Not here. Back at the hotel."

When we're safely locked inside our room, I turn to Colin. "We need to find Walker. He's the key to all of this."

Colin's eyes widen and the color drains from his face, giving him a sickly pallor, and his nostrils flare with each exaggerated breath. Even though both of us were kidnapped by Walker, only Colin was brutally tortured to get information. But that's how I know Walker is the key.

"Do you remember the Project Blackbird memo?" I ask.

He nods.

"Jack found it not long after you were kidnapped. It seemed to indicate we knew enough to bring down their operation. How could they know that? Walker's the only one who knows how much we knew. He's gotta be behind the memo. The more I think about it, the more sense it makes."

Colin stares at me with unblinking eyes, before giving his head a hard shake. "What exactly are you thinking?"

# Making Plans

*Evan*

After spending the day brainstorming with Colin, I still don't have a clue how to go about finding Walker or what we'd even do if we found him.

Lying on my bed, hands clasped across my belly, I stare up at the ceiling until my eyes lose focus. Walker has a house out in the Ruins, but he must also have some sort of headquarters here. It's pretty clear he's working with people in the Union, which means there's a digital trail. The trick is finding it.

I absently rub the bedsheets between my thumb and index finger while I think. They're harsh compared to the supple Egyptian cotton ones in our posh Northwestern Province hotel, but there's something oddly comforting about the texture of these.

Jack's dad has been looking for Walker since Colin was kidnapped. Max had us work with a forensic artist to come up with a digital representation which they ran through facial recognition, but nothing turned up. We know he's here somewhere, so there must be a way to find him. My eyes close and my thoughts drift before I bolt upright.

I know how we can track Walker down.

"Colin?"

His only response is a loud snore. I guess it can wait until morning, but my mind is too busy to join him in slumber.

Apparently I managed to doze off, because a chorus of bangs disrupts whatever dream I was having. I glance around the room for the cause of the commotion.

Colin slams the dresser drawer. "Bout time you woke up," he grumbles.

Oh joy, grouchy Colin is here. When I glance at the clock, I decide not to engage him since it's after nine-thirty, well past his feeding time. I forgo a shower, because I don't think he'll wait that long, and change into something I didn't sleep in before schlepping off to find breakfast.

Once Colin has something in his belly, he stops scowling, so I figure it's safe to talk to him.

"So, I was thinking last night while you were visiting dreamland, and I think I came up with an idea."

"Yeah, what's that?" he asks between mouthfuls of granola, milk dribbling down his chin.

"Once we find Walker, we need to break into his place and see what we can find."

His spoon stalls on its approach and he stares at me with dark, incredulous eyes.

"He's the brains behind everything, I'm sure of it now, so if anyone is going to have the master plans, it'll be him. First we have to find him, and I think I have an idea."

He continues to stare at me, spoon midair, milk dripping on the table.

"Are you going to say something?"

"Have you lost your fucking mind?"

My mouth falls open. I get he isn't crazy about the plan, but Colin rarely swears and never drops the "f" bomb.

"Have you've forgotten what that psychopath did to us? Breaking into his place is like the stupidest idea you've ever had. I love you, and I support you, but I'm not following you into his asylum of torture."

What Walker put Colin through is so much worse than what he did to me, so I can understand. I'll just do it without him.

"Oh no you don't," he says, as if he can read my mind. "I know what you're thinking and no way. I'll text Jack and Bryce right now and tell them what you're up to."

"You wouldn't." Although the set of his jaw tells me he will. I get why he doesn't want to go with me, but he wouldn't betray me. Would he?

Colin drops his spoon into his bowl with a clank and a splash. "I would and I will. Lisa's out of her flippin' mind if she thinks you listen to me, but at least I know Bryce will lock your ass up before he lets you go off on some crazy, half-baked ill-fated mission, likely ending with your death."

Chewing on my bottom lip, I try to figure out how to go forward from here. I can't let Colin text Bryce. "Fine. We can wait until Bryce and Jack get back and let them handle the breaking and entering. But, why don't we at least try to track Walker down until then."

He eyes me, his brows drawing together, but doesn't argue. He picks up his spoon and resumes eating while I explain how we can talk to my sort of boss, Tony, and use the Provincial News' resources to locate Walker using the police sketch.

"That's not a bad idea," he says when I finish.

After breakfast, we head back to our room to grab our tablets before heading to Tony's office.

Pulling my sweatshirt hood up to cover my hair, I step off the elevator on the top level and survey the surroundings before working my way toward my old workplace.

A couple of blocks out, we separate and observe the crowds from opposite sides. I check for anyone who seems to be watching the front entrance, scrutinizing every person sitting on a bench, at a table, or sipping coffee, but no one appears even remotely interested in Western Provincial News.

Colin circles back around to me. "I didn't see anything suspicious."

"Neither did I. Okay, let's do this."

Heads down, we stride across the sidewalk and push through the elegant glass doors.

"Evan!" Stevie, the receptionist, launches herself from her chair and flies around the expansive desk to greet me.

I don't know her all that well, but we hit it off the short time I worked here. She turns toward Colin, her gaze traveling over him, mischief lighting up her blue eyes. "And who is this?"

"Oh, sorry. Stevie, this is my friend, Colin. Colin, Stevie."

She grins, tilting her head. Colin returns her smile before shifting his attention back to the lobby.

"Tony will be thrilled to see you." Stevie pivots and leads the way, her long blond ponytail swinging gracefully. "Come on back."

She knows I know the way, so I suspect this escort is for Colin's benefit rather than mine.

We find Tony sitting at his desk, glaring at his tablet. He glances up as we approach, recognition erupting on his face, and he comes out into the hall to greet us.

"Evan, Colin, good to see you. How's the shoulder?" he asks, ushering us into his office and closing the door.

"Eh," I say with a little rocking hand motion.

He indicates the chairs across from him. "Sit down, sit down. What are you doing here?"

Tony returns to his chair and I launch into our plan to find Walker so we can have Jack and Bryce check him out.

I push my tablet across the desk, the composite image of Walker up on screen. "When Jack's dad ran this through facial recognition six months ago, he didn't get a hit."

Tony studies it, taking notes as Colin and I share everything we know about Walker. I show him on his map where Colin was taken after he was kidnapped last summer, then zoom out to the large empty space outside the Union labeled RUINS.

Tony taps on his tablet and brings up an old satellite photo of the United States. It's all pre-war, so the buildings still stand tall.

"Do you know where the Mesa Verde power plant is?" I ask.

After another quick database search, he zooms into the southwest. "Here." He taps the map in what was once the state of Arizona.

I walk over to the display wall, narrowing my eyes at a huge concrete structure that is now nothing but a pile of rubble.

"Wow," I say on a breath.

It's unreal that it's the same place. Running my finger along the road we crossed, I dip into the wooded area and the river that ran through where Cyrus and the others lived. I find Tanque Verde falls, which I'm sure is what they now call Green Valley. I trail south until I spot houses dotting orderly streets up against a small mountain I believe is the one I crossed after escaping from Dantel.

"Here. I think this is where he was holding me."

Tony sighs and rubs the stubble on his jaw with his fingers, staring at the map. "Technically, you're still an employee here, Evan, so you have access to all the Western Provincial resources. I'll help you in any way I can."

"Okay, then, let's get started."

## Cyrus

"How many more days are we gonna sit around doing nothing?"

Rainey stares at me over her margarita glass, eyelids droopy. "We're not doing nothing. We're…observing."

"You're doing a bang-up job of observing your third margarita." I push my bottle across the bar and toss a few dollars next to it. "I'm going to the room."

The ceiling fan rocks, unbalanced and rattling, above where I lie on my back. Inaction isn't my thing, and Rainey getting hammered is just pissing me off. But I need her. I can't speak the language, which leaves me frustrated most of the time.

The door opens and I turn my head to see my partner, clear-eyed and pissed as all hell. "What do you think is going on here?"

"I think we're wasting time."

"Look, you don't just show up and start asking around about weapons down here unless you want to end up dead. Especially as a foreigner." Rainey lifts a brow and crosses her arms.

"I understand, but you getting drunk isn't helping."

"I'm as sober as you are." She actually looks and sounds it. "But I'm listening. Lots of conversations going on around us in that bar. They're not paying much attention to the couple vacationing from the Northern Territories. Probably because they think we don't understand what they're saying."

"Okay." I sit up and swing my legs over the edge of the bed. "What are they saying?"

"The Uprising is providing them with a steady cash flow. They're not necessarily trusting, wary of anyone not referred to them, but they're greedy. I think we can make that work in our favor."

"How so?"

"We have enough money to attract the attention of just about any arms dealer." Her mouth lifts in a sly smile. "Your girlfriend's loaded. You might want to think twice before cutting her loose."

I narrow my eyes and shake my head. "Any idea on the safest ones to approach?"

"Not yet. Give me another day."

Great, more waiting.

"Follow my lead," Rainey whispers in my ear before pushing up.

I trail her across the bar to the corner, where a hulking figure in white hunches in the shadows. Rainey murmurs a few words in Spanish, and he leans forward, half his face lit by the surrounding lights.

He says something to Rainey but never takes his dark, suspicious eyes off me. Throwing a couple dollars on the table, he stands. His thick head and neck are screwed on to a broad frame that stops well short of six feet. His gait is steady, powerful, as he leads the way. Rainey is tiny compared to this dude, but I take comfort in the fact I can see the top of his head. Greasy black hair stands at attention, and tattoos of fierce animals, flames, and death wrap both arms from biceps to elbow.

My gaze moves between this guy, Rainey, and our surroundings, unsure where we're heading but not about to ask Rainey. If he hasn't figured out I don't speak Spanish, I'm not going to clue him in. Nothing about Rainey, aside from her size, screams helpless, but it's clear now my role is that of the silent bodyguard, watching and nodding while they talk.

Rainey and the guy keep up a steady conversation through town. We wind through narrow streets, past stained buildings with broken tile roofs and decaying balconies before turning into an opening at the end of a long row of doors set into a low building.

The opening leads to a dark room, and I grab Rainey's arm, pulling her against me until my eyes adjust to the lack of light. She doesn't fight me, which means this situation has her on alert as much as it does me. My hand instinctively reaches behind my back where my gun sits in my waistband.

The guy says something to Rainey in rapid Spanish and she responds with slow, deliberate words. He laughs and returns to where we're standing inside the doorway, backs against the wall. Rainey's shoulders relax against my chest and she steps forward.

I follow her, but not without a quick glance back to make sure our escape route is unblocked. We walk down a shadowy hall to another door. He opens it, laughter and conversation drifting up, and heads downstairs. Light pours up the stairway in a wide arc, throwing long shadows behind us.

Rainey's chin juts up in a confident pose as she marches down, like she does this all the time. My gaze sweeps the area with each step I take. A room comes into view filled with men and women, dressed in all white, similar to our escort.

We're stopped at the bottom of the stairs by a dude even bigger than me, arms crossed over his chest like a bouncer up in the Northern Territories. He barks something at Rainey, and she lifts her hands, then slowly reaches into her waistband and grips her gun by the handle between her thumb and forefinger, handing it over to him.

My body stiffens. We're about to be unarmed in a roomful of dangerous-looking strangers. This is by far the dumbest thing I've done, and I give a quick thought to getting the hell out of here.

Rainey reaches down and pulls the knife from where it's strapped to her calf and glances up at me. Her eyes are wide, but she nods, begging me to cooperate. Clearly she's no surer about this situation than I am. I may have to wring her neck if we survive.

I pull out my weapons, following her lead, and hand them over, then let them frisk me. I watch as he frisks Rainey, making sure his hands don't go anywhere they shouldn't. When we're cleared, we enter the room, all eyes on us.

Conversation halted the minute we hit the bottom step, and I feel dozens of pairs of eyes on me as I take in our environment. The only door in the windowless room is behind us.

The man who escorted us speaks to the group while I study Rainey's body language for clues. The muscles in her neck and shoulders are tense, her jaw clenched, but her balled hands relax at her sides. She says a few words and nods at me, then her shoulders drop, even though the tenseness remains, as if she's trying to give the appearance she's relaxed.

Shit, I really wish I understood Spanish. This is frustrating as all hell.

Rainey approaches a man sitting on our left with long stringy hair and a tattoo of a knife cutting across his face from temple to jaw. He uncrosses his legs and stands, towering over Rainey with a stringbean-like frame accentuated by sculpted biceps and forearms.

I move up behind her, keeping only six inches between us as they speak. The pace of their conversation picks up, but the tone never gets over a low conversational level. Neither smiles, but neither scowls nor tenses further. This is a business discussion and nothing more.

Soon they shake hands and I pick up one word in Spanish I recognize, "mañana."

*Tomorrow.*

# Plans in Action

## Cyrus

"**L**et me do all the talking," Rainey says.

"Like I have a choice." I've never felt this out of my element, not even when I first stepped into the Union with Evan's unconscious body. But at least then, I was doing something. Now, I'm just following Rainey around, pretending I understand what the hell's going on.

"You know what I mean. It could get hairy in there, but let me do the negotiating."

"Got it. I'll be big and silent. Like always."

She sighs. "This isn't an attractive side of you."

"Oh hell, Rainey, I'm not trying to win any beauty contests here. We're supposed to be getting weapons and I'm as impotent as a nine-year-old boy. Why didn't you just come down here alone?"

"Stop being an asshole."

I run a hand through my hair and blow out an exasperated breath. "Fine," I mumble. "You do the talking. Let me know what we decide."

She shakes her head and stops at a small house at the end of a rumpled street, knocks three times, then twice. Someone slides open a metal cover and peeks out. Rainey says something and the door swings wide.

Again, we're checked for weapons, and again they take our guns and knives. Again, I stand in the corner, watching the group and the door as Rainey does all the talking.

The room is filled with men and women, all rougher looking than even the most jaded Uprising recruiter. Dark eyes shift between me and Rainey, hands resting on holstered guns.

Rainey moves around the room as if it's some sort of cocktail party, conversing and sometimes even laughing. The crowd has been assembled by Marco, the stringy-haired dude with the dagger tattoo we met yesterday. He's not here, but supposedly these are eager arms dealers who want our business.

Rainey flashed enough cash to let Marco know we're legitimate and whoever we work with will give a cut of the sales to Marco for making the introduction.

I've seen a lot in my nineteen years, but this is the most fucked up situation I've been in. The bunch in this room would make even Dag, the asshole who turned Evan over to Walker, shit his pants. I can't hide a smile at that thought.

The woman Rainey is speaking to glares at me, probably thinking I'm smiling at something she said. As if I understand a damn word. I give a slight shake of my head, and Rainey speaks quickly before shooting me a dark look over her shoulder and moving on to talk to a tall kid leaning against the wall. He's been watching Rainey with hunger since we arrived. Probably has no clue she'd fry his nuts and eat them for lunch if given the chance.

He stands up straight, rolling his head on his neck like he's preparing for a fight. Only his fingers messing with the hem of his faded green T-shirt hint at his nervousness. His smile is genuine, though, as he bends down and says something to Rainey. Her cheeks darken and her shoulders tense, but she stands her ground, not backing away from the invasion of her personal space.

The conversation is brief, the handshake firm, then Rainey's gaze locks with mine before she turns and heads back toward the bouncer. He escorts us out, returns our weapons, and we walk back down the street in silence.

Once we're several blocks away, Rainey lets out a long sigh. "He'll send word to our hotel in a couple of days about where and when to meet. He's got product and we've got money."

"Why him?"

"All of them were shady, and the fact they're willing to deal with us on only Marco's recommendation is suspect enough. I get the feeling Marco is a bit of a loose cannon, but this guy, Fredo, struck me as less predatory than the others. He could be hiding it, but we don't have a lot of options. We'll just have to watch our backs."

"Let's figure out the best way to go into this to make sure we can get out of it."

She glances up at me, a smirk pulling at her lips. "Now that's the real challenge, isn't it?"

The bustling café overflows with the clanking of dishes and low murmur of voices from the lunchtime crowd. The door chimes as someone enters. My head pops up, ever alert to our surroundings, only to see someone thoroughly uninterested in us, and return my attention to my clam chowder.

"This feels like a lost cause," Colin says, mouth stuffed with burger.

We spent the last few days searching through the massive databases within Western Provincial News as well as the external ones they connect to and came up dry.

I glance at Tony sitting next to Colin. "Is it possible for there to be no trace of someone living in the Union?"

He dips a french fry into ketchup and gives me a thoughtful look. "Sure. If he wasn't born here and no identity was created for him, we wouldn't be able to find much. Especially if he only arrived in the past year or so."

"Is that even possible?" I ask. "Can the mastermind of an intricate plot to bring down the Union be someone who landed here recently?"

Colin wipes his mouth with his napkin and sits back in his chair, temporarily satisfied. "Seems unlikely."

"I tend to agree," Tony says. "From everything you've told me, he's got his hooks in at all levels of government. Those are not short-term relationships."

I rip a piece of the sourdough bread bowl and dip it in the chowder as a thought occurs to me. "What if he used to be someone else? I mean, what if he was born here but has a new identity now? Is that possible?"

"I suppose," Tony says. "But facial recognition should have found some trace of his former identity."

Ugh, he's right. I pull off another chunk of bread and pop it in my mouth, leaning back in my chair, defeated. Unless...

"If they can add people to the database like they've always lived here, why can't they remove someone?"

Tony swirls his iced tea with his straw, the ice cubes clinking against the glass. "It's a little more complicated unless they grew up down below. They'd have to meticulously delete every record, one by one. There isn't any easy way to do it — one of the fun little things the Union built into their privacy code. You're entitled to privacy, but if you use the Union's resources, like the PrintPad system, or public transportation, it leaves a traceable footprint."

I chew my lip, processing how many records are out there of me. Could a kid who grew up on the lower levels make the kinds of contacts Walker would need in the upper levels of government? It's unlikely, so it's more likely he deleted himself.

"What if he missed one?"

"Where are you going with this, Evan?" Tony asks.

"If he decided to swap his old identity for a new one, he'd have to erase his history, but he might've missed something along the way. Do you have software that could take that image of Walker and reverse age it?"

A slow smile spreads from Tony's lips to his dark eyes, crinkling them at the corners. "You're going to make a damn fine investigative reporter someday."

I stand and stretch, the bones in my back cracking after bending over Tony's desk swiping through records on a tablet for hours. We've only been searching since yesterday afternoon, but I swear it feels like a week. The odor of stale coffee and grease overpowers his small office.

"I think I found something," Tony says.

For the first time in days, hope buds in my chest. With a quick swipe of the screen, a poster-sized image is transferred to Tony's display wall. It's a photo from at least twenty years ago. I walk over and examine it up close.

Colin tilts his head, studying the image from various angles. He runs his hands through his hair and squints at the display. "It could be him."

"It's the eyes," I say. They're hooded like now, but not as much and he has the same long face. The hair is different, and his cheeks were fuller then, but I'm sure.

"Okay," Tony says. "Give me some time and I'll see what I can find now that we have a little more information."

"I could use a break," Colin says.

"Same here."

We say goodbye to Tony and head back to our room. After searching through databases for Walker, I'm a little more paranoid than normal. I've learned how easy it is to be spotted on camera.

I insert the key card into our door and push it open. "Hey, Col, let's move to a different hotel."

"I was thinking the same thing."

We toss our stuff into our bags and head south one borough to another low-rent hotel.

"You hungry?" I ask him after we claim our respective beds.

His dips his head and glances at me out of the top of his eyes, making me laugh for the first time today.

"So that's a 'yes,' then?"

He grins and leads the way to a deli a few blocks away that smells like warm bread and fresh coffee. The glass display case is filled with ham, roast beef, mortadella, provolone, Muenster, and Havarti. Loaves of fresh-baked bread are piled high on the table behind the counter. A teen with dark locks tucked under a hair net is cutting salami into paper thin slices with a mandolin.

I swallow back the saliva flooding my mouth, not realizing how hungry I was until we walked in here. We order grilled paninis and wait impatiently until they're ready, taking our sandwiches to a table with a bright yellow tablecloth. The toasted bread crunches with my first bite, a long string of melted cheese trailing.

"You're not going to wait for Bryce and Jack to get back, are you?" Colin asks.

Stopping mid-chew, I glance at him, a knot forming in my stomach. I set my sandwich down and wipe my hands on the paper napkin.

He shakes his head and takes another bite.

"Colin, you don't have to—"

"I don't have to do what?" He raises his head to glare at me. "Go with you? Then what? What if something happens to you? I'll never forgive myself. I'll have to live with that the rest of my life, which won't be very long, because Cyrus'll kill me as soon as he finds out."

I chew on my lip as he talks, not sure what to say. "Col—"

"Save it, Evan. You're stubborn and you do whatever the hell you want. It's what you always do." The hard set of his jaw releases a fraction and he gives me a crooked little smile. "But I know why you're doing it. And I have to admit, I'm pretty pissed they stuck me here babysitting you."

"So you're not going to tell Jack and Bryce?"

"No. The more I think about it, the more I realize your plan is better than doing nothing. And who knows, maybe we'll actually be able to pull it off."

My tablet dings with a text. Tony. "Hey, Tony said he found something. He wants us to meet him at the office."

"Are you sure it's him? No offense, but you're quick to trust texts from people."

I roll my eyes, but he's right. When he was kidnapped, Walker texted me as Colin and lured me to where they were holding him.

When we get back to the hotel, I pick up the phone and call Tony.

He answers on the first ring. "Yeah."

"It's Evan. Did you want us to come by?"

"Yeah, didn't you get my text?" Great, he sounds irritated.

"Just making sure," I say, trying to soothe him. "We'll be there in twenty."

The knot in my stomach is still there, balling tighter as we head back to Tony's office. Nervous excitement about what Tony found mixes with apprehension about what that means. As much as I want to do something, to not sit around and wait while my friends are all putting themselves in danger, running into Walker again is about the last thing I want to do. By the end of the twenty-minute commuter train ride from our hotel to the express elevator, I'm ready to hurl.

"You're freaking me out EvTay," Colin says. "Take some deep breaths."

I nod and close my eyes, concentrating on my breathing during the ride up to the top level of the Union. When the doors open, I feel a little more in control, and wipe my sweaty palms on my jeans before stepping onto the sidewalk.

Tony is waiting for us in the darkened lobby. He lets us in and leads us to his office, sliding his tablet across his desk.

I pick it up and start sifting through the information. "What is this?" I ask, staring at the front of a building of some sort.

"A warehouse Walker is renting in this borough."

Glancing at the screen again, I swipe to a map and see it's not far from where we are now.

"How?" I ask.

"Everyone leaves a footprint if they're here long enough. Unless they never leave the lower levels."

"Thanks," I say.

"We're going to do something that isn't exactly legal," Colin says. "So it might be best if you pretend you didn't find this."

I shoot Colin a look. I told Tony we'd let Jack and Bryce handle it. Now he knows I lied to him.

"I'm going home." Tony's eyes spark with anger as he snatches the tablet back, but I've already memorized the address.

He escorts us outside, the doors clicking shut and locking behind us. Without a word, he turns and heads south.

Colin glances at me, and with a deep breath, we head north.

# Plans Gone Wrong

## Cyrus

The stench of dead fish left out in the sun too long is overpowering as we stand in front of a large warehouse in the center of town. Ocean breezes don't reach this far inland, leaving the air stale and rancid. I pull my shirt up to cover my nose and mouth.

Wearing a backpack full of cash, Rainey quivers beside me, a bundle of jacked-up nerves. I adjust my own backpack stuffed with bags for hauling our purchases back to the Union. If all goes well, we'll be back at our beach campground before sunset.

Sweat prickles my skin before sliding down my chest, trailing into the waistband of my cargo pants. The door opens, and I put my hands up, ready to be frisked. Once again our weapons are removed. Rainey cuts uncertain eyes my way, but at this point, we're in too far to back out. We either succeed or die trying.

With a clang and a rumble, a huge rippled steel door slides to the right, exposing a dimly-lit cavernous room. Fredo glances at Rainey, eying her curves.

She shudders under the visual assault, and I want to beat the crap out of him even more than the first time. He sweeps his hand, inviting us in. The fishy odor is less overpowering in here, which helps me focus my senses on evaluating our surroundings.

Fredo slides the door closed behind us, and I tense. Although we left some cash under a loose floorboard beneath the bed in our room, we've still got a shitload of it on us. I pause, waiting for my eyes to adjust to the sudden reduction of light.

Folding tables are arranged in a semicircle in the center of the warehouse. Two armed guards ranging in size from big to huge, dwarfing Rainey and making me feel like the runt of the litter, stand on each end. Fredo fires off a string of commands, and Rainey takes another tentative step forward.

Screw this. We're here as buyers and shouldn't be acting like a couple of scared kids. I push past Rainey, approaching a table as if I'm picking up supplies at the trading post, and peruse the merchandise. Handguns, rifles, rounds of ammo for both types of weapons, and blocks of plastic explosives are arrayed for us to scrutinize.

Rainey moves next to me, and although I can sense she's on edge, she's working hard to act as if this is an everyday activity. She asks questions, listens to their answers with a thoughtful expression, and fingers several of the semi-automatic handguns.

She hands one to me and I pull back the slide, making sure it's unloaded, before pressing the trigger a few times. It's light and fits naturally in my hand. Glancing at the inventory, I don't see any way to conceal the rifles, but the handguns should suit our purposes well. I nod at Rainey and she handles the negotiations while I begin loading the bags with guns and ammo. When the first bag is full, I set it down and fill the next one, repeating the process until four bags are stuffed. I want more than we think we'll need because I don't want to have to come back down here.

When I'm finished, Rainey and Fredo negotiate the price and she pays him. He counts it out twice and gives her a toothy grin, his eyes roaming her body again. I grab her arm and hand her one of the bags, grabbing the other three, backing out, so I can keep my eyes on everyone.

When we reach the door, I wait for Fredo to open it for us, figuring our weapons won't be returned to us, but once we're out of this place, I plan on loading a couple of the handguns in the closest bag.

Instead of opening it, though, Fredo crosses his arms and smiles. Unease drips through me, and the hair on the back of my neck rises, standing on end. As much as I want to know what's going through Rainey's head, I don't take my eyes off Fredo.

A gun is jammed between my shoulder blades while angry Spanish words float over my head.

"Shit," Rainey whispers next to me, dropping her bag at her feet.

Whoever's behind me grabs my bags from my hands. This situation can't get much worse, so no point now in hiding the fact I speak English.

"What the hell, Rainey?"

She shrugs. "Sorry. I didn't see this coming. They want the guns and the money. I thought Fredo, while sketchy, was the most trustworthy of the bunch we met the other day."

I let loose a long string of profanity, each word louder than the last. My immediate concern is for Rainey's safety the way that asshole, Fredo, is eying her like she's dessert. The door behind us slides open, and I grab Rainey's arm, pulling her closer to me while I evaluate the situation.

Two guards approach, barking orders at us in Spanish, jerking their rifles in our direction.

"Follow my lead," I whisper to Rainey.

Her head snaps up, her eyes pleading with me not to do anything stupid, but if we leave without the weapons or the money, there's no point in going back to the Union. We need guns and ammo to accomplish anything.

Formulating a plan in my mind, I bide my time, walking with a shuffle, until the opportunity presents itself. My foot catches on the slider and I stumble. The guy behind bumps into me, and I thrust my elbow back into his gut, forcing the breath from his lungs.

I whirl around and step back, squaring myself. When he rights himself, I bring my left fist up and hook him across the jaw, sending him to the floor with a single well-placed punch that sends shards of pain up my arm. Shaking out my hand, I reach down and grab his rifle.

Rainey swears loudly, but she spins, kicking her guard hard in the chest. She's small but mighty and soon has the guy on his belly in a headlock, his firearm secured. I offer her a hand and pull her up just as a chorus of cocking rifles comes from behind.

When I turn, I see two more guards plus Fredo with weapons trained on us. Shit, where'd those other two come from? I close my eyes and let out a sigh of defeat, dropping the rifle and putting my hands behind my head, realizing I've probably just guaranteed both of our deaths.

I managed to push all thoughts of Evan from my mind over the past few days, but now all I can think of is how I left things with her, how I treated her. Now she'll think...hell, I don't even know, but she won't have any idea how much she means to me. I ruined every moment we could've spent together because I was too pissed to see beyond my own issues.

Worst of all is knowing Rainey would've been on her way back to the Union now.

"Sorry," I mumble a lame apology.

She cuts her eyes my way and begins speaking rapidly in Spanish, even faster than normal. I may not speak the language, but I pick up a few key words, including gringo estúpido and el Unión. I can't tell from their expressions if anything she's saying is working, but when Rainey's words slow, and her breathing gets a little deeper, I take that as a good sign.

Fredo says something to the bigger of the two guys still standing. The dude glares at me, but nods. Rainey's shoulders drop and she lets out a long breath.

"What?" I whisper.

"We're being taken back to the coast. They'll make sure we get on a boat. Please don't screw this up, too."

A guard jabs his rifle into my back and shoves me out of the warehouse, Rainey following. We walk in silence the thirty minutes it takes to get to the beach where we're escorted to a boat operator.

The guy on my right, the taller of the two with a mean scar down the side of his neck, hands a wad of cash to the operator, jerking his thumb at us. The guy takes the cash and nods, indicating his boat.

I glance at Rainey, but we have no choice other than to comply. As I take a step toward the water, the dude with the scar whips around and clocks me. I stumble to my left, pain exploding across my jaw, white bursts of light flashing behind my eyes.

He spits at me and laughs as I right myself. I follow Rainey into the boat, trying to clear my head, realizing I'm lucky I'm still standing. The boat operator and the goon shove us through the sand out into the water, fueling my dizziness. I swallow hard, refusing to puke in front of those two assholes.

Goon boy stands on the shore, arms crossed over his chest, watching the boat, with us in it, move up the coast and out of sight.

*Evan*

Our footsteps echo off the back wall of a restaurant where a waste bin piled high with the day's garbage gathers flies. We turn and make our way through another alley leading to a sidewalk dotted with potted plants, benches, and small trash receptacles. In the

Union, you can never go more than a couple hundred yards without finding somewhere to properly stow your trash.

Since leaving the commuter station, we've only seen a few people. During the day, this section of the borough bustles with business activity, but goes as dormant as winter grass back east once the sun sets. Glowing streetlamps illuminate small evenly spaced patches, but dark shadows prevail. When we reach the intersection of the alley and sidewalk, we pause behind a large potted tree.

We're still three blocks from our target, but for several long minutes neither of us moves, like we're as rooted to this spot as the tree is to the pot.

What the hell was I thinking coming here tonight? And bringing Colin with me? Every brave thing I've ever done in the past was because I didn't have a choice. If I hadn't shot Dantel, Cyrus would have died. I jumped into a raging creek only because Bryce was drowning. Colin and I escaped from Walker because if we hadn't at least tried, we'd both be dead. But this...this is deliberately putting ourselves in a dangerous situation.

When five minutes have passed and we still haven't moved, Colin leans down and whispers in my ear, "Are we gonna do this or what?"

I glance up at him, swallowing.

"We can go back to the hotel if you want," he offers with a shrug.

Do I want to bail on this plan and go back to waiting for everyone else to return? We located Walker's warehouse, we can leave it to Jack and Bryce to search. They're trained for this sort of thing. But Lisa is out in the Ruins right now looking for Mateo. If she can do that, I guess I can do this.

I shake my head and press my lips together. "Let's do it."

Tucking my hair inside the hood of my jacket and pulling the cord tight around my face, I take a deep breath and step onto the sidewalk. Colin follows me and we quickly cover the remaining distance. I spot the address on the left and pull Colin back between two buildings. A wrought iron trash can surrounded by shrubs provides ample cover for us to observe the front of the building.

Two narrow windows are perched above a steel door on either side like narrowed eyes. Lights angle out of them, painting harsh rectangles on the pavement below. I reach into my pocket and fist my knife, reassuring myself of its presence, as we hunker down to watch and wait. Time passes and my legs cramp, but no one enters or leaves the warehouse.

"I can't feel my feet," Colin whispers. "Let's get up and stretch. Plus we need to check out the back before we can make a plan."

"Okay."

We leave our protected nook and move north until we find an alley winding behind the low row of buildings. A combination of steel swing and roll-up doors line the length. Lights above each one cast triangles of dingy light downward, allowing us to locate the backside of Walker's warehouse. An enormous cobweb stretches from the bottom of the handle to the doorstop jutting from the wall.

"Doesn't look like they use this one much," Colin says.

I nod and we return to our spot out front, settling back down. We barely get ourselves situated when three men approach from the south. When they pass beneath one of the streetlamps, my throat slams shut — Hopp and Rush, two of the men who held me captive in the Ruins.

I don't even realize I'm shaking until Colin whispers in my ear. "Evan, what's wrong?"

"We made a mistake coming here." I back up, moving down the alley, away from the warehouse and Walker's men.

Colin follows, grabbing my arm. "Evan?"

"I have to get out of here."

"Okay." He nods. "Let's go."

My heart pounds, but I don't move. "Those guys. They were with me in the Ruins. One of them…" I inhale a sob. "He was there…when Lucien…"

Colin puts his arms around me and rubs my back. "They just went inside. We can leave now. The coast is clear."

"I'm sorry I didn't listen to you." We turn and start to head back. "You said this was a bad idea."

Colin halts in front of me, and I slam into his back. I peek around him and see Rush, Hopp, the guy I don't know, and Walker leaving through the front, heading down the sidewalk away from us.

The warehouse windows are dark.

Colin glances over his shoulder. "I can't believe I'm saying this, but this might be our chance. Do we go in or back to the hotel?"

Chewing my lip, I glance from Colin to the door and back again. If the warehouse is empty, this could be a perfect opportunity. I take in a deep breath and hold it before blowing it back out.

"Umm, let's do this."

We scrunch down behind the shrubs again and plan our strategy. "What do you think?" Colin asks, no trace of the fear that colored his face a few days ago when I first mentioned finding Walker.

"I think we don't know how long they're gonna be gone, so if we're doing this, it's now or never."

He nods. "Let's find out if we're lucky enough they left the place unlocked."

We squeeze between the shrubs and cross the walkway to the door. A streetlight a hundred feet away supplies enough light to see, but isn't shining directly on us.

I reach out and yank the handle, but it doesn't budge. Based on the cobweb on the back door, it's unlikely that one has been used recently, but it'd suck to spend a bunch of time figuring out how to break in, only to find out later the back door was unlocked the whole time.

"Let's try the back door," I whisper.

We scoot down the sidewalk, going around to the back side again, but it's also locked.

"Now what?" Colin asks.

"Break a window?"

We head back to the front and stare up at the windows. Colin points to the one on the right. Narrowing my eyes, I notice it's open a fraction of an inch. Not much, but enough I can tell it's not latched. The opening's too small for Colin to fit through, but not me.

"Looks like I'm up," I say, swinging my arms and pretending I'm not scared shitless to dive head first into the unknown.

Colin squats, allowing me to sit on his shoulders. He stands, gripping my knees and moves next to the building, positioning me under the window. I'm still below the ledge, so I have to reach up with my fingers and feel for the lip of the frame.

Grime and dust greet my hand, and something tickles its way across my wrist. I yank my hand back, shaking it violently. A black dot falls to the sidewalk and skitters into the shadows. Cobwebs cling to my nails and I wipe them on Colin's shoulders before reaching up again.

Wedging my fingernails into the small crack between the window and the frame, I wiggle them until I can get my fingertips into the opening.

Colin sways under my weight and I hiss at him to hold still. He answers me by slapping my shin, but moves his feet apart and plants himself in a more stable stance. With a final shove, the window slides open.

"I need to stand on your shoulders," I whisper.

He nods and lets go of my legs, bracing his hands against the wall while I twist and claw my way to standing. His body wavers beneath me as I grip the inner edge of the frame and begin pulling myself up.

My left shoulder screams in protest and it hits me I might not be able to do this. The implanted meds mask the pain, but don't speed the healing process. Beads of sweat break out on my forehead, but I bite my lip and push through the pain.

My right arm does all the work, my left only along for the ride now. Colin pushes up on the bottom of my shoes, and I make the final lunge, my teeth cutting into my lip, drawing blood. My hips rest on the window sill while my head and shoulders squeeze through the shallow opening.

The ground is a long way down, but I close my eyes and shove off, dropping head-first, remembering to tuck and roll when I hit the floor. I'm no gymnast, nor particularly graceful, so what I envisioned as a daring ninja-style landing, is more of a thud and slam as I crash, flopping to my back.

"You okay?" Colin whisper shouts from outside.

"Yeah."

I get up slowly and wipe my hands on my jeans before unlocking the door and yanking him inside.

He closes and relocks the door while I wait for my eyes to adjust to the reduced light. I spot a chair across the room and drag it next to the wall to climb up and close the window.

Colin pulls out his tablet and turns on the screen to use as a flashlight. We're in a small office with one door leading off to the right and another straight back. A desk faces the door, littered with so much crap it resembles a pre-Union garbage heap. Greasy, crumpled food wrappers, mugs ringed with old coffee, boxes, and some stuff I don't recognize are shoved to one side. A couple chairs are piled with more junk, and an overflowing wastebasket and dying plant sit in the corner. Beside the desk is a short metal chest with two drawers.

Colin and I glance at each other, and with a shrug he starts on the desk. I could hug him right now for taking the worst job, and make my way over to the chest.

"Just garbage here," Colin announces.

"The chest is empty. Both drawers."

We head to the door on the right, which opens into another office with desk, chair, sink, mini fridge, and some strange looking machines. Unlike the cesspool out front, this desk is empty. Colin begins opening drawers while I check the machines.

I've just started searching when Colin whispers, "Jackpot!" and holds up a tablet.

Can we really be that lucky?

Colin shoves it into his jacket. "Let's go."

"We can't take it. They'll know someone's been here. And if it contains what we need, they'll know whoever took it has that information. Which means whatever we learn will be worthless. We have to get the information without them knowing we have it."

His eyebrows draw together and a scowl crosses his face. "So we just leave it here?"

"Yep. But after we copy whatever's on it to our tablets."

A clicking sound from outside makes me freeze, and an icy chill slips across my skin.

*Someone's at the front door.*

# Contingency Plans

*Evan*

**M**y heart slams against my rib cage, and I struggle to drag in a breath. The door creaks open in the front room, and Colin and I stare at each other, eyes wide and unblinking in the soft glow of his tablet. He turns off the screen, plunging us into darkness.

I dive under the desk and scoot into the back corner, pulling my knees to my chest, and hold my breath. Colin makes scuffling noises as he searches for his own hiding spot.

The next thing I know, Colin is next to me, bumping his head on the underside of the desk. He stifles an obscenity that begins and stops in his throat. I press my lips together, praying whoever's out front didn't hear. It wasn't loud, but the building is so quiet.

Colin folds his long legs in half and crushes them against his chest.

Footsteps come toward us, and I squeeze Colin's arm. He presses his forehead to mine as someone enters the office and flips on the light. I shrink back farther into the shadows and Colin squeezes even closer.

The chair rolls and squeaks with the weight of a body, knees stopping mere inches from Colin's back. It's only a matter of time before the warmth from our bodies is enough to give us away.

I palm my knife, my thumb poised over the button as a large hand pulls open the drawer on the right.

The hand reaches inside and removes something. My lungs burn with long-held air, black spots swimming in front of my eyes. Moments before I pass out, the guy rolls back and shoves the chair under the desk, bashing Colin's side.

Slowly, as if I'm under water, I let my breath out through my nose, straining for any sound to give me a clue where the guy is. I'm sure he isn't gone yet. Colin and I wait like statues, our breaths and nervous sweat mixing, turning the air in our small space balmy.

No sounds come from the room we're in or beyond, as if whoever's here is listening for us to make a sound. I left the chair beneath the window in the front room instead of moving it back, maybe he knows someone's been here. My heart pounds, echoing in my ears, until it's all I can hear, and fear burns through my veins like acid with every passing second.

Scuffing sounds near the office door are followed by receding footsteps. A few seconds later, the front door closes and locks.

Colin and I remain still, breathing shallowly in case he's tricked us.

When I've counted five minutes in my head, I shove Colin and he tumbles out, stretching his joints. I crawl out after him, working out my own kinks.

I'm ready to grab whatever information is on that tablet and get the hell out of here, but it's gone. Disappointment presses hard against me as I stare at the spot on the desk where the tablet was, hoping it will magically reappear until my vision blurs.

"Come on," I say, with a sigh of defeat.

"Wait, let's check out the backroom before we go. Might as well."

"Are you nuts?"

"Look, we already broke in here. We'll never get this chance again. I didn't risk my ass for nothing."

Resigned, I follow him through the second doorway, leading into a dark room. The sudden coolness of air makes it feel as if we've entered a large area. We both pull out our tablets and turn on our screens, illuminating a huge warehouse. Stacks of boxes reach like fingers toward the exposed rafters above. Row after row form a grid filling the enormous space.

I step closer to one and shine my screen on it. Holy shit, the boxes are filled with ammunition. Lots of ammo. When my heart starts beating again, it practically pounds its way out of my chest. There is no good reason to have this much ammunition in a warehouse. Only bad ones. Horrific, deadly bad reasons.

From somewhere in the distance, Colin announces, "Bingo!"

I rush to the far side where a workbench butts up against the side wall. Colin holds up a small external drive. He pushes the pin into the port of his tablet and downloads the contents. Seconds later, he sets it back on the workbench, and grabs my hand.

"Come on, EvTay. Let's get out of here." He leads me back up front, dropping my hand to unlock the door. He yanks, but the door doesn't open.

I push him aside and try. The handle moves, but the door won't budge. *Shit.* There's a deadbolt I didn't notice earlier that requires a key. Who the hell uses keys anymore? Colin checks the desk drawer for a key, and I go to the other office and do the same. My hand frantically skimming drawers, coming up empty.

Colin shakes his head, his shoulders dropping when I return empty-handed. The window I came through catches my eye and I climb back up to open it, but even if I can get back out, Colin can't fit through. I sink into the chair with a sigh.

"What about the back door?" Colin asks.

I shrug. It's worth a try. We head to the back, and Colin unlocks the door, but it's also secured with a deadbolt. He heads over to the workbench and begins searching for a key to the back door, while I work hard to fight the rising panic boiling in my gut.

"There's no key," Colin says, his voice unnaturally high.

"What are we going to do?"

"You can go get help. Go back out the window."

"And leave you here?"

The sound of the front door creaking has us both diving for cover behind the stacks of boxes. I clutch my fist to my chest, attempting to mask my ragged breaths, and grab my knife, switching open the blade.

Like a flash of lightning, an idea blasts into my brain — we need a diversion. I turn on my tablet and send a quick text to Tony.

And then we wait.

The air is musty, smelling of dust and sweat. The overhead lights flick on, flooding the warehouse with light while simultaneously carving dark shadows. Colin and I wait together next to a stack of boxes. Tony should have been here at least ten minutes ago.

Heavy footsteps head toward where we're hiding, and I push to my feet, remaining in a crouch, listening. Colin crawls to the end of our row and peers around the corner, then motions for me to follow.

The footsteps stop for several moments before resuming and stopping again.

"He's taking inventory," Colin whispers. "We just need to stay ahead of him until Tony gets here."

I nod, inching up behind Colin, staying low. Minutes tick by as Walker's goon shuffles his feet again moving to count the next stack. A loud pounding on the back door makes me jump, and I smack into a box. Colin pulls me around in front of him, putting his hand over my mouth.

The pounding comes again and the man yells, "Hold on, hold on." The metallic sound of a gun being cocked is followed by jangling and a click. I close my eyes and silently hope this plan doesn't result in Tony being shot.

We creep in the other direction as the door is yanked open behind us. "Let's go," Colin whispers.

We rush to the front office, and I cross my fingers as Colin unlocks the door. When it opens, I sigh with relief. Colin pokes his head out, looking both ways, then grabs my hand and yanks me out, closing the door quietly. We scurry across the sidewalk and take cover behind the shrubs where we camped out earlier.

"What now?" I mouth.

He takes my hand and pulls me down the alley until the buildings at the other end obscure us. We walk south until the path joins up with the one that runs in front of the building we escaped from only moments ago and wait in the shadows for Tony.

"What if the guy at the warehouse doesn't believe he was just in the wrong place?" I ask.

Colin shrugs.

"We need to make sure he's okay." I grab Colin's sleeve and pull him after me.

Knife in hand, we slink toward the alley, stopping in the deep shadows of a couple of trees on the corner. Tony and the warehouse guy, the dude from earlier I didn't recognize, are still in the alley. I can't hear what they're saying, but the man points and Tony nods. Laughter follows, then Tony says, "Okay, thanks. Sorry to bother you."

The guy closes the door, and Tony makes his way toward us, weaving.

"Is he drunk?" Colin asks.

I shrug. "Maybe. I mean, he might've stopped at a bar after we left."

We pull back further behind the trees until Tony reaches us.

"Pssst," Colin calls out.

Tony's head swivels in our direction, and with a quick glance back down the alley, ducks in to join us. I throw my arms around him and hug him tight. He doesn't smell like alcohol.

"Thank you, Tony."

He puts his hands on my shoulders and pushes me back. "Let's go."

I yank Colin's sleeve and drag him behind me as we trail Tony back to the commuter station. While we wait for the next train, Tony turns to me, his usually brilliant blue eyes are dark and angry.

"I should never have let you two go there by yourselves. I don't know what I was thinking."

"You didn't let us." I shrug. "We just did."

"But I knew what you were up to." He shakes his head. "I was already in the process of getting dressed to come check on you when I got your text."

"Well, it's a good thing you weren't with us or all three of us would be stuck in there right now," I say.

He grunts a response as the train pulls in. It's a short ride before we get off and follow Tony into the darkened lobby of Western Provincial News. After locking the front door, he leads us to his office and collapses into his chair.

"At least tell me you found something."

Colin pushes his tablet across the desk to Tony. "We can do better than that, we can show you."

Tony turns it on and begins swiping through files. Colin and I move behind Tony so we can read over his shoulder. Tony lifts his head and turns toward us, a smile spreading across his face.

*Holy shit.*

We hit the jackpot.

# Jackpot

*Evan*

"**W**ow," Colin says, glancing around the beach. "This place is packed."

I nod, taking in the overwhelming number of teens crisscrossing our path. A few are in shorts, clearly visiting from somewhere far colder, but many are dressed like us, in jeans and sweaters.

"What's the deal?"

"No clue, but I hope they still have tents available."

After spending a week and a half with Tony, sorting through the information we found in the warehouse, we're both more than ready to reunite with the others.

My level of anxiety only increased with our arrival at the campground. I miss my friends, and I'm worried about where things stand, or rather don't stand, with Cyrus. There's also a nagging worry in the back of my mind that someone won't make it back.

As we approach the registration tent, two guys tossing a football back and forth shift to lobbing it over our heads rather than pausing to allow us to pass.

A girl in a ridiculously small bikini, given it's not even March, argues with the front desk clerk, her hands flying out to her sides before returning to her hips in a huff. She shouts something obscene and turns, halting when she spots us, her face reddening before marching outside. She stops to say something to the two football guys.

Colin tears his eyes away from her ass, giving his full attention to the harried clerk. "We need four tents."

The kid behind the desk snorts. "Right. At the end of midwinter break. You're funny."

That explains why it's as crowded as the shopping district on Christmas Eve and why everyone is dressed inappropriately for the weather.

"Do you have *any* tents?" I ask.

"I can get you two small ones on the outer edge of camp."

Well that sucks, but this is where we're supposed to meet, so it's not like we can go to a different campground. "Fine," I say. "We'll take them."

Teeny bikini storms back in. "You know what? This place is for losers. We're leaving." She turns and stomps back out.

The clerk closes his eyes and sighs. "I can give you a third one now. The big one in the middle of camp."

"Great," Colin says. "Thanks."

"Yeah, not a big deal. But we don't have any strawberry-flavored ice cubes. Just so you know."

Colin and I glance at each other, and I stifle a giggle. That's what she was worried about? She needs to spend a day out in the Ruins if she wants to experience real problems.

Thirty minutes later, a porter leads the way to a large tent in the center of camp, similar to the one Rainey and I shared last time.

"I'll take this one," I say. "Unless you want to share the giant bed with someone."

"No, I'm good. You gonna share with Lisa and Jack?"

"Haha, funny boy. No. I figured Lisa, Rainey, and I can manage and you guys can fight over the cots and floors of the other two tents."

"Works for me."

He slings his bag over his shoulder and saunters down the path behind the porter to the next tent.

I drop my stuff on the floor next to the bed, kick off my shoes, and run out to catch up with Colin. The second tent is all the way down at the southern edge of camp. Colin tips the porter for both of us and heads in to dump his stuff before rejoining me.

"Now what?" he asks, swinging his arms.

I shrug. "I don't know. We didn't have a plan beyond meeting back here in two weeks. Bryce texted from the train they'll be here in a couple of hours. Let's go see if the others are back yet."

We set out, lapping the campground twice, weaving between tents, checking the mess tent and the beach before accepting no one else is back.

"Coffee?" Colin asks after we wrap up our second tour.

"Sure."

We head to the massive canvas tent anchoring the western edge of camp and grab coffee, taking it down to the water. The wind blows a frigid salty mist, pelting my face with water smelling of fish and seaweed. A group of teens, wearing nothing but swimsuits, run up and down the sand, throwing a Frisbee.

Colin and I make our way south to the jetty and climb up onto the rocks. I scan the horizon for sailboats. Plenty of boats bob and roll on the waves this morning. I hope Cyrus and Rainey are aboard one of them.

After an hour of watching boat after boat pass without coming ashore, I give up. "I'm heading back to camp."

Colin nods and follows me. When we reach the mess tent, Bryce and Jack are sitting at one of the outdoor tables sipping coffee. My heart skips a beat, and I stumble run through thick sand the last hundred yards to them.

Bryce stands and wraps his arms around me, pulling me in for a long hug. When he releases me, I move over to Jack and give him a quick squeeze while Bryce and Colin do the guy-bro handshake back-patting thing.

Bryce and Jack pick up their coffees, and Colin and I show them to the third tent to drop off their bags. The four of us head down to the beach, away from any potential eavesdroppers, to talk. Colin launches into our adventures with Tony and the warehouse.

Bryce stops and grabs my hand, turning me to face him. "I thought you were going to take it easy."

"So that didn't happen," I say. "But…it was totally worth it. Tell 'em what we found, Col."

Colin shares what we discovered on the thumb drive, and my smile grows as Bryce's eyes widen and Jack's jaw drops.

"Holy shit…" Jack whispers.

I nod. "Yeah. So-holy-it's-nearly-heavenly shit."

Jack shakes his head, his own smile growing. "I can't believe you two and Tony figured out in less than a week what my dad couldn't in six months."

Colin laughs. "Well, it was Evan's idea to do the reverse aging thing, but Tony's the one who found the warehouse."

"We should turn this over to my dad to investigate further," Jack says.

"No way," Colin says, his face darkening as he runs a hand through his dark locks. "If you do and they move in, then what? We lose the element of surprise. They don't know we have this information. If they figure it out, everything we risked our asses for will be worthless."

"We can't just leave a warehouse of ammo sitting there. I'm sorry, but the potential for what could happen is too much for me to just sit on."

"Jack, please," I say. "Can't we talk about this first?"

He shakes his head, "No. Look, my dad isn't going to go in guns blazing, but he's been trying to find Walker for months. This is the first solid lead. He needs to know what you guys found. He knows what's at stake, Evan."

This is an argument I can't win, so I nod, shoving my hands into my pockets, and trudge back to my tent.

The smell of pine mixes with smoke as we gather around our own private bonfire. Snapping and popping of the burning wood rises above the pulsing waves behind us. No one else has returned yet, and a palpable tension hangs over us like a storm cloud. I feel a rare kinship with Jack when I see my own anxiety reflected back in his eyes.

"We spent a few days staking out Benton's place before I cornered Alivia on the street and got into the apartment," Bryce says. "The level of activity was significantly higher than it was last fall."

"We needed to get in to see what was going on," Jack says with a shrug, as if apologizing for using my arch-nemesis yet again.

"Sneaking away from Alivia for any length of time wasn't easy," Bryce says. "So I told her I was visiting my family for a couple of days and had to leave soon, but wanted to make sure I could see her next time I was in town. She showed me how she sneaks in and out of the apartment."

"Wait, so you broke into the mayor's apartment?" Colin asks.

Bryce shrugs. "It wasn't so much breaking in as it was entering uninvited. A little less risky than what you two did."

"Semantics," I say. "So, what did you find?"

"We got our hands on the identities being entered into the database. Benton's not doing it himself, he's got some computer guy working for him."

"We should turn the list over to Jack's dad so he can start tracking them down," Colin says.

"Can he do that without tipping anyone off?" I ask.

"Remember what I said before?" Bryce asks. "If we have a specific target to focus on that's not the Ruins, we have a better chance of stopping this without risking innocent people in the Ruins."

"Yeah. And we know who that is now. Walker."

He rubs his head with his hand before leaning back against a log with a sigh. "But not just Walker. He's working with Benton and who knows who else. If we keep an eye on who he's bringing in, we improve the odds of getting everyone involved. They won't just be turned loose in here. They'll be working with others. We need to find out how high this goes. Benton's too much of a yes-man to be the top dog."

"Okay, but can Max track them without them finding out?" I ask again.

Jack blows out a long breath. "I don't know. I hope so. Because until we know who we can trust, anyone investigating this thing is in danger, my dad included."

"But an even bigger problem," Bryce says, "is there are more coming every day. We're going to head back and get more names. The more information we have, the better prepared we'll be."

"Tony was able to locate the warehouse through his research, maybe he can help Max," I say. "It might be easier that way and maybe less likely to draw attention to what they're doing."

Jack nods. "Not a bad idea. I'll talk to my dad about it tomorrow when I meet with him." He pushes up and wipes the sand off his pants with his hands. "I'm gonna take another walk around camp and turn in."

"I'll come with you," I say, getting up to join him.

But we both know no one else is coming tonight.

*Cyrus*

"Rainey—"

"I swear, Cyrus, if you apologize to me one more time, I'll slice your balls off and feed 'em to the sharks."

I swallow hard, convinced she means it, and take another swig of beer.

She stares at me, licking the salt on the rim of her margarita. "I'm not even so much pissed anymore that you almost got me killed, although mostly because I try not to think about it. But you did exactly the thing you claim is the reason you're so torqued at Evan. It was reckless and stupid. You don't do dumb, which means your head's not on straight. I get you've got your shit, we all do, but unlike you, I don't have a death wish." She takes a big gulp of her drink and sets it down hard on the table.

"I don't have a death wish," I mumble, but she's right about the rest.

"Well you sure could've fooled me." She turns and gazes out the window overlooking the beach below. "You got a second chance here, dude. You should be dead now, we both should. Don't fuck it up."

"You ever gonna tell me what you said to those guys?"

Her head swivels back to me, eyes narrowed. "Nope," she says, dragging out the n and popping the p.

The remnants of the paper label of my beer litter the table, and I push them around with my finger. "You don't have to do this with me, I'm not asking you to."

"I haven't been hanging out in a hotel for the past week so I could let you do it alone. But I need to know your head's in the right place, that you're not gonna do something idiotic again. We've got a pretty good plan. Stick to it and if it starts to fall apart, we cut and run. Okay?"

"Yeah. I don't think it's gonna fall apart though. We've been watching them for a week, they're so routine it's stupid."

"Anything can go wrong, and no doubt something will, but I'm not any more thrilled about going back empty-handed than you are."

I toss back the rest of my beer and set it down, the label pieces fluttering. "I'm heading back to the room to get some sleep. I want to leave before dawn."

"I'll be up in a bit." She takes another sip of her drink and turns her attention back to the beach.

I throw a couple of crumpled bills on the table and walk back across the street.

After we paid the boat operator to let us off the minute we were out of sight of Fredo's goons, we circled back to our hotel and grabbed our stuff before checking into a new room across town. We've been staking out those assholes ever since. The warehouse is only guarded by one young kid early in the morning, and he spends most of his time watching porn on his tablet.

I let myself into the room and fall back on the bed with a groan. Rainey's right, I've got a second chance, and she wasn't only talking about this deal. I have a second chance to make things right with Evan.

My gaze travels from the spiked heels of Rainey's boots up her shapely legs to the tight skirt hugging her hips. Her long hair is styled straight and sleek, covering the scar on the left half of her face, while the right is tucked behind her ear, revealing how pretty she really is.

Damn, she's hot. I let out a whistle.

Possibly for the first time ever, Rainey blushes, shoving me in the shoulder as she brushes past. "Stop looking at my ass."

I chuckle, unwilling to admit that's exactly what I was doing.

Rainey's gun is strapped to her thigh under her skirt, and mine's tucked into my waistband, my loose T-shirt hanging over it. We make our way down the cobbled street, polished smooth by centuries of wear, toward the warehouse under the cover of darkness, those kick-ass heels of hers making a racket.

"Hold up a sec," she says, bending forward to unzip her boots and peel them off.

We make the rest of the walk in relative silence. When we get a block away from the target, I motion for Rainey to stay back before I move closer, scoping it out to make sure they haven't changed things up. Peeking around the corner, I see the kid, staring at his tablet, his chest rising and falling rapidly. Idiot. This is almost too easy.

I signal to Rainey that we're a go, and when she waves back, I head around the side of the building, listening for the clicking of her heels as she approaches the guard.

From my spot behind a large trash bin, I watch the dude glance up from his tablet when she nears. He fumbles the thing, nearly dropping it before stuffing it into the pocket of his cargo pants. The sound is still on, though, and the heavy breathing and moans from whatever video he was watching echo off the walls until he reaches in and shuts it off.

The plan is for Rainey to tell him she's the new bartender at one of the exclusive twenty-four-hour underground nightclubs and ask him for directions. I can't understand what she's saying, but he seems to be buying it, although his eyes never rise higher than her chest.

I slip up behind him and press the barrel of my firearm against the back of his neck. He freezes, mid-laugh, and Rainey reaches forward to relieve him of his rifle.

I don't need a translator to get the gist of what he says. Rainey grins before whispering something to him in response.

The kid's face turns purple, but he nods, pressing his fingerprint to a device mounted next to a metal door. It clicks, and I twist the handle, pushing the door open.

"Hang on," I whisper to Rainey, entering first, my senses on alert.

When no one fires, Rainey enters behind me, dragging the kid with her.

"Did you frisk him?" I ask.

"Yeah. He's clean."

She's got his mouth taped and hands secured behind him with the duct tape she stashed in her bra. With every day that passes, I'm more and more glad we're on the same side. I'd hate to have to go up against her.

After our eyes adjust, we work together sweeping the warehouse until we're sure no one else is here. I toss Rainey a bag and we both begin loading up, grabbing the guns and ammo we paid for. When the first one's full, I zip it up and start on the next, trying not to get too cocky over how flawlessly this is going.

A loud pop from behind makes me whip around only seconds before a bullet zips past my head. Too close.

"Rainey!"

"I'm okay," she calls back as more shots ring out, bullets pinging off metal shelving.

*Shit.* Dropping to my knees, I peer over a stack of crates at two dark shadows near the door. I crawl over to Rainey at the end of the row, reaching her as another barrage of bullets fly, tearing up the boxes we're using as cover.

Rainey stuffs her handgun in her waistband and levels the rifle she took off the guard. "These guys are pissing me off. Cover me."

I fire off a half-dozen rounds and they both duck, but Rainey's ready and hits one in the knee. He goes down, screaming, while the other one disappears out the door.

Rainey peels off her boots and stands. "I've got this." She runs toward the door, her bare feet slapping against concrete.

I take off after her, kicking the rifle away from the guy writhing on the floor as I pass.

Rainey pops her head outside only to pull back mere seconds before a bullet rips into the door above where her head had just been. I reach around and fire a couple of shots while Rainey ducks down and squares herself, lining up another shot. A head and shoulder appear around the corner, and Rainey fires, but misses.

"Go finish grabbing everything," she says. "And grab that C-4, too. It could come in handy. Take everything we can carry. I figure we're due an incentive after what they put us through."

I'm not comfortable leaving her in the door alone, but we need to get out of here, so I rush back over and load up the bags. When they're stuffed, I fill my pockets with cartridges and spare magazines for easy access. Grabbing the bags, I return to Rainey.

She fires off two more rounds and pops up from the floor, tossing a backpack on and grabbing another by the straps. I square one of the backpacks on my back, and grab the rest in my right hand, using my left to hold my weapon.

Rainey and I back out of the warehouse, moving away from where the shooters are taking cover. At the corner, we turn and run down the alley. No more than ten steps later, a bullet tears past my ear, and I jerk back against the wall. Turning, I fire off a few shots until they stop shooting at us, allowing Rainey to make it to the end of the alley.

"Come on," she yells, firing to provide me with cover.

I reach her, huffing to catch my breath. The extra weight of these bags is taking its toll. "Now what?"

"I'm about out of ammo. I need to reload. Can you cover me?"

"Yeah. Load a couple for me, too," I say between breaths.

Rainey reaches into the side pocket of my cargo pants and pulls out cartridges and magazines, loading them with fingers blurring like the Uprising pro she once was, while I keep our pursuers at bay. She hands me a freshly loaded gun, taking mine to refill. It takes her less than three minutes to load up four guns, but it feels more like hours. I'm itching to get the hell out of here.

A sudden shot from behind us has us both hitting the ground.

Rainey and I lock eyes, simultaneously arriving at the same conclusion.

They've circled around us.

We're penned in.

# Escape Plans

*Cyrus*

**B**ullets bite the ground around us. I cover my head with my right arm, firing off rounds with my left. Rainey works on fending off whoever's behind us, letting loose a stream of profanity that would make me laugh if we weren't in so deep.

"What now?" I yell over my shoulder.

"I've got an idea, hang on."

"Hang on to what?"

"Cover me for a sec. I need to reload."

I twist and fire two shots behind me before returning my attention to the guys in front. They duck back behind the wall, but it's only a matter of time before reinforcements arrive.

"Okay," Rainey calls to me.

"Okay?"

"Just follow me."

I have no idea where, but I've got nothing better and nothing to lose at this point.

Rainey gets up, one gun in each hand, and fires in both directions as she backs up across the alley.

I doubt we can shoot our way out of this, but I'm not going down without a fight. Might as well go with it. Pushing up, I adjust the backpacks and bags and follow Rainey. I can't shoot straight for shit with my right hand, but I guess it doesn't need to be straight.

With both of us firing two guns, the guys momentarily retreat around the corner, allowing Rainey to lead the way to a narrow alley between two buildings.

"What the hell are we doing, Rainey? We went from penned in to being fish in a barrel."

"Trust me. There's a door here. The kid up front told me about this entrance when he thought I was trying to find my way into the nightclub. Here." She yanks open a door and ducks inside, pulling me with her. "They'll figure out where we went in a second, so we have to hurry."

The room is black, and I bump into something hard. A table. It rocks on its base before righting itself as we move past.

"Come on." Rainey runs through the dark room and opens another door.

We step into an empty hall and halt. I'm unsure which way to go, but the sound of the door in the alley opening and slamming into the wall behind us has me moving.

"This way." I grab Rainey's arm.

At the end of the hall, we push through another door that leads to a set of stairs heading down. Going downstairs sounds like a good way to get ourselves cornered, but going back isn't an option. Down it is.

Dingy yellow lights hanging from cords in the ceiling illuminate our way, but just barely.

"Watch your step," I say, noticing a broken bottle on the floor.

I reach around and swing Rainey into my arms, carrying her over the glass shards before setting her down, kind of wishing now she hadn't taken her boots off.

We jet through the hallway where we're greeted by a loud thumping, rhythmic and heavy. I halt and Rainey slams into my back.

"Go," she says, shoving me between my shoulder blades.

Voices from behind, combined with Rainey's prodding, push me into action. I haul ass the last fifty feet, dumping into a dark room with pulsing lights, loud music, and sweaty dancers moving in time to the beat, holding drinks high overhead. At five o'clock in the morning.

Bodies press against me, forcing me left then right. A pretty girl with long black hair smiles up at me, never missing a step as she dances past.

Rainey grabs my arm and yanks me, threading her way through the crowd.

Over the tops of bouncing heads, I spot two guys with rifles enter the club. Ducking, I follow Rainey across the room and out into another hallway. We dash to the end to find more stairs, one set going down and another leading up.

Rainey looks to me for a decision.

I shrug and head up. I'd rather take my chances on the street.

At the top of the stairs we find another club. This is crazy. It's like a maze of nightclubs. We weave through the crowd again, entering another leg of this crazy-ass labyrinth.

"Which way now?" I ask.

"Let's stay down here as long as we can. We have a better chance of hiding out in the throngs. And they're less likely to shoot into a large group of people. I hope, anyway."

We continue threading our way through hallways, nightclubs, and staircases, up and down, in and out, zigging and zagging until I'm drenched in sweat and struggling to catch my breath. After we've gone through several clubs without seeing our friends, I'm pretty sure we shook them.

I lead the way up a set of stairs to street level, and push through a door into gray morning light. With my finger on the trigger of my gun, I look both ways.

My back against the wall, I slide the last few feet to the end of the alley and peer around the corner.

Straight into the barrel of a gun.

*Shit.*

### Evan

Anxiety gnaws on my stomach like a squirrel on a piece of bread. Except this is more like a pack of squirrels fighting over a single crumb.

The possibility that the others have returned and are waiting for us in the mess area propels me out of bed. I throw on a pair of jeans and Eddie's sweatshirt before heading out to get coffee. The only person I recognize at any of the tables is Bryce, and he's alone. Steam rises from a mug in front of him, his hands wrapped around the base of it.

I duck into the mess tent and grab my own coffee before taking the seat next to Bryce.

"Morning," I mumble.

He nods. "Good morning."

Ten minutes of silence pass before Colin and Jack join us, before the four of us spend a long, agonizing day waiting in vain for our friends. As one hour passes into the next, tension becomes a steady companion. Eating is impossible, so I try walking the campground to ease some of this fear trickling through me. As the morning transitions to afternoon, nausea replaces the emptiness in my gut.

By the time the sun hovers over the horizon, I've lapped the campground more than a dozen times, my eyes constantly scanning the ocean for boats heading this way. Finally I take a seat on the jetty and pull my knees up to my chest, wrapping my arms around them.

"Hey," Colin says.

I tear my gaze away from the water long enough to acknowledge him. "Hey."

Dark circles mar the skin beneath his eyes and gravity tugs at the corners of his mouth, as if holding his lips in a natural state of rest is an effort. He climbs up and sits next to me, draping one of his long arms across my shoulder.

He presses a kiss to the top of my head. "They're going to be okay."

"You don't know that."

He sighs. "No, I don't, but I need to believe it."

"Me too," I whisper.

The sun dips beneath the sea, turning the sky from cobalt to crimson.

Colin pushes off the jetty. "I'm going to get dinner. Coming?"

I follow him, not because I'm hungry, but because I don't want to be alone. We eat a sullen dinner and find a fire to gather around.

When it's too late to do anything except go to bed, I trudge off to my tent, but sleep is no easier tonight than it was last night even though I'm exhausted. Every time I allow myself to think my friends might not come back, I feel like I'm drowning, my heart pounding, trying to break free of my chest.

The morning begins the same as yesterday, except I'm far more bleary eyed. Coffee helps. A little. We spend another long, nail-biting day with no news and no activity. By lunch, we're all snapping at each other, and I've had enough commiserating.

I push up from the table, needing to get away from the rest of them. "I'm going for a walk. Alone."

My feet take me down to the water's edge, and I tell myself it's so the sound of the surf can soothe me, but my eyes scan the horizon the way they always do. Hours pass, the waiting futile, frustrating, nerve-wracking.

The tears I've refused to allow will no longer be denied. They gather and fall freely down my cheeks. What if they never come back? I wipe angrily at my eyes, refusing to let that thought get a foothold. So there's no reason to cry. Too bad my stupid eyes can't get with the agenda as tears continue to pool and escape.

A warm body presses against my back, startling me, and brown arms wrap around my shoulders. "I'm sorry," Bryce says.

He thinks I'm upset because of all of our petty arguments today, but the comfort he's offering, no matter the reason, is exactly what I need. I turn and bury my face in his chest, letting him hold me while I sob. He pats the back of my head until I'm all cried out. The front of his shirt is damp with my tears and snot, and I rub it with my sleeve, but that only makes it worse.

"God, I'm such a mess," I say.

"We all are, but you're the only one who isn't pretending you're not."

"How's Jack holding up?"

"About like you. Minus the tears."

I wipe my eyes and nose on Eddie's sweatshirt, which is a couple of days past needing a wash as it is. "I'm better when I have a plan, but I don't know what to do. We all agreed if anyone was late, we'd go look for them. But I never thought we'd be missing four. Do we go after Lisa and Simon first or Cyrus and Rainey? Or do we split up, half going to Mexico and the others out to the Ruins?"

He only sighs and pulls me back against his chest, resting his chin on my head. He smells like brine and soap, and it's oddly comforting.

His arms stiffen and his breath notches before he lifts his chin. "Looks like we're only missing two now."

Shifting, I follow his gaze, and my heart skips a beat before it takes off at a sprint. Cyrus and Rainey are trudging across the beach, weighed down by backpacks and duffel bags. I rip myself from Bryce's arms and stumble run through the sand, throwing my arms around them both, a cross between a sob and a laugh escaping my mouth.

Cyrus drops his bags and wraps two strong arms around me, sighing as he rests his stubbled cheek on my head. I close my eyes and melt into him, almost forgetting Rainey is part of a three-way hug.

Rainey lets go and I wrap my other arm around Cyrus, but he stiffens and releases me. Reality slams into me like an angry wave, reminding me how things are between us. Rejection and defeat edge out the relief I was harboring. I turn away and start back toward camp, a hollow ache in my chest.

Bryce approaches Rainey, catching my eye for a second before reaching down to take her bags. "How'd it go?"

"We can talk about it later," Rainey says, glancing at Cyrus, something silent and heavy passing between them.

I lead the way to my tent in silence. Rainey drops her stuff off and then we go in search of Colin and Jack, finding them at a bonfire. They pop up off the ground as if someone lit their shorts on fire.

"Hey, when did you get back?" Colin asks, throwing his arms around Rainey.

"Just now."

Colin reaches around Rainey to shake Cyrus's hand.

"I'm starving," Cyrus says, running a hand through his hair.

"Same here," Colin says, because he's never let anything like a missing friend get in the way of his appetite. As Colin leads

Rainey and Cyrus to the mess tent, I overhear him telling them we're still waiting for Lisa and Simon.

Jack sits with this forearms propped up on his knees, staring into the fire, and I drop down beside him. Sparks jettison skyward before burning out and disappearing into the thick marine layer blanketing the stars.

I turn and study his profile, note his grinding jaw. "She'll be back, too, you'll see."

He sighs, keeping his gaze locked on the flames. The others return with their meals, the smell of grilled meat turning my stomach.

Colin sits next to me. "Want a bite?"

I shake my head, not even a little interested in food. I watch as Rainey sandwiches herself between Bryce and Cyrus.

"So what happened to you guys?" Jack asks.

"We ran into a little trouble," Rainey says, but something in her voice makes me think the trouble wasn't as little as she's trying to play it off.

"What kind of trouble?" Jack asks, narrowing his eyes.

She shrugs. "Let's just say we might not have a lot of friends south of the border."

I turn to Cyrus, but his gaze is fixed on the flames, face expressionless, as if he's not paying attention.

"What's in the bags? Did you at least accomplish the mission?" Bryce asks.

Cyrus glances at Bryce before turning back to the fire. "Yep."

Thick silence wedges in the spaces between us like an unwelcomed guest. It soon becomes clear Rainey and Cyrus aren't offering up anything more.

Jack launches into what they found back east. He pauses mid-sentence and says, "Hang on," before taking off for his tent and returning a few minutes later with his tablet. He turns it on and hands it to Cyrus. "Here are the names and photos of who we have so far. Let me know if any of them look familiar."

Cyrus swipes through the photos, Rainey leaning over to look at the screen, too. Cyrus stops and narrows his eyes before shaking his head and continuing. When he's done, he gives it back to Jack. "Nope. No one I recognize."

After another lull in conversation, the topic turns to Lisa and Simon. "We shouldn't be surprised they're not back yet," Colin says. "They had a tough assignment. Plus, they wouldn't abandon their mission just because time was up."

"Maybe," I say. "But they knew we'd be worried. They could've at least reported back in or something. Unless they can't…" I shut up and peek at Jack, his jaw is working overtime.

"Simon knows his way around out there," Rainey says. "And he can talk his way out of pretty much any situation. I'm sure they're fine."

"Let's wait till tomorrow," Cyrus says. "See if they show up. If not, we'll plan our next move."

No one argues or offers an alternative, so silent agreement wins by default. An awkward quiet rolls in like morning fog, and Jack clears his throat, glancing at me.

I shake my head. No way am I volunteering our information tonight.

He rolls his eyes and shares with Cyrus and Rainey what we found in the warehouse. The awkward lulls in conversation from before are nothing compared to the deafening silence that follows Jack's tale.

For several long, torturous moments, the only sounds are the crashing surf behind us and the fire snapping and spitting in front of us.

"Your job was to make sure that kinda shit didn't happen." Cyrus says with scary-dead calm, directing a deathly glare at Colin.

Colin tenses next to me and inhales sharply. "I'm sorry, but have you actually met Evan? She does whatever the hell she wants. You're out of your damn mind if you think she was gonna listen to me."

After two days of no sleep and almost nothing to eat, being talked about like I'm not here pushes me over the edge. I stand, ready to unleash a mouthful, but words fail me. Instead I open and close my mouth like a fish before turning and marching back to my tent. Once inside, I let loose a torrent of obscenities.

I'm sick of the way Cyrus is always pissed at me. Whether it's Bryce, me not following orders, or something else, I don't know, but whatever the problem is, it might be something I can't fix.

And that scares the hell out of me.

## Cyrus

"Are you being an asshole just for the sake of it?" Rainey asks as we head back toward our tents.

I cut my eyes to her. "What does that mean?"

"You couldn't wait to get back here to work things out with Evan. What the hell happened?"

I run a hand through my hair and blow out a long breath. "Nothing."

"Bullshit."

I stop and turn toward her. "Fine. Seeing his hands all over her...I...I can't, okay?"

"You can't what? Shit, Cyrus, you go down to Mexico, take on arms dealers, but you can't tell the girl you love how you feel? You're a bigger pussy than I thought."

"Shut up, Rainey."

"You know what?" She stops and shakes her head. "Never mind. You're an idiot, though." She stomps off toward the tent she's sharing with Evan.

I head down to the water to clear my head. I didn't come back to fight with Evan. Hell, I don't want to fight with her, but damn it, I can't stand that she slept with that tool. Seeing them on the beach tonight only reminded me he's been with her in a way I haven't, and it pisses me off.

If I can't get past this, maybe I don't love her the way I thought I did.

If I believe that, I'm an even bigger idiot than Rainey thinks I am.

# Frustrated

## Evan

ool, moist air greets me when I emerge from my tent.
Morning sun reflects off low clouds, casting the sky in a
soft gray. The sand scrunches under my bare feet as I
make my way over to the mess tent for coffee.

Bryce and Jack are sitting at one of the tables nursing their
own cups when I sit down to join them. Jack's face is pulled tight,
and the deep purple rings beneath his eyes are even more
pronounced than yesterday. Golden stubble dusted with flecks of
darker whiskers give him a rugged appearance that would look
good on him if he wasn't so worn. Yesterday, Jack and I were in
this together. Today, at least I know the boy I love is safe, even if
he hates me.

I reach out and place my hand on Jack's arm. "Rainey's right, Simon's a resourceful guy. Plus he knows people in all the right places."

His gaze rises to meet mine for a moment before dropping back to his coffee.

Colin ambles up, thunking his tray — overflowing with eggs, toast, and a towering stack of pancakes — on the table and begins shoveling food into his mouth.

"Colin and I will go look for them," I tell Jack.

Colin turns to me. "Huh?" His bottom lip goes slack and a piece of egg falls out, hitting his plate. So gross.

"You and me. We can go find Lisa and Simon."

He nods vigorously and returns to chewing, washing it down with a mouthful of coffee. "Yeah. Totally. We can leave today."

Jack glances up again, the heaviness of his fear apparent in his hunched shoulders. "I want to go with you."

"I thought you were heading back east," Colin says.

"Not until I know she's safe."

"We can't afford to wait," Bryce says. "But I can handle it on my own."

"No. We agreed everyone pairs up." I turn toward Jack and squeeze his arm. "We have this. Give me your tablet."

Jack reaches into his back pocket and pulls out his tablet, handing it to me.

I locate the town where Sonia, Marcus, and the others live near the border of the Northern Territories on the map app. "Here's where we'll be in two weeks. Head to the bar in the center of town and ask for Ally. She'll get you to us. All of us. Lisa and Simon, too. I promise."

Jack's gaze locks with mine, and after a few long seconds, he nods. "Okay. But if you don't get her, I'm calling in the cavalry. I'll do whatever it takes to get her back."

"Fair enough." I take a sip of coffee and swallow, remembering something else. "Oh, hey, what did your dad have to say about the warehouse and the identities you found?"

"He's staking out the warehouse, but so far, he said there's no movement. He's worried they've already abandoned it."

My shoulders drop. We should have turned the information over to him as soon as we had it, instead of sitting on it for nine days. Sure they had no clue we'd been there, but maybe Tony knocking on the back door spooked them enough to move.

"He's working with Tony to track the people on the list I gave him. If they're on the grid, they'll be able to monitor their movements."

"And if they're not?"

"Then at least we know they're here, even if we don't know where. But it makes no sense for them to go to the trouble of getting official credentials just to hide out on the lower levels," Bryce says, checking his watch. "We'd better get going if we're going to catch the morning train."

Jack pushes up and the two of them head off to pack.

Rainey and Cyrus wander over to the mess tent within minutes of each other. I try to pretend it doesn't bother me. Cyrus scratches his hand through his hair and studies me with an indecipherable expression before heading inside to get breakfast. Rainey mumbles something that might be "good morning" and plops down at the table next to us.

When Cyrus returns with his food, Colin says, "Bryce and Jack are going back east this morning to get more IDs," leaving off the part where he and I are going into the Ruins to find Lisa and Simon.

Cyrus nods and Rainey mumbles something else. Jack and Bryce reappear, bags in hand. Glancing between a sullen Cyrus and an incoherent Rainey, I push up. "I'm coming with you."

"Me, too," Colin says.

The trip to the top level is quiet with no attempts made at small talk by anyone. Jack shuffles off to get tickets and rejoins us, handing one of them to Bryce.

The train eases into the station, and I hug Jack tightly. To my surprise, he wraps his arms around me and squeezes, a sigh escaping his mouth.

"We'll find her." He presses his lips together and stares at me with brilliant blue eyes overflowing with worry. "We will."

Pulling me back in, he whispers, "Okay," before releasing me.

I reach out to give Bryce a quick hug. "Be careful."

He gives me a dimpled smile. "Always."

Jack and Bryce throw us one last wave goodbye and disappear into the train. Colin drapes his arm over my shoulder and we watch as they pull away and disappear from sight.

"So now what?" Colin asks when our feet hit the sand.

"Now we break it to Cyrus and Rainey that we're going to find Lisa and Simon."

"It's not gonna go over well."

I sigh. "Yeah, I know."

Rainey and Cyrus are still at the table outside the mess tent, heads together, reviewing the information on Colin's tablet from the warehouse. There's no way they can deny the importance of what we found.

"Hey," Colin calls out.

Their heads shoot up, and Cyrus glances at me briefly, but his eyes won't meet mine.

Rainey stands and hands Colin his tablet. "Come on, let's go for a walk."

We follow Rainey down to the water where the remaining cloud cover has burned off, revealing a brilliant azure sky. A flock of squawking seagulls glide above the calm surf, one diving down to grab breakfast. A few other campers stroll along the sand, enjoying their last day of mid-winter break.

"We've been talking," Rainey says. "Cyrus and I'll go get Lisa and Simon while you two head up north to the house."

"Colin and I already decided we're going. We figured with you two both being former commanders, it's more dangerous for you."

She lets out a laugh that sounds more like a bark. "No offense, but you almost got yourself killed last time."

"No offense, but I'm guessing things didn't go according to plan south of the border," I shoot back. She and Cyrus exchange a loaded glance, but neither tries to deny it. "Okay, so we all go together."

"No," Cyrus says, hands stuffed into the front pockets of his jeans, gaze fixed on the horizon. "We can't risk losing more people. The fewer of us that're together at one time, the less chance we'll diminish our numbers. After reviewing the data you got, I have an idea, but it's going to take all of us and more to pull it off."

I reach out to grab his sleeve, forcing him to face me. His expression is like a mask, betraying nothing. "Then we'll have to keep each other safe. Lisa and Simon are missing, and up until last night, so were you and Rainey. We were going to head down there to look for you."

For just a second, his mask slips and surprise flitters across his features. He folds his arms over his chest and turns back toward the water. "Mexico was…an unknown. The Ruins aren't."

"Shit, Cyrus." His head snaps back to me. "Colin and I are trained Uprising soldiers, stop treating us like we're children who need to be protected. Seriously, if we can't do this, we've got no chance in whatever plan you've come up with."

He narrows his eyes, his jaw clenching.

"Look," Rainey says. I drag my gaze away from Cyrus and turn to find her watching us with an amused expression. "It's not about you not being capable. Lisa and Simon were heading to the same camp you two busted out of. They know you there, but no one knows me. I can get in and out. Cyrus is only providing backup since they know him, too."

I can tell I'm not going to win this argument, and if anything, they'll disappear in the middle of the night again. "Fine. But I swear, if you're even six hours late meeting up at the house, Colin and I will come after you."

"We won't be late," Cyrus grunts before turning and heading back into camp.

The camp feels deserted as we sit at one of the many available tables for dinner. With classes starting back up tomorrow, only a handful of other campers remain.

Next to me, Colin shoves half his burger in his mouth in one bite. Boys can be so gross. Turning away, I poke at my salad, popping one of the candied walnuts in my mouth. I stop mid-chew when Rainey and Cyrus set their trays down opposite us. I figured they'd be gone already.

The superficial conversation Colin and I had before their arrival halts, and we mostly eat in silence. Colin makes a few comments on our meal, but what else can you say beyond the juiciness of the meat or the crispiness of the bacon? As has become our routine, when everyone is finished eating, we make our way to one of the bonfires.

After settling into the sand, backs against the logs, Colin turns to Rainey. "What's your plan?"

She explains how she's going to slip into the camp and grab Lisa, then send Lisa after Simon while she gets Mateo, and they'll all meet us at the house near the border.

I stare into the fire as they talk, taking it all in but not contributing. When conversation winds down, the butterflies in my belly scramble. Cyrus is leaving again and I'm left once more to wonder if and when I'll see him next.

Cyrus stands, brushing off his jeans, and I turn to look out at the water so I don't have to watch him walk away without saying goodbye. Again.

A large hand reaches down to me, and I startle before glancing up into amber eyes that give me no hint of what he's thinking.

"Can we talk?"

I take the offered hand and let him pull me up. Other than our spontaneous hug on the beach last night, it's the first time he's touched me in weeks. But as soon as I'm on my feet, he drops my hand, turns, and heads toward the water. It takes me a few extra quick steps to catch up to him.

The warm air near the fire quickly gives way to cold, moist air that makes my breath float, faint and wispy. I pull my hands inside the long sleeves of my sweater.

Cyrus stops a few feet from where the beach turns into the hard packed surface, sculpted by the earlier high tide. He shoves his hands into the front pockets of his jeans and stares out at the ocean, flat waves pushing in.

I dig my heels into the still warm sand and wiggle my toes until they're buried. A full moon provides ample light for me to see absolutely nothing on his face. A sudden gust of wind blows my hair back, pelting me with a chilly spray of water, and I shiver.

Gaze still locked on the waves, he says, "I don't want to fight anymore."

I swallow back unexpected tears, making my words thick. "I never wanted to fight in the first place."

He sighs. *Great.* Neither of us wants to fight, glad we got that straightened out. Good talk. When several minutes pass with no further attempt at conversation on his part, I give up and turn to head back to my tent.

"You're the most frustrating girl I've ever met."

I whip around, anger building. "You've made that abundantly clear."

He turns to look at me for the first time since we left the bonfire and runs a hand through his hair. "You drive me insane on nearly a daily basis, but I love you, Ev. I don't love you in spite of that, I love you because of it." He blows out a slow breath and drops his hand to his side. "Everything you do that drives me crazy and frustrates the hell out of me is what makes you...you, the girl I'm completely, hopelessly, forever in love with."

I gape at him, all anger flooding from me like a popped water balloon. It takes a second before I realize my mouth has joined my eyes in the whole gaping thing, and I slam my lips together. His words penetrate my dumbfounded haze.

Cyrus moves toward me with tentative steps and swallows hard. "You're all I have left."

He pauses in front of me, the heat from his proximity warms me, but I shiver anyway. I can smell that clean mix of sun and soap, that's all him. His arms wrap around my shoulders, in a hesitant hug, but that's all I need to press against him, melting into his chest.

He sighs, squeezing me tighter and says so softly it's almost a sigh, "I don't know who I am without you anymore."

The tears that have been threatening all day flood my eyes as I rest my head against the boy I love so fiercely it terrifies me.

"Ev," he whispers.

I lift my head, wiping my eyes, and glance up at him. The depth of emotion in his eyes slams into me, leaving me speechless.

He lowers his face inch by agonizing inch until I feel the soft brush of my favorite lips. His mouth moves with mine in a way that's both familiar and somehow different, desperate and exciting, drawing out emotions until my heart is spiraling.

His teeth nip my lower lip seconds before his tongue slides into my mouth. He kisses me urgently, as if he needs to kiss me more than he needs to breathe.

My hands find their way behind his neck, pulling him closer to me, matching his need with my own. His soft, amazing lips are addictive, like a drug, and I'm in bad need of a fix.

We cling to each other on the beach, passion and fear and love all tangling with lips and tongues and teeth. When he pulls back, his hands slide up to cup my cheeks.

I stare into beautiful eyes no longer trying to hide anything from me. He wraps me in his arms, pulling my head to his chest, his body shuddering.

The steady, rapid rhythm of his heart beneath my cheek makes my own race, and I realize what I want.

What I've wanted for so long.

What I've always wanted.

I step back and take his hand, lacing our fingers, and lead him to my tent.

# Fierce Love

*Cyrus*

**E**van's fingers shake as she ties the tent flaps together. I don't know if it's from fear or anticipation. I want to believe it's the latter, but it's probably a little of both. There's something comforting in knowing she's as nervous as I am.

I've never been nervous. Excited, hell yeah, but not anxious like this. It's only been four months since I've been with a girl, but I feel like a fourteen-year-old again. It's not my first time, but it is my first time with the only girl I've ever been in love with. A girl far less experienced than me, and I want this to be perfect for her.

She turns, her eyes darting around, looking everywhere but at me. God she's beautiful. My fingers twitch, longing to reach out and stroke her face, bury themselves in her hair.

She peels off her sweater and tosses it on the chair, revealing a simple white tank top and a pair of tight jeans that hug her curves. I've never seen anything sexier.

The soft glow of white lights strung overhead provide enough illumination for me to make out the red creeping up her neck and flushing her cheeks. I hate that she's uncomfortable, but I'm powerless to help her. My mouth is dry, and my heart pounds against my ribcage.

As cold as the outside was, it's balmy in here, and getting warmer by the second. I reach between my shoulder blades and grab my sweatshirt, pulling it off and dropping it on the ground, never taking my eyes off Ev.

She coils and releases her fingers at her sides, her gaze now fixed on the floor.

I take small, careful steps forward until I'm in front of her. Her breath hitches, the only indication she's aware of how close I am. Reaching out, I skim my fingertips down her arm. Goosebumps rise across her skin and she shivers.

As much as I want to grab her and kiss her senseless, I exercise my limited self-control to remain patient and follow her lead. I slide my fingers back up until my palm rests on her cheek.

With a sharp inhale, she lifts her face and presses it against my hand, closing her eyes. I take in every curve of her face, study the freckles dotting her nose, thick lashes fanning smooth cheekbones, her full, perfect lips.

She lets out a small sound, somewhere between a whisper and a moan that nearly brings me to my knees. My control completely shot, I pull her against me and trail kisses up the side of her neck, breathing in her sweet scent.

Nuzzling the spot beneath her ear, I relish the way her breath catches with each soft kiss. I move higher, skimming my nose along her jaw, until I reach her chin.

She tilts her head back, and I work my way down to the hollow at the base of her throat. When she whimpers, I'm done. My lips find hers and I kiss her like I've never kissed her before, pouring everything into this moment.

She pushes into me, twisting her hands in my T-shirt. I lift her off the ground and she wraps her legs around my waist as I carry her to the bed, laying her down, never letting my mouth leave hers. I kick my shoes off as we inch further up the blankets, our greedy hands exploring each other.

Her fingers dip beneath my shirt, and I suck in a breath. That only seems to encourage her, and her lips become more urgent. Clothing is discarded at a steady rate until there's nothing between us.

She whispers my name like a plea, and I'm falling, stepping off a cliff into the unknown. But I'm ready to take the plunge with her. With one, long, deep kiss, I roll away to grab my jeans.

"Where are you going?" she asks, her voice all breathy and hotter than shit.

"Just grabbing a condom."

"You don't need one."

I freeze, confused. "Oh," I say, trying like hell to hide my disappointment. I turn back toward her, wrapping my arms around her waist and pulling her against me while I try to get my racing heart under control.

"What's wrong?" she asks.

"Nothing. I'm happy just to hold you." It's only partially a lie.

"But...I thought..."

I glance down at her and she's chewing on her kiss-swollen bottom lip, which isn't helping. At all.

A sudden smile tugs at her mouth. "I mean you don't need a condom because I can't get pregnant. I got a shot that protects me, plus I've been vaccinated against all known STDs."

"Oh." My own smile joins hers, spreading wide as that sinks in. Because hell, I've never had sex without a condom, and because she's the only girl I trust enough to even consider it with.

I grin wider and roll her onto her back, nipping her lip before kissing her slowly, taking my time, trying to make this night last forever.

## Evan

With his left arm wrapped around my waist and his lips pressed to the top of my head, Cyrus's heart rate gradually returns to normal beneath my ear.

Whatever that just was, it was unlike anything I've ever experienced. I mean, sex with Bryce was fun, it made me feel alive and for a short time helped me forget the horror in my life. But what Cyrus and I just shared was so different, intense, soul-drenching...*perfect*. For me, anyway. He's being awfully quiet.

I know there are plenty of girls in his past, and I'm sure some of them were very good at this, so maybe this wasn't what he'd been hoping for. I'm not stupid enough to believe that me not really knowing what to do would have gone unnoticed or that my inexperience doesn't matter. I only hope it doesn't matter a lot.

My hand runs up his side, over sculpted muscles until I reach his shoulder. I trail my fingertips down the bulge of his right bicep until they dip into the scar cutting across it. The scar he got from Dantel's knife the day Lucien was killed.

Cyrus's words from earlier come back. *You're all I have left.* Is that why he's still with me? Would he have given up on me by now if Lucien was alive? Suddenly, I need to know how he feels about this, about us.

I prop my chin up on my fist on his chest. "Cyrus?"

His eyes are closed, but a slight smile tips up the corners of his mouth. "Hmmm?"

"What are you thinking?"

He opens his eyes briefly before closing them again. "That I get it now."

My face scrunches in confusion. "What?"

"I used to give Lucien shit for settling down with Draya when he was still so young." His words are slow and heavy, as if he's fighting off sleep. "He told me when I found the right girl, I'd understand." His hand tightens around my waist. "He was right. I get it now."

My heart stops for a split second before restarting, warmth blooming through my chest and spreading until it swallows me whole. I had no idea it was possible to love someone this much, to want and need him in a way that both fills me with peace and scares the crap out of me.

I don't know what to say in response to his beautiful words, so I don't say anything.

Instead, I scoot up until my lips find his and kiss him until I'm dizzy, and blood races through my veins.

## Cyrus

I love the way she feels in my arms, her bare skin pressed against mine. My fingers glide up her spine, and I press a kiss to the top of her head.

"Tell me what happened in Mexico."

"Don't you ever sleep?" I tease her.

"Cyrus, we've barely talked to each other in a month unless it was to argue about something. I'm making up for lost time."

I try to fight a smile, but it's a losing battle.

"Tell me," she insists.

"Fine." I blow out an exaggerated sigh and tell her.

As the story unfolds, I toy with the idea of sugar-coating it, but I know that's not what she wants. So I share everything, all the while tracing circles with my fingers on her back, enjoying how goosebumps rise up in response. When I tell her how close we came to being executed before Rainey managed to talk our way out of it, she stiffens.

"All I could think about was how messed up everything was between us and how you'd never know how I felt about you." I pause and pull her closer. "That's why I wanted to talk tonight. I couldn't leave again with things the way they were."

"I thought you hated me." Her voice is soft, but has a rough edge to it that tightens my chest.

I lift her chin, guilt ripping through me, as a tear slips out of her eye, trailing down her cheek. I wipe it with my thumb, struggling to find the right words. My throat is thick and all I manage to get out is, "I could never hate you." I swallow around the fist in my throat and try again. "I could *never* hate you."

*Shit.* There are a thousand other things I should say, starting with how sorry I am to ever make her feel that way, but the words are locked down tight. Instead, I crush her against me, and stare up at the tent, working to get a grip.

Her soft mouth kisses a path up the side of my neck, and I close my eyes and sigh. I don't deserve her. Once I've got myself under control, I reach down and press my lips to her forehead before continuing with my story.

"Oh my god," she says when I get to yesterday morning. "So how'd you get away? The guy had a gun to your head, Cyrus!"

I smile, thinking about how it all went down. "Rainey saw my body go rigid and dove back inside. She slipped around to the other side to scope it out. She was hoping they didn't have enough manpower to cover every exit, and she was right. The next door she tried was unguarded, so she snuck up on the guy. By then, he had me disarmed and all the bags on the ground. He was so busy congratulating himself, he never heard her approaching. The guy was a greedy idiot. He should've been calling for backup, but he wanted to see if I had anything he could pocket before he called the others."

She shudders and her hand slides up my chest before coming to a rest on my shoulder. "And you worry about me?"

She has no idea how much. "Every minute of every day. You attract trouble like no one I've ever met."

Pressing closer to me until there's no space between us, she kisses the side of my neck.

"Are you ever going to let me sleep?" I tease.

But when she takes my bottom lip between her teeth, I forget how to breathe.

She owns every last piece of me.

With a stretch, I roll over, eager to cuddle with my girl and possibly interest her in a little early morning fun. My hand only hits sheet, though, and I pry my eyes open to find an empty space beside me.

"Ev?"

No response. I scrub my hands over my face and glance around. My clothes are folded in a neat pile on the table next to the bed. Quickly dressing, I head into the cool morning and find everyone at a table outside the mess tent.

Ev's eyes meet mine and a shy smile slips onto her face. Although I hate to admit it, I had a momentary fear that maybe she left before I woke because she regretted last night. But that smile and the warmth in her eyes tells me I don't have anything to worry about.

I take a seat beside her and wrap my arms around her waist. She leans against me, and I nuzzle her neck until the smell of bacon and coffee hits me hard.

"I'm gonna grab breakfast." I kiss the side of her head before going in search of food.

I've still never tried coffee but the rich odor is dark and earthy, and since Ev loves it so much, perhaps I'll give it a shot today. Rainey introduced me to breakfast burritos down in Mexico, so when I see those on the menu, I order one to go with my coffee.

The pounding surf to my right is interspersed with screeching birds overhead as I make my way back to the table. I resume my spot on the bench next to Evan and take a bite of burrito. The buttery soft eggs and crisp salty bacon are laced with melted cheese, and it isn't anywhere near as greasy as the ones I had down south. I take a swig of coffee to wash it down, and my tongue is hit with a bitter harshness that nearly chokes me.

Setting my cup down, I turn to Evan. "I don't understand what it is you like about this stuff. It tastes like burnt piss."

She reaches over and takes a sip, a smirk pulling up the corner of her mouth. "That's because you're used to tea, and you got black coffee. You just need to know how to order it." She grabs my hand, dragging me back into the mess tent. "Can I get a cappuccino, extra foam, with a caramel drizzle?"

A few minutes later, the girl hands me a drink, and Ev studies my face while I try it. It's really good and tastes more like it smells. It's creamy with a touch of sweetness that's similar to the tea with milk and honey my mom made me when I was a kid.

"Well?" Ev asks, her left eyebrow notching up in that completely adorable way she has.

I smile and take her hand, leading her back to the table. "Better."

"I'm anxious to get going," Colin says when we rejoin them. "All this waiting is pointless. The sooner we can find Lisa and Simon, the sooner we can plan our next move."

Evan pushes her food tray back and grabs her coffee cup with both hands. "We need to stop by Eddie's first. If they make it back here, they'll check in with him when they don't find us here. Plus, I want him to know where we are…and we need more cash."

Colin and Rainey nod in agreement, mouths full of food.

I wolf down the rest of my breakfast while everyone else talks, then grab Ev's hand and pull her to her feet. "We'll be back," I tell the others.

Lacing our fingers together, I walk her down to the water. Not knowing if or when I'll ever get back here, I want one last look, this time with my girl by my side. I stop short of where the ocean creeps up the sand and draw Evan in front of me, wrapping my arms around her waist.

I place a kiss on top of her head. "I'm gonna miss this. When you were in the hospital, I went to the beach every day. There's nothing in the Ruins that even comes close"

For a few quiet minutes, I appreciate the girl in my arms and the scene before me. Something tells me moments like this will be rare going forward.

# Rare Moments

## Cyrus

The tension around Eddie's eyes appears more pronounced than I remember from our visit three weeks ago. He visibly relaxes as he wraps his daughter in a hug. When he releases her, he reaches out to shake my hand first before doing the same with Colin and Rainey.

He opens the door wider. "Come on in."

"Where are the kids?" Ev asks, her head swiveling.

"Liam's at school and Talia took Quinn down to Seaport Park when you texted me you were on your way." Eddie walks into the kitchen. "You guys hungry?"

"We just had breakfast." Ev says.

Colin plants himself on one of the stools at the counter. "I could eat something."

I have a healthy appetite, but Colin can eat me under the table.

Eddie gets busy, pulling out pans and slicing bread. "Grilled cheese okay?"

"Yeah, that sounds good, Eddie," Evan says, joining him. "Let me give you a hand."

While they work, Colin and Evan fill her dad in on the past few weeks. I'm surprised she doesn't hold much back. Her dad's head whips around to the bags by the door when he finds out they're filled with guns and explosives.

"It's C-4," I explain. "Stable. I wouldn't have grabbed it otherwise."

His head swings to me, eyes narrowed, and though we've talked multiple times, I get the feeling he's sizing me up in a way he hasn't before.

After our late morning snack, Eddie leads the way outside to an enclosed garden area I never noticed before off the living room. He's explaining some of the plants and shit to Rainey, but Ev's in the kitchen cleaning up, so I slide the door closed and go help her.

"Hey," she says, her voice all soft and sweet.

"What can I do?"

She wipes a stray hair from her face with her shoulder. "You can dry. Towel's over there."

I grab the towel and begin wiping away drops of water from one of the pans. She places the plates and silverware into a tray and shoves it into a large opening, like an oven.

She turns and catches me watching. "It's a dishwasher. It uses high-pressure water, heat, and special soap to clean them." She fidgets with the hem of her shirt. "So, um…we talked it over and we're coming with you guys. Me and Colin. To get Lisa and Simon." I open my mouth to object, but she puts her hand up to stop me. "Hear me out. It makes sense. Colin and I know the camp. Rainey doesn't. And I don't want to split up. I came too close to losing you in Mexico."

"It's a really bad idea, Ev."

"I'm not backing down on this. You can either be pissed at me, and we can fight the whole time, or we can work together."

My jaw clenches so tightly, I'm pretty sure I'm going to crack a tooth. She has no clue what she's asking of me. Letting her go back to where she was almost killed? Hell, they'll shoot her the second they recognize her.

"Your logic is flawed. You want to go because you don't want to split up. That's a stupid ass reason to put yourself in danger."

Her nostrils flare. "Why do you need to fight me on every little thing?"

I toss the towel on the counter, working hard to control my temper. "This isn't little. Fuck, Ev, you almost died."

Her head snaps back and I realize I swore at her. Shit, I didn't mean to. I reach for her, but she steps away, anger burning in her eyes. She spins and begins attacking another pan with the sponge.

"Ev…" She pauses and I wait for her to look at me. "We have to be able to talk about this stuff without fighting."

"I don't want to fight with you either, but damn it, Cyrus, you have to quit treating me like I'm fragile. It pisses me off."

"I don't think you're fragile." The words are out before I have a chance to think about them, but it's true. She's tough, fierce, brave, but she also has a habit of acting without thinking.

"Then why don't you want me to do...*anything*?"

I rub my hand across the back of my neck and stare at the counter. "It's not that I think you're not capable, I don't want you to have to." I lift my head, waiting for her to stop scrubbing the shit out of the pan and her eyes to connect with mine again. "You have no idea what it was like...when they told me they weren't sure you were gonna make it...Ev, I *can't* lose you, too."

Her jaw slackens and the fire goes out of her eyes. She sets the sponge down and wipes her hands on her jeans. It only takes two small steps for her to reach me and wrap her arms around my waist.

"You're not going to lose me. You're stuck with me now, whether you want to be or not." Her voice is thick and soft. "Okay, so I can't make that promise, but you can't just send me away until it's all over. Do you remember what you said to me at the bridge the day we parted?"

"I said a lot of things."

"That you believe in me."

"Ev..."

"Cy..." She's never called me anything but Cyrus, and that one simple syllable slays me. "Did you mean it?"

"Yeah, but that was before you got shot."

"What does that mean? You no longer think I'm capable? Or is it something else?"

"It means I've never been more afraid in my life."

She lifts her head and we stare at each other for a long moment. As much as I need to protect her, it's not my place to tell her what to do. I think she sees the resignation in my eyes, because she pushes up on her toes and presses her mouth to mine.

My hands snake up to the back of her head, tangling in her hair and I kiss the hell out of her. At least until someone clearing their throat behind us makes her separate from me as if she'd been struck by lightning. I glance behind me and see her dad.

"Sorry," she says, touching her lips with her fingertips, her cheeks turning bright pink.

I swallow hard as I watch her return to the pan, knowing I won't survive if something happens to her.

## Evan

Morning light streams though the window when I open my eyes. A quiet snore comes from Rainey lying next to me. I slide out of bed without waking her and trudge downstairs.

Eddie glances up from where he's busy cutting up a cantaloupe. "Hey," he says, dark skin ringing his eyes, making my stomach twist with guilt.

When we filled him in on our plans last night, he argued, but only superficially. I assume it's because I'm an adult and he can't control me, but maybe a little because he realizes I don't have a choice. My best friend is missing and horror is about to rain down on the Union if we don't find a way to stop it.

I move next to him and kiss his cheek.

He gives me a small smile in payment, and I rest my head on his shoulder. How is this the same man I used to despise for abandoning me? He doesn't seem like the kind of guy who would do that. But then that guy was a teen, not much older than I am now, when my mom got pregnant with me. He ran for the hills because parental responsibility terrified him, but the man standing next to me risked his life to save me. I may never be able to reconcile these two truths.

"What can I do to help?" I ask.

"Why don't you scramble some eggs?"

I open the fridge and pull out a tray of white eggs, so different from the brown and blue ones I collected out in the Ruins last summer. Eddie dumps the cubed fruit onto a platter and rinses the cutting board to start on onions. Grabbing a whisk, I beat the eggs, fishing a piece of eggshell out of the bowl. After starting a pot of coffee, I grab a block of cheese and begin to grate it.

Colin tumbles down the stairs as the smell of brewing coffee wafts through the house. He stretches, scratching his belly when he reaches the bottom step.

Cyrus follows a minute later, his hair sleep-tousled, wearing sweatpants and a white T-shirt that fits him like a second skin. His eyes find mine, and he gives me a smile that lights up his whole face, making my heart spin. Walking up behind me, he wraps his arms around my waist and bends down to nuzzle my neck.

Eddie clears his throat and Cyrus releases me before taking a seat next to Colin at the counter like a scolded puppy.

A bleary-eyed Rainey enters the kitchen and reaches for a cup. Eddie sets one in front of her and pours some coffee into it.

A few minutes later, Talia slinks up to Eddie, kissing him on the cheek. So that's how it is. Talia can kiss Eddie, but Cyrus can't kiss me. I resist the urge to roll my eyes.

"Sorry we missed you yesterday," Talia says. She picked Liam up after school and didn't get back until after the rest of us had gone to bed.

"Yeah, me, too. I want to see the kids before we leave. Do you think they'll be up soon?"

As if on cue, Quinn and Liam come screaming down the stairs.

Quinn skips in and grabs my hand. "Eban, Eban, Eban!"

"Hey, QuinnyBee, what's going on?"

"I not a bee." She glances around the room, her gaze landing on Cyrus. Her hands fly to her hips. "What's you name?" she demands.

"This is Cyrus," I tell her. "You met him the last time we were here, remember?" Her right eyebrow notches up as she studies him, then nods, sending red curls bouncing. She marches over and sits at the kitchen table and waits to be served.

Liam is staring at everyone, not nearly as outgoing as his younger sister. "Hey buddy." He makes his way over to me. "You remember Rainey and Cyrus, and I know you remember Colin."

He nods, still not ready to talk, and takes the spot next to Quinn. But as breakfast progresses, he comes out of his shell, contributing to the conversation.

The meal is lighthearted and fun, the way everything is always brighter with kids around. When everyone is done, Talia ushers Liam upstairs to get dressed for school while the rest of us clean up the dishes before heading upstairs to pack.

I zip my duffel bag closed and carry it downstairs, setting it by the front door before going in search of Eddie. He's out on the patio. I grab my tablet and pull up a map of the Ruins.

"This is where we're going. If Lisa and Simon show up here after we leave, let them know where to find us, okay?"

He nods and takes the tablet from me, shoving it into his back pocket. "When will you be back?"

I shake my head. "I don't know. At least a month or two. Maybe longer."

The color drains from his face. "Can you find a way to communicate?"

"How?"

He sighs, his head falling forward. "I don't know. Through Tony, maybe?"

"There's no communications network in the Ruins, so I don't know how. But the Northern Territories are close, so if I can find a way, I will."

"If I don't hear from you, I will come looking for you," he says, lifting his head to glance at me.

"I know, I'll try."

Colin slides open the door. "Time to go."

"Where you going?" Liam asks, slipping out the door.

"Evan and her friends are going camping," Eddie says, saving me from having to come up with something.

"I thought you just went camping."

"We did," Colin says. "But we're going to a new place this time."

Liam nods as if this makes perfect sense.

Quinn shoves her way past Liam to join us, not one to be left out of anything. "What you doing out here?"

"Coming inside," Eddie says, sliding the door open and ushering us back in.

I kneel and pull my brother and sister into a long hug. "I'll miss you, but I'll be back soon."

"Kay," Quinn says, wriggling out of my arms and bouncing to the living room with an agenda only she knows.

Talia joins our little group and reaches out to embrace me. "Take care." It's awkward, I barely know her, but she's sleeping with my dad, so I squeeze her back. "And take care of my brother," she whispers.

I stiffen for a second, not realizing she knew what we were up to, but nod. When she releases me, Eddie drags me to him and hugs me for so long, I'm afraid we're going to miss the train.

Colin grabs my sleeve and yanks me along. Eddie follows us out and closes the door behind him.

"I told Mom I was going back undercover and wouldn't be able to contact her, but that I'd get word through Tony. Can you check in with her like every week or two?"

He sighs and rubs his face with both hands. His hands drop and I swear he's aged another couple of years. "Yeah."

After giving Colin a quick hug and shaking hands with Rainey and Cyrus, he and Cyrus exchange what seems to be an entire conversation with just a look. Then the four of us turn and head toward god only knows what.

# Book 2 – The Ruins

# Unknown

## Evan

**M**y lungs expand, filling with clean, fresh air, while my eyes drink in the raw beauty of the Ruins. As much as the Western Province felt like home only weeks ago, I can't fight the feeling *this* is where I belong.

Cyrus reaches down and takes my hand, lacing our fingers, as if he senses what I'm thinking and maybe feels it, too. The forest soon swallows us, surrounding us with stillness and aromas of wet dirt and cedar, pine needles and twigs scrunching beneath our feet.

Everything from the people I'm with to my surroundings is so right, I almost forget what we're here to do. Almost. While we walk, we discuss strategy for when we get to the camp. Rainey has plenty of ideas and Cyrus throws out insider information about the workings of the camp that could only come from the former commander.

"So, what are the odds all three of them are together?" I ask.

"It's possible, but I don't know how likely," Rainey says. "Simon and Lisa have been gone three weeks, which isn't a good sign."

She turns and studies me, then Colin, as if she hasn't known us for months. It sort of creeps me out.

"How far did you two get in your Uprising training?"

"We finished Basic and started on our specialty," Colin says. "Why?"

Rainey and Cyrus exchange a glance before they both stop. Cyrus drops his packs and reaches into one, pulling out a handgun. "Were you trained on these?"

"No," Colin and I say in unison.

Cyrus hands us each a gun.

All I can do is stare at the weapon in my hand. I knew this was coming, I mean, they went down to Mexico to get them. But holding it makes my skin crawl.

"It won't bite you," Cyrus says, his voice laced with humor.

I know it won't bite, but it can cause a great deal of destruction to the human body. And a shitload of pain. My shoulder begins to ache for the first time in days, reminding me what bullets are capable of.

"Hey." Cyrus takes my arm and turns me to face him. "I know this isn't easy, but it's important. If you can't learn to load, unload, and shoot this, you can't come with us."

I swallow and nod, staring at the ground, my boots, his boots, anywhere but at the gun in my hand.

He lifts my chin, forcing me to look at him. "These aren't Uprising rifles. No spiral bullets. No less deadly, but it's not the same. Okay?"

My heart pounds in my chest, but I nod again, I have to do this or be left behind. I stare at the smooth, dark gray titanium weapon in my hand. It's much lighter than either the gun I used to kill Dantel or the one I picked up from Walker's lackey when Colin was kidnapped.

Cyrus pulls a magazine from one of the bags. "These load the same way you learned, but they only hold twenty rounds."

Colin and I press cartridges into the clip the way we did in the Uprising and push it up into the handle of the gun. When fully loaded, it weighs nearly twice as much. Guess the ammo isn't made from the same lightweight material.

"The safety is on the side, here. Flip it and pull back on the slide to load the first round in the chamber."

My hands shake, but I do as instructed.

"Aim at that tree over there, lining up the indent in the back with the bar in the front. These have a decent kick, so be prepared for it. If you know it's coming, you can compensate." Cyrus moves behind me. "Wrap your fingers around your right hand and put your left thumb over your right." He places his hands on my shoulders to steady me while I support my right hand with my left. "Exhale first, then fire."

When he lifts his hands and backs away, bile rises in my stomach, but I follow his orders, swallowing down my fear. It's in my hand and I'm doing the shooting, not the other way around. I close my eyes, take a deep breath, then exhale, opening my eyes and fire, hitting the tree. The recoil is crazy wild, sending a shock wave back to my shoulder.

"Good job, baby."

I take little satisfaction in any of this, because once again, I know why I'm learning this and it isn't to shoot trees.

Colin and I spend the next twenty minutes practicing before Cyrus and Rainey decide either we're good enough or we've wasted enough ammo. Cyrus takes my hand, and we hike until sunset before making camp.

By the time I crawl into the tent, I'm so exhausted, I'm asleep before my head hits the ground.

I wake to a warm heavy arm draped across my waist and smile. I love waking up next to Cyrus. Like the other morning on the beach, he's sound asleep. He grunts as I dislodge myself, but doesn't stir.

Rainey and Colin are sitting next to a fire when I crawl out of the tent. Long shadows from the early morning sun stretch across the ground where I take a seat beside Colin.

"Morning," I say.

"Hey, EvTay." He gives me some dried fruit and a piece of jerky. "It's not good, but it's better than nothing."

Rainey hands me a steeping cup of tea.

"Thanks."

Colin stretches out his back. "This sleeping on the ground crap is for the birds."

I smirk. "Pretty sure birds sleep in trees."

He wads up his used tea bag and flings it at me, but my hand shoots out and catches it before it hits me.

"Any more tea?" Cyrus asks from behind us, his deep voice rough from lack of use. He sits next to me and I hand him my cup, taking a fresh one from Rainey, letting the tea steep while I finish off my dried cranberries.

As soon as we're done with breakfast, we pack up and move out, hiking on through the day, only stopping for lunch, until night falls again. The next day is a repeat. I swear it didn't seem like we walked this far before, but then we covered more than half the distance on motorbikes.

Early in the afternoon on the third day, we reach a wooded area that feels familiar, and I know I've been here before. I may have been high on painkillers, but these are the woods surrounding the camp where Colin and I trained, where Cyrus was last commander, where I was shot.

My hands begin to shake, and a thin layer of cold sweat coats my skin. Soon I can't catch a complete breath, like my lungs won't fully inflate.

Cyrus clamps his fingers around my right hand, steadying the shakes. "Hold up," he calls to Rainey and Colin.

Dropping my hand, he takes my shoulder and turns me to face him. My gaze darts around, searching for sentries with guns and spiral bullets.

A vision of my friends lying on the ground, ripped apart and bloody, fills my head, and I close my eyes, trying to make it go away.

"Hey." The word comes from far away even though Cyrus is standing in front of me. "Breathe."

I nod and pull in a short ragged breath. It was stupid for me to come, this is why he didn't want me here. I'm freaking out.

"What's wrong with me?" I gasp.

"Panic attack. You need to breathe."

My heart races, and I gulp in a mouthful of air, but I still feel like I'm suffocating. I hear Colin and Rainey nearby, voices, words, but nothing that makes sense. Like they're speaking a foreign language.

"Listen to my breaths, Ev. Copy me. Breathe in."

He takes a breath, and I try to do the same, but I'm choking.

"Baby, you're okay. This is just your body reacting. Try again."

I suck in another shuddering lungful of air.

"Good. Now let it back out. Slowly."

My breath whooshes back out, and Cyrus pulls me against him.

"Breathe with me." His chest rumbles beneath my ear. "Feel my breaths. Match my rhythm."

Squeezing my eyes closed, I inhale with each breath he takes, hold it, and exhale when he does. After a dozen of these, the muscles in my neck begin to relax, muscles I didn't even realize were tight. My shoulders drop and I wrap my arms around Cyrus's body, clinging to him as I take a trembling breath of my own, my heart rate returning to something less stratospheric.

"What the hell was that?" Colin asks.

I turn to face him, feeling like an idiot. God, that was embarrassing. "I-I don't know, it was like I couldn't breathe."

Rainey's dark eyes study me and I'm sure she's convinced I'm a total liability. "Post-traumatic stress-induced panic attacks," she says with a nod. "I used to get them all the time."

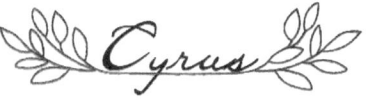

Watching Evan unravel freaked me out. I had a panic attack after the tornado. Sonia helped me through it, which is the only reason I recognized it and knew what to do. But shit, seeing that wild look in her eyes, feeling her body trembling, drenched in sweat…nearly killed me. Rainey admitting she got them, too, probably did more to ease Evan's concerns than anything I could've said.

I haven't let go of Ev's hand since, and she hasn't uttered a single word. Just keeps her eyes on the path, following Rainey and Colin. It only takes about twenty minutes before we're about as close as I'm comfortable getting to camp until nightfall.

"Let's hold up here," I say.

Rainey halts in front of me, her head pivoting to take in our surroundings, the commander in her is assessing everything. It's the same thing I'm doing. We should be safe for now. Unless there's been a dramatic change since we left, the sentries are clueless we're in the area. Their job is to keep people from leaving, not keep anyone out, because who in their right mind would break into an Uprising camp?

Thick trees obscure us to the casual observer, and dense ground cover muffles our low conversation and slight movements. If shit goes south later, the dense vegetation should provide enough protection for us to escape. I take a seat on a moss-covered trunk, pulling Ev down next to me.

Rainey scratches the side of her face. "I'm going in alone."

My head snaps to her. "Rainey—"

"You three are a liability if they recognize you. The odds we don't run into anyone in camp who recognizes you are about zero."

"I don't like it."

She rolls her eyes. "You don't like anything."

I shake my head but can't argue. We're all a liability in there. Shit, I can't believe I let Ev come here with me. "Alright. Fine. But I'm coming after you at the first gunshot."

"You're such a cowboy." Pushing off the log, she sweeps the ground with her boot and picks up a stick. "Okay, tell me everything you remember about this place."

We spend the rest of daylight drawing a map of the camp in the dirt, using rocks and leaves to represent tents, the vehicle depot, and other landmarks. Evan, Colin, and I fill her in on the finer details of daily activities. When it gets too dark to see, Rainey pulls a flashlight from her pocket and illuminates the diagram, staring at it, memorizing it.

She points at the leaf representing the girls' sleeping quarters. "If Lisa's here, she'll be in her bunk by now."

I indicate another leaf on the map. "If Mateo's still here, he'll be there."

Rainey slaps a fresh magazine into her gun and pulls back the slide. Then, moving with the stealth of someone who spent time training in Special Operations, she slips into the darkness and disappears.

Time passes at a record slow pace, the chirps of a million crickets fill my head until it becomes unbearable. I push up and destroy the dirt map with my boot, dragging leaves and pine needles over it. Then I pace, checking and rechecking my piece to make sure a round is in the chamber. I keep one eye on Evan as she sits on the log, chewing on her bottom lip. I swear she's going to bite through it.

Colin thrusts a hand through his hair every few minutes. An owl calls out four times before quieting to crickets again. I still strain, listening for voices, shots, footsteps, anything, but only hear the sounds of the forest surrounding us.

Rainey's been gone too long. I need to go in there after her, but now I'm not sure about leaving Evan and Colin alone. Ev's panic attack from earlier has me concerned about her ability to focus in an emergency. If bullets start flying, will she make solid decisions, or will she panic again? I feel like shit for doubting her, especially after I said I didn't, but that was before I saw her freak out.

The snapping of a twig nearby jolts me. I freeze for a second before grabbing Ev and dragging her behind a tree, covering her small body with mine.

She doesn't gasp in surprise, nor does her body tremble beneath me. I peer around the tree, my body rigid, Evan's small frame rising and falling with each rapid breath. She might be afraid, but I have to give her credit, my earlier fears about her mental state are replaced by growing respect.

"Hey," Rainey's raspy whisper comes from nearby.

My shoulders ease, and I flip on the safety, tucking my gun in the back of my waistband. I release Ev, pressing a quick kiss to her temple before stepping out.

Mateo wears a stupid shit-eating grin and reaches out a hand. We shake, slapping each other on the back. Damn, it's good to see him. Mateo steps back and takes in Colin and Evan. His eyes travel over my girl's body, and suddenly I'm not so glad to see him.

He nods and directs a slow smile at her. "Looking good, 172. I wasn't sure you were gonna make it."

That's enough of this shit. I reach out and take her hand, pulling her next to me. The move's not lost on Mateo, and his grin grows wider. *Ass.*

He shifts his gaze to Colin, reaching out to take his hand. "173. Good to see you."

"Where's Lisa and Simon?" Ev asks.

Rainey shakes her head, "No sign of them."

Mateo scratches an eyebrow. "No one matching their descriptions has arrived in the past month. In fact, the last group of recruits was well over a month ago."

"So what do we do now?" Colin asks.

I run a hand through my hair. "Well, we can't stay here. As soon as they figure out Mateo's gone, they'll start searching for him. We don't want to be anywhere in the area when that happens."

"Where are we going?" Evan asks.

"Away from here. We can make camp and regroup in the morning."

Her sigh is the only response I get. A sigh that can be taken many ways.

I cut my eyes to Rainey as we move out. "What took so long?"

"Getting in was easy. These are the most pathetic group of sentries I've ever seen."

Her accusation is clear, and I throw my free hand up. "Hey, I was only commander for a few weeks."

"The new commander's a dipshit," Mateo says.

"Anyway," Rainey continues. "Mateo was where you said he'd be."

Mateo directs a sly smile at her. "She's lucky she didn't get her head blown off. You sneak up on a guy in his bunk in the middle of the night, bad things can happen."

"You let someone sneak up on you in the middle of the night. If I was there to take you out, you'd be dead."

"Oh my god, it's like a game of 'who's the biggest badass,'" Evan says. "Seriously? How about we all agree you're both terrifying, each in your own way."

Mateo lets out a noise that sounds like a cross between a snort and a growl. "I'm snoring away when I feel something on my arm. I realized it was a hand and couldn't think of any good reason a hand would be on my arm. I pretended I was asleep, reached for my piece, and turned it on her."

Rainey scoffs. "I knew you were awake. I heard the change in your breathing. I didn't expect you to go for your gun, though. I was expecting you to open your eyes."

"So, here's this tiny girl standing over me. She doesn't appear very threatening, but she doesn't look familiar either."

"Hey, I'm not tiny."

Now it's Mateo's turn to scoff. "Yeah you are."

"I told him I was here with you guys and that you were waiting out here for him. I was ready to have to sell it, but he just got dressed and followed me out."

"How'd you get past the sentries?" Colin asks.

"Shit," Mateo says. "The two idiot sentries were making out. We could've walked right by them and they wouldn't have noticed. We didn't have to, though, just cut a large berth around them. They put a bunch of horny teenagers together, what the hell did they think was gonna happen?" he says with a shake of his head. "Whatever this started out as, it's turned into a joke. They've got these kids at some sort of hormonal summer camp, give 'em guns, and train 'em to kill. But they don't give a shit about any of 'em. There's not a single one of those kids that's getting out of this alive."

# Getting Out Alive

**M**ateo studies Colin's tablet, poring over the stuff we discovered in Walker's warehouse. His own tablet sits next to Colin's as if he's comparing information.

He glances up, his eyes meeting mine. "I think I know where your friends might be." I lean over his shoulder as he points at a camp farther south. "If they came in anywhere along here," he says, indicating a portion of the Northwestern Province wall, "they probably got caught up in a sweep around that time. Those 'recruits' were taken here."

"Okay, then shouldn't we be heading south?"

He shakes his head. "No. We need to plan this out. Rainey coming in and grabbing me is one thing. I knew the behavior of the sentries, but this other camp is unknown. We can't go in unprepared."

"Let's go," Cyrus says from behind us. His voice is rough, like he's irritated, but I have no idea why. We've been hiking for a day and a half since we found Mateo, so it's not like the Uprising is coming after us. He takes my hand and tugs me along behind him.

Mateo stands, shoving his tablet into his side pocket and hands Colin's back to him. Hoisting one of the large duffel bags containing weapons over one shoulder, he grabs a second one and catches up to us.

"I get we need a plan," I say to Mateo, then shift my gaze to Cyrus. "But why do we have to go north to do that? Wouldn't it make sense to head toward our destination?"

Mateo and Cyrus exchange a glance before Cyrus answers. "We need more than just a plan. To do it right, we need supplies. Stuff we have to get from the Northern Territories. We'll get them soon, I promise, but it has to be done right."

I have no argument for that, and we lapse into silence as one hour passes into the next, heading farther north, closer to where Sonia, Marcus, and the rest now live. Before long we're approaching the outskirts of town. The last time I was here, I was hoping I'd see Cyrus and was crushed when I found everyone but him. This time, he's with me, his fingers tightening around mine. We pass businesses, a few people calling out to him or Rainey.

A lanky guy, all limbs and teeth, waves from across the street. "Hey, Rainey, where you been?"

"Traveling. I'll see you later," she calls back. "Shit," she mutters under her breath. "Remind me to stay away from the bar tonight."

I can't hide my amusement. "He seems quite excited to see you."

"Yeah, the way a puppy is happy to see its owner at the end of the day. I don't need to talk to Travis tonight. Or ever. I swear he slobbers."

I laugh, feeling sorry for Travis. He clearly has it bad for Rainey.

"Cyrus, when'd you get back?"

I turn to see a big guy, bigger than Mateo. Cyrus drops my hand and reaches out to shake with the guy. "Bolt. Hey, just got back."

Bolt turns steel gray eyes on me before letting his gaze sweep the rest of the group, then back to Cyrus. "Stop by later so we can catch up."

"I'll do that."

Bolt crosses the street and enters one of the stores without a glance back.

"Bolt?" I ask.

"Nickname. Rumor has it he survived a lightning strike, but it's more of an urban legend, I think."

"So does everyone around here know you guys?" Colin asks.

"Small town," Rainey murmurs and picks up the pace.

We make good time through town and as we get closer to the house, my heart rate notches up with excited anticipation. I can't wait to see the others.

My excitement is nothing compared to Colin's, though. Nervous energy pours out of him with every bouncing step he takes. He very nearly sprints the last block, but when he reaches the walkway leading to the house, he pauses. Dropping his hands to his sides, his fingers move as if strumming the strings of his guitar.

I pull up next to him. "You going in?"

He lifts a hand and runs it through messy dark locks. "Yeah."

Cyrus pushes past us and heads up the stairs to open the door. "Hey, is there anything to eat around here, I'm starving."

Even from out here, I can hear Ally's squeal. "Oh my god, Cyrus, is that you? You're never going to believe who—" The words die on her tongue when her gaze locks on Colin.

Ally rushes from the house and flies past me, never taking her eyes off Colin. She throws her arms around his neck and kisses him. I stand awkwardly beside them for a second, before hurrying into the house, Rainey and Mateo on my heels.

Cyrus's mouth is pulled tight as he takes in a lip-locked Colin and Ally, his hands balled into fists at his side. "What the hell is that about?"

Oops, I guess in all the time we had together, we failed to mention Ally and Colin. I grab his arm and try to pull him away from the door to give them some privacy.

"I'm serious," he growls. "What the hell?"

"Cyrus." I yank him hard, making him face me. "She's a big girl. Old enough to decide who she kisses."

He narrows his eyes, but at least he leaves them alone.

Will pokes his head out of the kitchen, plate in one hand, dish towel in the other. The plate hits the floor with a clatter, and he drops the towel on his way over to greet us. He wraps his arms around my waist, lifting me off the floor.

I ruffle his blond hair. "Is it possible you grew more in the past three months?"

"Doubtful." He sets me down and reaches out to shake hands with Cyrus.

Cyrus pulls him into a bear hug, and they pat each other's backs in that way guys do when they want to hug, but don't want anyone to know it.

"This is Mateo," Cyrus says, indicating the big guy with us.

Will shakes his hand then hugs Rainey. Before I have a chance to ask where everyone else is, they spill into the house from the backyard through the door off the kitchen, kicking dirt off their shoes.

"Guess who's here," Will calls.

Sonia's hand flies to her mouth, tears pooling in her beautiful light brown eyes. Cyrus crosses the living room and pulls her into a long hug, whispering something to her while her arms wrap tightly around his waist.

"Hey there," Marcus says from behind me.

I spin around into his arms, he embraces me warmly, kissing the side of my head.

The next half-hour is filled with more hugs from smaller people, laughter, and even some more tears. It's the nicest homecoming ever, and I want it to last forever.

After the initial pleasantries are finished, we spend a couple of hours bringing everyone up to speed on what we've been up to, what we've learned, and what we still need to do.

"Wait, you were shot?" Sonia screeches.

I nod. As much as I'd like to say it was no big deal, it really was.

"That's why I took her to the Union," Cyrus says, quietly. "She needed medical attention she could only get there."

"Can I see it? The wound, I mean?" Sonia asks.

"Sure." I get up and follow her into her bedroom before pulling off my sweater.

Her fingers brush my bare shoulder. "Wow."

"Yeah. Not gonna sugar coat it. It was bad. And then I developed an infection. They told my family they didn't know if I'd make it." I reach down and grab my sweater off her bed and pull it over my head, stuffing my hands through the sleeves.

Sonia sinks onto the bed next to me and stares at her hands. "I'm sorry about how...about when you were up here—"

"Sonia, we don't have to do this again. I know. It's okay."

"It's not, though. I didn't realize how close I came to losing you, too. We've lost too many people. Life is too precious to take anything for granted."

I sigh and put an arm around her. She's right, and a lot more danger awaits us before this is over. A knock at the front door has both of us raising our heads.

Sonia stands, pulling me to my feet, and we head back down the hall to find out who's here.

## *Cyrus*

A loud knock on the front door draws our attention, and I instinctively reach for the gun in the back of my waistband. Marcus's eyes go wide and he shakes his head, glancing at the boys. Yeah, I'm definitely different than I was before my time in the Uprising.

Ally opens the door and I almost wish it was a situation I could take care of with my gun, because this is so much worse.

Bridget crosses the room and throws her arms around me. "Cyrus! I heard you were back."

Before I get a chance to react, her lips land on mine. My hands settle on the sides of her waist to gently push her back, grateful Sonia dragged Evan into the bedroom. That's a shit storm I don't need.

"Hey, Bridge."

She pulls back, her eyebrows drawing together. I take her hand and guide her toward the door, eager to get her out of here as soon as possible.

"Come on, let me walk you home." When we get outside, I drop her hand. "So, yeah, I was gonna come by and see you, but we literally just got back."

"We?" One thin blond eyebrow rises.

"Yeah. We."

"I want details."

I laugh. "I knew you would." While we make our way across town, I fill her in on the past four months since I left. We've reached her front porch by the time I'm finished.

"Well, I cannot say I am not disappointed for me, but happy for you. This is what you wanted, no?" Her French accent is as thick as ever, and I'm not used to it anymore, so I have to pay close attention to catch all the words.

I nod, hell yeah, this is what I wanted, and if it hadn't been for the girl standing before me, I never would've gone after Ev. Bridget introduced me to Simon and encouraged me to find the girl I love, whatever it took.

"When I heard you were back, I assumed it was because you did not find her. I hope I did not cause you any trouble."

I shake my head, "No more than usual."

The corners of her eyes crinkle and she reaches up to run a delicate hand along my face. "You look happy. The sadness that haunted your eyes is gone."

"I am."

"So why are you back here if you found your Union girl?"

"We've got to stop the Uprising, Bridge. What they're doing is wrong. Whatever their plan is, it's not what they're telling us. I've got a lot to tell you. Can we get together later this week? If we're going to pull this off, I need your help."

Her eyes search mine for a few seconds. "Okay. Wednesday night, after work. Meet me at the school."

"Thanks," I say, reaching out to squeeze her shoulder. I owe her more than she'll ever know.

As soon as I open the front door, I know I'm in deep shit. Conversation halts and everyone turns toward me. Everyone except the one I need to talk to. My gaze circles the room and Marcus inclines his head toward the backyard.

"How bad is it?" I ask as I pass through the living room.

"She's pissed off like I've never seen her," Colin says.

*Great.* I let out a long breath before opening the back door.

She startles, but doesn't turn around.

I step outside and make my way across the deck. "I'm sorry."

Her head pivots slowly until she's facing me, a mixture of anger and pain swirling in her beautiful eyes.

"Ev…"

"Don't," she hisses.

"I should've told you about her."

"Well, it's not like you had days of endless hours with nothing better to do. Oh, wait, yeah you did."

I drop my head. She's right, there's no excuse.

"Did you think you were going to waltz into a town where everyone knows you, and your girlfriend wasn't going to find out you were back?"

I close my eyes and let out a long breath through my nose. "It wasn't like that. She's not my girlfriend."

"Really? So you were just friends then? And, what, she tripped and her lips happened to land on yours?"

Oh crap, she saw everything. "Hey, I didn't kiss her."

One look at Evan tells me that didn't help. Silence takes root, growing, becoming dark and looming. My hands itch to reach out and take her in my arms, hold her, tell her Bridget never meant anything to me, that she was only a distraction, but none of those words will fix this.

"Just go," she whispers.

"No. Not until we talk." Hell if I'm leaving now. We spent close to a month angry and apart, and that doesn't work for me.

She tenses, her head whipping around, fire in her eyes. "You want to talk? Fine, let's talk. You go first. How could you?"

"How could *I*? What about you?"

Her hands fly out from her sides. "What *about* me? You left me half-naked in the middle of making out in your hideaway.

Remember? God, do you have any idea how humiliating that was? Then you told me to go home and walked away from me."

Running a hand through my hair, I struggle to find the right words. "I…shit, Ev…"

She shifts further away as this goes from bad to epically fucked up.

"How can you even compare *her* to Bryce? It's completely different. You sent me back with him, knowing how he felt about me, knowing I was in love with him before I met you, or at least I thought I might've been. But you didn't even meet this girl until after you were supposed to be in love with me."

Hearing her say she's in love with that douche is more than I can take. Pissed off doesn't even come close, but if I don't walk away and cool off, I'll end up saying something I regret.

"You're right, it *is* different. Because you're the only one I've ever been in love with."

I shove up and head back inside, slamming the door behind me.

# The Only One

Evan

I wipe tears as I head down the sidewalk away from the house, silently cursing myself for not remembering to grab a jacket and less silently cursing Cyrus.

I'm getting awfully tired of watching the boys I love kiss other girls. The little voice in my head that keeps me from being too self-righteous reminds me I kissed Cyrus in front of Bryce. I blow out a shaky breath full of emotion that puffs in front of my face like a cloud.

Picking up the pace, I soon reach the center of town and the bar where Ally works. My fingers are numb and my cheeks raw as I pull open the door. A blast of warm air mixed with voices and loud music welcomes me.

Ally glances up, rag in one hand, two empty glasses in the other. She stares beyond me, confusion and concern crossing her face. When she finishes wiping the table, she tips her chin at it for me to sit. She drops off the glasses and picks up a tray, delivering drinks to a rowdy table of guys in the corner.

Placing the tray against her hip, she makes her way over to me. "Are you here alone?"

My puffy eyes and swollen lips probably tell her enough, because she doesn't ask any more questions.

She glances over her shoulder. "I'll be right back," she says, disappearing to deliver another order.

The last time I was here with Rainey, she said something about drinking to get numb. That sounds like a pretty good idea, so when Ally doesn't return after a few minutes, I go up to the bartender and get a beer.

The level of noise rises and falls with conversation, laughter, and music. The thunk of a dart hitting the board to my left is followed by a whoop and cheers, drawing my attention to the small group of kids around my age.

My gaze drifts around the room as I return to my table. In just the time I was getting my drink, the two empty stools at the bar are now taken and only one table remains unoccupied.

I study the scarred wood of my own table, tracing my finger over marks left behind from decades of use. A vision of the tall, leggy blonde throwing her arms around Cyrus, kissing him, fills my head, unbidden, coiling my stomach. Watching that was about a thousand times worse than Bryce kissing Alivia.

"Haven't seen you around here before." A husky voice startles me, and my hand flies to my chest. The guy's at least a decade older than me, scruffy, but not bad looking. "What're you drinking?"

I notch an eyebrow in his direction. The beer in my hand should make the answer obvious.

Ally suddenly appears next to the table. "Scott, how's it going?"

He glances between me and Ally, and mumbles something before wandering off.

"What was that about?" I ask.

She shrugs. "Nothing. He hits on every new girl who comes into town. I figured you didn't need that."

"Thanks."

"So what are you doing here alone?"

I peel the corner of the label from my bottle. Everyone else knows by now, she'll find out soon enough. "Bridget."

"Oh." She drops into the chair across from me and sets her tray on the table. "Do you want to talk about it?"

I shake my head.

"Ally, order up," the bartender calls.

"I'll be back in a few minutes."

After she delivers the drinks, she returns to the bar and plugs a handheld tablet into some sort of docking station, types something, and shoves it back in her pocket as a large group of teens spills in the front door.

A half-hour later, I'm nursing a warm beer when Marcus takes the seat Ally vacated. Damn them and their new technology and their ability to read and write. There's no hiding out here anymore.

Marcus signals to Ally. "Two beers."

She sets the bottles on the table, taking my old one, and I get busy working on the new label.

Marcus reaches out and puts his hand on mine, stopping me. "You shouldn't walk around out here alone at night."

"I'm armed."

His eyebrows fly up.

"First lesson I learned in the Uprising."

He nods and takes a long pull on his beer. After a few minutes, he sets his bottle down, his head swiveling, then grabs my hand and pulls me up. "Come on. Let's play darts."

He writes our names on the board and we lean on the bar, sipping our drinks while we wait. When we're up, Marcus hands the darts to me. I position my foot against the toe-line, lining up my shot and release, hitting just left of center. The next two land near the first, and when I turn around, Marcus's mouth is hanging open.

"Where'd you learn to play like that?"

"Back home." I shrug. "They're like tiny little knives. I'm good at throwing knives."

"Remind me to stay on your good side," he mumbles.

Soon a line of challengers forms, and one by one, I kick their asses, although I refuse to take their money. For a few hours, I manage to forget my jealousy and anger. At least until Colin arrives to walk Ally home. His eyes find mine across the room, and I swallow back the lump in my throat.

I hand my darts to the next challenger. "I'm done."

Colin pushes his way through the crowd and hands me my jacket. "Here."

"Thanks."

We stand awkwardly next to each other while I wait for him to tell me what an asshole Cyrus is.

"You should cut him some slack. It's not like you weren't with someone else."

My head jerks up and I stare at him open-mouthed. "Are you serious?"

"I don't think you're being fair."

"For real? Cyrus sulked and brooded for two weeks, then disappeared to Mexico without saying goodbye simply because Bryce had the nerve to show up in the Northwestern Province. But I'm just supposed to get over it ten minutes after watching my boyfriend kiss another girl. You saw her, right? All five foot ten of her. She looks like a model, and that French accent..."

Colin glances around, and I realize I'm yelling. He grabs my arm and pulls me outside into the frigid night air. I shove my arms into my coat and button it up.

"I was sitting right next to them when it went down. He didn't kiss her. She kissed him and he pushed her back."

I study his face, he seems sincere. "Really?"

He nods. "Really."

"Still, it's not only that. Why didn't he tell me? Do you think he still has feelings for her?"

"I think if he did, he wouldn't have pushed her away. He thought you were still in the bedroom with Sonia. He didn't know you saw them until he got back."

My eyes narrow, and Colin shifts his gaze away, probably realizing he said too much.

"Got back from where?"

He doesn't answer and refuses to look at me.

"Got back from where, Colin?"

He sighs and shoves his hands into his pockets. "He walked her home."

I close my eyes and turn away. Cyrus was holding her hand before I turned away, unable to watch them any longer.

The front door opens and Marcus pokes his head out. "I'm ready to go whenever you are."

Colin ducks back inside leaving me and Marcus on the sidewalk. A couple, arm-in-arm, glances at us before heading into the bar, giggling. Stupid people in love.

"So how long were Cyrus and the blonde together?" I can't even bring myself to say her name.

Marcus gives me a sideways glance, as if he doesn't want to answer. The question hangs out there until he finally mumbles, "It wasn't anything serious."

"But it was something?"

He starts walking in the direction of the house, turning to make sure I'm following. Rolling my eyes, I take a few quick steps to catch up to him.

Marcus opens his mouth, as if to speak, closes it, then seems to wage some sort of internal battle before turning toward me. "Look, Evan, when Lucien died and you left, Cy was a mess. He tried to hide it, but...after he met Bridget, I don't know, he seemed better."

Something between jealousy and shame twists my insides. I never should have left him, and I *hate* that someone else was there for him. Someone tall and beautiful and all long blond hair and French accent.

"Evan…it *wasn't* serious. She was just someone to, I don't know, kill time with."

I shove my hands into the pockets of my jacket and start walking again, trying to dislodge images of Cyrus and Bridget killing time together in bed.

"Shit," Marcus says under his breath. "I'm probably making things worse. He's crazy about you. Yeah, there were other girls, hell there were always girls, but no one like you. He loves you. I mean, he *really* loves you."

How is this supposed to make me feel better? If there were so many girls, girls who look like Bridget, what does he even see in me? It makes no sense.

Marcus continues as if he can't stop talking, like he realized he dug a hole and is trying to fill it with a never-ending stream of verbal vomit. "I don't know why he got involved with Bridget when it's clear now the whole time he was planning on going to find you."

He's watching me expectantly, as if he needs reassurance he didn't screw things up even more for his best friend, but I'm not sure what to say. Marcus didn't make things worse by telling me the truth, the truth Cyrus should have told me. I drop my gaze to the sidewalk and watch my boots striking the pavement.

"Aw, hell, Evan, I'm not saying you have to pretend tonight never happened, but just listen to him, okay? Give him a chance."

With a sigh, I lift my head and study his face, all pinched with worry, and decide to let him off the hook.

"Okay."

The windows are dark when we approach the house, but I notice a light on the porch. A light they didn't have last time.

I turn to Marcus. "Did you guys get power?"

"Yeah, we only got a small set of panels, but it's more than we've ever had." He gives me a wide grin, acknowledging they were paid for with the money I left when Colin and I joined the Uprising.

Marcus unlocks the front door and pushes it open for me. My eyes adjust to the dark, and I see Mateo sprawled out on the couch, arm flung across his face, mouth slack. It's the most relaxed I've ever seen him.

Everyone else must be in bed, but then it's after two in the morning, so that's not surprising. I glance around, not sure where I'm supposed to sleep. If Cyrus and I weren't fighting, I guess I'd be in his bed with him. Or not, remembering the condoms I found in his dresser when I was here last fall. I can't sleep in the same bed he slept with Bridget in, no matter what happens with us.

"'Night," Marcus calls to me before heading down the hall to his room.

There are two sets of bunks in Ally and the boys' room. The boys share one and Ally sleeps in the other. I can take the top bunk, except Colin's probably going to be sleeping there. The chair in the corner it is.

I head to the closet off the kitchen to hang up my coat and grab a blanket when a shadow outside catches my attention. Through the window over the sink, I see Cyrus, hunched over on the deck, upper arms resting on his knees. The full moon illuminates the hard lines of his face. I button my coat up again and ease out the back door.

Cyrus doesn't move a muscle as I approach, even though there's no way he doesn't know I'm here. I cross the wooden deck and take a seat next to him, pulling my legs up and wrapping my arms around my shins. I rest my head on my knees and study him. His jaw ticks, but he never looks my way. Neither one of us speaks for several endless minutes.

I take a deep breath before diving in. "When are we going to stop fighting about stupid shit?"

He doesn't respond, and I'm not sure what else I'm supposed to say. My attempt to break the ice didn't work, so I guess I'm going to have to dig deeper.

I let out a small sigh. "I suspected there was someone else while I was gone, but I didn't ask because I didn't want to know." I pause to take a breath and give myself a chance to put my feelings into words. "But when I saw you with her...damn it hurt...I had no idea...I think I finally realize how much I've been hurting you. I'm sorry, Cyrus."

He turns and studies me, his jaw still ticking like mad before glancing down at his hands. "That night in the hideout, I left because it was wrong."

His words pierce my heart and I swallow around a giant ball of pain in my throat. "Wh-what?"

"Why did you let things go as far as they did that night?"

"Because...I was ready, I wanted to."

"Yet the day before, you couldn't back away from me fast enough when things were nowhere near as serious. What changed?

Were you really ready, or were you just trying to prove to yourself you'd made the right decision?"

My thoughts drift back to the night in his hideaway when I was ready to have sex with him for the first time. The night he walked out on me. "A little of both, I guess."

"And the other night on the beach?"

The other night? That night meant *everything* to me. Tears spring to my eyes as pain mixes with confusion. "Are you serious? I can't...what do you *want* from me?"

He stops studying his hands and glances at me, anger burning in his eyes. "I bared my soul to you the other night, Evan. I said things to you I've never said to anyone." He pushes up and turns toward the house.

I'm used to him calling me "Ev" or "Baby," and the way he spits out "Evan" as if it's a bad taste in his mouth has me recoiling.

He pauses on his way to the door. "For once, I'd like to know where the hell I stand with you."

Thick tears coat my throat and I turn away so he won't see me cry, not sure what to say. Is he right? I told him I loved him. Once. But that was seconds before I thought we were both going to die, so maybe it doesn't count. The other night he gave me beautiful words that buried themselves deep in my heart forever. I gave him a part of me, too, but in his eyes, it was something I'd given to Bryce first.

When Eddie appeared in my life, I was awful to him, I tested him, made him prove he was ready to be my father. I pushed him hard to see if he'd stick around even if his daughter was a total monster. Am I testing Cyrus, too? Maybe I'm trying to push him away to see if he'll actually go, or if he loves me enough to stay.

I hear the door open and panic claws through me, turning my blood to ice.

"Cyrus, wait. *Please*," I beg, fear threading my words.

The door closes, but when I turn toward the house, he's on this side of it. I sigh with relief and wait for him to come back, but he stays next to the door, watching me.

"Can you please…just come back and sit by me."

He stares at me for a few moments before crossing the deck and taking a seat beside me, but far enough away the heat from his body doesn't reach me.

"This isn't easy for me," I say, hoping he'll cut me some slack.

He doesn't. His eyes flicker with a combination of hurt and anger. I have nothing to lose by laying it all out there, so I push up on shaky legs and move in front of him, desperate to touch him yet terrified of being rejected. Before I can talk myself out of it, I crawl onto his lap and take his whiskered face in my hands, my eyes locking with his.

With a deep breath, my heart finally lets go of the emotions it's been selfishly guarding for so long. "I love you, Cy. I love you more than I've ever loved anyone. More than I knew I *could* love someone. The way you make me feel…" I swallow and shake my head. "I never knew it was possible to feel this way, like I'm falling whenever I'm around you. You make me feel alive. It's intense and exhilarating, but it scares me." Then I whisper the words that are the hardest to say. "The way I need you terrifies me."

A sigh rolls through him and his body shudders, but he never breaks eye contact. The anger from before has been replaced by something deep and powerful.

Suddenly his mouth is on mine, fierce and full of emotion. This isn't the skillful, practiced kissing I'm used to from him. This kiss is deeper, raw, real, as if he's *truly* kissing me for the first time.

His kiss ignites a fire that consumes me, our lips and tongues speaking without words. He tangles his hands in my hair, pulling my face closer. If this is makeup kissing, I can't wait for makeup sex.

He pulls his mouth from mine, his forehead falling to my shoulder, his breathing erratic, and he swears softly. "I gave my room to Colin and Ally. I didn't think we'd need it."

A giggle escapes before I can stop it. He lifts his head and stares at me, which only makes me laugh harder.

He smiles and presses his lips to the sensitive spot below my ear. "God, I love you, Ev."

Then he slides me forward and stands. I wrap my legs around his waist as he carries me into the house.

# Letting Go

**Evan**

**M**y face is pressed against warm skin, my back up against the wall. I inhale, and my senses fill with the scent of the boy I love. We decided to share one of the empty bunks in Ally's room last night. It's a little crowded, but neither one of us wanted to sleep apart from the other. It must have gotten too hot for Cyrus during the night, because he peeled his shirt off.

The rough denim of his jeans brushes against my stomach where my tank top rode up. I shift to pull it down, and stop mid-tug when I see his tattoo.

The sun's rays reach beyond a ring of barbed wire encircling names that surround the U all Uprising soldiers are branded with.

As they move up in rank, tattoos become more elaborate with everyone choosing personal elements to include. Cyrus added his siblings' names — Lucien, Penelope, and Bartholomew — along with two more, Benjamin and Calliope, whom I assume are his parents.

Across the bottom is a single name that opens an aching hole in my chest. *Evan.* Tears fill my eyes as I reach out a finger to trace it.

He grunts at my touch and rolls over, pulling me into his arms. "Good morning, beautiful."

A tear slips out and runs down my cheek.

"Hey, what's wrong?"

How do I tell him what an idiot I've been? How foolish I was to doubt him.

I shake my head. "Nothing. Everything's perfect." I swipe the tear away. "I love you. I'm sorry it took me so long to tell you."

His lips capture mine in a soft kiss. "I want to wake up next to you every morning."

"Mmm, I'd like that."

"Gross," Ty says from the bottom of the other bunk.

I laugh, and Cyrus tosses a pillow at him. "Someday you won't think so." He picks his T-shirt up off the floor and pulls it on before taking my hand and tugging me to my feet. "Come on, we have a lot to do today."

Cyrus reaches out as we pass the dining room table and grabs a piece of melon, popping it in his mouth.

Mateo's in the kitchen, apron on, frying sausage. I turn to hide my smile. Never in a million years could I have pictured Mateo doing anything domestic. In my mind, he shoots and stabs things.

"I want to get going right after breakfast," Cyrus says.

Mateo glances at our locked hands, and grins. "Works for me."

"Where are we going?" I ask.

"You're heading into town with Ally to pick up supplies. The rest of us are going across the border to do some shopping," Cyrus says.

"Wait, across the border? Like the Northern Territories?"

"Yeah."

"I promised Eddie I'd try to send him a message. I can do that from up there, right?"

Mateo shrugs. "Ally and Will can get the supplies, I guess."

"I want to check in with him, make sure Simon and Lisa haven't shown up back there."

Mateo cuts his eyes to me. "I doubt it. I mean you can ask, but they likely got swept up by the recruiters."

I hate to admit it, but he's probably right.

Ally and Colin shuffle into the kitchen staring at each other, all dopey eyed. Colin follows his nose and zeros in on the plate of bacon, grabbing a piece.

With lightning quick reflexes, Mateo turns and raps his hand with the spatula. "Were you raised in a barn? Wait until it's served."

This time there's no hiding my smile. I love this version of Mateo.

"Border" is a term I'd only loosely apply to what's before me. And yet, entering the Northern Territories from the Ruins is a little like

Alice stepping into Wonderland. With one step, I'm in a world where a steady stream of cars hum over smooth, paved roads, colored lights control the flow of human and vehicular traffic, and tall buildings made of glass and brick line either side of the wide streets.

We walk a couple of blocks into the center of a bustling hub, where cars whiz past disturbingly close to pedestrians and other vehicles. It's a crazy contrast to Union life where the only vehicles are for emergencies or available for hire for short hops on the ground level.

We stop out front of a busy coffee shop. "You can send a message to Eddie in there," Cyrus says, kissing my cheek. "We'll be back in an hour."

I watch my friends disappear around the corner at the end of the block before pushing into the café. A heavenly aroma envelopes me, drawing me straight to the order line.

A dreadlocked guy with a pierced eyebrow and colorful tattoos dancing down his forearms smiles when I reach the front. "Can I help you?"

"A cappuccino with a drizzle of caramel. And, um, I need to send a text message."

He nods his head toward the windows. "Tablets are built into the tables over there."

I glance over my shoulder at several people swiping the surface of a long, high table overlooking the street. Dreadlocks returns with my coffee, and I take it to an open stool. A rectangle illuminates, directing me to scan my fingerprint. Yeah, that's not going to work, but being so close to the Ruins, they must accept other forms of payment. I hop down and make my way back to the counter.

"Back so soon?"

"Can I pay with cash?"

The pierced eyebrow goes up, but he says, "Sure. Five bucks an hour."

I hand him a bill, and he hands me a card with a series of numbers, letters, and symbols. Using the code, I log on and find the text app. I wonder if the network up here connects to the Union's. Only one way to find out. I enter Eddie's tablet ID and type up a short note.

*Me: I'm good. Did you hear from L or S?*

I wait to see if I get an error or a response, but nothing comes back to me, although it appears the message sent. Eddie could be out and not have his tablet with him, or the message went into a black hole because I can't communicate with him from here.

I click back out and search through other apps, finding one that promises me the latest news. I launch it, but everything's in French. Closing it out, I open another news app and read about life in the Territories. Lots of political drama as they seek to reunify under a central government. The ideas on how best to do that appear as varied as the candidates running for the top spot in the new government.

The girl sitting next to me clicks long nails against the glass as she enters something in an app. She swings waist-length dirty blond hair over her shoulder and gives me a tight-lipped smile when she notices me watching her.

I return my attention to my own workspace and spot a blue flag in the corner signaling I have a text. Excitement and nervousness combine, making my fingers shake as I swipe back over and read the note from Eddie.

*Eddie: Good. No. No word. Take care.*

The small balloon of hope that Lisa and Simon had found their way back to the Union deflates, and I log off. My square of counter becomes dark as the display turns off.

I grab my cup and head outside to wait. A woman gets up from a small metal table on the sidewalk, wadding up and tossing her trash. I drop into the chair she vacated and take in my surroundings.

Two pigeons cautiously approach my table, their heads bobbing and twisting as they move with short, quick steps. A car zooms past and they scuttle away, only to scuttle back over again. Four shiny silver motorbikes with knobby tires and scrunchy suspension pull up to the curb and the birds beat their wings in a frenzy to flee the area.

Cyrus smiles and inclines his head toward me. "Wanna ride?"

It's such a cheesy line, I can't help laughing. I swallow the last of my coffee and toss my cup into the recycling bin before climbing on behind Cyrus.

I glance over at Colin perched atop one of the other bikes. Rainey and Mateo riding don't surprise me, but Colin does. An image of Colin on a motorbike the day Rainey and my dad came to rescue us after I was shot comes to mind.

"When did you learn to ride?" I ask Colin.

"Summer before last. I thought you knew. It's easy." A grin spreads across his face. "I'll teach you when we get back."

Before I can answer, Cyrus hooks his hand behind my knee and slides me forward so my chest is against his back. "Hang on tight," he says, easing away from the curb.

We slice through traffic on smooth streets until we hit the border and the pavement turns to crumpled ruins. We bounce along, the wind tossing my hair, and I scoot a little closer to Cyrus and hold on a little tighter.

"It's like riding a bike, EvTay," Colin says.

I straddle the motorbike, leaning it over so my foot reaches the ground.

"Lean into the turns, don't fight it," Cyrus says. "Remember to be smooth, and relax. Don't forget to breathe."

Shoving an errant curl from my face with my shoulder, I let out a huff. "One teacher at a time."

Colin pushes Cyrus toward the house. "I've got this."

Cyrus's jaw clenches and his gaze shifts to mine.

I nod. I'd rather have Colin teach me so I don't make an idiot of myself in front of my boyfriend.

He presses a soft kiss to my cheek and heads inside.

Colin focuses his full attention on me. "You need to go fast enough to stay upright, but really you'll be surprised how easy it is. Oh wait." He runs into the house and returns with a large duffel bag, one of the ones they brought back from our shopping trip this morning. He reaches in and pulls out a helmet, hands it to me and waits for me to strap it on.

"This is the brake, that's the throttle, start button's here, and these are the gauges. This one is your speed. It's in kilometers, though, but don't worry about that for now."

I nod, repeating everything in my head, taking it all in, memorizing it. The bike is lightweight for its size so it feels like a heavy bicycle. A tall, heavy bicycle. I hate that I can't reach the ground with both feet. The brakes are similar enough to a bicycle, but the handlebar throttle instead of the bike pedals I'm used to is different enough this isn't going to be the piece of cake Colin promised.

"Smooth is the key. Ease on the throttle, same with the brakes."

He takes off down the street, making it look effortless before swinging around and heading back to me.

"Now you go."

I twist the throttle with my right hand, jerking forward with enough force I lose my grip and slam to a halt.

"Again, EvTay," Colin says.

I glare at him, but try again, slower this time.

"You need to get up enough speed to balance." He crosses his arms over his chest as I sputter along, passing him. "You have to go faster."

A few choice words swirl around in my head, but I decide to keep them to myself.

"Faster."

At the end of the block, I slow and do an awkward turn, heading back toward him. As I pass, he swings his foot out, kicking the back tire. The bike goes one way and I go the other, landing on my ass.

I get up and yank my helmet off before shoving Colin's shoulder hard enough that he stumbles back a couple steps. "What the hell was that?"

"You needed to see falling isn't a big deal. Now that you've done it, you don't have to be afraid of it anymore."

Slamming my helmet back on, I march across the street and pick up the bike. Anger floods my veins as I hop back on, and I'm more focused on being pissed off than I am on riding. At least until I realize I'm going fast. And with the speed comes more stability. Meaning Colin was right. Which sucks.

On the next pass, he signals for me to stop, a huge grin plastered across his face. "See."

I refuse to admit he's right, though.

He gets back on his bike and takes off, calling over his shoulder, "Let's hit the dirt."

I follow him to the end of the street and make a gentle turn, cutting through an empty lot until we reach the wilderness outside town. Dirt is way more challenging, and I lay the bike down several times, each time hitting the ground a little harder.

Colin creates a trail through the plants, and I try to keep up. He circles around behind me, and when I turn to look for him, my front tire hits a rock. I go flying and land hard on my back, the wind whooshing from my lungs.

Colin stops next to me and hops off. "You okay?"

"Y-yeah," I wheeze.

He reaches down and pulls me to my feet. "You want to call it a day?"

"Are you kidding? I'm seconds away from owning this thing."

He laughs and helps me pick up the bike. We spend the next few hours together as I practice, increasing my confidence until I'm exhausted and hungry, which means Colin must be starving.

He races me back to the house, and beats me by a good thirty seconds. We stash the bikes in the backyard and drag ourselves into the kitchen. I grab some ice out of their new freezer and wrap it in a towel, applying it to my aching shoulder while Colin rummages around for something to eat.

The others are in the dining room discussing plans for Operation Break-Out Lisa and Simon. Cyrus glances up when we approach, his eyes zeroing in on the ice pack, and no doubt taking in the dirt on my clothes and the twigs in my hair.

He pushes up from the table and approaches me. "What happened?"

"She fell a few times," Colin calls from the kitchen.

I decide not to mention the first time was because he made me. "Just a couple of bumps and bruises."

Cyrus cuts his eyes to Colin.

Colin puts his hands up. "Hey, she's mostly in one piece. *And* she can ride."

"I'm fine." I take Cyrus's arm and guide him back to the table. "What have you all been up to this afternoon?"

"Details and shit," Rainey says.

I laugh as I take a seat, Colin dropping down next to me, and the others bring us up to speed.

The boys are reading great on their own, but they still insist I read to them at bedtime. Connor and Ben are nestled against me as I sit on the edge of Ty's bed, a new book full of bright pages and exciting adventures in my lap.

I'm transported back to last summer when this was our nightly routine, and for a short time there is no room for thoughts about what we're doing in the morning. Ty's chin hits his chest, his eyes going from hooded to closed before I finish.

I bend down to kiss his head before tucking him in. After quick hugs, Connor scuttles up the ladder to his bunk, and Ben disappears down the hall to the room he shares with his brother, Will.

Cyrus is leaning on the wall beside the door frame, arms crossed, when I close the door behind me. He reaches out for my hand and pulls me against him, wrapping his arms around my waist.

He presses his forehead to mine. "You're amazing, you know that?"

"What do you mean?"

He shakes his head, the corners of his mouth lifting. "The way you are with the boys, how you just up and decided to learn to ride today and then did." His eyebrows pinch together. "Speaking of, how's your shoulder?"

"Still sore, but okay. Getting banged up seems like part of life these days, but after being shot, it's no big deal."

His face darkens and I immediately regret saying it.

I shrug and change the subject. "So, Eddie said no word from Lisa or Simon."

He brushes his lips against mine. "When you didn't mention anything, I assumed as much." His words are slow and heavy, as if he's not fully aware he's speaking.

He bends forward to kiss me again, softly at first before deepening it. I lean into him as his kisses become more persistent. He pulls his mouth from mine, his eyes glazed over, making my skin burn.

"I can set the tent up in the backyard for us."

My heart ratchets up a notch and I close my eyes savoring the energy racing through me. At least until I remember what we're doing in the morning.

"Mmmm, tempting, but neither one of us slept much last night. We both need a good night's sleep tonight. Inside. In beds. Alone."

His fingers slip under the edge of my shirt and glide across my ribs as he leans in to nuzzle my neck. "I'll sleep better if you're with me." His voice is so low and sexy next to my ear, I want to give in to him.

But I can't. "The last time we spent the night alone in a tent together, not a lot of sleeping was going on."

"Fine," he groans, his lips moving to rest on my forehead. "But I'm not gonna like it."

"Noted. You can have the top bunk if you want."

"Oh, I definitely want to be on top," he says, waggling his eyebrows.

I roll my eyes and slap his shoulder before pushing off him and getting ready for bed.

# On Top

*Cyrus*

I drag myself down from the top bunk, noticing the empty bed below before making my way into the kitchen to find my girl with a mug of tea.

She hands it to me before turning around to make another. I switch the cup to my left hand, circling my right around her waist and pull her against me so I can kiss her neck. I love seeing goosebumps rush up to coat her skin.

"Morning."

She tilts her head back and smiles. "Morning."

"Scoot, everyone into the dining room," Sonia orders.

The younger boys set the table while Will places a bowl of chopped melon in the middle. Living up here limits access to fresh fruit in the winter, but melon is brought up from the south year-round.

I grab a piece of honeydew, but it's nowhere near as good as when it's picked ripe. Before long, the smell of sizzling bacon and frying eggs makes its way to me, and my stomach lets loose a small roar. Not long after, a feast is laid out before us, and I dig in to piping hot scrambled eggs, crisp bacon, and fresh-baked bread, loading up before our mission.

"We'll take care of the dishes," Sonia says, pushing back from the table. "You guys go get ready."

I stand and kiss her cheek. "Thanks."

She smiles then gives me a playful shove down the hall.

I head to my room and dress in the stuff we got yesterday that closely resembles Uprising uniforms before returning to the front room. Grabbing one of the backpacks, I begin shoving spare batteries into it, then grab another and do the same.

Ev walks past, her fatigues hugging her ass with perfection, distracting me. She stops and turns toward me, catching me staring, a grin lighting up her face.

Quirking her left eyebrow, she nods toward the backpacks. "What's all this?"

"Extra power. We'll need it."

She comes up beside me and grabs one of the packed ones, shrugging it onto her back.

Sonia hands me a small wrapped package. "Sandwiches. For the road." Then she reaches up and kisses my cheek. "Be careful."

"I'm always careful." I give her a confident smile, deciding to never fill her in on what went down in Mexico.

The front door opens and Mateo pokes his head in. "Time to go."

We file outside where Mateo has lined up the bikes on the sidewalk.

"Where's Colin?" Rainey asks.

I glance around but don't see him. Marcus yells something inside the house, and Colin comes out the door with a guilty expression, Ally's hand clasped in his. It's one thing to know what they're doing in my bed, it's another to have to see evidence of it. She's like my little sister, although I know she's not, and she'd kill me dead on the spot if I interfered with her love life.

"Can we finally go?" I ask Colin when he reaches his bike.

"Sorry," he mumbles.

Rocks crunch beneath the tires as we pull away, the quiet hum of the electric motor giving way to wind noise as we pick up speed. I love the feel of Ev's hands around my waist, her chest pressed against my back as the hours pass. We only make a quick stop for lunch and to swap out depleted batteries with fresh ones, arriving at the outskirts of the camp by twilight.

I ease to a stop next to Mateo and help Ev down before stretching and shaking out my limbs after riding all day.

Colin grabs his tablet and I move beside him to study the camp layout he got from Walker's warehouse. Colin passes it down until everyone's had a chance to review the map.

Mateo checks his watch. "Everyone knows the plan, right?" We all nod. "Alright, then. It's show time."

Before we split up, I take Ev's hand and drag her to me. Brushing hair from her face, I lock my eyes with hers to make sure she's really listening to me. "Watch your back, if things start to go south, get out. We can try another way, but promise me you won't do something like you did with Willow."

She glances away and swallows hard. I know I'm being rough with her, but she can't afford to be reckless here.

"Ev, look at me." Her gaze shifts back to mine. "Promise me." She nods and I let out a breath I hadn't realized I was holding. "You can do this."

I bend down and kiss her softly until Mateo slaps me on the back, scaring the hell out of me.

"Let's go, Romeo."

Rainey grabs Ev and the two of them head left. I watch them go over my shoulder, hoping like hell she isn't going to risk everything to save Lisa. If it all turns to shit, we'll figure out another way to get Lisa and Simon, but we can't do that if she gets shot again. Or worse.

We move silently, and I'm impressed Colin picked up as much as he did in the short time he spent with Mateo in special ops. Kid's a natural. A sentry stands fifty yards ahead, back to us, watching for soldiers trying to escape.

A single gunshot is fired into the air signaling shift change, and the sentries begin walking in. Their attention is focused toward camp, on alert for anyone looking to take advantage of the switch in personnel to sneak out. Keeping a low profile, we cover the distance with sure, light steps. The lightweight hunting boots we bought in the Northern Territories are like a second skin, helping me to avoid snapping twigs.

Hushed voices carry across the clearing, and Mateo puts up his hand. We freeze, waiting for the bodies that accompany the voices.

A boy and girl, sixteen at most, head toward us, clutching each other, oblivious to anyone or anything around them.

Once they pass, we circle the clearing and make our way to the sleeping tents. As night wears on, the temperature continues to drop, until our breaths become visible. We arrive next to the tent that was marked as the boys' quarters on the diagram on Colin's tablet.

Mateo stands guard since he doesn't know what Simon looks like, and Colin and I duck inside, waiting by the entrance while our eyes adjust to the even lower light levels in here.

According to plan, Colin heads left and I go right, searching each bunk for Simon. The first one I come to has a dude on the bottom with dark curly blond hair who could be Simon. I slink around to the other side to get a look at his face. The guy on top groans and shifts in his sleep. I freeze because me creeping around his bunk in the middle of the night will raise alarms and could lead to me having a knife to my throat. When I'm sure he's asleep, I check the lower bed.

Not Simon.

I move on.

Frustration settles in after I make it through half the bunks without locating Simon. While it's possible they're not in this camp, or they're in the hole, it's unlikely. I'm moving to the next bunk when someone grabs my sleeve. I whip around, gun in hand, to find Colin.

He makes a hand motion toward the entrance where Simon's sitting on the floor, pulling on his boots.

I nod and head outside to grab Mateo, anxious to get the hell out of here, but he's gone.

"Shit," I mutter.

"Something wrong?" Simon asks, coming up behind me.

"Where's Mateo?" Colin asks.

I shake my head. "No clue. We're supposed to meet at the rendezvous spot if we get separated. Let's go."

I lead the way back through camp, keeping my eyes peeled for Mateo, the girls, or soldiers. Simon hasn't even finished basic training yet, and makes as much noise as a pack of wolves. I tense, turning to glare at him.

He shrugs. "Sorry."

"Just try to keep it down."

He gives me a grin and a thumbs up, and we continue on, easing around the side of the tent and working our way back toward the wooded area near the perimeter.

The plan to get past the sentries is to act like commanders. Sentries tend to be the least talented of the bunch, and often are just happy to follow directions. Since most of them have little to no contact with their commanders, it should be easy enough to pull off. It's the same way Rainey was able to overpower a group of recruiters the night I took Ev into the Union after she'd been shot. But, in the off chance someone with half a brain is on sentry duty, we've got contingency plans.

Footsteps head toward us accompanied by hushed voices and a giggle. I slink further into the shadows, waving for Simon and Colin to join me, although I realize there's no way we can escape notice. Time to implement the backup plan. Nodding at Colin, I tuck my gun into my waistband and stand to my full height, squaring my shoulders as Colin drags Simon the other way.

The couple comes around the corner, nearly slamming into me. The boy's eyes slowly shift up to mine and he swallows hard, pushing the girl behind him.

"Who are you?" he asks in a squeaky voice, puffing out his chest.

"What are you doing out of quarters?" I bark.

His eyes widen and he takes in my face and fatigues.

"Uh…we uh…" He stammers.

"Return to your tents now."

"Yes, sir."

He and the girl turn and run off in the direction of the sleeping quarters. That was almost too easy.

"Who the fuck are you?" a deep male voice growls from behind me.

Before I can reach for my gun, he's on me, kicking the back of my knee and tackling me to the ground.

I roll over, taking him with me. He squirms, reaching for my weapon, but it's knocked aside in the scuffle. After the way Lucien died, I really don't want to wrestle on top of a loaded gun. I get in a few quick, well-placed punches, and he falls back, his eyes closing.

Shaking out my hand, I move to push up, but he swings at me, landing a direct hit in my gut that knocks the wind out of me. Damn, he's strong.

I see the next punch in time to roll to my side, evading it.

He reaches into his fatigues and pulls out his knife, flicking open the blade.

Shit, I didn't want to have to hurt anyone, but he's making it hard. I dodge the first strike, but he's quick to sweep back and narrowly misses my forearm.

The guy's been around longer than I gave him credit for, and he definitely knows what he's doing.

When he lunges next, aiming for my midsection, I'm ready for him. At the last second, I roll into him, slamming my knee into the side of his wrist. The impact deflects the blade from its target, giving me a chance to grab his arm.

He's strong, but I'm stronger, and in seconds I have him on his back. I grab his wrist and twist, bashing it against a rock until he drops the knife. With a solid left hook, I watch the lights leave his eyes before pushing up.

"Will you quit messing around, we need to go."

I whip around to find Mateo standing over me, a half-grin on his face. He reaches down to yank me up and hands me my piece.

"Thanks for your help," I mutter.

"You had it handled." He glances past me. "Where's Colin?"

"He took Simon to the perimeter. They're waiting for us."

"Let's go."

We only take two steps before a bloodcurdling scream cuts through the night.

And it's coming from the direction of the girls' sleeping quarters.

# Screams

## Cyrus

**M**ateo halts in front of me, swearing loudly. I look beyond him and my lungs seize. A girl stands behind Ev, holding a knife to her throat. The girl is taller, but appears young and maybe even more terrified, which is a bad combination. The way her hand shakes, she may end up cutting Evan's throat by accident.

Ev's eyes are wide as they shift between Lisa, Mateo, and me.

"Stop," the girl yells, a tremor in her voice.

"Frankie, don't," Lisa pleads.

"I'm not asking again. Where're you going?" the girl, Frankie, demands.

"We don't belong here," Lisa says.

The girl lets out a short laugh that sounds more like a bark. "None of us belongs here."

Frankie's grip tightens around Evan, pushing the blade up against the skin.

My heart trips, and I take a step toward them, ready to end this, but Mateo shoots out his arm to block me. I lift my gun, steadying it with my right hand and aim at Frankie's head, confident I can put a bullet between her eyes faster than she can move that knife.

"Stand down," Mateo growls.

My gaze flickers to him, and in that second, I realize he's right. But shit, standing here watching this go down is about the most useless I've ever felt. I'm not good with useless.

"Frankie? Is that your name?" Mateo asks. The girl glances at him. "What's going on here?"

Her eyes sweep the area, taking us all in before landing on the gun in my hand. She yanks Ev's arm behind her back, the sharp blade drawing blood from a small nick in her neck.

Anger pulses across my skin, and I'm beginning to think Mateo doesn't have it all figured out.

Frankie flexes her bicep, pulling the knife even closer. "Drop it."

Ev's eyes bug out, drifting from my gun to my eyes and back again.

Fear nudges out some of the anger as it sinks in that I'm not in control of anything in this situation. My shoulders drop and I lower my weapon to the ground, never taking my eyes off Frankie's arm.

"Kick it over here," Frankie commands.

"Let's talk," Mateo says.

"No! No talking. Kick the gun over here. Now!"

Mateo nods, his gazed locked on mine, silently communicating he's got this handled. Frustration over my lack of control makes me kick a little harder than I intended, sending my piece skidding to a stop near Frankie's boot.

The girl hasn't taken her eyes off us since we arrived, but her gaze drops for a second before returning to us. So fast it's practically a blur, Frankie goes for my gun, yanking Ev with her.

In a single, fluid motion, Mateo retrieves his weapon from the back of his waistband and trains it on Frankie before she realizes what's happening.

Evan rolls to her side and jams her elbow into Frankie's gut, forcing the air out of her lungs. Frankie's grip on her knife falters and Evan reaches for the gun. But instead of picking it up and using it to protect herself, she tosses it out of the way.

*What the hell is she doing?*

Frankie points the knife at Evan, but now Evan has positioned herself between both us and Frankie, so neither Mateo nor I have a clean shot.

Evan turns to face Frankie and throws her arms out. "Stop! We're leaving, and you can't stop us."

Frankie lunges at Evan and all the blood drains from my head. Evan jerks back just in time to miss being gutted. I take a faltering step to the side, trying to find some oxygen.

Lisa points her gun at Frankie. "Don't move, Frankie. Drop the knife."

Frankie's gaze darts from Evan to Lisa and the knife slips to the ground before Frankie sinks to her knees.

Mateo reaches down to grab her knife and glances around before turning to me. "We need to tie her up."

Lisa shifts on her feet. "Um, she knows too much."

"What do you mean?" I demand.

"When she first caught us and she had the knife to Evan's throat, demanding answers, I told her a little about what we're up to."

I let loose a string of profanity. This wasn't part of the plan, and I don't want to have to kill kids, but leaving her here isn't an option now.

Mateo strides up to Frankie, covers her mouth with tape, and tosses her over his shoulder. She kicks and pounds her fists against his back, but his only response is to increase his grip.

He stows his piece in the front of his waistband, well out of her reach. "Let's go."

I take Ev's hand and pull her along. "Where's your gun?"

"Lisa has it."

I cut my eyes to her. "How did that happen?"

"It's a long story," she says, averting her gaze.

No doubt it's one I'm not going to like.

### *Evan*

Cyrus hauls me behind him, and I have to run to keep up with him.

"Where's Rainey?" he asks, his voice so low it's a little scary.

"She went with Simon and Colin."

"That wasn't the plan."

"No, but Lisa had to tie her boots, and the five of us hanging around was going to draw attention. So I told her to go and we'd meet up with her at the rendezvous spot."

"So how'd Lisa get your gun?"

Yeah, he's going to be pissed about this. "Well...I saw Mateo and he was alone. I wanted to find out where you were because I knew where Simon and Colin were. I gave Lisa my gun and told her where to find the others, and then I followed Mateo."

He stops and turns to stare at me before shaking his head. He mutters something and yanks me along until we catch up with Mateo and Lisa. Mateo makes three soft hoots, like an owl, and Rainey signals back, acknowledging the call and confirming she won't shoot us.

Cyrus tightens his hold on my hand. "We're not done talking about this."

I couldn't get that lucky.

The rest of the team is at the designated location behind a stand of trees where we can covertly observe the bored sentry.

"I checked out both of them while you were getting Simon," Mateo says. "This one has the least interest in what he's doing. He's either daydreaming or playing some weird game with rocks."

Sure enough the guy lines up small stones on a log while mumbling to himself.

Rainey pulls out her ponytail holder and shakes her head. "I've got this."

She moves toward the sentry, fluffing her hair with her fingers. When he notices her, he aims his rifle at her chest, and I suck in a breath. What if he's got a girlfriend? Or a boyfriend? This isn't going to work.

I take a quick glance around our little group and notice someone else is missing. "Where's Colin?" I whisper.

Cyrus doesn't answer, but movement to my left catches my eye where Colin's sneaking up behind the sentry. The guy's deep in conversation with Rainey now, and based on body language, I'd say even if he has a girlfriend, he's not one to let labels get in the way of flirting with a pretty girl.

He leans forward, putting his head down next to Rainey's ear, and Colin reaches around from behind, grabbing him in a chokehold. Within seconds, the guy is limp in Colin's arms.

Frankie continues to flail over Mateo's shoulder, hands secured behind her back, muffled yells caught in her mouth.

I glance at the boy on the ground as we make our way past before he regains consciousness. Damn, he's young.

Less than five minutes later we're at the bikes. Mateo studies Frankie as she glares at him, angry hatred pouring from her eyes. He rubs his jaw then shrugs off his coat and peels off his T-shirt. For a fraction of a second, she stares at his perfectly sculpted chest before trying to run. Mateo's on her in seconds, yanking her back.

Colin moves in and holds her arms while Mateo tears his shirt into strips. When he finishes, he hands the strips to Colin and throws on his jacket before straddling his bike. Then Colin binds Frankie to Mateo's torso with the T-shirt strips so she won't fling herself off or go flying if he hits a rock.

She wiggles and slams her forehead between Mateo's shoulder blades. He lets out a loud curse and turns to say something to her. His voice too low to make out what, but she stops fighting him and her shoulders slump in defeat.

Noises behind us in camp have all of us freezing.

Cyrus grabs my arm and tugs me to his bike. "Time to go."

Lisa climbs on behind Colin and Simon behind Rainey, and we're off and into the woods in under a minute.

Cyrus is pissed. I'm not sure how I know since his back is to me and we can't really talk, but there is no doubt in my mind. Maybe it's the way his body is rigid against mine. Or maybe it's because he hasn't reached out to put his hand on my knee or any of the other little affectionate things he did on the way to the Uprising camp. Nope, our ride back home is one long anger-fueled standoff.

Fine. He's pissed. Pretty sure it's because I gave Lisa my gun, but she needed it more than I did. I had the situation with Frankie under control. Mostly. At least until Mateo and Cyrus showed up and she freaked out.

Terror makes people act irrationally, even someone who's already irrationally holding a knife to my throat. She was scared enough before, but with Mateo and Cyrus pointing guns at her, she flipped the switch to completely terrified.

When we stop to swap batteries and eat a snack, my suspicions are confirmed when Cyrus doesn't even look at me, much less speak to me. I take a seat beside a tree and lean back to munch on my trail mix and wash it down with water from my canteen.

Lisa drops down next to me, and I hand her a bag of food. "Thanks. So how'd you find us?"

"Mateo figured you got caught up in a recruiting sweep last month," Colin says, sitting down across from us. "He thought that was the most likely camp they'd have taken you."

"Is that what happened?" I ask.

"We came into the Ruins too far south," Simon says, shoulder braced against the trunk of a tree. "But we didn't figure it out until we'd already been walking for a day. It didn't make sense to go back and take the train further north, so we kept going. We were making good time, and thought we'd even be back before anyone else. But they rolled up on us when we were sleeping. I wasn't expecting them to be out recruiting at night or we would've slept in shifts. We never saw them during the day, so we weren't even aware they were in the area."

"I remembered everything you told us," Lisa says. "So we went along, acted the part of good little recruits, biding our time until we could escape."

Colin pops another handful of trail mix into his mouth. "How were you gonna do that?"

"Simon played poker with some of the guys who'd been there awhile. He was earning favors left and right. It was only a matter of time before he had enough people owing him, and he could cash in and get us out."

Simon grins, shrugging. "Just using what I know. Like always."

"I'm glad you found us, though, I was getting tired of being there," Lisa says. "The food was awful."

Wiping his hands on his pants, Cyrus stands and moves toward the bike. "Let's go," he calls over his shoulder.

I roll my eyes and climb up behind him. We ride the rest of the way home without further stops, arriving shortly before ten o'clock in the morning.

"I'll take Frankie with me," Mateo says when we roll to a stop in front of the house.

"And then what?" I ask.

"I don't know. We'll take it one day at a time," he says.

After being awake for a full twenty-four hours, adrenaline running on overdrive, I'm ready to collapse and sleep for the next three days. The front door flies open, and Ally rushes out, straight into Colin's arms.

I grab his bike and push it into the backyard for him, then head into the kitchen to find Sonia, Marcus, and Will.

I reach out to hug Sonia. "What're you guys doing home from work?"

"We took the morning off. I couldn't concentrate. Plus, I wanted you to have a hot meal when you got back."

Lisa trails in behind me, and Sonia's eyes snap to her. "I know you. You came to the house looking for Evan."

Lisa throws her arms around Sonia and hugs her. "Thanks so much for opening your home to me."

This is Lisa being Lisa, and just one of the many reasons I adore her.

"You're welcome to stay as long as you like," Sonia says, patting Lisa's back.

Sonia calls over her shoulder to the boys to set the table, and soon we're in the midst of a returning heroes' breakfast that rivals even the best Thanksgiving feast.

# Homecoming

*Evan*

After feeding us, Will, Marcus, and Sonia went to work, leaving the boys with us. Ally's the only one who can keep her eyes open, so she's in charge by default. Cyrus disappeared into the boys' room and crashed in one of the bunks. I give some thought to joining him, but since he's not speaking to me, I opt for the couch instead. No sooner has my head hit the cushion than I'm tumbling into dreamland.

The front door opens, startling me, and I pop up. Marcus closes the door behind him and walks past me on his way to hang up his coat. I try to drift back off, but I'm too awake now. If Marcus is home, the rest will be along soon, so I head into the kitchen to start on dinner. Ally and the boys join me and everything's ready by the time Will and Sonia get home.

Cyrus enters the dining room, raking a hand through his hair. Our eyes meet and he immediately puts up a wall between us. I wonder how long he's going to give me the silent treatment this time.

Dinner conversation centers around our rescue adventures, and after, because Ally and I cooked, we're relieved of cleanup. Needing some fresh air, I grab my coat and head outside, taking a seat on the deck.

I dangle my legs over the side and lean back on my hands. The quiet chirping of crickets mixes with children's laughter from one of the neighbors' yards. Stars begin to blink to life as the sky transitions from soft gray to cobalt. It's unseasonably warm, hinting at the spring to come.

The back door opens, and I turn to see Cyrus striding toward me, his shoulders tense. I guess we're going to talk now. On the one hand, I hate that he's dictating this whole thing. We don't speak when he's mad and we do when he feels like it. On the other, I'm glad he's not going to drag this out for weeks like last time.

I push up and face him.

He rubs a hand down his face and sighs. "What the hell were you thinking out there?"

"Which thing are you referring to?" I ask, not sure what he's most pissed about.

His jaw gets a workout as he stares at me. "Everything. You didn't stick to the plan, you gave your gun to Lisa, and you risked your life, again. All to protect a girl with a knife to your throat."

"Okay, first I stuck with the plan until things went off script. Simon and Colin weren't supposed to come after us. Why weren't you with them? Why didn't *they* follow the plan?"

"I was looking for Mateo."

"Oh, so, you're allowed to abandon the plan, but not me? I adapted to the situation the best way I could."

"She could've killed you, and there wasn't a damn thing I could do to stop it."

"But she didn't."

"You don't get it, Evan. I saw my parents, my siblings…" He shakes his head and sighs. "I watched Lucien die. I came close to watching you die. I can't do it."

A stinging energy rolls across my skin, plunging inside and gripping my heart. "What are you saying?"

"I can't do this anymore."

My chest constricts until I can barely breathe. "Do what?" I squeak.

His eyes fall away from mine and he lets out a long breath through his nose.

"Cyrus…"

"I need to talk to Frankie."

He turns and heads across the yard and out through the side gate, leaving me more frustrated than before.

Lisa takes the spot next to me on the deck. "Hey. What are you doing out here alone?"

"Just needed some fresh air."

"I'm sorry. About what happened. With Frankie."

"It's not your fault."

"I should've been paying attention. I should've stopped her, shot her, something. I froze."

"Yeah. I froze the first time I was in a situation like that, too."

"What happened?"

"I ended up killing the guy before he could kill Cyrus."

"Oh." She drops her head and stares at her hands.

"But, Lis," I turn to her and wait for her gaze to meet mine. "He tried to rape me. He wasn't my friend or a scared kid."

"*You're* my friend. I care more about you than Frankie. I had no idea she was so wound up."

"Why do you think she did it?"

"I don't know. She never said much. I mean we talked, but never about anything more superficial than what we were having for lunch or what an ass our instructor was." She's quiet for a minute then rubs her palms on her knees. "I'm sorry I told her all that stuff. I thought maybe if she knew a little of what we were up to, she'd let you go."

"Do you think she's into the whole Uprising cause?"

She shakes her head. "No, but something's definitely going on with her." She leans back on her hands and turns to study me. "So what all did I miss?"

A small snort escapes me. "What didn't you miss," I say, bumping her shoulder with mine. Then I bring her up to speed on what Bryce and Jack are up to, Cyrus and Rainey's trip down to Mexico, and my adventure with Colin in Walker's warehouse.

"Wow. So that's how you knew how to find us?"

"Well, that's how we knew the layout of the camp. Mateo knew some stuff about recruiting sweeps and figured out which camp they probably took you to. But that was based on what we discovered in the warehouse. So yeah, I guess that's how we found you."

She smiles. "Thanks for coming for me." She stares across the yard, chewing on the inside of her bottom lip. "When will Jack get here?"

"A few days."

She opens her mouth to say something, closes it, then sighs. "What's up with you and Cyrus?"

"He's mad because I gave you my gun."

"I don't understand."

With a deep breath, I recap our most recent argument.

When I'm done, she turns to study me for a moment. "So where is he now?"

I stare at my clasped hands, rubbing my thumbs together. "He went to talk to Frankie."

Lisa puts her hand on my shoulder until I turn toward her. "Ev...he's scared. I know I was."

"Yeah, I get that, but...I'm not sure what he wants me to say. I don't think I did anything wrong."

She reaches over and takes my hand, lacing our fingers. It feels so small compared to Cyrus's. "Maybe he just wants to know you'll do everything you can to make sure the girl he loves survives."

"Maybe. But he has a crappy way of communicating that."

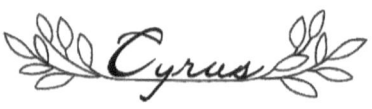

Cyrus

The stone walkway has been swept of leaves and dirt, and though still dormant, the yard is neat, planters weeded and ready for spring. I'm having a hard time picturing Rainey living here.

I knock on the door and glance around as I wait for someone to answer. The neighbors' houses aren't quite as well maintained as this one, but it's a clean part of town.

The door cracks and a blue eye peers out at me. "Yes?"

"I'm here to see Rainey."

She opens the door wider and studies me. She's tall and pretty. "Who're you?"

"Cyrus."

She smiles, throwing the door open. "I'm Ilona. Come in."

The front room is dark without solar panels to provide light, but a dozen or so candles create a warm glow.

"I'll get Rainey. Hang on."

She disappears around the corner, her long hair swaying.

Rainey calls from somewhere deep in the house, "Come on back."

I head toward Rainey's voice and spot her standing beside an open door at the end of the hall.

Inside the room, Frankie sits on the bed, her back against the headboard, arms folded over her chest. The scowl leaves a crease between dark eyes.

Mateo leans on the wall, ankles and arms crossed. "Took you long enough to get here." The small smile tugging at his lips is in direct contrast with his words. He's loving this. Mind games are his specialty, and the longer Frankie waits for whatever comes next, the more on edge she'll be.

"Can I get something to drink?" Frankie asks, a small tremor the only indication she's anything but royally pissed.

Ilona disappears, returning a few minutes later with a glass of water. Frankie guzzles half of it and wipes her mouth with the back of her hand. A tall dude walks up behind Ilona and wraps his arms around her waist, resting his chin on her shoulder. He cuts his eyes to me for a second, then pulls Ilona back down the hall.

I turn my attention back to Frankie. Her long stringy hair is pulled back into a ponytail, revealing a bruise under her eye I didn't notice before. "Where'd you get that?" I ask, nodding toward her face.

She smirks. "The red-headed bitch clocked me with her elbow."

A mixture of pride for my girl and anger at Frankie for her comment war inside me, but in the end, anger wins out. I cross my arms. "Start at the beginning."

"Which one?"

"Whichever one gets us to how you ended up here."

She thrusts out her chin. "You all kidnapped me. That's how I ended up here."

"Try again."

She sighs and tosses her head back until it thunks on the wall. Wincing, she leans forward and rubs it with her palm. "My brother signed up for the Uprising. My mom was devastated because he's only fourteen. So I signed up to keep an eye on him. My brother hates the Union for what they did to my dad."

Mateo uncrosses his arms and pushes off the wall. "What'd they do to your dad?"

"My dad ran our local market. He had access to stuff from Mexico and the Northern Territories that was illegal in the Union. Drugs, weapons, that sort of thing. But more important than the stuff, was the information he dealt in. He knew people in the smuggling trade and acted as a middle man. He'd help this guy from the Union get information, and in exchange, he provided a market for what the smugglers were selling. We lived pretty good."

"Doesn't sound so bad," Rainey says.

"Not at first. But the Union guy, some official, kept bugging my dad about a dude named Vaughn and whether the guy had been poking around, asking about him and stuff."

"What was the official's name?" Mateo asks.

"He called himself Bailey, but I'm sure that wasn't his real name."

"How do you know he was from the Union?" Mateo asks.

"You could tell. I mean, his fingernails were clean, and his hair was all perfect, and he looked like he was terrified he was one wrong move away from contracting a deadly disease every second he was out here. His clothes were another giveaway. Neat, tailored, even though he was trying hard to blend in. He always had this other guy with him, though. That guy was definitely comfortable out here."

"What was *his* name?" I ask.

"Wells or Wilson or something."

"Walker?"

"Yeah, that was it."

I blow out a breath. That asshole's into everything.

"So what happened to your dad?" Mateo asks.

"One day, we – my dad, my brother, Martin, and me – were in the market getting ready to open, when Bailey showed up with some guy I've never seen before. The guy said, 'We took care of you and you shit all over us. We told you not to talk to Vaughn.' Then he shot my dad in the back of the head and took off. Martin was only ten and it really scarred him. He's wanted revenge against the Union ever since."

"Okay, so you joined up. How'd that end up with you holding my girlfriend at knife point?"

Her head snaps to me and she swallows, eyes wide. "Uh...Martin went missing a week ago. Kids are disappearing regularly. So when I saw her," she says with a nod toward Rainey, "and the redhead slinking around camp, I decided to follow them." She pauses and examines the back of her hand, like she's seeking answers there.

"Go on," I say, getting tired of her stalling.

She glares at me before stuffing her hands under her thighs. "They came out with Lisa and then a couple of guys I didn't recognize came running up. I thought they were taking Lisa like they took my brother. So I was gonna follow them, hoping to find Martin. Then, her..." she points at Rainey again, "and the guys took off and it seemed like maybe Lisa knew the redhead. I just wanted answers. I wasn't gonna hurt her, but I needed Lisa to believe I would. And she did, so she told me you're all Unis." She pulls her hands out and narrows her eyes. "Where's my brother?"

Mateo moves next to the foot of the bed. "First, you're not in any position to be making demands. Second, we're not all from the Union. Third, tell me more about the missing kids. How many?"

She shrugs, "One every week or two, I guess."

Rainey's eyebrows fly up. "How is this going unnoticed?"

"It's not going unnoticed. Aren't you paying attention?"

Rainey moves toward Frankie, her fists balled.

As much as Frankie could use a little slapping around, it won't help us, so I grab Rainey's arm and yank her back.

"When did it start?" Mateo asks.

"I don't know. We signed up a little over two months ago, but it was going on the whole time I was there, and I got a feeling it'd been going on for a while."

None of this makes sense. "Why do you think they're disappearing and not being shot while trying to escape?"

"Because, the only kids who are disappearing are the ones who believe in the cause. They'd never walk away."

Mateo's gaze shoots to mine. That wasn't going on in our camp when I was there. He shakes his head, telling me it didn't happen after I left either. There's a lot more going on here than any of us realized.

"First round's on me," Rainey says, setting three beers on the table before taking the empty seat between me and Mateo. "So what do we do with Frankie?"

Frankie's only one of many problems we need to deal with, and I don't know how to approach any of them. Lack of sleep is finally catching up with me.

Mateo takes a swig of his beer and cradles it in his hand. "I want to talk to this Lisa before I decide if I believe Frankie. But if she's telling the truth, I doubt she's dangerous. Still, we can't release her. She has nowhere to go, and we don't need her deciding that intel about what we're up to is the price she pays for information on her brother."

"Agreed," I say.

"She can stay at our place for now. Between all of us, she'll be guarded twenty-four seven," Rainey says. "But what do you think's up with the missing soldiers?"

"No clue," Mateo mutters before turning to study me for a second. "Your contacts up in the Northern Territories include any hackers?"

"Not that I know of, but I can ask. Why, what're you thinking?"

He runs his tongue along his back teeth and takes another sip. "I'm thinking if this is going on, there'll be chatter. I want to find out how widespread it is, and what the theories are."

I nod and take a long pull on my beer before sitting back in my chair and looking around the bar. We purposely chose someplace other than where Ally works. This place has a rougher vibe to it. Mostly guys in here. Guys who look like they've seen a lot of shit go down and don't care who we are or why we're here. The handful of girls in the place also have a hardness to them. One girl in particular, sitting near the door, is throwing me seductive smiles. She's attractive in a natural way.

Rainey glances over her shoulder at the girl, then back at me, eyebrows raised. Not going there with her.

I turn back to Mateo. "I'll ask Bridget about talent. It probably won't be cheap."

He finishes his beer and sets the bottle on the table before pushing up. "Okay. Let me know what you find out. I'm trashed. See you guys tomorrow."

Rainey signals for two more beers, but she lets me pay for them when the guy drops them off.

"So, what's up with you and Red?" she asks.

"We're not talking about this."

"You need to talk to someone."

"Nope."

"Really?" The corner of her lip tips up. "Because when we left camp this morning, the pissed-off ball of anger rolling off you nearly steamrolled me."

I down half my bottle, turning away from her, hoping she gets the message.

She doesn't. "What's got your shorts all up in your ass crack?"

"What part of 'we're not talking about this' don't you get?"

"The part where we're not talking about it."

For whatever reason, that makes me laugh, breaking some of the tension that's been eating away at me all day. I slowly turn to her, wondering if I do need to get some of this off my chest. "We're just having a...disagreement."

"Again?"

"I know you think this is all a big joke, but she continually does shit without any consideration for her own safety, and...I just don't...hell, I don't even know."

Rainey stares at me for a long time before sitting back in her chair. "We all have baggage. We've all had people we love die on us. And it sucks. Every single time. But I've seen more than my share of people who shut down when they lose someone. They disappear into themselves, shun the world, wind up bitter and alone. Trust me, they're no better off than the rest of us."

I finish my beer and signal for another. "You want one?"

"Naw, I'm heading out." She leans forward, her elbows resting on the table. "You're gonna do whatever the hell it is you do, but my suggestion is to enjoy the time you guys have together. Stop wasting it fighting, because that girl freaking loves you, and I'd kill for what you two have." With that she pushes up and walks out of the bar.

After a third beer, I order a scotch in honor of Lucien. I give a silent toast to my brother and wonder what he'd say to me if he was here. Something tells me he'd agree with Rainey.

# Baggage

*Evan*

**M**y eyes fly open, and my heart races as someone or something attacks me. I turn to fend off the blows only to realize a small foot is wedged under my chin. Taking care to avoid waking the sleeping boy it's attached to, I crawl out of the stuffed bed. Colin and Ally gave up Cyrus's bed last night to Lisa. With no better place to go, I joined her. Sometime after that we were invaded by Ty, Connor, and Ben.

I open the bedroom door and slip out, padding down the hall to the kitchen to make tea. Indoor plumbing is just another thing up here to love. The thought of going outside to the creek in the freezing morning air to fetch water makes me shiver. After filling the kettle, I rummage around in the drawer for some matches to light the stove.

"Hey," a deep voice rumbles behind me.

I startle and spin to find Cyrus looking adorable with his sleep-tousled hair. We stare at each other for several long seconds as I try and fail to come up with a response.

He glances away and runs a hand through his hair, and I struggle not to gape at how his shirt pulls up, revealing a couple inches of taut abs or the way his bicep bulges as his hand rests on the back of his head.

"Look...can we...get out of here. There's a place in town we can get coffee."

The unexpected nature of his request leaves me sputtering. "I uh...um...okay."

I set the teapot back on the stove and head back to the bedroom to dress in a pair of jeans and my Uprising boots. The supple leather molds to my calves where they stop just below my knees. They may not be something worthy of M Clothing, but they're the most comfortable footwear I own. The oversized soft evergreen sweater I yank on over my tank top *is* from M Clothing, though.

When I get back to the living room, Cyrus is nowhere to be seen. I grab my navy pea coat from the closet and head outside where he's waiting for me on the front porch. He leads the way down the concrete steps to the sidewalk.

To give my fingers something to do, I fasten the buttons as we walk. Apparently my hand thinks it belongs nestled in Cyrus's, so when the top button is secure, I shove my fists in my pockets to keep from reaching out to him.

The soles of our boots strike the uneven pavement, breaking the otherwise tranquil morning. I sort of assumed we were going to pick up our conversation from yesterday, but he walks beside me in stoic silence. We travel several blocks without speaking until the dead air between us looms like a monster, breathing down my back. If he just wanted to go for coffee, why drag me along?

I open my mouth, but it closes again when I realize I don't know what to say. By the time Cyrus halts at a glass door in the center of town, my nerves are gnawed into a frayed mess.

I step into warmth, surrounded by the heavenly aromas of roasted coffee beans, chocolate, and baked goods. There's no line so we make our way up to the counter and order. The barista calls out our names as I'm hanging my coat on the back of a chair. I grab our drinks and hand one of them to Cyrus before sitting.

He glances around before taking the seat across from me. His fingers fiddle with the cardboard sleeve of his cup and only stop when he takes a sip. I study him, waiting for him to totally unravel. He opens his mouth to say something, but before he can get a word out, the tall, leggy blonde who was kissing him the other night enters the café.

*Unbelievable.*

Cyrus follows my gaze, turning toward the door. She spots him, her face lighting up with recognition. As she makes a beeline for our table, I slink down in my chair feeling small and plain. She's polished and perfect with shiny brushed hair and flawless makeup, while I have dark circles under my eyes from a fitful night and hair that would happily house a family of rats.

Cyrus clears his throat and shoves his left hand into the front pocket of his jeans. "Bridget, this is Evan. Evan, Bridget."

Bridget reaches out a graceful hand to shake mine, her skin as smooth and beautiful as the rest of her. "Evan, it is very wonderful to meet you." The way she says my name, it sounds like Avon, and I hate her. "I have heard so much about you."

I can't say I've heard much, or anything really, about her, but that's not her fault, so I swallow my bitterness. "Good to meet you, too."

She turns back to Cyrus. "I know we are to meet tonight, but Ilona said you needed to ask me something."

Wait, what? They're meeting tonight? This is news to me. You'd think after the other night, he'd have mentioned he was getting together with his ex-whatever. Yet he has the nerve to be pissed at me for giving my gun to Lisa. Whatever conversation he's hoping to have is going to have to wait, because right now, I'm ready to unleash a steaming load of red-headed fury all over his ass.

I stand and push back my chair so fast it topples over. My face burns with frustration and embarrassment as I bend down to right it, grabbing my coat. "I was just leaving. It was nice meeting you."

"Evan wait," Cyrus says, standing and taking a step toward me. "Why?"

He stares at me with pleading eyes, but doesn't say anything.

Yeah, didn't think so.

I shove through the door before I say or do something I won't be able to recover from. Anger burns through my veins like acid while I stomp down the sidewalk. When I reach the corner, I make a detour, deciding to stop by to see Ilona, Alexander, and Zak. Their house is only a block away.

Rainey cracks the door, squinting at me from the other side. "You're up early this morning."

I wiggle my coffee cup in front of her. "Needed caffeine."

She opens the door, letting me in, and Ilona, the cheery strawberry blonde I first met with Rainey last year, squeals, rushing over to hug me. Tall, hunky Alexander, who may or may not be involved with Ilona, pops his head out from the kitchen before grinning and joining Ilona.

"It's good to see you guys." I glance past them, looking around. "Where's Zak? Did he go back home?"

"He's still sleeping. He worked a late shift last night," Ilona says. "But he'd kill me if he didn't get to see you. His room is the second on the right."

I head down the hall and rap on the door. There's no response so I knock a little louder and am answered by a muffled groan.

"Are you decent?" I call out.

Rustling comes from the other side, followed by a thunk and a few swears before the door flies open. Zak stands in a rumpled T-shirt and sweatpants, a huge grin plastered across his face, revealing two little dimples.

"I thought that was your voice." He throws his brown arms around me and lifts me off the floor. "What took you so long to stop by?"

"We've been sort of busy since we got here."

"You eat?" Rainey calls.

I shake my head. "Not yet."

Zak tosses one long arm over my shoulders and walks me out to the dining room.

Rainey sets two more plates on the table. "Sit then. We're getting ready for breakfast."

I take a seat, glancing around again. "Where's Frankie?"

"Sleeping," Alexander says, stuffing a biscuit into his mouth. "Mateo's watching her."

Even though I'm not particularly hungry, I eat some eggs and a piece of bacon, washing them down with the rest of my coffee just as Mateo wanders down the hall with Frankie in tow.

I'm finished, so I take my plate into the kitchen, making room at the small table for Mateo and Frankie, and clean the dishes. Alexander and Ilona are putting their coats on in the living room when I rejoin the others.

"Gotta get to work," Ilona says. "Will we see you later?"

I wave. "I'm sure you will."

Alexander reaches down to take her hand and they head outside. I guess that answers that question. Definitely involved.

"Sit," Mateo orders me.

I roll my eyes. It's like he can't stop being an Uprising leader But, I do as instructed and turn to face him.

"Frankie here says some kids are going missing. Kids loyal to the cause. Lisa say anything to you about it?"

"No, but we were all pretty tired last night."

He nods. "I want to talk to her. C'mon, let's go." He wanders into the kitchen to say something to Rainey before heading to the front door.

"Sorry I woke you," I say to Zak.

"I'd have been pissed if you didn't," he says with a grin. "I'll try to catch up with you later this week."

"Cool." I turn and follow Mateo outside, taking extra steps to keep up with him. The guy can walk fast. "What do you want to talk to Lisa about?"

"I want to find out how much of Frankie's story is true. If Lisa can corroborate any of it, that'll go a long way toward me trusting her."

"Why would she lie?"

He cuts his eyes to me. "Why wouldn't she?"

Lisa stretches her legs out on the deck and leans back on her hands. "Mateo is hot. Scary as hell, but crazy hot."

"Yeah, I guess."

She glances at me. "What's going on?"

I take in a deep breath and let it back out. "I thought Cyrus wanted to talk this morning. He invited me to coffee, but…his ex was there and…"

"And you flipped out and stormed off?"

The way she says it makes me laugh, and I close my eyes, nodding. "Yeah."

She puts her arm around my shoulder. "Oh, Ev."

"Okay, fine, I'm predictable." I open my eyes and turn toward Lisa. "But she said they were going to meet tonight. He never mentioned he was getting together with her. After the way he was about Bryce…I don't know, I thought maybe he'd get it, you know?"

"So are you two still fighting about what went down at the camp?"

"That's the thing, I don't really know."

She shakes her head. "You two have some major communication problems."

"Thanks."

"No, I'm serious. You get pissed and stomp off, he gets scared and lashes out. It's not healthy. You've got your issues because of Eddie, and he's got his issues, because…who the hell knows, but you gotta find a way to talk about this stuff."

I nudge my shoulder into hers. "I want to be mad at you, but I can't, because you're right."

She grins. "I'm always right. I thought you knew that."

"Fine. I'll try to talk to him when he comes home." I lie on my back and stare up at the sky, searching for patches of blue peeking between large white puffs. "So, what did Mateo want?"

"He asked about Frankie and the missing soldiers. I told him everything I know. She definitely joined up with her brother, and she was a wreck when he disappeared. I didn't know her all that well, she was in the class before me, but we talked sometimes. Everything she told Mateo fits with what I know about her."

"What do you think is happening to them? The missing soldiers, I mean."

She turns toward me, our eyes locking. "Nothing good."

# Nothing Good

## Cyrus

I stare at the door where Evan just walked out, wondering if there's any way I could possibly have fucked that up more. The plan was to talk things through this morning, not make it worse. I had this whole speech planned out, rehearsed it in my head on the way here, but I never got to say it.

"Are you okay?" Bridget asks.

Dropping back into the chair, I indicate the one Evan vacated. "Yeah. Fine. Have a seat."

"So you needed to ask me about something that could not wait until tonight?"

I scrub my face with my hands and get my head back in the game. "Yeah. I know you need to go, so I'll make this quick and explain everything tonight. I need someone with computer hacking skills. Do you know anyone?"

She eyes me for several long seconds. "Are you in trouble?"

"No. Not really. We need access to information." I glance around the coffee shop and stand, reaching for Bridget. "Come on. I'll walk you to work."

We head down the sidewalk on our way to the school where I met her last year not long after we arrived up here. I'd wanted to continue learning to read, and Bridget taught at the local adult-learning center.

"What is going on?" she asks.

"We found out soldiers are disappearing from the Uprising."

"That does not sound so strange. You went missing, no?"

"Yeah, but this is different. The ones who are missing are the ones most loyal to the cause, so it's unlikely they're escaping or being sent to the Hole."

"How can a hacker help?"

"We want access to the Uprising's satellite, find out what they're saying to each other."

We reach the end of the block and cross the street, heading down a narrow street that leads to the school.

"I will ask my friends. I am sure there is someone who can do it. You can pay?"

I nod.

"Okay. I will get you a name tonight."

"Thanks, Bridge."

She gives me a soft smile. Opens her mouth to say something, then shakes her head. "I am off at five. I will see you then." With that, she turns and heads inside, leaving me with nowhere to go.

Cyrus was gone all day and didn't even come back for dinner. By the time he rolls in after the boys are in bed, I'm seething. I want to unload on him so much it physically hurts to hold it in. And I would if I hadn't promised Lisa I'd work on communicating better. We're so good at talking about everything else, but when it comes to complicated issues with us, he clams up and I go a little crazy.

Cyrus's gaze sweeps the living room and pauses when it lands on me, his face an unreadable mask. I start to head back to the room I'm sharing with Lisa, his room, the room he used to have sex with Bridget in. Damnit, I can't sleep there.

Someone knocks on the front door, and I stop mid-step, spinning to see Marcus letting Mateo and Rainey in.

"Hey," Mateo says. "Team meeting."

I love the way he gets straight to the point. Cyrus could take a lesson from him. Will heads to the kitchen and makes some tea, delivering mugs to everyone as we settle in at the dining room table.

Mateo turns to Cyrus. "You get a name?"

"Yeah. A girl by the name of Hillary. She'll meet with us tomorrow. Half upfront."

"What are you guys talking about?" Colin asks.

Mateo swings his head around to look at all of us. "Frankie. She mentioned some disturbing information."

"The missing kids?" Lisa asks.

"It doesn't make sense," Mateo says. "The most dedicated soldiers aren't being eliminated. So where are they going?

Someone in the Uprising must know something. We're looking to hire the services of a hacker to access their communications, see if there's any chatter. The network we used was old pre-war technology, so the satellite only passes overhead for about twenty minutes every two-and-a-half hours. Meaning she'll have to hack in fits and starts."

"What do you think's going on?" I ask.

"I have no idea, but it's not a coincidence those who're missing are the ones with the biggest beefs against the Union."

"How does hacking a satellite help us?" Lisa asks.

"It gives us access to whatever's being sent back and forth. We need to see what they're saying."

"What about everything else?" I ask.

Mateo sits back, his gaze meeting mine, something I can't quite place in his eyes. "I don't want to put any plans into action until we know everything we're dealing with."

I let out a long sigh. It makes sense, but it means more waiting. "How long will it take?"

"Depends on how good Hillary is, but it's such old technology, it should be a snap for anyone with even rudimentary skills."

Our team meeting was short, and after Rainey and Mateo left, everyone drifted off to bed. I can't bring myself to sleep in Cyrus's room tonight, which means it's the couch for me. I flip off the last of the lights, tripping over someone's boots on my way back to the living room.

Pulling the blanket from where it's draped over the arm of the chair, I lie down, using the throw pillow under my head, but I can't sleep. The floor creaks and the walls groan as the sounds of night wrap around me.

After tossing and turning at least a dozen times, I pad to the kitchen to make tea and run into a solid chest. I step back to allow him to pass, but he doesn't move.

"I'm sorry." His voice is low, gruff, and still sexy as hell.

I swallow around the lump in my throat and struggle with a response. It's not okay that he keeps avoiding me when he's angry, but I need to forgive him so we can be okay again. "Cyrus—"

"Wait." The word is a command, and I bristle, but he quickly softens his tone. "I have more to say…I'm not good at this, but if I don't get it out now, I may never…and I need you to understand."

"Okay," I whisper.

"I hate not being in control. Nothing good happens when I'm not in control. The tornado, that day with Lucien, when you were shot, what happened to you with Frankie…when I can't control the situation, everything falls apart. I know that's my problem and I have to figure out how to deal with it…but give me a chance to do better, to *be* better."

Tears flood my eyes and I blink them back, inhaling a deep breath through my nose until I find my voice. "You don't have to change who you are, Cyrus, just…talk to me."

"I'm good at a lot of things. Building, surviving, fighting, but I'm not good at talking about this kind of shit."

"You know what I'm not good at?"

The corner of his mouth lifts. "Remaining calm and rational when you're pissed at me?"

I shake my head and let out a soft laugh. "Ha, ha. No, funny boy. Reading your mind. So when you don't talk to me, I start trying to figure out what's wrong and end up assuming the worst."

"And what would that be?"

"That you might be done with me."

He inhales sharply. "That's not gonna happen, trust me. I can't be around you and not be with you. And I can't *not* be around you. Us, you and me, it's the only thing in my life that feels right." His head drops and his hand flies to the back of his neck, gripping it tightly. "I've never felt more helpless than when Frankie had a knife to your throat, and I hated that. But when I came home last night and couldn't find you, when I went to bed and woke up alone, I hated that even more."

I blink again, my vision blurring. "You're actually better at this shit than you think."

He lifts his head and gives me a small smile. "If something happens to you, it'll destroy me."

"I know," I whisper. "Because I couldn't bear it if anything happened to you."

His body unwinds before my eyes, as if all the tension coiled inside him gradually releases. A long, low sigh flows from his lungs, and he steps forward until he's only inches away. I lift my gaze to meet his, and the deep emotions pouring from his eyes steal my breath.

In a swift, desperate move, he cups my face and his lips crash into mine. He guides me back until I'm pressed against the wall and tips my chin up with this thumbs so our tongues can tangle.

I reach up, weaving my fingers in the soft waves of his hair, and sigh into his mouth. He leans in, pinning my body beneath his, and nips my bottom lip, deepening the kiss.

His hands slide down to rest on my hips, his kisses coming harder. He draws back and redirects his lips down the side of my neck. Goosebumps break out across my skin and I'm pretty sure I squeak.

When his mouth finds its way back to mine, it's more demanding, and I push into him, trying to get closer. Winding his arms around my waist, he lifts me off the floor and pivots, walking us toward the living room, his lips never losing contact.

Our chests rise and fall with exaggerated breaths as he tips me over the arm of the couch, falling with me. He runs his hands up my thighs, over my hips, under my top, and I wrap my legs around his waist.

He groans and his lips drift down my neck again, whiskers raking across sensitive skin, making me gasp. I twist my fingers in the soft cotton of his tee and tug. He separates from me only long enough to allow me to pull his shirt off before his mouth returns to mine, warm, desperate, wild.

The emotions I've tried to bottle up the past two days begin to spill forth like water overfilling a glass.

Whether he feels the tears on my cheeks or senses a change in my breathing, he slows his pace. His kisses become sweet, his lips lingering on mine, our tongues slow dancing, as if he's telling me he needs me as much as I need him.

My hands grip his shoulders, and although I can't feel it, I know the tattoo is there. The one with my name, silently reminding me of his vow to protect me, to keep me safe, to not lose me the way he's lost everyone else whose name is inked on his skin.

## Cyrus

Smooth bare legs tangle with mine and I lean in to press a kiss to her tattoo. I noticed it the night on the beach but was distracted before I had a chance to ask about it. She sighs as my lips travel from her shoulder up the side of her neck.

"What does this mean?" I ask.

"What?"

"The leaves and dots?"

She twists so she's lying on her back staring up at me. Her hand reaches up to stroke the scruff on my jaw. "It's supposed to represent my two halves. The leaves are wild and random, representing the Ruins half of me. The dots are ordered and precise, like my Union half. I guess I don't see myself as belonging in only one or the other, so I'm fighting for the survival of both."

That's not the answer I was expecting, although I don't know what that was. Once again, I'm awed by her, by the way she thinks, by who she is. I press my lips to her forehead and wrap my arms around her, pulling her to my chest. Being with her like this, soft skin warm against mine, is the most perfect thing I've ever known.

"What do you think is happening with the missing soldiers?" she asks.

"I'm not sure." I roll back and slide my palm to her hip, propping my head up on my hand. "But it's not random, nor a coincidence. It's part of the plan somehow."

"Do you think this means they're close to attacking?"

"I think it means they're closer, but how much, I don't know."

"What did you talk to Bridget about all day?"

"I wasn't with her all day. This morning I asked her about the hacker, then I spent most of the day at Rainey's, trying to get as much information out of Frankie as possible. She doesn't know much, though, and I don't think she's dangerous."

"But Bridget said you were meeting tonight."

I knew this discussion was coming, but somehow I'm still not prepared for it. With no better idea of where to start, I go to the beginning. "When we first got here, we knew we wanted the boys to go to school. We also knew they'd need a tutor first."

"Oh yeah, Alphonse," she says, snuggling into my shoulder. "I met him."

"He came later. Sonia, Marcus, Will, and Ally all found jobs, but I was excused from work because I was in mourning, plus someone needed to stay with the boys. So I was put in charge of finding a tutor." My hand drifts to her back and begins tracing slow circles. "People are always moving in and out of this area, so there're a lot of classes for adult learners as well. One night after I walked Ally to the bar, I wandered around and stumbled into one of those classes. Afterwards, I asked the teacher if she'd be interested in tutoring three small boys."

"Let me guess. The teacher's name was Bridget?"

"Yeah. That's how we met." Pausing to gather my thoughts, I pull her closer, as if I'm trying to reassure her, but really I think

I'm reassuring myself. "She always knew my heart belonged to someone else, and eventually that became a problem for her. But she encouraged me to find you and introduced me to Simon. She's from the Northern Territories, which you may already have figured out. Not everyone up there is neutral. There are pockets of people who hate the Union and are helping the Mexican cartels. After the war, the world's largest economy imploded. Canada was hit much harder than Mexico because of the huge influx of refugees from the States, and it collapsed under the strain."

I grab the blanket and pull it up over her shoulders when I notice the goosebumps on her skin. She makes a soft sound, and I almost forget what I was saying.

"So?" she asks.

"Right. So there are a bunch of fourth-generation refugees up in the Northern Territories who are pretty bitter toward the Union. Bridget grew up with a group of these kids. She may not be a fan of the Union, but she doesn't agree with what the Uprising is doing. It was one of the things we had in common. When she came to the house the other night, I told her I'd fill her in on everything after we got back from getting Lisa. So that's why I met her tonight, to bring her up to speed on what we discovered and ask if she knows anything new."

"Does she know anything new?"

"No, but I'm hoping she can find some answers for us on timing and what's going on with the missing soldiers. She's going to ask around."

"So she's like a secret agent?"

"I guess." I'm not sure if that's true, but it might be the best description.

She's quiet for a long moment, and I want to know what's going on in her head, but we've just spent the last ten minutes talking about a girl I slept with. There's no way I'd still be on this couch with her if we'd been talking about Bryce.

"Did you love her?"

Her question throws me, but I reach down and hook a finger under her chin, forcing her to look at me. "I told you the other night you're the only girl I've ever loved."

She blinks a few times. "No. You said I'm the only one you've ever been in love with. You can love someone without being *in* love with them."

"True." I pause, giving some thought to my answer. "She was a friend when I needed one, and I care about her, but I never saw a future with her." I lower my face and run my lips across hers.

"Was there anyone else?" she asks, tipping her head back. "Besides Bridget, I mean. Any girls at camp?"

"No." My voice comes out harsher than I intended and she recoils. I wrap my arms around her and pull her back. "No one else. My life was all wrong before I met you. The only time it's ever been right is when I'm with you. I knew that by then. I didn't want anyone else."

She reaches her hand between us, her fingers finding my bottom lip, and tilts her face up. Soft perfect lips deliver a single sweet kiss that leaves me desperate for more, the way she always leaves me. I'll never get enough of her.

"Do you ever think about what you want to do when this is all over?" she asks.

"No."

"But, do you want to live in the Union or the Ruins? You really haven't thought about it?"

"I don't care, as long as I'm with you." I don't tell her I'm terrified to think that far ahead.

She sighs and is quiet for a few more minutes. "What's your last name?"

I peer down at her. "What?"

"Your last name. I just realized I don't even know what it is."

"Matthews."

"Cyrus Matthews. I like that. What's your middle name?"

"Alastair."

Her eyes soften and a small smile plays at the corners of her incredible mouth. She reaches a hand around the back of my neck and pulls my face close to hers, her breath tickling my lips. "I love you, Cyrus Alastair Matthews."

My full name on her tongue slices through me, cuts me open, and bares my soul. "I love you, Evan Delilah Taylor," I say before crushing my lips against hers, our names and mouths colliding.

# Colliding

*Evan*

The room is bathed in soft gray as morning gains a foothold, edging out night. I reach down and grab my clothes where they're piled on the floor next to the couch and pull them under the blanket, wiggling into my pajama pants.

"What are you doing?" asks a deep, sleepy voice behind me.

"Getting dressed. You should do the same."

He gently tugs me back against his chest. "What if I don't want to?"

"It's almost morning. What if someone wanders in here?"

He nuzzles my neck. "Fine, but I'm doing it under protest."

"Noted." I smile and turn my mouth to find his. His kiss almost makes me abandon my plan, but just the thought of getting caught is enough to make me resume dressing.

I hand Cyrus his boxers and jeans, and he pulls them on before sitting up and wrapping an arm around my waist again. "Coffee?"

I laugh. "I feel like I've created an addict."

His lips graze my ear. "I'm addicted to you."

I shiver before pushing him away with another laugh. "That was corny, you know that right?"

He smiles. "Yeah, but that doesn't make it any less true."

"You're such a dork."

Dorky or not, I'm seriously in love with this boy. I head into the bathroom to get ready, and as I brush my teeth, I replay our conversation from last night. It's a simple thing, knowing his entire name, but it's like he's finally mine, completely.

Cyrus is waiting for me by the front door, dressed for the cool morning. I shrug into my coat and he takes my mittened hand as we walk into town.

Bryce and Jack are due today, and I'm not sure how that's going to go. Even though Cyrus and I are on mostly solid ground, it still seems fragile in some ways, and I'm worried how Bryce's arrival will shake that foundation.

When we arrive back to the house, the guys still aren't here, and Lisa is pacing the floor, biting her thumbnail.

"Hey, Lis, it's still early," I say. "They'll be here."

I kind of wish I'd thought to bring her a cup of coffee. To take her mind off Jack, I drag her into the kitchen with me to start breakfast. Cyrus joins us, and for a short while we have fun making crepes. My Ruins friends are about to partake in the Lisa

Kendall experience as she whips the flour and eggs, adding a dash of this and a pinch of that. Cyrus chops stuff for the filling, while I grate the cheese. The others pour out of their rooms as the smell of sautéing onions wafts through the house.

With his first bite, I'd swear Marcus was dying based on the sounds he makes. "Damn, man, these are awesome," he says when he recovers from whatever mouth stroke he just had.

Lisa beams, if only for a second, before she starts to gnaw on her thumbnail again.

Marcus, Sonia, and Will take off for work while the rest of us clean up. One hour dissolves into the next, and Lisa morphs into a nervous ball of energy. I'm just about to take her into town to keep her from imploding when someone knocks on the front door.

Cyrus pops up and makes his way over, peeking out the side window before opening the door.

Lisa flies off the couch and into Jack's arms, while Bryce stands behind him, looking a little lost. His eyes find mine across the room, and I can't just leave him hanging. Cyrus will just have to understand. I mean he spent hours with his ex-girlfriend yesterday.

I head outside and pull Bryce into a hug. "I'm glad you made it."

He wraps his arms around me and sighs before stiffening and pulling away. I turn around and see the hard set of Cyrus's jaw and roll my eyes. It was only a hug and a G-rated one at that. Lisa and Jack, on the other hand, are locked in a very PG-13 kiss, bordering on something more R-rated.

Once Lisa removes her lips from Jack's, the guys drop their bags in the corner of the living room and Lisa and I head to the kitchen to put together a light lunch. We return to the dining room, where Cyrus is filling them in on how we got Mateo, then rescued Lisa and Simon.

After setting sandwiches and mugs of tea down on the table, Lisa parks herself in Jack's lap. He keeps one arm around her, eating with the other.

Colin saunters in the front door with Ally, a lopsided grin pulling at his lips. "Hey, when'd you guys get here?"

"About a half-hour ago," Bryce says, getting up to shake his hand.

Jack tips his chin in acknowledgment, but it can't escape his notice that Colin's arm is draped across Ally's shoulders or that her hand rests on his waist.

"Is that lunch?" Colin asks, eyes fixed on the sandwiches.

"Yes, Col," Lisa says. "Bread and meat and cheese are in the kitchen. Help yourself."

He reaches back to take Ally's hand and drags her into the kitchen with him.

Ally pops back out a few minutes later with a plate and takes a seat next to me. "I just texted Rainey and Mateo. They're on their way."

Lunch is a noisy affair with everyone trying to bring the others up to speed on what's been going on. Although the subject matter is rescuing people from training camps, staking out corrupt politicians, and preparing for a covert operation, somehow the atmosphere is light.

"It's a constant stream of couriers getting IDs," Jack says when it's their turn. "The numbers aren't huge though, so I'm not sure what the endgame is."

"What do you mean?" I ask.

"They don't have enough to stage an attack from within the Union, so I'm guessing they're cherry-picking people, but I can't find a common denominator." He reaches into his back pocket and pulls out his tablet, handing it to Cyrus. "See if anyone looks familiar."

Cyrus swipes through images, his eyes glazing over after awhile, until he freezes mid-swipe, the color draining from his face. I walk around to the other side of the table and peek over his shoulder, my heart slamming to a stop. A pretty girl with piercing blue eyes stares back from the screen.

*Draya.*

Why would she be involved with whatever's going on in the Union? She and Lucien had planned to infiltrate the Uprising to learn more about it, but after he died, she packed up and left. No one's seen or heard from her since. She was devastated by Lucien's death, and she blamed me. Cyrus said I embodied what she feared the most — the Union. Could she really be helping to bring it down?

"I take it you recognize her?" Bryce asks.

Cyrus nods before pushing up and disappearing into the backyard.

I take a step to follow him, but Jack grabs my arm, holding me firm. "Give him a minute."

My head drops, knowing he's right. "Yeah, okay." I take the chair vacated by Cyrus and pick up the tablet, staring at Draya's picture. *What are you doing, Draya?* "She was his brother's girlfriend," I say, more to myself than anyone else.

Tears blur my vision and I wipe them with the back of my hand before swiping through the rest of the pictures, but I don't recognize anyone else. I hand the tablet back to Bryce as the front door opens and Mateo and Rainey enter, stomping their boots on the entry mat.

The noise draws Colin and Ally from the bedroom where they were doing god only knows what. Colin zeroes in on me, his eyes searching mine, sensing something's wrong.

"Can I see that again?" I ask Bryce, reaching for the tablet. I find the image of Draya and hand it to Ally.

Her eyes widen, "Draya? Where'd this come from?"

"She's one of the people being brought into the Union. We still don't know why," Jack says.

"No," Ally whispers, her lip trembling. "She wouldn't."

Colin wraps his arm around her shoulders, and Rainey takes the tablet from me, swiping through the rest of the images while Mateo looks over her shoulder.

"Hey, that one," Mateo says pointing to an image. "I met him early on. Mean son-of-a-bitch."

The kettle whistles, and I return to the kitchen to make two more mugs of tea. My gaze is drawn to the window over the sink, or rather to what's beyond the window.

Cyrus sits on the steps of the deck, staring down at his hands, his shoulders hunched against the late afternoon chill.

After delivering tea to Rainey and Mateo, I slip into my coat and grab another mug before letting myself out the back door.

Cyrus glances up, and before he has a chance to mask it, I glimpse the pain in his eyes. Draya was like a sister to him, his brother's love. They grew up together. I hand him his jacket and wait while he shrugs into it before handing him the tea.

I drop down next to him, our thighs and knees touching, neither one of us saying anything for a long time. Clouds roll in, blocking what's left of the sun, dropping the already cool temperatures another notch.

"Are you okay?" I finally ask.

He takes a sip of tea. "Yeah."

"I don't understand why she'd be with them. After everything that happened, why sign up to work with the people responsible for killing Lucien."

"She probably doesn't know," he says quietly. "She didn't stick around long enough to find out the details."

"She has to know, Cy. She knew who was looking for me. If she knew enough to blame me, she knows enough."

He shakes his head. "She knew you were kidnapped by smugglers. It's unlikely she knows Walker's in the Uprising up to his eyeballs. We didn't discover that until later."

"Maybe, but she'll find it out eventually, and then what?"

"I don't know, but I can guarantee she's doing whatever she's doing because she hates the Union and blames them for Lucien's death. When you're deep in grief, it can be hard to think rationally. Draya's channeling her pain and anger into action. I get that." He finishes his tea and sets the mug on the deck before reaching over to take my hand, threading our fingers together. "What are they going to do with the names and photos?"

"Turn them over to Jack's dad to investigate."

His thumb draws little circles on the back of my hand, his gaze focused on the trees by the back fence. The branches are empty, without even a hint of the buds to come.

"I need to find her before they do. After we're done, I'll go look for her. Can you ask Bryce to remove her information before Jack gives it to his dad?"

"Of course. And I'll come with you. We'll find her together."

He leans over and kisses the top of my head. "It's cold, you should go inside."

I start to protest, but realize this is his way of telling me he'd rather be alone. "Okay." I push up and grab his mug, heading back to the house.

Jack and Bryce are deep in conversation with Rainey and Mateo when I return to the dining room. "Hey," I say, and wait for them to stop talking and glance up. "Can I ask you for a huge favor?"

"Depends," Bryce says.

I swallow hard. "Can you delete Draya's record for now? Cyrus wants to try to find her. It's important to him, to everyone here."

"Okay," Bryce says, and Jack nods his agreement.

## Cyrus

Marcus pounds the last stake into the backyard, securing a second tent to the ground. "Two tents gonna be enough?"

"Yeah. Ally and Colin want one, and Ev and I'll take the other."

He lifts an eyebrow at me. "Who's sleeping in your room?"

"Lisa and Jack."

He throws his head back and laughs. "Man, everyone but you's had sex in your bed."

"Shut up," I growl.

"Where does that leave loverboy?"

"I swear on all that's holy, if you call him that again, I'll beat your ass until you can't move."

He puts his hands up. "Fine, fine, I get it. Sensitive subject."

"What if some guy Sonia slept with was hanging around, staring at her all dopey-eyed?"

"Dude, that's not even a little funny."

"Bryce is sleeping in Ally's bunk with the boys." I glance over my shoulder into the house where everyone is cleaning up after dinner. "Hey, I'm going over to Rainey's. Can you let Ev know if she asks?"

"Yeah. You guys going at it again?"

"No. But she'll ask questions I don't want to answer right now. Why do girls always think you want to talk about your feelings?"

He lets out a robust laugh and pats me on the back. "That's the great unanswered question, my friend."

With Evan busy in the kitchen, I slip out the side gate and pop in the front door, my eyes searching for and finding Jack on the couch.

I incline my head and he pushes up, making his way over to me.

"What's up?"

"I have a theory I want to check out. Can I borrow the tablet?"

"Yeah, sure." He disappears down the hall, returning a minute later with the device. "You want to fill me in on what you're thinking?"

"It'll take a while to explain, but if I'm right, I'll bring you up to speed."

He studies me for a few beats and nods. "Okay."

I grab my hoodie off the arm of the chair and yank it on as I head out the door. When I arrive at Rainey's, a tall dude with dark hair and eyes answers the door this time.

"S'up?" he asks.

"Rainey here?"

"Yeah, hang on."

He's about to close the door when Ilona pops up behind him. "Hey, Cyrus, c'mon in. This is Zak. Zak, this is Cyrus, Evan's boyfriend."

He reaches out his hand, a ghost of a smile on his face. "Cool. Good to meet you."

"They're in the kitchen," Ilona says.

Rainey is standing on her toes, trying to reach something in a cabinet, while Mateo leans against the counter with an amused smile.

I shake my head and push past him. "What d'you need, shrimp?"

She whirls around, fire shooting from those coal black eyes of hers. "I got it."

"That's what she says," Mateo says with a laugh. "It's been entertaining as hell watching her 'get' it."

"So this is what you all do for fun around here?"

Rainey jumps up and grabs a box of something and flings it at Mateo. "You don't even pay rent. I'm not sure why I'm feeding you."

Mateo catches the box with one hand and puts the other up in surrender. "Hey, I offered to find my own place, but you wanted help with the prisoner."

"Speaking of," I butt in. "I want to talk to her. I have an idea."

They both stop and turn toward me. "What's that?" Mateo asks.

"I have a theory on where the missing soldiers are going, but I want to check it out and need Frankie's input."

"What's this theory?" Rainey asks.

"You'll see," I say with a smile that makes her roll her eyes.

Rainey leads the way down the hall and knocks on the door at the end. "Frankie, you awake?"

"Mhrm?" comes a sound from the other side.

"You've got company."

"Oh, joy." Her snarky tone is laced with the heaviness of sleep.

Frankie opens the door, glances at me, and flops herself back onto the bed, looking generally pissed off. "What do *you* want?"

"Information."

She snorts. "Why on earth would I want to help you?"

"Because if I'm right, I might know where your brother is."

She pops up, eyes wide. "Really?"

"I hope so."

"What d'you wanna know?"

I grab the tablet out of my back pocket and pull up the images, filtering by age and gender, then hand it to Frankie. "Swipe right to left with your finger and let me know if you recognize anyone."

As she swipes, I lean against the door and study her face. Now that she's cleaned up some, she's not bad looking. Her brown hair isn't stringy and the black eye Ev gave her is fading.

Her expression doesn't change, but her hands begin to tremble, so I move over to her before she can hide the image, although I doubt that's even on her mind. Her eyes are transfixed on a scrawny kid with deep-set dark eyes and the same mousy-brown hair as Frankie.

"Where'd you get this?" she whispers.

Mateo and Rainey both eye me, putting the pieces together. "Is that Martin?" I ask.

She nods slowly. "Is he…is he alive?"

"I believe so."

"Where is he? You said you might know where he is."

"I'm pretty sure he's in the Union."

The walk home is colder than the hike over, and now I'm wishing I'd grabbed my jacket instead of this sweatshirt. I shove my hands into the pockets and pick up the pace.

Now that we discovered who's going into the Union, we can try to figure out why. Knowing they're moving the most motivated soldiers inside doesn't tell us what they're planning to do with them. With any luck, Hacker Hillary can give us some answers.

The gate creaks as I pull it open and slip into the backyard. We really need to think about beefing up security around here. I climb into the tent where it's warm and filled with the soft sounds and sweet smells of the girl I love. After securing the opening, I kick off my boots and crawl up behind her.

"Hey," she says, voice thick with sleep. "Where were you?"

"Over at Rainey's. Didn't Marcus tell you?"

"Yeah. He didn't say you'd be gone this long, though. Is everything okay?"

"Yeah. We'll talk in the morning. Go back to sleep."

She tips her head back and kisses the bottom of my chin. "Love you."

"Love you, too, Ev."

I wrap my arm around her waist, tucking her against me, reminding myself of the reason I'm doing this.

# Reasons

## Evan

"**M**oss Mouse," Mateo says.

Lisa's brows pull together. "Muss-what?"

"MOSS MOUSE," Cyrus says slower, before spelling it out. "It stands for Mass, Objective, Surprise, Security, Maneuver, Offensive, Unity of Command, Simplicity, and Economy of Force."

"Ohhh-kay," Lisa says, apparently having no more of a clue than I do.

Mateo pushes off the wall he's been leaning against and uncrosses his arms. "Principles of War. The Uprising is relying on some of those, including mass and surprise, but it's apparent now that objective — directing all resources toward a clearly defined goal — security, and unity of command are probably not part of the strategy. We'll go after them using the same principles, only doing a much better job. We don't have mass, but we'll have a clear objective, an offensive strategy, economy of force, the ability to maneuver, unity, security, simplicity, and most importantly, surprise."

"So how do we do all that?" Colin asks.

"We've been working on a plan for the past few days," Cyrus says. That explains why I've barely seen him. "We're still waiting on some intel, but we've got something outlined so far that we can refine later."

Jack squares his shoulders, hands stiff at his sides. "What is this master plan?" The set to his jaw makes me think he isn't enjoying his current status of "not in charge."

"Teams of two will sneak in and take out their weapon and ammunition stores," Rainey says. "The information Colin and Evan found in Walker's warehouse gives us the location of every Uprising camp along with detailed layouts of each camp. There's a tentative plan of attack set for May, and the last shipments of arms and ammo are due in a few weeks. We want to wait to strike until we know they won't be able to recover in time."

Bryce lifts his head and directs his gray eyes at her. "What intel are we waiting for?"

"We know what the training camps are planning, but that's only half of it," Mateo answers instead. "The other half is whatever's going on inside the Union's walls. Walker may or may not be involved with that operation as well, but it wasn't with the plans from the warehouse. Lucky for us, the security piece is missing from their MOSS MOUSE, and Hillary has managed to hack the satellite. She's grabbing the data in chunks as it travels to and from the satellite, but the camps only know their piece of it. The bigger picture is still beyond our reach."

"How exactly are we supposed to take out their weapons?" I ask.

Rainey turns toward me, a wicked grin lighting up her face, making her appear impish. "With the plastic explosives your boyfriend grabbed down in Mexico."

A chill churns through my belly before radiating out. "With what?" It comes out more screechy than I intended.

"Don't worry," Mateo says, his voice far too calm considering what we're discussing. "For the next two weeks, we'll practice. We'll be so fucking prepared, the Uprising won't know what hit 'em."

## Cyrus

Rainey tacks a map of the Ruins to the wall in their living room. Over the past week, Ilona sketched the information from Colin's tablet onto a huge sheet of butcher paper so we can all see it at the same time.

Mateo scratches the back of his neck as he studies it. "Twenty-five camps and six teams. It'll be tough, because we only have so much time before the satellite passes overhead again and allows them to alert the other camps what we're up to. But if we cluster them right and time it well, it's doable."

"What if you had eight teams?" Ilona says from behind me.

I turn toward where she's standing by the couch, clutching Alexander's hand.

"We're in," Alexander says. "Simon and Zak, too."

"You know what we're doing, right?" Mateo asks.

"We do and we're in. They need to be stopped," Zak says.

Mateo smiles. "Eight teams will definitely make it easier. Three camps per team with the exception of one, which will have to take out four." He grabs a pen and begins writing on the side of the paper.

I move up to see what it says. Names. Teams. Teams I don't like.

"What the hell?"

Mateo glances over his shoulder at me. "I'll explain in a minute."

"Yeah, not gonna happen."

His shoulders tense as he continues with his list, but it's a bullshit list. When he finishes, he turns and locks eyes with me for a moment. "Look, I'm teaming those with Uprising experience with those without. It has nothing to do with who's currently sleeping together. It's economy of force and nothing more."

He's out of his mind if he thinks I'm not going to be with Ev when this shit goes down. A knock at the door breaks some of the tension in the room, but not by much.

Rainey opens the door and everyone else files in, filling the room to capacity. Evan and Bryce are the last to enter and that takes my mood to an even darker place.

She smiles when she spots me, coming to my side and slipping her hand into mine. "Hey, the map looks good, Ilona."

Ilona beams. "Thanks."

Evan steps away from me and studies the list on the side. "What's this?"

"The teams," Mateo says.

"No it's not," I remind him.

Mateo all but ignores me as he explains his teaming logic.

"It makes sense," Ev says.

"No it doesn't," I growl, staring at the names.

Colin/Ally

Cyrus/Sonia

Evan/Marcus

Lisa/Jack

Mateo/Will

Rainey/Bryce

Simon/Ilona

Alexander/Zak

"What about the boys?" Ev asks. "If everyone's going, what will happen to them?"

I've already given this some thought "They can stay with Bridget."

Ev turns to stare at me, and I can tell by the set of her jaw she's not happy about it. It has nothing to do with my relationship with Bridget, though.

"She was their tutor," I explain. "They know her and are comfortable with her."

She shakes her head, arms crossed. "I'll take them to Eddie's. They'll be safer there."

I start to protest, but she has a point. If anyone figures out we're behind what's about to go down, the kids could be in danger.

"What about Frankie?" she asks.

"She wants to find her brother," Mateo says. "We still don't know what's going on with the kids taken into the Union, so Frankie's staying here for now. We'll figure it out when we get back."

Lisa flips her long hair over her shoulder. "Is that a good idea? Can we trust her here by herself?"

"I think so," I say. "But just to be safe, Bridget's going to keep an eye on her."

I turn my attention back to the teams, determined to fight Mateo on this, although I have to admit it's probably a losing battle. If Ev and I team up, that leaves Marcus and Sonia, who've never set foot in an Uprising camp. I can't do that to them, but this whole thing is starting to leave a bad taste in my mouth. Like everything is building up to some sort of giant shitfest I have no control over.

## Evan

Cyrus's jaw is tight on the walk home from Rainey's, his grip crushing my hand.

"I know you're not happy with Mateo's plan, but you're cutting off the blood supply to my fingers."

"Sorry," he mumbles, easing his hold. "You're right, I don't like it, but I can't argue with the logic."

We lapse into silence for a few blocks, and every time I glance up at him, his jaw is ticking away. "It's gonna be okay."

He stops midstep, turns, and faces me. "Maybe. But if it's not? So much can go wrong, Ev."

"But we're totally planning this thing out. You, Rainey, Mateo, you all have experience as commanders or leaders. We have intel from Bridget and whatever Hillary can get off the satellite. Lots can go wrong that can't be planned for. You know that better than anyone, but even if we're together, that doesn't guarantee anything."

He narrows his eyes. "I trust Marcus like he's my own brother. It's just..." He glances away. "If it can't be me with you, I wish at least it was Bryce."

My mouth falls open, and it takes a few seconds for me to realize I'm not blinking. "What?"

He turns back toward me, anger flashing in his amber-colored eyes. "I want to beat the shit out of him every time he looks at you, but he's the only one besides me who loves you enough to put your safety first."

"Ohhh-kayyy." We stare at each other for several long seconds as what he said sinks in.

Without further conversation, he takes my hand again and pulls me along the sidewalk. I don't know what to say, because I'm not sure there is anything to say, but wow, that was just...wow.

We slip into the backyard through the side gate, and I head inside to hang up my coat and brush my teeth. It's late enough everyone's either in bed or on their way.

I flip off the light in the living room and notice a figure sitting on the bench on the porch. Bryce. I grab my coat again and button it up as I slip out the front door.

He glances up and scoots over, patting the spot next to him. We haven't spoken much since he and Jack arrived. I've been trying to be sympathetic to Cyrus's feelings, but I miss talking to Bryce.

"So how do you feel about the plan?" I ask.

"I think it'll work. Based on everything we know, the training camps are filled with teens who'd rather be anywhere but there. But I also think we'd be making a huge mistake to underestimate them."

"True." We sit quietly for a few more minutes. "How do you feel about being teamed with Rainey?"

He smiles. "Like I won the lottery. She's small, but man she's fierce."

I laugh. "Yeah, she is." After another pause, I turn and study him. "Are we okay? You and me, I mean."

He turns those slate gray eyes toward me, and I can't help but remember the first time I looked into them. It seems like a lifetime ago he walked into my English lit class back home, and my heart tripped over itself. He swallows hard and picks up my hand.

It feels weird to have my hand in his again after all this time, but I can't bring myself to pull it back. This boy means the world to me. I may not be in love with him, but I'll always love him. He'll forever occupy a piece of my heart. How can he not? He was my first crush, the first guy I slept with, and though he lied to me about who he was, there's still something there, some beautiful thing that's more than friendship, but so much less than what I have with Cyrus.

"I love you, Evansville. And I know you don't feel the same, but I'm starting to be okay with that. Not so okay that it's easy for me to see you with someone else."

Tears prick my eyes, but I get it. I doubt I'd ever be able to handle seeing Cyrus moving on with someone new. Just the little glimpses I've seen of him with Bridget were enough to cut me to the bone.

"I never wanted to hurt you," I whisper.

"I know." He gives me a sad smile. "And I never wanted to hurt you, and yet I have. Repeatedly."

"What are you going to do when this is over?"

"I don't know." He turns away and drops my hand, staring down the street. "Go back to work, I guess. Figure out what happened to my dad."

A bolt of energy zips through me. "Oh my god, why didn't I think of this before?"

He twists to face me, his brows drawn together. "What?"

"Frankie! The girl from camp staying at Rainey's. She said some guy kept asking about someone named Vaughn. Could that be your dad?"

"What are you talking about?"

"Frankie. She said the Union killed her dad because he was talking to the wrong people, or something like that. Cyrus can tell you more, but the name Vaughn is in there somewhere."

A nervous energy seems to flow from him and he pops off the bench. He starts pacing the small front porch. "He would have used an alias if he was undercover."

"Maybe the guy didn't know his alias."

"I need to talk to her."

"Okay. It's too late tonight, but I'm sure tomorrow. Do you want to talk to Cyrus tonight? I only heard secondhand information, but he was there when she told her story."

He shoves his hands into the front pockets of his jeans and nods.

# Secondhand Information

**Cyrus**

**H**illary clicks and swipes on the tablet so swiftly, her fingers blur. She glances over the top of her glasses. "Stop looking at me, you're making me nervous."

"Sorry," I mumble and turn away.

Clothes are tossed onto furniture, electronic devices stacked on flat surfaces, and last night's half-eaten dinner sits on the small table in the eating area. I'm not sure I want to sit anywhere, so I opt for leaning against the wall while she works. Head down, her eyes zip back and forth across the screen.

"You're doing it again."

I throw my hands up. "What am I supposed to look at?"

She lifts her head and large dark eyes study me behind heavy-rimmed glasses, making her appear owlish. Her upturned nose is dotted with freckles and her heart-shaped mouth presses into a pucker. "I don't know. I didn't have time to eat last night. You could go get me a muffin and some coffee."

"Sure."

Glad to have something to do, I head into the center of town. Cars amble along the Northern Territories streets, and a handful of other pedestrians tip their heads in acknowledgment as they pass.

I stop at the nearest café and study the pastry display. I have no idea what kind of muffin she'd want, and there are far too many choices. The line behind me grows as I stare at about a dozen different kinds of muffins in the display case.

"Anytime, dude," calls a guy from somewhere in the middle of the pack.

Normally, I'd turn and glare, but he's got a point. Girls like chocolate, right? But she could be allergic. "Shit, umm, banana nut muffin and two cappuccinos. With caramel drizzle."

I don't even know what type of coffee she likes. When did getting someone something to eat turn into a freaking nightmare?

Grabbing the bag and two coffees, I push through the door and collide with a body.

"Cyrus! I was going to come find you later. I have news."

"Oh, hey, Bridge. I'll wait for you. I'm heading back to Hillary's now."

She goes inside, and I sip my coffee until she rejoins me.

"What are you doing up here?" I ask.

"I met with my friend last night." She shrugs and blushes. "He is one who likes pillow talk. He told me the final shipment will arrive in the camps next week. It is a lot. They are putting all of their…how do you say…eggs in one basket?"

I shake my head. "I don't know what that means."

"This is the plan. They are counting on it working. Meaning if you disrupt it, there is no backup plan."

Understanding dawns. They might have backing from Mexico, but it's not unlimited. "Did he say anything about what's going on inside the Union? With the kids they're moving in there?"

"They are for phase two, but he did not elaborate, and I did not ask."

I roll that around in my head a bit. So if we can bring down the Uprising, this might be the end of it. For the first time since we went to that bombed-out power station and overheard rumors of an attack, I feel like maybe we can succeed.

"Where're you headed now?"

"Back to my friend's place. He is expecting me."

"Bridge." I grab her arm and stop her. "Are you in danger?"

She shakes her head. "No. He is only a middleman. Businessman. He will not care if the plan does not work. But he will care if he thinks I shared private information. Especially with a former lover."

"What are you getting yourself into?"

Bridget jerks free. "It is not like you think. He is a good man and he loves me."

I search her eyes for any sign she's afraid of him, but I don't see anything. "And you?"

"I am fond of him. And what about you? Are you happy?"

"I'm not sure I can live in a constant state of fear and be happy."

She hooks her arm through mine and resumes walking. "When you love deeply, you have much to lose."

"I have good news and bad news," Hillary says. "Which do you want first?"

I grip the back of my neck and blow out a slow breath. "Let's get the bad news over with."

"No one seems to know what's going on with the missing soldiers." She pops a piece of muffin in her mouth. "They're all talking about it, though. Going back several months. Even a couple of commanders have gone missing and at least one leader." She eyes me. "The description of one of the commanders sounds an awful lot like you."

I nod, but don't answer.

"So, if you're part of this, remind me again why you have me hacking the satellite?"

"I'm not a part of it."

She pushes her tablet away and sits back, taking a sip of coffee.

"So what's the good news?"

"Uh-uh. I want to know what's going on first."

"That wasn't the deal."

"You can keep your money and pay me in information instead."

We stare at each other, an obvious standoff under way.

She sighs and blinks first, pushing her glasses up her nose. "I don't agree with what the Uprising is doing. They need to be stopped, and I can help you."

We have enough information now, I'm not sure we need her help anymore. Pulling cash out of my pocket, I decide to pay her what we agreed on and toss the bills on her desk.

"Wait," she calls out when I reach the door. "I have family in the Union, but I haven't seen them in years."

If we're still playing the game, it just took an unexpected turn. I spin to face her. "Where were you born?"

"In the Northeastern Province. I grew up there. On the lower levels. I met up with a group of anarchists and followed a guy out here. It didn't work out with the guy, but I feel at home here. My parents are still in the Union, though."

"Okay, let's say I believe you. How can you help?"

"If you tell me what you're going to do, maybe I can help."

"Not gonna happen."

"You can trust me. If I wanted to turn you in, I would've done it already."

"Good point. Let me think about it."

"Okay, but you don't have a lot of time. The attack has been moved up. They're going to start staging it in less than a month."

This is the first solid information we've had on timing and it fits with what Bridget said on the shipment of weapons. I decide to take a chance and give her an overview of our plan. When I'm done, she gets a big grin, showing a row of bright white teeth. "I can get you something money can't buy."

"Oh yeah? What's that?"

She sits back in her chair again, crossing her arms over her chest. "Time."

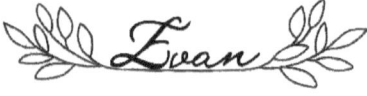

Mateo steps back and crosses his massive arms over his chest. "Try again, Evan."

It's like being in the Uprising camp all over again, and I scowl at him. Still, I take the lump of clay, masquerading as plastic explosives, and shove the blasting cap and wires in before hooking it up to the timer while Mateo times me with a stopwatch.

"You have to be faster than that. You've got a dozen of these to set."

I swipe a piece of hair out of my face with the back of my wrist and go again, the muscles in my back and shoulders aching.

"Hey," says my favorite voice from somewhere behind me, but I know better than to turn around.

I finish my exercise, and Mateo clicks the stopwatch, the corner of his mouth lifting a fraction. Guess I'm not as slow as he wanted me to think. *Ass.* Pushing up, I wipe my hands on my pants and head over to Cyrus.

"We're not done here yet," Mateo says.

"I'm taking a break. Torture someone else for a while."

He narrows his eyes but calls out, "Lisa, you're up."

She groans and heads over to take my spot, leaving me free to return my attention to my boyfriend. I wrap my arms around his waist, and he bends down, giving me a quick kiss before dragging me inside.

"Everything okay?" I ask.

"Yeah. I think so, anyway. I just need to talk something over, and I need your perspective."

"Okay…"

"Hillary found chatter on the missing soldiers. Including us."

"I guess that makes sense. Of course people would notice we were gone. It helps us blend in, in a way, doesn't it?"

He nods, then blows out a long breath. "I might have done something stupid."

A slight tremor rolls through me. Cyrus doesn't do stupid. "What?"

"I told Hillary our plan." His gaze meets mine, and the uncertainty in his eyes unnerves me.

"Why would you do that?" I'm starting to not like this Hillary chick.

He throws his hands up and turns away. "I don't know. She said she grew up in the Union, that the Uprising has to be stopped, and she could help."

"She grew up in the Union?"

"That's what she said. She talked about growing up on the lower levels and hanging out with a group of anarchists or some shit. I wanted to believe her…because we need help."

"Wait…"

He turns to face me, the creases in his forehead deepening. "Wait, what?"

"She grew up on the lower levels?"

He shrugs. "That's what she said."

"Unless she's been there, or knows someone who did, the chance she'd know how the Union works, and that the antigovernment crowd tends to roam down there, is pretty slim. She's probably telling the truth."

Tension floods out of him in waves and as a smile tugs at the corners of his mouth.

"So, can she help us?"

"Yeah." He nods, his smile growing. "She can help us in a way I never anticipated."

Although this part of the Ruins seems to have forgotten we're a week into spring, all the bodies packed into Rainey's living room make it uncomfortably warm inside. I cross to the window and slide it open to let in fresh air. A slender girl in a short skirt, ripped leggings, and combat boots makes her way up the front walk. Her hair is in some sort of crazy bun thing, with streaks of indigo running through her root beer brown locks.

She knocks on the door and Zak opens it, taking in the girl, head to toe, a small appreciative smile gracing his lips.

Cyrus walks to the door and takes her hand, pulling her inside. "You found it okay?"

She nods and pushes up her black-framed glasses.

"This is Hillary," Cyrus announces.

Hillary pivots, glancing around the roomful of people and steps closer to the door.

"They look scarier than they are," he says with a grin.

Her eyes scan the crowd and stop when they reach me, recognition lighting up her dark eyes. "Hey, I know you."

I stiffen, sure if I'd met this girl before, I'd remember.

"You're Eddie McIntyre's daughter."

And there it is. The part of my life I'd temporarily forgotten. The one where everyone knows the sordid details of my family drama. I nod but don't want to talk about it with a complete stranger.

"So what did you figure out?" Cyrus asks.

She tears her eyes away from me and moves toward the map on the wall. She studies it for a few minutes. "How far apart are the camps?"

"Roughly two hundred miles," Mateo says.

She looks around the room again, her lips moving as she counts the people in the room. "Is this everyone?"

"Yes," Cyrus says. "We have eight teams of two. Every team will have to hit three camps, with one taking care of four."

"How are you moving from one camp to the next?"

"Motorbikes," Rainey says.

"How fast do they go?"

"With the terrain, we'll be lucky to average seventy miles an hour," Cyrus says.

Hillary's lips move again and she adds her fingers to the mix this time. "So, you'll need at least six hours of travel time, plus time to get in, do what you need to do, and get out again. So let's say eight hours total. The satellite the Uprising uses passes overhead every two-and-a-half hours. They don't have real-time communications, they can only upload new messages and download anything new. Still, I don't think that's not enough time. But…I wrote a bit of code today and uploaded it. I can send up a message, activating the code to knock out communications for up to two hours. I can resend the message every time it passes overhead, buying you more than enough time."

"Are you sure it'll work?" Cyrus asks.

She turns to him, smiling, revealing two dimples. "I already tested it."

He reaches up a hand and she high-fives him before swinging her hips in a little dance.

I'm not sure we can trust her, but if we can, I have to admit, this more than doubles our odds of success.

# Odds of Success

*Evan*

Sonia settles beside me on the front porch bench, handing me a mug of tea. "What are you and Cyrus going to do after all of this? Are you coming back here?"

"I don't know yet." I wrap my hands around the cup to warm them. "He wants to find Draya first, but after that, I'm not sure. He says he doesn't care where we live, but he must have some feelings about it."

"What do you want to do?"

"I don't know. I want him to be happy. He says he'll go wherever I want, but I want to know what *he* wants." I shove a piece of hair out of my face. "I can see settling up here, or back down south, or even in the Union, but honestly, I don't think I can pick just one place. There are so many people I love and care about who don't live anywhere near each other. I don't want to have to choose between them anymore."

"We want you to stay here, of course, but I understand your family's in the Union."

"Would you guys consider moving to the Union?"

She stares down the street, taking her time before answering. "I don't know, Evan. Maybe. But I'm not sure how that would work. We're making a life here and it's going well. What would we even do in the Union?"

I shrug. "Anything you want."

"Marcus and I will talk about it, and I'm sure Ally is already considering it." She shifts on the bench next to me, her long thin braids swishing. "I just need to get through the next few days first. I'm almost afraid to plan beyond that."

Her words cut through me like little guilty knives. They're doing this only because of me. They could remain here and not be affected by the Uprising, but her loyalty won't allow her not to help.

"You can't think like that," I say. "Having a plan, something tangible you can see, is the only way to get through."

"My plan is to see Marcus and everyone else again when this is over. That's the tangible vision I have. Beyond that, nothing much matters."

A warm body is inside the tent when I crawl in, startling me. Cyrus hasn't slept here the last few nights, opting to spend the night on Rainey's couch instead. He says it's because by the time he's done hashing out last-minute details with Rainey and Mateo, it's too late to walk home. While I believe him, there's been a massive ball of tension surrounding him the past week, driving a wedge between us.

"Where were you?" he asks.

"Talking to Sonia. Umm…what are you doing here?"

"What do you mean?" He asks, propping his head up on his hand, his T-shirt pulling tight across his chest.

I drag my eyes away from his muscles and meet his gaze, his pupils dilated, making them appear darker than normal. "Well, we're leaving in the morning, I figured you'd be doing last-minute planning."

"I don't think there's much more we can do now."

I sit next to him and peel off my boots. "Do you feel comfortable with everything?"

He runs his free hand through his hair and glances away. "Comfortable? No, but I think we've planned the hell out of this, and everyone's trained. Too much relies on luck and elements outside our control, which I hate, but this is the best chance we'll ever have, so we have to go for it."

I crawl under the blankets and lie on my back staring up at him, watching the tic in his jaw. "Are we okay?"

His gaze drops to mine. "Yeah. Why?" He sounds genuinely surprised by my question.

"I don't know. You've been distant lately. I know there's a lot on your mind, but I'm used to you talking to me about those things."

A softness fills his eyes and a smile tugs at his mouth. "For once, I was trying not to be a jealous asshole. As much as I tried to hate Bryce, I really don't. He's not a bad guy." He shrugs. "I feel like I got the girl we both wanted, and I didn't want to rub it in."

"Seriously?"

He nods, leaning down to brush his lips across mine. "Seriously."

That might be the single most amazing thing he's ever said to me, and I think I just fell completely, infinitely, irrevocably further in love with him. I wrap my arms around his neck and pull him closer, kissing him hard.

"I really love you, you know."

"I know."

And that might be the second most amazing thing he's ever said to me.

*Cyrus*

The girl next to me is the one good thing in my life right now, and I hate that she thought something was wrong with us. By trying to keep my fears from infecting her, I kept my distance. And yeah, part of it is I didn't want to be a total tool, but I'd never let that interfere with what Ev and I have.

Glancing down at her, I take in her beautiful face, the perfection of her mouth, and my heart slams into my ribcage. She's so much more than a pretty face, though. She's everything, and I can't lose her.

I lower my face to hers, inhaling her scent, tasting her lips, memorizing every detail.

Every curve of her body.

The softness of her hair against my face.

The silkiness of her skin beneath my hands.

Every sound she makes.

Cementing each memory to carry me through the moments we're apart.

"Come on, Cyrus," Sonia yells from inside the house.

I double-check the backpack one more time. Spare batteries, C-4, blasting caps, wires, flashlight. Before every trip, the feeling I'm forgetting something gnaws at me, and this is no different. Satisfied I have everything, I zip it up and stuff my arms into the straps before pushing the motorbike through the side gate.

Sonia ushers Ben, Will, and Ty out the front door, loaded down with their own backpacks.

Mateo ambles up the sidewalk from the direction of town and reaches out to do the bro handshake with me. "Here," he says. "All synchronized." He hands me two watches. One for Ev and one for me.

I glance around for my girl, but don't see her.

"Why are you busting my balls if Evan and Marcus aren't ready yet?" I ask Sonia.

"They're ready. They're inside saying goodbye. You might want to do the same."

Right. After securing the bike, I take off my backpack and hang the straps on the handlebar before heading into the house. Ally and Colin are talking to Lisa and Jack. I head over and do a quick goodbye.

Ally pulls me in for a hug, her body trembling with unshed tears. "Be careful," she whispers.

"Yeah," I say gruffly. "She's the closest thing I have to a sister," I say to Colin over the top of her head. "Take care of her or I'll kick your ass."

"If something happens to her, you'll have to get in line behind me."

My eyes find Will in the kitchen cooking breakfast, and I make my way over to him. "Hey. Mateo's solid. You'll be good. Just follow his lead."

His eyes lock with mine, and for a split second, raw fear swims in them before he throws me a forced smile. "I'm excited to see the Union. I hear the ocean's awesome."

I return his smile with a genuine one, remembering my last night on the beach with Ev. "Yeah, it is. See you soon."

I turn to head out, but he wraps his arms around my shoulders from behind in a tight hug. Closing my eyes, I sigh and grip his arm across my chest, giving it a firm squeeze. "Be careful."

"You, too."

*Evan*

"Take care of her," I whisper to Jack as he hugs me goodbye.

He kisses my cheek. "I will. You take care of yourself."

Lisa and I are in tears before Jack even releases me. "Promise me you'll be careful," I say.

She nods and wipes her eyes. "I will. You, too."

She clings to me tightly before Will rips me from her embrace. He squeezes me, lifting me off the ground. "This is going to work, Evan, I know it."

He sets me down, and I take his face in my hands. "Watch your back, okay? Ben will be safe with Eddie, I promise."

"Yeah. Thanks for that."

Mateo is leaning against the wall, watching us. His gaze locks with mine, and the uncharacteristic emotions swimming in his dark eyes steal my breath. He pushes off and grabs my wrist, pulling me to his chest and wrapping me in his strong arms.

"Everything's going to go as planned," he says, kissing the side of my head and releasing me. He gives me a quick smile before turning to say something to Will.

I stare at his back for a few seconds, wondering what the hell that was all about.

Before I can process it, Ally shoves a couple of books at me. "Give these to Ty. Do you think your dad will read to him?" Her big blue eyes are shining with moisture.

"Yeah. He will. The boys are going to have so much fun, Ally."

She nods, tears slipping out and trailing over her cheeks. I move closer and for a moment, we cling to each other.

"Hey, what about me?" Colin asks. I lift my head and our eyes connect, making my heart feel as if it's been squeezed in a press. He pulls me from Ally, and I burrow into his warmth. "Be careful, EvTay," he says, his voice thick.

"I can't believe we're going to be apart for this. We've done all our crazy shit together."

He laughs, his chest rumbling beneath my ear, and squeezes me tighter. "I love you."

"I love you, too, Col," I whisper.

He presses his lips to my forehead as the front door swings open. Simon ambles in, eyes sparkling with mischief.

"What are you doing here?" I ask. "You guys aren't leaving until tomorrow."

"I couldn't miss the big send-off this morning."

Colin lets me go and Simon gives me a brief hug before his eyes sweep the room, landing on Rainey filling her canteen from the kitchen. She turns the faucet off and spins to face us, giving Simon a brief nod before turning her attention to me.

"Promise me you'll look after him," I say, my voice so choked with emotion it barely comes out above a whisper. She might be almost a foot shorter than Bryce and weigh half as much, but she's one of the toughest people I've ever met.

"I will." She sets the canteen on the dining room table and makes her way to where I stand beside the couch.

"Make sure you look after you." She reaches out to hug me, which is so out of character it catches me by surprise. Not nearly as much as the tears she wipes away when she pulls back, though. "You'd better come back, or it'll kill him, and I doubt there's anything I can do to protect him from that."

"Yeah." I turn away before I start crying again and spot Bryce sitting alone on the back deck.

I slip out the back door, and he glances up, slate gray eyes the color of the early morning sky piercing mine.

My throat is so clogged with tears, I'm afraid I'll choke on them. Taking a seat next to him, I lean my shoulder into his. "I don't want to imagine a world you're not a part of. Please be careful."

He takes my hand and fiddles with my fingers. "I will." He pauses for several long moments then sighs. "I talked with Frankie."

"You did? What did she say?"

He shakes his head. "She never met him, nor does she know anything other than a name, but if he was investigating smuggling, it could have brought him out here. I need to find out what happened to him. It's the first real lead I've ever gotten."

My eyes search his. The hope that his dad was alive was something I used to sense in him, but I'm not sure it's still there.

The back door opens, and Marcus pokes his head out. "Time to go, Evan."

"Coming," I yell before turning back to Bryce.

He leans over and kisses my forehead. "Stay safe, Evansville."

With a sigh, I push up and follow Marcus, leaving behind the first boy who won, and then broke, my heart.

Ty's arms are wrapped around my waist, his cheek plastered against my lower back, and he squeezes tighter with every bump. I grip the handlebars with white knuckles, afraid of hitting something and throwing his little body off the back. At least since I'm concentrating on the terrain, I don't have time to dwell on what we're about to do.

Up ahead, Cyrus puts up his hand, signaling a stop. I ease back on the throttle and pull up behind the rest of them. Sonia helps Ty down and hands me a bag.

I take a seat on the ground next to Cyrus and open my bag to find a granola bar, dried fruit, and some of the venison jerky Marcus made in the smokehouse. Cyrus drapes an arm around me, pulling me against his chest as we eat.

"You'll love the Union," Cyrus says to the boys. "The first thing you'll notice is how noisy it is. That takes some getting used to, and there's no way to escape it. Eventually you learn to tune it out, like bad smells."

"When we get there," I say, "we'll walk through a concrete tunnel to an elevator that'll take us up to the top. Then we'll catch a train that goes super fast — more than three hundred miles an hour."

"It's similar to the Territories in some ways," Cyrus says. "Everything is paved, but there aren't cars or anything, and it's unnaturally clean."

"We have cars," I insist with a sideways glance. "Just not many. The Union's built kind of like half a pyramid. It's tall where the back wall meets the Ruins, but as you near the beaches, it gets lower to the ground. Oh, you'll get to see the ocean. Cyrus loves it there."

He cinches his arm around my waist and kisses the side of my head. "Try not to stare too much. Unis don't think their world is strange. For them, it just is."

Marcus glances at his watch. "We should get going."

I sneak a peek at Cyrus, wondering if he feels it, too. Every mile takes us closer to the Union, closer to saying goodbye. Soon we'll be going our separate ways.

We resume our ride, and the lump in my throat grows with each hour that passes, and the knot in my stomach expands until it's the size of a basketball. By the time we reach our destination, my guts are so twisted, I'm pretty sure I'm gonna puke.

I blow out a heavy breath while I dismount and lean my bike against the wall.

"Give us a minute," Marcus says, taking Sonia's hand and leading her away from the rest of us.

My hands are shaking so much I stuff them into my pockets so the boys don't notice.

Cyrus picks up our lunchtime conversation, distracting the boys. "The ocean smells like nothing else, and the sound of the waves coming ashore is something you need to experience for yourself. Oh and wait until you try the food. There's nothing like it in the Ruins, although the stuff Lisa cooks comes close."

I shake my head and smile. "You're building up their expectations. They're going to be disappointed, you know."

He lifts his eyebrows. "Hardly. You can't relate to what it's like to see all that for the first time because you grew up with it."

"Hmm, maybe, but I still think you're making it sound both better and worse than it is."

His gaze shifts beyond me, and I twist to see Marcus and Sonia approaching. I turn back to Cyrus, and our eyes lock, the knot in my stomach tightening.

"Come here, boys, look at this," Sonia says before their voices drift away, leaving me and Cyrus alone.

He leans against the wall and wraps his hands around my waist, tugging me against him. I stare up into beautiful amber eyes that for once aren't hiding anything from me. His lips brush mine and he slides one hand up to cup my face, his thumb stroking my cheek. He deepens the kiss, words he can't say pouring through his lips and tongue. Every unspoken thought is in this kiss, comforting and frightening me in a crazy cyclone of emotion.

He draws back, his mouth a breath away. "I love you, Ev. I need you to come back to me."

The watermelon in my throat prevents me from answering. My lips move, but no sound comes out.

"We need to go," Marcus says.

Cyrus lifts my chin and kisses me one last time. A soft, lingering, fearful kiss that leaves me aching. His thumb traces my trembling bottom lip as he releases me.

I grab my bike, and push it through the opening, glancing over my shoulder once last time at the boy who owns me heart and soul.

# The Union

*Evan*

"Wait here." I leave Marcus and the boys and head down a narrow hall, trying doors until I find one that's unlocked.

A musty odor greets me when the door swings open. My eyes adjust to the lack of light, and I take in the small storage locker just large enough to house the motorbikes. Judging by the thick layer of dust and abundance of cobwebs, no one's been in here in ages.

Marcus and I push the bikes down the hall and park them inside. We set our backpacks with the explosives and our changes of clothes on the ground, grabbing the depleted batteries. After closing the door behind us, I lead the way to the elevators. The doors open on the top floor, blasting us with the sights, smells, and sounds that make up Union life.

"Remember, try to blend in," I say.

The boys' eyes are wide, and their little shoulders are hunched as they try not to swivel their heads to take everything in. Even Marcus is speechless. I guess maybe they're not disappointed.

"I'll be right back." I leave them on the platform to stare out the window while I cross the station to buy tickets.

When I return, Marcus is pointing at something in the distance, and all three boys are craning their necks to see. A smile breaks out on my face at the overabundance of cuteness.

I pull my tablet from my backpack and shoot off a quick text to Eddie.

*Me: Hey, you around?*

*Eddie: Yeah. Everything OK?*

*Me: Yeah. On my way to your place*

*Eddie: Great!!!!!*

*Me: Need a HUGE favor*

*Eddie: Uh-oh*

*Me: Brought some friends with me. Can they stay with you for a couple days?*

*Eddie: Sure. When will you be here?*

I check the schedule.

*Me: 3 hours give or take*

*Eddie: See you then*

Twenty minutes later we board, sitting on the west side so they can look at the Union as we travel. The train pulls out with the boys' faces smashed against the window, even the six-feet-plus boy. Before long, though, they settle into the seats around me.

Connor leans his head against my arm. "Are you scared?"

We told them what we're going to do; they have a right to know since their siblings are risking their lives. I don't want to scare Connor, but I don't want to lie to him either.

"A little." And because I don't want them to dwell on it, I change the subject. "You're going to stay with some of my family tonight. My dad, my brother, and one of my sisters. Oh, and you'll probably meet Bryce's sister."

"What are they like?" Ben asks, now paying close attention to our conversation.

"My dad's super nice, and because my sister and brother are little, he's used to doing fun stuff with kids."

"What kind of stuff?" Ty asks, crawling into my lap, kicking Connor in the chin in the process.

"Hey," Connor yells.

"Sorry," Ty says with an impish smile that makes me think he's not sorry at all.

"All kinds of things. He'll take you guys anywhere you want to go."

"Does he have books?" Ty asks.

"Well, we read on our tablets, but Ally gave me your favorite books. They're in the backpack."

He nods and slips off my lap, leaning back against the seat, quiet for the first time since we boarded.

By the time we arrive in the Western Province, the boys are asleep. Ben's eyes crack open when the train pulls to a stop, his head still lolling to the side. Marcus picks up Ty and carries him while I take Connor. Connor wakes almost as soon as I pick him up and wiggles down.

Once we're in the terminal, Ben and Connor's eyes widen. It's different enough from the northwest where we got on that their wonder has returned in full. They're non-stop chatterboxes all the way to the commuter station where we catch a ride to Eddie's borough.

Ty wakes when Marcus sets him on the seat next to us.

"Where are we?"

"Almost there," I tell him.

The setting sun paints the sky a soft purple with highlights of orange and pink when we emerge from the terminal on the other end. Eddie is on the front porch with Talia, Liam, and Quinn when we approach after the short walk from the train. His gaze drops to my little friends and his eyebrows disappear into his hair.

Quinn and Liam duck behind Eddie, watching the boys. Eddie turns and hands off the kids to Talia, then makes his way down the path to us. I set the packs down and launch myself into my dad's arms.

He hugs me impossibly tight, and I relax in his embrace. For a few moments, I feel safe.

When he releases me, I turn toward Marcus and the boys. "Eddie, this is Marcus, Cyrus's best friend. Marcus, this is my dad, Eddie, and his girlfriend, Talia. Talia is Bryce's sister." While they shake hands, I squat down to Quinn and Liam's level. "This is Ty, Connor, and Ben. They're going to stay with you for a couple of days. Do you think you might have some toys they could play with while they're here?"

Liam nods but doesn't move. Quinn stares at the boys, blue eyes wide.

"She has hair like yours," Connor says, staring at Quinn.

I smile. "She does."

Eddie leads the way into the house, and once inside, the boys' shyness evaporates before my eyes. They take in their surroundings, dozens of questions firing, most of which are of the "what's that" variety. The clean lines and smooth modern appliances are so different from either of their homes out in the Ruins. Eddie flips on the monitor and the wall lights up with images from the beach cameras dotting the coastline of the Union.

"I can take you down to the water tomorrow, if you'd like," Eddie says using his dad voice.

The boys turn to him, eyes still wide, and Ben nods.

Talia, who has yet to utter a word since we arrived, suddenly finds her voice. "Would you like to see the rest of the house?"

More nodding.

She takes Liam and Quinn by the hand and the other three trail after her, giving us some privacy.

After our apartment was bugged last year by someone, I'm still paranoid about talking openly in the house so I incline my head toward the door. We head outside and across the expansive walkway to the park.

As we stroll the meandering path, Marcus and I fill Eddie in on our plans and why we brought the boys with us. Under the path lights, I watch the color drain from my dad's face before it returns with angry redness.

A long stretch of heavy silence takes over when we finish our story. Then, without a word, Eddie turns on his heel and marches out of the park, disappearing into the night.

I heft my backpack onto my shoulder and head across the hall to where Marcus is staying. He opens the door before I can knock.

"Ready?" I ask.

"Ready as I can be."

Downstairs, Marcus unplugs the battery packs and stuffs them in his bag while I grab a handful of protein bars from the pantry.

I unlock the door and pull it open.

"You're not going to say goodbye?"

Adrenaline floods my veins, making me jump before I turn to face Eddie. "Sorry. I didn't want to wake you."

He makes his way down the stairs and wraps me in a lingering hug. "Be careful."

"Always, Dad."

He releases me and turns to Marcus. "Take care of her."

Marcus smiles that smile of his that consumes his entire face. "Cy already told me not to bother coming back if anything happens to her, but something tells me she's going to be taking care of me."

Eddie shakes Marcus's hand and leans against the door frame as we make our way down the sidewalk.

We reverse our trip from yesterday, both of us dozing on the A-Train, trying to bank sleep for tonight. We arrive in the Northwestern Province just after noon and retrieve our motorbikes and backpacks from where we left them. We turn our backs on each other to change into our Uprising uniforms before snapping in freshly-charged battery packs.

With a heavy sigh, I follow Marcus, pushing my bike out of the storage closet and through the opening in the back wall. We mount up and ride toward our first target.

# Book 3 – The Uprising

# First Target

"**M**orning," Sonia says, sitting up and stretching next to me. "You get any sleep?"

"Some." I scrub my hands across my face trying to wake up. Truth is, I didn't fall asleep until probably an hour ago.

Sonia hands me my breakfast, a bag of jerky.

"Thanks."

We sit beside each other, chewing in silence. There's still a full day of riding ahead of us before we reach our first camp.

I shove the last piece of jerky in my mouth and crumple up my bag. "Should we take the tent with us?"

She presses her lips together before answering. "It's one more thing to carry. Let's leave it."

I nod and we both head out into an overcast morning. Last night when we made camp, it was too dark to see much, but now I take a good look around. The land here is more open than up north, but not quite the desert landscape from down south.

I tear down the tent and lean it against a tree before we mount up and take off. Someone will come upon it someday and consider themselves lucky.

My thoughts are grim and filled with worry as we travel. I try not to dwell on the worst possible scenario, but the morose images worm their way in anyway, like an invasive blackberry bush.

After a quick stop for lunch, we continue on until sunset, arriving within a few miles of our first target.

"How many batteries do we have left?" Sonia asks.

"Four. We'll need one each to make it to the next two camps. After that, we'll ride as far as we can until we lose power and walk the rest of the way."

"Okay, I guess that's the best we can do."

Sonia's unusually quiet. No doubt she's as worried as I am, but it's not like her to keep it all inside. Although I should get her talking, I don't because then she'll expect me to talk. Unfortunately that's how conversation works.

We still have more than two hours before we move out. After checking and rechecking all our gear, making sure everything is ready, we still have an hour.

I join Sonia on the ground and lean back against the tree trunk next to her.

She tears pieces off a leaf and throws them. "Evan says you won't tell her where you want to go when this is over."

"I said I didn't care, not that I refused to tell her."

She shrugs. "Same thing."

"Not really."

"Telling her she's all you need to be happy is too much responsibility to put on her. Don't you remember how you freaked out when you thought she was staying in the Ruins for you?"

"Yeah. I get it. I just…she has family, and I'm not going to take her away from them, but I'm not willing to be away from her again. I'll go where she goes, and maybe that makes me a giant pussy, but you know what, I don't give a shit."

She laughs. "I never thought I'd see the day. Lucien would be proud of you."

At the mention of my brother, I drop my gaze to the ground, staring at the dirt and leaves. I wonder if he really would be proud of me.

"He would," she says softly, reading my mind. "He might not have agreed with all of your methods, but you're doing the right thing for the right reasons. This…" she sweeps her hand in front of us. "…is the right thing. Maybe at first you wanted to do something because of a girl you fell in love with, but I've noticed a change in you since you came back. You've seen the Union and the people who live there. You're doing this as much for them as you are for her. Maybe more."

"Everything we thought we knew about the Union is wrong. You know that right?"

She nods. "I think I knew on some level after the first time I talked to Evan last summer. I just didn't want to believe it."

"So the attack should be well under way back east," I say, changing the subject.

"I guess we'll find out if Hillary was able to do her thing."

"Or if she set us up."

"Do you think she would?" Her breath catches.

"No. If I did, I would have fed her false information."

"Well I'm glad we don't have to chase the satellite. I'm not sure this was really doable without her help."

"It would've been harder, but not impossible."

She wiggles her wrist. "We didn't need these expensive watches after all."

"It's still good to all be on the same time and schedule. Speaking of which. Ready to head out?"

"Yeah, I guess. Let's do this."

## *Evan*

"It's showtime," Marcus says, glancing at his watch.

My nerves ratchet up another notch. We hid the bikes behind a rock outcropping about a mile from our first camp. I take one more look at the map before stuffing it in the side pocket of my cargo pants and follow Marcus.

We approach the perimeter and crouch, moving with careful steps. A half-moon lights our way, but also makes us visible. We drop to our bellies and crawl the last hundred yards. The sentry is standing with his back to us, his body language suggesting boredom.

I check my watch. Thirty seconds to shift change.

Like clockwork, at midnight, without even a cursory glance around, the sentry begins walking toward camp.

Marcus taps my shoulder and I nod. We crouch-walk a dozen or so yards, then stand and saunter in as if we belong here. When the replacement sentry makes her way past us to assume the vacated position, I duck around a tree, yanking Marcus with me.

Mateo said they don't protect the camp from break-ins, but I didn't realize how lax it would be. This is crazy. They're betting an awful lot on the fact that the Union doesn't know what they're up to. An army of teens with no real defensive strategy, I can't help thinking we're missing a big piece of the puzzle.

Everything is silent as we make our way to the supply tent. We stop fifty yards away behind a tall evergreen and drop our packs. I flip the safety off my gun and slip around the tree to survey the area. Two soldiers guard the front opening, leaving the sides, and more importantly the back, unguarded. I return to Marcus and nod.

He grabs the backpack with the explosives and disappears around back while I cover him. Marcus shoves the pack under the tent, wiggling in after it.

I can't believe this is all they have guarding their entire stash of weapons. Although when your army consists of kids, you probably don't fear a well-coordinated mutiny.

My eyes sweep our surroundings again. The guards are as bored as ever, and no one else is even in the vicinity. A light breeze rustles branches near my head, sending fresh pine wafting through my nose. The low murmur of voices from the two guards is the only sound I can hear over the pounding of my own heart.

Seconds tick by as Marcus sets the explosives. It feels like a lot longer than the five minutes he's been gone before I see him crawling back out. He rejoins me, and we make our way back toward the perimeter. We have forty minutes before the charges detonate. Enough time to get the hell out of here, even if we run into a little resistance.

We make good time back, halting when we spot the sentry. She's young, maybe sixteen or seventeen. There's no way I can shoot this girl. I glance at Marcus, noting he's a little green. Guess he's not any more comfortable killing a teen girl than I am.

Shaking my hands out, I revert to my Uprising self, the whole reason we're teamed up. "You need to distract her so I can move up behind her," I whisper to Marcus. "She's trained to shoot anyone she thinks is escaping, so make sure she doesn't think you're making a run."

He swallows. "You want me to talk to her?"

"Yeah. Use that Marcus charm of yours."

"She'll know I'm not from here."

"Not necessarily," I whisper. "I was in a camp for six weeks and never met everyone there. Most of the girls, yeah, because we shared a tent, but not all the guys."

"Why would I be out here talking to her if I wasn't trying to escape?"

"You're a teen boy, she's a girl. Hormones rage. Trust me, just smile at her, and we'll be fine."

He grimaces, but nods and slinks off to the side while I get into position. Marcus exits the trees and swaggers toward her, grinning. He calls to her and she spins, rifle pointed at his chest.

I suck in a breath, suddenly doubting my plan.

"I saw you the other day in the mess tent," Marcus says, laying on the charm. "I've been trying to find you ever since. Has anyone ever told you…" the rest of his words die on the wind, but based on her body language, she's eating this up.

I slink up behind her while she's preoccupied with flirting. Marcus keeps his eyes on the girl, but he must know I'm here. Damn, he's good. Summoning my training, I move so fast, she doesn't feel me coming until my right arm is around her neck. I line up my forearm and bicep the way I was taught and squeeze them together while pressing my left hand against the back of her head, cutting off her oxygen.

The second she goes limp, I loosen my hold and gently lay her on the ground.

Marcus gapes at me before snapping out of it. "Remind me to stay on your good side."

We take off at a run, putting maximum distance between us and the camp before she wakes. As we ride away, I'm still breathing hard, trying to catch my breath, but a momentary bout of euphoria fills me. I can't believe how easy that was.

We're only about ten miles from camp when an explosion tears through the night behind us, like an angry lion roaring his displeasure. I hadn't expected it to be such a big blast. Yeah, take out the weapons, but now I'm wondering about everyone there, and not just the two guarding the front. I trained and worked with kids just like the ones in that camp. Most of them were only there because they had no choice.

I close my eyes and try to convince myself no one was injured in the blast.

## Cyrus

"Stay down," I hiss.

A soldier passes no more than ten yards away, and Sonia's head drops back to the ground, her cheek pressed against dirt. The kid appears to be on his way to the latrine, which might be the only thing that saves our asses.

Sonia's entire body trembles, and if I don't find a way to calm her down, she'll give us away. I scoot over until I'm next to her and cover her hand with mine. The wild fear floating in her eyes would be comical if we weren't actually in a life-and-death situation.

I lean closer and put my lips against her ear. "Breathe with me. In...out...in...out." It takes a good minute for her breathing to return to a normal rate. Twisting my fingers with hers, I pull her hand to my chest. "We're going to move on three, okay."

She nods.

I tap her hand once, twice, three times before rolling away and pushing up to a crouch. She follows me seconds later and moves away from the fallen trunk we were hiding behind. I'm worried about her state of mind now and whether or not she can provide adequate cover.

We reach the back side of the supply tent, and I drop to the ground, signaling Sonia to do the same. From a prone position, I scan the area for guards and find two posted in front, same as the last camp.

I bend close again. "Can you handle setting the charges this time?"

Her head whips around. "Why?"

"It's easy. Trust me. You'll be in and out in five minutes. I've seen you in training, you're better than me."

She swallows hard and nods, switching backpacks with me. I creep forward to get a better view of the guards while she slinks to the back. I check my watch and start mentally tracking her time.

The two idiots out front are rating the girls in camp on a numbered scale of hotness. One minute passes, then another, and another. After four, I crawl back to wait for Sonia. Her hand reaches out from under the tent only seconds before a twig snaps.

I swivel and see someone walking toward the back of the supply tent. Large form, definitely male. *Shit.* I glance back at Sonia, oblivious to the fact she's about to pop out and into the path of an unsuspecting soldier.

Only one thing to do.

Hopping up, I stride across the field, approaching the guy. He turns away from Sonia's position, zeroing in on me.

"Hey," he calls. "Who are you?"

Here we go again. I take a deep breath. "Why are you out of quarters?" I demand, reverting to the commander I once was.

Instead of freezing, though, he continues toward me, reaching for his gun. Just my luck, the one guy we run into isn't some mindless kid. Nothing left to do now except shoot our way out. My gun is drawn and pointed at him before he realizes what's happening, and he drops to the ground. I fire two shots over his shoulder, chancing a quick peek at Sonia. She's out and standing behind me, frozen.

The gunshots drew the attention of the two guys out front, though, now running toward us, rifles waving back and forth as they jog. These guys are total idiots.

"Head for the perimeter," I call to Sonia over my shoulder.

She nods and takes off in the other direction.

"Stop," I order the guards.

They halt, their eyes traveling between me and the guy at my feet.

"I want some answers. Now."

"Who *are* you?" one of them asks.

"The guy that's going to send you to the Hole if you don't tell me what the hell is going on right now."

It has the desired effect and both kids go slack-jawed, allowing me to focus on the one on the ground. He's not the commander or he'd have already shot me. Likely he's a leader with an eye toward advancement.

I cross my arms over my chest. "I was transferred here to oversee the operation, and so far, I'm not impressed. All three of you, report to the commander's tent now. We'll be having a talk as soon as I inspect the perimeter."

"Yes, sir," the two guards say and scurry off in the other direction.

I nod at the guy lying in the dirt. "What are you waiting for?"

He glares at me, but pushes up and stalks off after the other two.

We have five minutes at the most before the commander figures out what's going on and sends out reinforcements. I sprint to the rendezvous spot and find Sonia.

"Now what?" she asks.

"Now we get the hell out of here. Same plan as the last camp."

She nods and waits for me to do my thing. Approaching the sentry, I bark commands, he obeys, heading into the center of camp. Sonia and I run to the bikes and hop on. I power mine on, and have barely flicked up the kickstand when the first bullet flies by my head.

Sonia screams.

"Go, Sonia. Go! A moving target is harder to hit."

She takes off and I follow her, putting me between the shooters and Sonia.

"Zigzag," I yell. "If you're unpredictable in your movements, they can't line up the shot."

She darts off to the left as a bullet zips past, piercing my jacket sleeve. I duck my head and fall in behind Sonia.

"Left, left, left," I yell as another flies past, pinging off the back of her bike. Sonia zags left and I pass her, taking the lead. "Follow me," I call over my shoulder.

I weave and dodge until we're out of range, but continue on full-speed for a good ten miles before I pull over to catch my breath and make sure Sonia's okay.

Her hands shake and her face is as pale as a black girl's can be. I run my hands over her arms, back, legs. She's good.

"We still have one more camp to hit. Are you up for it?"

She nods, eyes wide.

I hope she still feels that way a couple of hours from now when we get there.

# One More

Evan

The near-silent hum of the electric battery is comforting as we make our way to the final camp. We've been lucky so far, but the nagging voice in the back of my head says it can't last. Although perhaps this isn't luck at all, but just how it is. Rainey had no difficulty getting Mateo out, and we didn't meet with much opposition when we got Lisa and Simon.

We reach the outskirts of the third target in under two hours, thanks to being able to use paved roads for a good part of the way. Sure they were old and torn up, but it was still faster than riding on dirt.

We're in a more densely wooded area with more options for hiding the bikes closer to the perimeter. Marcus pulls to a stop, and I glide in behind him. I turn off my bike and unclip the battery pack, replacing it with a fresh one, then do the same for Marcus's while he brings up the map for this camp on the tablet.

We've been studying the three maps over the past week, so it's mostly a refresher at this point. He turns it off and stuffs it in his pocket before hoisting his backpack onto his shoulders.

"Ready?"

"Yep."

We move closer, going from tree to tree, until we spot the sentry then drop to a crouch. Shift change is coming up in a half-hour, but dawn isn't far behind. We catch a break five minutes later when the sentry ducks behind a tree to take a leak. Heads down, we crouch-walk past him and into camp.

There is an eerie silence, as if it's too quiet. If we hadn't seen the sentry, I'd be convinced they'd bugged out. I glance at Marcus and his jaw is clamped shut. His eyes meet mine, wide and unsure, as if he senses something's off, too.

We make our way to the supply tent, my stomach knotting tightly. I wipe my sweaty palms on my fatigues, my eyes sweeping the area while Marcus disappears around the corner to set the charges.

I gnaw on my lower lip as time crawls, waiting for Marcus to reappear. A twig snaps behind me, and I spin to face a soldier five yards away, pointing a rifle at my chest. The moonlight is enough that I can make out his face. He's young, no more than fifteen or sixteen — he could be Will. Our eyes lock, and fear laces his as it does mine. My gaze drops to his trembling finger on the trigger. My own gun trembles in my hand, but I cannot kill this boy. He doesn't know that, though, and I suspect he may not have the same qualms about shooting me.

The soldier's eyes flick to my gun and stay there. He swallows hard, but still doesn't shoot, even though by not doing so he's putting himself in mortal danger.

Beads of sweat form on my forehead and upper lip, and anxiety burns through my chest. The sound of my heavy breathing fills my ears as I stare at the boy, and he stares at my gun.

I watch as his trigger finger quivers. Terror floods me, and I know I should shoot him, but I can't bring myself to do it. Instead, I squeeze my eyes shut, hoping I die instantly. I don't want the excruciating pain I had before. Anything would be better than that.

My last thoughts as gunfire ricochets across the clearing is that I've let everyone down. My family, my friends, and most of all Cyrus. A single tear of regret slips out and rolls down my cheek while I wait for the searing pain to rip through me.

It never comes.

Did he miss?

Even if he's a terrible shot, he couldn't miss from that distance. When I open my eyes, Marcus is heading toward me, yelling something I can't wrap my brain around. The kid lies on the ground, bleeding.

Marcus's words finally break through the mind fog. "Go, Evan, go!"

But I can't. I can't take my eyes off the boy who could be Will. The boy who probably didn't even want to be here. I walk over to the Will-like boy and kneel beside him, feeling for a pulse, but I know he's dead even before I touch him. His eyes are frozen open, staring into nothingness.

He was going to shoot me. Marcus did what he had to in order to save me, but what gives me the right to live over this boy? He probably has people who love him, too.

The popping of gunfire draws my attention away from the dead boy. Something flies so close to my hair it creates a breeze, ruffling my curls. Whipping around, I spot a boy, younger than the one lying on the ground, aiming at Marcus.

Without thinking, I grab my gun and shoot a couple of rounds past him. The boy dodges behind a tree as Marcus grabs my sleeve and drags me to my feet.

The boy pops out and shoots several times. I fire twice more, sending the kid ducking for cover. Another soldier rounds the corner of a tent and spots us. She kneels, lining up her rifle. There's no way the sharpshooter is going to miss.

I take a cleansing breath, aim, and fire three rounds, one of them hitting the girl in the forehead.

The gruesome nature of what I just did plunges me into a surreal state of focus. My head whips to a kid rolling out from behind the tent.

"Let's go," Marcus yells, taking off at a full sprint.

I fire, striking the boy in the chest. His eyes widen before he stumbles and falls. Marcus runs back to me, takes my hand, and yanks me along with him.

I stumble, tripping over the dead Will-kid at my feet, my hand sliding into the sticky blood seeping from his chest. Swallowing bile, I scramble up, but before I can take a step, more shots whiz past us from farther back.

I turn and shoot at the three soldiers running toward us, firing their deadly automatic weapons with screw-like bullets designed to cut a body to shreds.

"Don't run straight," I yell at Marcus. "You gotta be unpredictable."

Marcus dodges to his right as a bullet drills into the bark to my left, dangerously close.

My heart hammers in my ears, muffling the deafening barrage of gunfire around us.

I lurch to the side and duck behind a tree, then push off and dart in the other direction. Marcus runs past me as a bullet tears through his backpack, scattering the contents behind him.

"Marcus!" I scream.

He turns, eyes wide, but doesn't appear to be shot.

I let out a quick sigh of relief as another bullet passes far too close. Dropping to the ground, I roll and fire off a couple of shots before crawling to where Marcus is taking shelter behind a felled tree. A bullet strikes the trunk near my head, doing its little spiraling thing before coming to a stop. My breath stalls in my lungs.

Marcus finishes reloading his weapon and gets off a few shots. "Come on, let's go."

But I can't. That bullet triggered something, and it's like I can't breathe again. I cover my ears and curl into a ball, unable to move, gasping for air.

A hand grabs my shoulder and shakes me hard. Marcus fires over the log, then puts his face down next to mine. "You need to get a grip. Now. We have to go."

I shake my head, unable to stand, unable to put myself in the line of fire. Unable to let myself be shot again.

Marcus pops off another couple of rounds, then kneels closer to me. "Evan, please. We have to go. I promised Cy. Please…" he pleads with me.

Cyrus. If he was lying on the ground, I'd want him to get up. I have to do the same. I owe it to him, my family. Myself. I focus on my breathing, trying to remember how to do that.

"Okay. Let's do this," I gasp.

Marcus points to a large redwood a dozen yards away. "I'm going to fire off five rapid shots. When I do, run to that tree."

Nodding, I push up to my haunches and wait for him to start shooting. With the first shot, I take off in a crouch, pine needles and leaves slick beneath my boots. Even slipping a few times, I manage to scramble for cover before Marcus fires the fifth shot.

Gun in hand, I lean out and fire in the direction of the soldiers. Marcus darts toward me while I fire until my clip is empty and Marcus is a good fifteen yards beyond me.

Marcus shoots, buying me time to drop my clip and slap in a fresh one.

The next ten minutes involve Marcus and me providing alternating cover for each other as we make our way closer to the perimeter.

On the last pass, he ducks behind another tree, but doesn't cover me. I turn to call out to him, but instead suck in a breath.

A sentry has Marcus on the ground, hands behind his back, gun pointed at his head.

# Cyrus

Other than our close call in the second camp, we've been lucky, and we need to ride this streak. I glance over at Sonia. She's doing much better after everything went so smoothly at the third one.

Rainey and Bryce are hitting four targets, the only team with that assignment. Mateo determined between the two of them, they were the most experienced team, even though Bryce spent zero time with the Uprising. Still his time on the force and his undercover work count. And yeah, I can admit I don't hate the guy, but I still feel like he's one-upping me with the fourth camp.

I've had this plan in the back of my mind for at least a week, and I knew it would depend a lot on how things went up until now. Shit happens for a reason. We're done ahead of schedule, and we're also too close to a potential fourth target to not at least check it out. Everything's lining up, it's gotta be fate.

I put my hand up and signal Sonia I'm going to stop and pull over. She rolls up next to me, putting her foot down.

"Everything okay?"

"Yeah. Fine. Look, we're only about fifty miles from the old Mesa Verde power plant." She nods, waiting for me to go on. "We have enough juice left to make it there and then some. I've been thinking…if they have an underground bunker there, it could be their headquarters out here. It's stupid not to take it out, too, if the opportunity presents itself."

She studies me for a few long moments without speaking, her nostrils flaring as she breathes heavily.

"You don't need to come with me. It'll be a piece of cake."

She glances around, but it's still an hour until dawn. "Okay, let's check it out. But, Cy, we accomplished our mission, even if we don't take out this bunker. So this is more like frosting on the cake. If it's as easy as you say, we can do it. Otherwise, we head back as planned."

"That's all I'm asking."

The ride south goes quicker than expected and soon we're pulling to a stop about a mile away, stashing the bikes and covering the remainder of the distance on foot.

The half-moon lighting our way earlier has dipped below the trees, making the darkness a looming presence. We approach the outbuildings where Evan and I first overheard talk of an Uprising only six months ago. It feels like years.

Being back here again, so close to where we used to live, is unnerving. I wasn't prepared for how it would affect me. I shake it off and motion Sonia to catch up to me as I crouch behind a couple of boulders.

"What do you think?" Sonia whispers.

"I want to get closer. You wait here."

She nods and I use my Uprising training to make it to the rubble, barely making a sound. Crickets provide background noise and an occasional hoot of an owl overhead on his end-of-night sweep for food.

I stalk over broken concrete, rocks, and brick zeroing in on the glow coming from the hatch Evan discovered when we were last here. Glancing back over my shoulder toward Sonia, I weigh my options. If I return to her, I'm only delaying. I have everything I need, all that's left is to plant the explosives, set the timers, and run back to the bikes.

With slow, cautious movements, I constantly scan the area until I reach the target and ease off my backpack. The zipper seems to echo off every exposed piece of concrete as I open the bag.

C-4 in hand, I inch forward and insert the blasting caps before attaching the wires. I place three around the steel hatch, then more farther out, hoping to cause an avalanche rather than just blowing the hatch open.

This time, I program the timers for twenty minutes instead of forty. Even twenty seems too long. Anyone could come up before then and discover them, but ten isn't long enough.

I set the last one and grab the backpack, turning to meet back up with Sonia. My foot catches on a rock and it skitters, clanging across the metal hatch.

*Shit.*

With one eye on the rocks underfoot, I hightail it over the rubble.

I'm almost to the outbuildings when explosive heat and a deafening roar from behind sends me flying.

## Evan

Behind me, soldiers continue shooting at us, bullets ripping chunks from the bark next to my shoulder. In front of me, a sentry has a gun pointed at Marcus's forehead.

There's no surrender. Even if they don't kill us on the spot, when the explosives go off, we're as good as dead.

I've got to get us out of this situation or die trying.

I fire off two shots in the direction of the approaching soldiers and launch myself at a tree ten yards away. Taking a second to collect myself, I peek around it, knowing what needs to be done, and line up the shot. The first bullet misses the target, but the second hits the girl in the chest. She falls forward, her long dark ponytail fanning out on the ground above her head.

The other two soldiers dive for cover, allowing enough time for me to make it to the next tree. Another dozen feet closer to Marcus. Either the sentry is deaf, or too consumed with fear to notice I'm advancing on him.

Reaching into my pocket, I grab my knife and flip open the blade. I take in a deep breath, hold it, then blow it back out, steadying myself.

One, two, three.

The knife sails across the clearing, hitting the soldier in the shoulder and he jerks backward. Raising my gun, I aim and shoot, never even coming close to missing my mark.

The Uprising trained me well.

Marcus scrambles for his weapon and fires beyond me, giving me cover until I join him.

"Thanks," he pants when I reach his side.

Adrenaline powers through me, and I yank Marcus to his feet. We turn and run away from camp like someone ignited our asses.

A roar unlike anything I've ever heard tears through the night, slamming me face first to the ground. My hands slide against dirt and rocks, ripping skin from my palms. The second blast slams the air from my lungs and sends something hard crashing into my skull.

Heat washes over me like a wave of fire, and I turn to stare at flames rushing toward the sky. My ears ring, and I cover them, trying to block the sound, but it's coming from within.

Dizziness spins me, making it difficult to get my bearings.

"Marcus!" I yell, but can't hear over the clanging inside my head.

I'm pretty sure when I yelled, I split my head in two; I reach up to hold it together. Kicking with my feet, I scramble up, but as soon as I stand, the world tilts.

Marcus is fifty feet away. He takes a step before turning back, his eyes zeroing in on me. His mouth drops open and he changes direction, sprinting toward me.

The ground continues to rumble beneath me, or maybe I'm rumbling. Something warm and sticky trickles down my face. Marcus reaches for my hand, but I don't take his, because mine are busy holding my skull together.

He yanks me up by my elbow and tugs me after him, but the earth, bitch that she is, lists to the right, making me stumble. Marcus turns to face me, worry lacing his dark eyes. His lips move but no sound comes out.

My stomach lurches and I fall to my knee, my hands slipping to the ground as I retch until there's nothing left. Steely knives pierce my brain and a pounding rhythm of pain strikes the inside of my head with each heartbeat.

Marcus's usually dark face appears ashen as he bends over and wraps his arm around my waist, hauling me to my feet. He tucks me against him and drags me away from camp. I hope he remembers where we parked, because I don't.

Every step sends excruciating pain slicing through my head, but I'm pretty sure my brains haven't fallen out, so I guess I didn't crack my skull.

We arrive at the bikes, and Marcus looks from me to my bike and back again, processing something. He undoes the clips and takes the battery from my bike and places it in the backpack with the spares and our changes of clothing, easing it onto my shoulders.

He pulls me over to his bike and hops on, reaching out his arm to steady me as I climb up behind him. He takes off as soon as I wrap my arms around his waist.

We bounce our way across the ground, making my head feel as if it's being torn apart. I grit my teeth and hang on tighter. About the only good thing is my hearing seems to be recovering.

When we finally, gloriously come to a stop to swap batteries, Marcus takes my arm and guides me from the back of the bike. He grabs his tablet from his pocket and switches on the light, shining it on my face.

He sucks in a breath. "You have a nasty gash on your head." He only sounds like he's in a tunnel now.

I curl in my top lip and bite it. "I'm sorry about what happened back there."

His brows pinch together. "What are you talking about?"

"With the kid. I don't know what happened. It was like I was looking at Will, and...I couldn't shoot him. I'm so sorry. I could've gotten you killed."

Tears pool in my eyes and begin to trail down my cheeks. Soon I'm crying hard and can't stop even though the sobbing is driving a nail through my head with a sledgehammer.

Marcus pulls me into his arms and holds me while I cry. His hands run up and down my back while he whispers soft things in my ear I can't quite hear. He presses his face to mine, our tears mixing as his body trembles.

When I've cried myself out, and I'm drained of all emotion and energy, Marcus releases me. "Are you okay now?"

I nod and we resume our trip, me leaning my cheek against Marcus's back as we ride. The throbbing in my head keeps me from dozing, which is probably the only reason I haven't fallen off. We swap batteries once more before arriving at the Union wall by late morning.

I dismount and make the mistake of turning east, the sun searing my eyes. Spikes of pain in my skull reignite the nausea, and I lean over and dry-heave.

I'm drenched in sweat and my stomach hurts almost as much as my head when I right myself. Marcus wraps an arm around my shoulder and guides me to the opening he's discovered. He eases inside, pulling me with him, the sudden darkness a welcome relief.

"We need to clean you up before we get on the train," he says before going off in search of a hotel room.

I slink to the floor in a dark corridor of the lower level, and lean my head back, closing my eyes as the world around me blissfully fades away.

# Fading Away

*Evan*

"**E**van...Evan...oh my god, Evan!"

I groan and lift one eye to find a freaked out Marcus squatting in front of me. "What? What's wrong?" Damn, my head hurts. Why does it hurt? Oh yeah.

A slow smile spreads across Marcus's face and he chuckles. "Shit, I thought you were dead."

"Not yet, but if you scream at me like that again, it may kill me."

"Sorry." He stands and reaches down a hand to pull me up.

He drags me down the corridor to a dank hotel a couple of blocks away. A handful of people openly stare at us, but most can't be bothered. Weirdness abounds on the lower levels, and we're probably no worse looking than many bottom dwellers.

Marcus opens a door, and I enter a small room with our remaining backpack sitting on the only bed.

I walk into the bathroom and flip on the lights, blinking against the harsh brightness and the sharp pain it reignites. My eyes adjust, and I almost gag at my reflection. Dried blood is matted into my hair, coating half my face before trailing down my neck and soaking my shirt. When I lean forward and examine the gash on my scalp, I actually do gag. It's deep and ugly, and I'm pretty sure that white stuff is bone.

After turning on the shower, I return to the bedroom to grab my clothes. "Can you go find some bandages or something? And a hat?"

Marcus hesitates, staring at me for a few moments. "Are you going to be okay?"

"Yeah. But, um, I need to clean my head and then hide it under a hat. So can you go?"

"Sure." He glances at me one more time before disappearing out the door.

I'm not sure I need the bandages, but I need him not to be here when I clean up. There's no easy way to do this, so I start by peeling off my filthy, blood-soaked clothes and dropping them on the floor. I take a deep breath and step into the shower. It's a perfect ninety-eight point six degrees, but it's going to sting like mother-freaking hell when it hits my scalp.

Clamping my lips together, I step under the stream and let loose a guttural yell as blinding pain shatters me into a million pieces. The edge of my vision goes dark, and I gulp in deep breaths of air to keep from blacking out. I grit my teeth and go all in, letting the water rinse the blood from my body. My stomach clenches as I try to hold it together long enough to wash my hair.

My hands shake from pain and adrenaline as I work the lather into my matted hair. On trembling legs, I lower myself to the shower floor to let the spray wash the soap away, no longer having the strength to continue standing.

By the time I turn off the water, a cold sweat covers my body and fresh blood flows from the gash on my head. I push up and grab a towel, applying pressure to the wound.

The door opens and Marcus barrels into the room, carrying a bag. "Hey, I got you—" His eyes go wide before slamming shut, and his free hand flies up to cover them.

Yep, I'm sitting naked on the toilet lid, pressing a bloody towel to my head.

"I'm so sorry, Evan."

"Not your fault," I say, kicking the door closed with my foot.

"I swear I didn't see anything."

"It's okay, Marcus. I just wanted to stop the bleeding before I got dressed. Who thought packing a white T-shirt was a good idea?"

"Hey, the girl at the pharmacy gave me this stuff you can squirt on your head to numb it."

Shit, why didn't I think of that? Showering would have been a lot less painful. "Thanks, Marcus. Umm…can you toss it in here?"

He doesn't respond, but I can hear him swearing on the other side of the door. He cracks it only enough to squeeze the bag in before slamming the door shut again.

It takes nearly twenty minutes to get the bleeding under control so I can spray the PainAway on, but damn, within a minute, the pain has dulled to a mild throbbing. I use some butterfly bandages to hold it together the best I can. After dressing in jeans and a T-shirt, I pull the ball cap down over my curls, hiding the gash. Satisfied, I open the door and head into the other room to find Marcus staring at his feet.

"Marcus."

"What?" He lifts head, his gaze bouncing around the room.

"Look at me." He slowly shifts his eyes to mine. "When I was shot, I think everyone and their brother saw me naked. It's no big deal, at least not to me, but if you're going to act all weird with me, I'll need to tell Cyrus why."

His jaw goes slack. "No. Shit, no. I'm fine. I promise." He launches himself off the bed and moves toward the bathroom, carving a large path around me. "I'm gonna clean up."

I lie on my back, fighting to stay awake, while Marcus takes an unbelievably long shower.

He finally emerges a half-hour later, a cloud of steam following him. "Hot showers?" His face erupts into a huge grin. "Damn, you must really love Cy if you were willing to give that up for him."

I let out a small laugh, but quickly sober. "Do you think the others ran into any trouble?"

His smile falls, too. "I don't know. I hope not." He crosses the room and sits on the edge of the bed, putting his hand on my shoulder. "You were great out there. Really."

"I almost got you killed."

"You saved my life."

His dark brown eyes fill with gratitude, and I realize he's right. I saved him, but he saved me, too. That's what partners do. We killed a lot of people to save each other, though, and somehow I have to find a way to live with that.

"You ready?" he asks.

I nod.

We head out, dumping our bags in the nearest trash can before going up to the top level and buying two tickets to the Western Province.

The train hums along, and soon my eyelids become too heavy to do anything but close.

Marcus reaches over and shakes my arm. "Hey, Evan, you can't sleep. I may not know as much as Sonia, but I do know you're not supposed to fall asleep with a concussion."

I drag my eyes open and attempt to focus on him. "I'll try. Talk to me. What made you decide to leave your family after the tornado?"

He shrugs. "I was ready for a change, and it seemed like the right time to move on. When Lucien and Cy said they were leaving, I decided to go. I didn't spend a lot of time thinking about it."

"How old were you?" It's bizarre to me that Ruins parents let their young teens wander off, but it's such a different way of life out there.

"Fourteen. Same as Cy."

"Were you scared?"

He laughs. "Hell yeah. But I was more afraid of being left behind."

"Did you know Sonia was the one for you?"

He smiles, white teeth standing out in contrast to his dark skin. "Naw. I liked her, but not like that. I was surprised when she wanted to come, too. Even more surprised her folks let her. One day while we were walking, she reached down and took my hand. That's when I realized she was into me."

I wait for him to elaborate, but he doesn't, so I nudge his shin with my foot. "And?"

"And, she's Sonia. Have you seen her? She's gorgeous. I'd have been stupid not to find out where things went. But I was still trying to figure out what all my feelings meant. Between my changing body and my changing life, I was kinda out of my element. Things were awkward at first, but we'd known each other for so long it wasn't awkward for long. By the time I was fifteen, I knew I was crazy about her. I still don't know what she sees in me."

The attendant walks by with the cart and stops beside us. "Would you like anything to drink?" he asks.

"I'll take a water. Evan?" Marcus says.

"Water's good."

The attendant hands over two bottles before moving down the aisle. I twist off the top and take a long swallow. The bottled desalinated water tastes funky to me after drinking fresh water out in the Ruins for the past two months.

"So what about you?" Marcus asks. "When did you realize you were interested in Cy? 'Cause I thought that was never gonna happen."

I take another sip and think back over our initial interactions. "Probably the day you guys first took me to the trading post. When I saw Lucy flirting with him, I was stupid jealous. Watching them together made my blood boil." Another memory from that day pops into my head, and I narrow my eyes at Marcus. "You set me up, didn't you? Cyrus seemed confused I thought he was involved with Lucy...now it all makes sense."

He shrugs and grins. "Hey, I knew he was nuts about you, but he wasn't doing anything about it. So I let you know Lucy was interested in Cy, figuring if you were interested, maybe *you'd* make a move before it was too late."

"You're an ass," I say, but I can't keep the smile off my face.

The A-Train pulls into the Western Province station, and I have to force myself not to shove my way to the front of the pack. Instead, I wait for the other passengers to disembark, fighting the feeling I'm coming out of my own skin. If my head wasn't killing me, I'd run to the commuter terminal.

I texted Eddie from the train, asking if everyone was there yet, but he still hasn't responded. I obsessively check my tablet, but there's never a reply, and I'm trying really hard not to read anything into that.

Hours later, but probably only minutes, the commuter train glides to a stop and I'm the first one in line to get off. The doors slide open and I launch myself out like a bullet, Marcus on my heels, but he soon outpaces me. I'm forced to slow to cope with the pounding in my head, and before long the crowd swallows Marcus.

By the time I reach Eddie's apartment, Marcus is walking out the front door, shoulders hunched, head down. My heart plummets and I start taking in long breaths through my nose and blowing them out my mouth to keep from losing it again.

"Marcus," I call, my voice quivering. "What's wrong?"

He lifts his head and shakes it. "They're not here."

Okay, that's not necessarily bad. They're just not here *yet*, although they should have been here before us. The last camp they hit was near where they lived out in the Ruins, a short A-Train ride to here. Maybe they ran out of juice and had to walk.

The door behind Marcus opens and Eddie pokes his head out. Deep worry lines melt as he closes the distance between us, yanking me into his arms and squeezing the breath out of me.

A steady stream of bodies pours out of the apartment, rushing up to us, asking questions, trying to get in on some sort of massive group hug. My eyes sweep the faces, and in addition to Cyrus and Sonia, Bryce and Rainey are also among the missing. They had four targets, though, so that doesn't worry me as much.

"Has anyone heard from Alexander, Ilona, Simon, and Zak?" I ask.

Eddie releases me and the crowd parts.

"Alexander texted your dad from a café in the Northern Territories about an hour ago," Will says. "They're good."

Lisa hooks her arm through mine and tugs me into the house. "I'm glad you're here. I was worried when you guys were so late getting back."

My eyes search her face, and I can tell the exact moment she realizes the impact of her words. "Oh, hey, Ev, I'm sure he's fine. They'll be here."

Ty, Connor, and Ben pound down the stairs with Quinn and Liam behind them. Small hands and arms clamp onto me and Marcus, and for a little while, their energy distracts me, keeps some of my fear at bay. The wall crumbles, though, as another hour passes with no word from our missing friends.

With my eyes glued to the door, I listen to the conversations swirling around me, picking up bits of stories. Colin and Ally had no resistance at all. Jack and Lisa had to shoot their way out of their last camp, Will and Mateo had trouble at two of their camps.

I break my trance and seek out Marcus, knowing he's the one person who feels the same way I do, but I don't see him. After checking upstairs, I ease outside and find him on the sidewalk, staring in the direction of the train station.

When I reach his side, he takes in a deep breath and puts his arm around my shoulder, pulling me against him.

We stand together, watching and waiting, until Eddie fetches us for dinner.

# Crumbling

I only managed to pick at my dinner, I couldn't even make the fork enter my mouth. The thought of food was enough to make me gag, actually trying to eat it would have ended in a mess.

Marcus and I resume our spot on the sidewalk as soon as the dishes are done. The front door opens and Mateo glances out. His gaze connects with mine, and he saunters over to join us, only giving us a gruff, "Hey," in greeting. He's worried about his friends even if he won't admit it.

The sun sinks behind clouds that have pushed in from the coast, dropping the temperature. I shiver, but I'm not willing to go inside. Mateo gives up, or at least I think he does until he returns wearing a coat and hands a sweatshirt to me and another to Marcus.

"Thanks, man," Marcus says, pulling it on. I recognize it as one of Eddie's and the sleeves don't even come to his wrists. The bottom band sits an inch above the waistband of his jeans, looking ridiculous.

Another hour passes, and I stop pretending I'm not falling apart. My heart fractures into a network of cracks as I face the probability no one else is coming back. The first tear rolls free, followed by another. There's no hiding them from anyone, but I feel like crap for bringing Marcus down any more than he already is. I walk over to the park so I can unravel without an audience.

Waves of fear and grief threaten to pull me under, and I wonder how I'm going to survive the next minutes, hours, and days when I sense someone beside me. Without even looking, I know it's Marcus. He doesn't say anything, he doesn't need to. The only other person who can relate to what we're feeling is Talia, and she's holed up inside with Eddie and the kids.

My hands shake, a combination of anxiety, lack of food, and a lingering concussion. I make my way over to the bench to sit. The streetlight above me begins to glow as darkness grows and surrounds us. Marcus takes a seat next to me and puts an arm around my shoulders. I think he needs to hang on to me as much as I need him.

With a sudden motion, Marcus launches himself off the bench, leaving me to fall back with a thunk. I right myself and follow his trajectory as he sprints down the path.

My breath catches, and my pulse quickens. Sonia is walking toward us, her hand on Cyrus's waist, his arm resting on her shoulder as he limps. Marcus reaches them and pulls Sonia into his arms.

Cyrus's gaze locks with mine, and I push up, propelling myself through the park at a slow run that sends pain quaking through my skull. I stop a foot away, trying to get a read on him, but his expression is unfamiliar.

We study each other for only a second before I throw my arms around his neck and burrow into his chest, knocking off my ball cap. Cyrus crushes me against him, his cheek coming to rest on the top of my head. I suck in a breath at the pain, but don't pull away.

I can't.

I never want to leave his arms.

## Cyrus

She feels perfect nestled against me, but it's not enough, I need more. More that doesn't involve an audience. My head pivots, searching, until I spot an alcove between her dad's apartment and the neighbor's place. I take her hand and drag her with me, doing my best not to let my leg keep me from what I need.

Pressing her up against the back wall, my lips descend on hers, and I kiss her hard, rough. My mouth seeking and finding reassurances, finding…home.

She matches my intensity with her own, and my body relaxes for the first time since we parted ways two days ago, melting into her. She lets out a little moan as her fingers dig into the back of my neck.

We may be in a secluded spot, but we're still outside, so I find enough self-control for the both of us. Dislodging my tongue from her mouth, I press soft kisses to her lips and breathe her name.

She whimpers and I nearly lose it. She pulls my face back down and kisses me with a tenderness that brings tears to my eyes. "I love you," she murmurs over and over.

Shit, this girl is everything. I rest my forehead against hers, my chest rising and falling at a rapid pace.

"Okay, you two, save some for later," Sonia says. "I need to look at that leg now, Cy."

Right, the leg. I scoop my arm around Ev, and guide her back to the sidewalk.

Sonia narrows her eyes, her gaze shifting to Evan. "And I should look at your head, too."

I twist around and only now do I see a wicked cut on her scalp.

Her fingers fly up to her hair and she gingerly presses against it, wincing. "I'm fine."

Before I can ask her what happened, the front door opens and a flood of people explodes from inside. Ally breaks free, leading the pack, and flings herself into my arms. She kisses my face, tears pouring down her cheeks.

"Hey, hey, what's wrong?" I ask.

She punches me in the chest. "We thought you were…" Her eyes dart to Ev, and she slams her mouth shut.

"You should have been back eight hours ago," Mateo says, walking up and giving me a one-armed hug, smashing Ally between us.

I reach back and find Ev's hand, weaving our fingers together, and follow Sonia inside.

Will claps me on the back. "Hey, we were pretty worried. What happened to you guys?"

I open my mouth to answer, but when my gaze flicks to Ev, I realize I need to tell her first. "It's a long story."

"Everyone out," Sonia orders.

Eddie approaches me and pauses before reaching out a hand. I take it and he pulls me in for a hug. "Don't ever do that to my daughter again," he growls.

"Dad, this is Sonia," Evan says. "Marcus's girlfriend."

"Hey," Eddie says, shaking Sonia's hand.

"Do you have a first aid kit?" she asks.

"Yeah. Hang on." He flies up the stairs and returns carrying a metal case with a big red cross on the front.

"Thanks." She takes it from him and turns to Evan. "You should go, too. I'll come get you when I'm done so I can check your head."

She shakes her head. "I'm not leaving."

"Ev..." I say.

She cuts her eyes to me. "I'm not leaving you, so don't bother."

I sigh. This isn't a battle worth fighting, but I'm about to scream like a little kid, which is something I'd rather she not see.

Sonia glances around, her eyes landing on the kitchen counter. "Take your pants off and climb up there," she commands.

I unbutton my jeans and kick them off, not totally comfortable standing in front of two girls in nothing but my T-shirt and a pair of boxers.

"Socks, too."

I peel them off and hoist myself up.

"Lie on your stomach."

"You get kind of imperial when you're in healing mode."

She lifts her eyebrows, mouth pinched, but doesn't respond. Probably not the best idea to give her shit before she starts digging around in my leg. I prop my chin up on my fist while Sonia unties the makeshift field bandage from my calf.

Ev sucks in a breath. "What happened?"

Sonia crosses to the sink to wash her hands. "After we hit the third camp, Cy had the brilliant idea of going after that underground bunker. You remember the one at the old Mesa Verde power station?"

"That wasn't part of the plan," Evan says. "I'm not sure if I should be impressed with the brilliance of your idea or pissed you went off script. Especially after you gave me such a hard time for doing the same."

I want to reach around and take her hand, but Sonia starts prodding the wound, and instead, all that comes out is a steady stream of profanity.

"There was something wrong with the timer, it went off before he cleared the bunker. Stuff was flying. Rocks and debris rained down on us. Something flew out and hit Cy in the leg."

"Are you sure he wasn't shot?"

"Yeah. Mostly anyway."

"I never saw anyone," I say through gritted teeth, a light sheen of sweat now coating my skin. "I set the timer for twenty minutes but it went off in less than five."

"Oh, wait!" Evan says and runs outside.

"Are you trying to get me into trouble?" I ask Sonia.

"You were going to lie to her?"

"No. But I would have found a more delicate way to tell her."

Ev bursts back into the house, breathing hard. "Here…use…this…" she pants, handing something to Sonia.

"This might sting," Sonia says.

I brace myself, but it's just cold, not painful. At least for a few seconds, then warmth spreads out until my leg feels weird. Like it's not even there.

"What was that?" I ask.

"It's called PainAway," Ev says. "It's only temporary, but it dulls it for a short bit."

Sure enough, I can feel pressure and tugging as Sonia does whatever it is she does, but no pain. I relax, laying my head down on my hands and close my eyes, nearly falling asleep before Sonia whacks my ass.

"All done."

A bandage covers my calf. It'll hurt like a mother when I peel it off my leg hair. After pulling my jeans back on, I slide up behind where my girl sits on the stool and wrap my arms around her waist.

Sonia peels the bandages off, and they pull at Ev's hair, opening the wound. Shit, that's nasty. Sonia digs around in the first aid kit, grabbing a bottle and squirts it in. Then she reaches into her cargo pants and pulls out a tube of something.

"What's that?" I ask.

"Surgical glue."

"Where'd you get that?" Ev asks.

Sonia grins and grips the back of Ev's head. "You'd be surprised at all the goodies I can find up in the Northern Territories."

Evan lets out a groan, and sways.

Sonia's eyes narrow. "Did you hit your head?"

"I don't know. Maybe. We had trouble getting out of our last camp. There was an explosion before we cleared the perimeter. I sort of went flying."

Sonia takes a small flashlight from the kit and shines it in Evan's eyes and performs the finger tracking thing she does whenever one of us conks our head. "Cy, can you get some ice from the freezer?"

"Yeah." I kiss Ev's shoulder before heading to the fridge and opening the door, but there's no ice.

"It's on the bottom," Ev says.

The bottom is a drawer thing, but there's a bin of cubes. I grab a handful and wrap it in a towel from the counter before handing it to Sonia.

"You have a concussion," Sonia says, placing the icepack on the side on Evan's head. "We'll need to keep an eye on you, but you should see a doctor here in the Union. Tonight."

Evan nods. "I will. As soon as Bryce and Rainey get here."

There's exactly one too many people in this room right now, but Sonia did just stitch me up and glue my girlfriend's head back together, so I'm not going to tell her to get lost. Just make her uncomfortable enough to leave.

I take the compress from Sonia, and with my free hand, sweep the hair away from Ev's neck. I trail a line of kisses up the back of her skin, loving the way goose bumps erupt across the surface.

"My work here is done," Sonia says.

"Thank you," Evan says, but it's mostly a whisper.

# Stitched Together

Evan

Cyrus trails kisses along the back of my neck, the rough stubble on his jaw raising goose bumps over my entire body. If I was lightheaded before, I'm downright dizzy now. I close my eyes and sigh, leaning back into him, only vaguely aware of Sonia leaving when the door closes behind us.

Cyrus spins me around on the stool, setting the ice pack on the counter. I wind my arms around his neck and he steps closer, nestling himself between my knees.

"I missed you," he says, pressing his forehead to mine.

We were apart less than 48 hours, but I know what he means. "You can't ever tell me I'm impulsive again, you know that right?"

"Mm-hm," he says, his lips finding their way back to my neck.

"Seriously, Cy. That was so off-plan. You did exactly the thing you accused me of."

"I know," he murmurs under my ear, making it damn near impossible to concentrate.

I push him back, not so far I can't keep my arms around him, but enough he's no longer so distracting. I lift an eyebrow. "What were you thinking?"

He sighs. "I was thinking we were chopping off limbs, but to kill the beast, we needed to cut off the head."

"Really? That's...kinda brilliant."

He smiles. "So, am I forgiven?"

"I don't know. I was terrified, like more than I've ever been."

"I'm sorry," he whispers, his lips finding their way back to my neck. "Never again. Anything else we have to do, we do together. Okay?"

I nod, my voice stuck in my throat as my pulse pounds beneath his mouth. He kisses his way from my ear, skimming my jaw, up to my mouth. I inhale his breath and push closer, savoring the feeling of his lips against the sensitive skin of mine. My lips part and his tongue dips inside. I'm lost in something so real the last few hours of panic, worry, and heartache are erased. He is *so* forgiven.

His movements are slow, languid, like honey being poured from a bottle, filling me with sweet warmth. He moves his hands up to cup my face, his thumbs gliding over my cheeks. I press closer to him, willing our bodies to become one. Our kiss outside was different, it was about overwhelming relief. This one pulls at me, demands more, and I want to give it.

His mouth becomes desperate, as if I'm the water his parched throat needs. He tightens his grip on me, and my hands twist into the back of his shirt, pulling him closer. A soft groan in the back of his throat ignites me.

I pull my swollen lips from his and peer up into his dark, hungry eyes. His warm breath dances across my face, sending a shiver down my spine.

"Do you think you can make it up the stairs?" I whisper.

He growls and wraps his arms around my waist, lifting me off the stool. "Which room?"

Before I can answer, the front door flies open, followed by stomping and loud voices.

*Rainey and Bryce!* I spin around, but my heart plummets when they're not among the others. Worry is etched into Talia's face as she ushers the younger kids in, making me feel like shit for trying to seduce my boyfriend while my friends are still missing.

"Bedtime," Eddie announces, eying me and Cyrus.

Cyrus takes a step back, and we help Eddie and Talia put five little kids to bed.

"I'm hungry," Colin says.

Lisa rolls her eyes. "Shocking." But she heads to the fridge and starts pulling out stuff for sandwiches.

To give myself something to do, I join her, grabbing a fresh loaf of rye and setting it on the cutting board. Eddie plugs in the sandwich press to heat up while I pull the serrated knife from the block and begin slicing the bread.

"You're going to let them make you something to eat?" Ally asks. "Go in there and help them."

I glance over my shoulder at them, and smile when she shoves Colin toward the kitchen. A sharp pain makes me yelp. My eyes locks onto the bright red flowing from my index finger, and something inside me clicks. My hands tremble and the knife clatters to the floor.

Suddenly I can't catch my breath. I don't want anyone to see me like this and find enough control to make it to the foyer before tearing up the stairs and into my room, closing the door behind me.

The voices from downstairs blur into the background until all I hear are soft drips hitting the wood floor. Darkness envelopes the perimeter of my vision, pushing in, obscuring my surroundings. I am no longer in my room at Eddie's, but back in the Ruins, staring at the blood of the kids I killed. My pulse pounds in my head, and I wrap my arms around myself, trying to hold it together, but I can't.

The next thing I'm aware of is lying on the floor, my whole body shaking, my breathing erratic. Strong bands wrap around me from behind, and I turn toward the body they're attached to, inhaling Eddie's spicy scent.

Burying my face in his chest, I let him try to stop me from quaking, because I can't, and I give in to whatever's happening. My body wracks with silent sobs as a soundless scream tears from my throat.

My dad holds me against him and strokes my hair, comforting me in a way he never has before. He missed out on all of the skinned knees and heartache of my younger days, but he's making up for it now in spades.

I'm not sure how much time passes before my body stops its crazy shaking, but Eddie continues to hold me long after I've calmed down.

He finally unwraps his arms and lifts me to standing, then examines my finger. It's still bleeding a little and there's blood on my shirt, jeans, and the floor, but he doesn't seem concerned about my cut. His eyes search mine for answers to questions he never voices.

I take in a deep cleansing breath that shudders in my chest and sink onto the bed. Glancing at Eddie, I wonder if I can tell him. He's my dad, he's supposed to love me unconditionally. That's what parents do. But will he still love me when he finds out what I did?

"I…" The words die in my throat before erupting unbidden. "I killed so many kids today."

The awful truth hangs in the air, and I drop my gaze, terrified of what I'll find in Eddie's eyes — disgust, disappointment, or worse. He squats at my feet and glances up at my face, but what's in his eyes is none of those. All I see are compassion and love. He puts his hand on my knee and waits for me to continue.

"I had to." The justification sounds lame even to me. "Because if I didn't, Marcus would be dead. Or me. But it's wrong to kill. They were just kids. No older than Will. They probably didn't even want to be there. They were only doing what they were ordered to do."

"Evan…" He pauses before blowing out a long stream of air. "What could you have done differently?"

I close my eyes and contemplate his question. Today, maybe nothing, but if I'd trained harder, thought faster on my feet, done any number of things differently before we went in, we might have been able to find another way. Even then, when the explosives went off...we knew what we were doing.

"I don't know," I whisper and fall back, throwing an arm over my eyes. All my thoughts begin to pour out of me, everything I pushed so hard to keep hidden. "I kept thinking this whole time that we could *do* something. We could stop the Uprising. That we could succeed where the adults had failed because we cared. I thought we were smarter, nobler, more principled than Walker. But when it comes right down to it, I'm no better than him. I killed innocent kids because I couldn't bear the thought of losing my friend, of having to tell Sonia I didn't protect Marcus. I'm just like him. I did it because I cared about what I wanted more than about what was right."

"Evan, you need to talk to someone, and I don't mean me. Someone who can help you cope with this."

I open my eyes and push up on my elbows. "What would I say? That I shot a bunch of kids out in the Ruins to prevent an uprising? Oh and by the way, there are actually people living in the Ruins and have been all along." I let out a harsh laugh. "No one would believe the truth. It's too crazy."

Eddie moves from his squat, sitting with his back to the wall and stretches out his legs. "Then talk to your friends. They'll understand because they were there, too. Honey, you're not the only one going through this. Those kids down there, they all did something they can never talk about to anyone but each other."

I thought they were all holding it together so much better than me, but maybe not. Jack's a cop, he's trained to kill, and my friends from the Ruins grew up leading very different lives. For them, life in the Ruins can be kill or be killed at times. Are they dealing with the same guilt?

Eddie sighs. "Cyrus loves you. I trusted him to take care of you because I see the way he looks at you. I knew he'd risk everything to protect you, and I have no doubt that extends beyond your physical safety. Talk to him."

Cyrus and I *are* overdue for a long series of talks about a lot of things. We've only scratched the surface over the past few weeks. I think about all the nights we talked on the rock while looking up at the stars, and it hits me. That's where I want to go, back out to the Ruins, back to where we fell in love, where we can *really* talk.

"I think I've always known Cyrus would take you away from here," Eddie says as if he can read my mind. "I missed too much of your life already, but I have no one to blame for that except myself. Cyrus makes you happy, and that's all I've ever wanted for you."

My heart squeezes in my chest and fresh tears threaten. "You're my father, you always will be. We're connected by so much more than where I live. I'm not going to disappear from your life. No matter what happens with me and Cyrus, I'm your daughter forever. Nothing will change that."

He sighs and pushes himself off the floor before taking my hand. "Let's get this cleaned up."

In the bathroom, he rinses my finger and applies some antibiotic ointment before bandaging it. I watch him as he works, thinking about what just transpired between us. We covered more ground in the past hour than in all the years we were in therapy together.

When he's done, Eddie heads downstairs. I return to my room, and for the second time today, change out of bloody clothes.

When I rejoin the others, I'm unsure of what to expect, but the only one who isn't acting like my crazy bolt from the kitchen didn't happen is Cyrus. His eyes search mine, and I give him a small smile.

The sandwiches have been eaten and the leftovers put away, so there isn't anything for me to do except fold myself into Cyrus's embrace. Letting him hold me doesn't change anything, but I feel better in his arms. For a moment, I don't worry about anything and only enjoy the boy I'm with and let him work his magic.

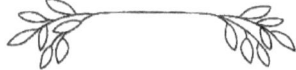

Eddie kicked us out of the house, using the sleeping kids upstairs as an excuse, but with one look at Talia I know that's only half the story. Taking Cyrus's hand, I lead him outside and across the sidewalk to the park, picking a spot where I can still see the apartment.

"If they're not here by dawn, we'll go search for them," Mateo says, draining the last of his beer and glancing at the two trash cans nearby.

I take the bottle from his hand and toss it in the recycling bin.

"That's better than waiting," Lisa says.

Mateo leans back against the light pole. "There's any number of reasons they're not back yet. If they ran out of battery power, they might have to walk fifty miles or more. That takes time."

I nod, knowing there's sound logic in that.

"We brought down the Uprising," Ally says. "A search party almost sounds easy."

Her words wrap around me, sink in. It's the first time I've thought about it in those terms. A part of me knows many of those kids wouldn't have survived an attack on the Union, but that wouldn't have been at my hands. Perhaps it's this weight of guilt that keeps us human. I doubt Walker's ever felt guilty about anything he's done.

Cyrus moves up behind me and wraps his arms around my waist. I lean my head against his chest while his thumbs trace small circles on my belly. There's nothing I wouldn't do to protect him and the rest of my family and friends, and maybe that makes me a monster.

I twist around so I can face the boy I love, force myself to stop thinking about everything else for now. He presses his forehead to mine as we talk about what we're going to do next. He tells me he wants to find Draya, and I tell him I want to eventually go back out to the Ruins.

I sense a change in the atmosphere only a moment before Cyrus's arms stiffen. Twisting, I crane my neck to see Rainey walking toward us and dislodge myself from Cyrus's embrace.

"It's about time you guys got back," I call out, relief flooding my veins.

Cyrus grabs my hand and pulls me back. I yank hard, trying to break free, glancing beyond Rainey for Bryce, but he's not there. Cyrus only grips me tighter, and when I turn to tell him to let me go, I'm confused by his expression.

I glance back to Rainey. "Where's Bryce?"

She stares at the ground, not acknowledging my question.

"Rainey, where's Bryce?" I ask again, a little louder.

She raises her head, her gaze meeting mine, tears running down her cheeks. My skin prickles and whatever breath I had whooshes out, as if someone has squeezed my lungs with a crushing blow.

Blackness envelopes me, and I'm falling with nowhere to land, as if I'll always be falling without any hope of relief.

"You were supposed to take care of him," I yell, struggling to get away from Cyrus, but he holds me firmly against him.

I want to hit Rainey, slap her, scream at her. A memory of Draya slapping my face after Lucien died surfaces and I go limp. It's not Rainey's fault Bryce is dead any more than it was mine Lucien died.

But it *is* my fault Bryce's dead. He was only in this because of me. I begged him to do it my way, and then I broke his heart.

Cyrus loosens his hold and turns me to face him. The first sob breaks free, followed by another, until they consume me.

# Consumed

## Evan

The days since Bryce died are still a blur. I remember
snippets — Talia's grief, Rainey's guilt, Jack's anger,
Lisa's tears. Rainey told us how the explosives went off
before Bryce even cleared the tent. She searched for him for more
than eight hours before giving up. I told her it wasn't her fault and
apologized for screaming at her, but I'm not sure that made a
difference.

Eddie's been doing his best to support both me and Talia, but
I've been pushing him away. There's nothing he can do for me,
but he can be there for Talia. Eddie says she doesn't blame me, but
I think he's just trying to keep me from spiraling any further.

Cyrus has been amazing. He holds me while I cry, leaves me alone to grieve in private, makes sure I eat and shower. It's as if he always knows exactly what I need. The problem is, I have nothing to offer him in return. If he minds, he doesn't let it show, but it must bother him. He needs a girlfriend, not the zombie I've become.

My mom, Joe, and my sisters arrived last night. Mom brought me a dress to wear to the funeral today. A freaking funeral. I've been to a few funerals in my life. For old people. Never someone so young. How am I going to make it through the day? I've been surviving in a fog of denial, but today is going to shatter that protective shell into a million pieces.

Mom and Eddie are surprisingly civil to one another, putting their differences aside out of respect for Bryce and for my sake as well as Talia's.

I take the emerald green dress with tiny white polka dots off the hanger and slip it on. It was Bryce's favorite color on me. He said it brought out the green in my eyes.

Someone knocks on my door.

"Come in," I say.

Mom enters, closing the door behind her. She studies me for a moment before settling me into a chair. Without speaking, she combs out my hair, piling it on top of my head and pinning it into place, pulling a few curls out to frame my face.

When she's finished, I slip into a pair of matching sling-back heels and examine the result in the mirror, but it's as though I'm seeing through myself.

Mom comes up behind me and wraps her arms around my shoulders. "You look beautiful, honey."

Her words are pointless. What the hell difference does it make how I look? I turn and head downstairs.

Cyrus is in the living room wearing a new tailored suit Eddie helped him pick out. With his clean-shaven face and some sort of styling product in his hair, he has a refined beauty I've never noticed before. He looks like one of the M Clothing models all the girls in school used to go crazy over.

He's more handsome than I've ever seen him, and yet I don't *feel* anything when I look at him. Why can't I feel?

Quinn and Liam, dressed in their finest outfits, stand beside Eddie. They rush to me, each taking one of my hands, and we walk outside, heading toward the elevators.

Mom clings to Joe while Eddie's arm is draped around Talia, holding her together. Cyrus reaches out to pick up Quinn before taking my hand and lacing our fingers. He squeezes gently, reassuring me he's here. He's always here. I don't think I could have made it this far without him.

We take the train from the lower level out to the beach where a small group of my friends are gathered on the boardwalk. Lisa hugs me, fresh tears pooling in her eyes. Colin wears a somber expression, and Ally is doing her best to remain stoic. Ty and Connor let go of Marcus and Sonia's hands and come over to hug me, then we all set off down the path to a grassy park nestled between the sidewalk and the sand.

Max stands with his fellow police officers, looking sharp in dress blues. For a fleeting moment, I wonder why Jack is in a navy suit instead of his uniform.

A petite middle-aged blonde with red-rimmed eyes and a flared charcoal dress approaches Jack. He wraps his arms around her while Max embraces Lisa. Max and the woman swap places and I realize she must be Jack's mom.

Max's eyes search mine before he pulls me into a hug. "Evan, this isn't your fault. You know that right?" he asks against my ear.

But it is my fault. We should have told Max what we were up to.

With his arm around me, Max leads us to another group of people standing under a large white tent. "This is Elisa Cooper, Michael's mother."

A beautiful woman with slate gray eyes reaches out a slender hand to me. Talia and Bryce definitely got their bone structure from her, but their dark coloring must have come from their father. I take her hand and swallow back tears.

"He loved you," she says, her voice kind, warm, loving.

I nod, not trusting myself to speak, and roll my lips inward to keep them from quivering. Taking a deep breath in through my nose, I let out a shaky sigh. "He adored you. He talked about you a lot."

She pulls me into her arms and holds me against her slight frame. She's comforting me, but I don't deserve it. Although somewhere in the back of my mind, I think maybe she's comforting herself by holding on to someone her son loved. She doesn't know I broke his heart, and I don't tell her. I let her believe in me, because she needs to.

She releases me and turns toward two girls on her left. "These are Michael's sisters, Rina and Bree."

They're gorgeous, but how could they not be? Both sisters reach out and hug me stiffly. Perhaps they know the truth. Maybe Talia told them.

My Uncle David arrives, escorting Rainey, Mateo, Will, and Ben. After more introductions and hugs, we take our seats and the service begins. There is no body and no ashes to scatter. This is a celebration of his life. The story is Bryce died in the line of duty, and he is getting a hero's send-off.

No one outside our group knows what he did, what he sacrificed for, how much of a hero he is, and that makes me angry.

When I'm angry is the only time I don't feel dead inside.

I take a seat on the patio and lean back against the cushion, rubbing my face with my hands. The door slides open, and Eddie walks out, carrying two glasses of scotch. He hands one to me.

"Thanks." I drop my gaze to my glass and notice gray squares instead of ice.

He chuckles softly. "Whiskey stones."

"What?"

"They cool the alcohol without diluting it."

"Genius." I take a drink, relishing the burn in my throat.

"She asleep?"

I nod and take another sip. It's been a month since we got back from taking down the Uprising, and for the first time, I'm beginning to wonder if what Ev and I have is going to survive.

Eddie sighs and leans forward, resting his forearms on his knees, his hands cupping his glass. "I just got off the phone with Max."

"Anything new?"

He shakes his head. Of course not, there never is. "His best guess is the group of kids they brought in are lying low, regrouping, but it's likely the Uprising won't be able to recover."

I run a hand through my hair and let out a sigh. "Any chance they're back out in the Ruins?"

"Max doesn't think so. They've been monitoring the perimeter."

So chances are, Draya's here somewhere, but Ev's in no shape to come with me, and I can't leave her like this. Everything is so fucked up. This isn't how it was supposed to be. We defeated the Uprising. We're supposed to be planning a future together. We were supposed to be *happy*.

"You know this isn't about you, right?" Eddie asks.

I lift my gaze to meet his. Logically I get that, but deep down it feels personal. If she's in love with me, why is she still so torn up over a guy she used to be with?

"She grew up differently than you did."

"I know—"

He puts up a hand. "Hear me out. She was raised to believe she has no more right to live than anyone else. She's struggling with what she did. On the surface, it seems like she's mourning Bryce, and she is, don't get me wrong, but not the way you think. His death represents every life lost that day, and she's taking it hard. She doesn't know how to cope with it, and I don't know how to help her. I'd hoped she'd talked to you…"

Setting my glass down, I stand and pace the small patio. "I tried. Hell, I've tried so many times to get her to talk, but she just shuts down, disappears into herself, it's like I'm making it worse."

Eddie stares at his drink for a long time before sighing and lifting his head. "Maybe she needs some time on her own."

"What do you mean?"

"I mean she's not dealing with it. She's worried about you, about how she's affecting you. I think she's holding a lot in."

I sink back down on the chair and put my head in my hands. "Did she say something to you?"

Loud silence is the only answer I need. I haven't wanted to see it, but now that it's out there, I guess I've known it all along. Even without all the guilt shit Eddie threw out there with Union life or whatever, she's got a healthy dose of survivor's guilt. I've been there myself, and I know her well enough to know she's trying to hide it from me, to protect me.

The rest of it, I don't get. They would have killed her or Marcus if she hadn't shot them. Ev's still never talked about what happened that day, but Marcus filled me in. How can she think defending herself is wrong?

"I suppose I could go out into the Ruins, check in with the others."

Eddie pushes up and pats my shoulder. "I know this isn't easy for you either, but some time apart might do you both some good."

"Yeah, okay." How the hell am I supposed to leave her when she's such a mess? It feels like a dick move, but at this point, I'll try anything.

I close the opening behind me and lean against the wall, staring at the endless trees spreading out before me. It's only a few days'

walk to the house from here, especially without the little kids slowing me down, but it seems more like a million miles. Blowing out a slow breath, I push off and start hiking.

Ev didn't seem upset or relieved when I told her I was going up to the border to check on everyone. She didn't seem to be...anything, but when I hugged her goodbye, she clung to me, burrowed her head into my chest, and I almost didn't leave.

Even now, I'm second-guessing my decision, hoping I'm doing the right thing by leaving her alone. Grief is hard enough, but grief coupled with guilt is a tough combination. Guilt I can't help her work through, because I don't think she did anything wrong.

Every step I take into the Ruins takes me one step farther away from her. Shit, I can't leave her. If this was the right thing to do, it wouldn't feel so wrong. Giving her space, sure, but I don't have to do that two thousand miles away.

It dawns on me I'm no longer moving. I'm not sure how long I've been standing here, but when I glance over my shoulder at the looming Union wall, I haven't walked far.

Turning, I take my first step back to where I belong.

I emerge from the tunnel into hazy sunshine less than a mile from the beach, and my bunched muscles begin to relax. The salty air, the sea breezes, and sand between my toes always have a calming effect on me.

The coastline up here is different from down south. Rocky, green, darker, colder, but it's where I first glimpsed the ocean.

When I close my eyes and think of the beach, this is how I envision it.

Eddie gave me a wad of cash, more than enough for a hotel, but I'd rather stay at a campground and earn my keep. As an official citizen of the Union now, I guess I can get a job.

When I reach the boardwalk, I sit on the concrete bench and untie my boots, stuffing them into the backpack. Slinging my bag over my shoulder, I make my way to the check-in tent. A young girl behind the counter smiles broadly, revealing a sliver of gum above large teeth. "Good morning, my name is Jessica. What can I help you with today?"

"I need a place to stay for a few weeks. I'm also looking for work. Do you have anything?"

Her face brightens. "Yes. We need a driver. Are you licensed?"

I shake my head. "No. Do you have anything else?"

Her face falls, and she genuinely appears disappointed for a moment. "Let me check. The season will be picking up soon, so we're just starting the summer hiring process, but our truck driver quit this morning. Can you hang on a sec?"

"Yeah." It's not like I have anywhere else to go.

She picks up a phone and I wander over and take a seat in one of the canvas chairs near the front. Jessica keeps one eye on me as she talks, and just before she hangs up, she gives me another one of her megawatt smiles.

"The manager's on his way up to talk to you."

"Thanks," I say, picking up a tablet from the table next to me and turning it on. I poke around on a couple of apps, but nothing grabs my interest so I set it back down.

After a few minutes, an average-looking dude enters the tent and zeros in on me. I stand to face him, wiping my palm on my pants. He's shorter and older than me, but his broad shoulders make him appear larger than his height would indicate.

He shoves his hand at me. "Hi, I'm Jeff. I'm the manager here. I understand you're looking for seasonal work?"

"Yeah, if you've got it."

"What experience have you had?" Jeff asks.

"None at a campground, but I have a lot of experience doing a variety of things."

"No vocation then?" he raises his eyebrows.

Shit, I drag my memory for conversations with Ev about vocations. She said she needed to choose something when she graduated, and I think she's only a year or so younger than me, so I should've picked something two years ago. I end up shaking my head, and Jeff doesn't question it any further.

"We need all the usual seasonal positions. Jess says you don't have your license, but you look strong enough to haul bags for guests and you can work in the mess tent. Do you have any physical limitations that would prevent you from performing those duties?"

"No."

"Okay." He runs his hand across his jaw. "Well, let's run you through the system and get you on board. When can you start?"

"Uh, today if that's okay."

Jeff's face lights up, and he turns and indicates for me to follow him to the desk. Jessica pulls out a small device and places it on the counter. It's similar to the one Simon used to collect my fingerprint out in the Ruins to get my Union credentials. I'm about to find out if what I paid for them was worth it.

I place my finger on the device and it beeps.

"It's nice to meet you Cyrus Matthews. Welcome to Woodland Park," Jessica says.

# Worth It

*Cyrus*

**B**efore zipping up my backpack, I check the space I've called home over the past month to make sure I didn't miss anything. Satisfied I have everything, I head up to the check-in tent to say goodbye to Jeff and Jess.

Jeff leans against the counter, talking to Jess. She lifts her head and throws me a smile, displaying bright white teeth. Unis have some glowing-ass teeth, I swear.

Jeff turns and shakes my hand when I approach. "Good luck. If you find yourself back this way again, we can always use you. You've got a great work ethic."

"Thanks, it was a good experience."

Jess walks around to hug me before planting a soft kiss on my cheek. I squeeze her back and give them both a quick wave before hiking back to the trains. She and Jeff are the only friends I made here. It was nice having someone to talk to.

I take the A-Train south, and anxiety churns in my gut the closer I get. I'm excited to see Ev, but wary of her reaction. By the time I finally enter the Western Province station, I'm close to losing my breakfast. I opt to walk the final distance to give myself some time to unwind.

It's a perfect, clear day, the beach visible even from here. The walkway to Eddie's place comes into view, and I pause, stretching out my shoulders and cracking my neck. With a deep breath I head to the front door and knock.

The door opens and a three-year-old mess of red curls and attitude stands before me. She smiles with recognition and launches herself into my arms. "Cywus!"

I wrap her up, lifting her off the ground and close my eyes. She smells like strawberries and fresh-cut grass. When I set her down, she takes my hand and leads me into the apartment.

"Is Evan here?"

She shakes her head. "No. She's at her mom's."

My heart dives into my gut. "When did she leave?"

She shrugs. "Daddy!"

Eddie ambles down the stairs, and he smiles genuinely, rushing up to give me a hearty embrace. "Cyrus, how are you? When did you get back? How is everyone?" He's a couple inches shorter than me, but still manages to hug me like I'm a little kid.

"Good. Umm…" I contemplate telling him where I've been for the past month, but I'm anxious to see my girl and don't want to get stuck in a long conversation. "I'm…looking for Evan. Quinn said she went to her mom's?"

"Yeah, back east." He opens the door wider. "Do you want something to drink?"

"No, I'm good. When did she leave?"

"A few weeks ago. Not long after you left." Shit, he makes it sound like I abandoned her. "She's staying in a hotel at the moment." He heads into the kitchen and starts writing something. He returns with a piece of paper. "Here's the address." An odd expression flickers across his features, but it's gone before I can figure out what it means.

"Umm…how is she?"

He sighs and runs a hand over his face. "Hanging in there. She's had a rough couple of weeks, but I think she's turned a corner."

Something like relief settles over me. This is good news, right? "Okay, well, I should get going."

He reaches out to shake my hand as Quinn wraps her arms around my legs. I reach out to ruffle her curls before taking off.

"She really does love you," Eddie says behind me.

I turn and glance over my shoulder at the father of the girl I love, appreciating the effort. I never felt like he wanted me to be with Evan, but him saying that now means something. I'm just not sure what. I nod and give him a tight smile before heading to the train station feeling even more unsettled than before.

## Evan

A seagull inches its way along the railing toward my feet, cocking his head and eying my bowl of cereal. I pick up one of the sugar-coated rings and toss it to him. He catches it mid-air, swallows and tilts his head expectantly. I shoo him with my hands, and he takes off toward the beach with an annoyed squawk.

This is the time of day I miss Cyrus the most. He needed to leave, I get that. Being around me had to be tough, but I hate that I haven't even heard from him in over a month. I guess it's too much to expect him to find a way to text me from the Northern Territories.

For a few fleeting moments after he left, I thought it might be easier with him gone, but I was wrong. I thought I was holding it together for Cyrus, so he wouldn't see how screwed up I was, or think I loved Bryce more than him, or that I was weak for not being able to handle it. It turns out, Cyrus was the one holding me together. Once he was gone, I fell to pieces.

Eddie made me go to a therapist, but it was a total waste of time. He sent me back to Mom when therapy didn't work. I think he just didn't know what else to do, but he said a change in scenery would do me good.

The first week, it probably did help. Mom took care of me, so did Joe, Katie, and Rachel. I even went to visit Uncle David. He's the only person I could talk to about everything, but being at his place reminded me of being there with Bryce, and I haven't been back since.

Eventually everyone fussing over me got to be too much, and I moved into a hotel. The one thing no one thought would be good for me turned out to be the best. Being alone has given me a chance to process everything the way I needed to. I've cried, screamed, and punched things, run on the beach, sat on my balcony for hours, thought about what happened instead of trying to avoid it. I'm still not sure how to deal with what I've done, but I don't let it consume me anymore.

More importantly, I figured out what's bothering me most about Bryce's death is that only a handful of people know why he died. What he did to protect the people of the Union. I wonder what would happen if they knew.

My tablet dings, indicating I have a text. I pick it up from the table beside me to find a message from Tony asking how I'm holding up. Clarity washes over me. Shit, why didn't I think of this before? I rush into the room and grab the phone to call him.

"Baxter, here," he answers with his gruff reporter voice.

"Tony. It's Evan."

"Hey, kiddo." His tone instantly softens. "How are you?"

"I got your text. Hey, um…I'm doing okay. I have an idea though."

"What's that?"

"What do you think about blowing the lid off of what's been going on around here? I think it's time we tell the citizens of the Union everything."

After hanging up with Tony, I came down to the beach to clear my head. For the first time since Bryce died, I feel a little more centered. Maybe when Tony and I are finished telling Bryce's story, I can put the things I've done, the kids I killed, into perspective so I can figure out what's next. Maybe by then Cyrus will be back.

I turn and trudge up the dry sand back to the pathway leading to my hotel.

"Hi, Mrs. Emerson," I call to the sweet elderly woman kicking back on the balcony next to mine. She's on her annual trip to visit the grandkids, but says it's too noisy to stay at the house with them.

"Hello, dear. How are you doing this evening?"

"Better."

"I'm glad to hear that. You're too young to be so sad." She says the same thing every night.

"Thanks, Mrs. Emerson."

"If you get lonely later, I'm going to be watching a movie with that Matthew Delacour you young girls like so much."

"I might take you up on that," I say with a quick wave.

I walk through the corridor from the beach to the hallway and let myself into my room. After packing most of my stuff, I hop into the shower and dress in a pair of lounge pants and a tank top. As I towel-dry my hair, I contemplate what to do about dinner, settling on a burger and fries from room service. When my food arrives, I take it out to the balcony to enjoy one last evening outside in the Eastern Province.

Feet up on the railing, I dip a french fry into ketchup and take a bite, the salty fried potato mixing with the sweet tomato-y ketchup on my tongue. The sun has moved behind the Union wall at my back, but the air remains warm, and there's enough light left for me to make out the silhouettes of people strolling along the sand. I finish my bottle of water and head inside to grab another out of the mini-fridge.

Someone knocks on the door while I'm chugging a fresh bottle, startling me. I wipe the excess water from my mouth with the back of my hand.

Must be Mrs. Emerson. She knocks again, a little more impatiently.

"Hang on," I call out, swinging the fridge shut and heading to the door.

I unlatch the deadbolt and crack it open. My heart slams to a halt in my chest and I gasp for air, as tears fill my eyes. The bottle falls from my hand, shattering against the tile floor, splattering my feet with icy water.

My fingers tremble as I undo the safety catch and throw the door wide. I take stubbled cheeks into my hands and kiss every inch of his face. His whiskers are rough beneath my lips, scratching me, but I don't care.

He wraps his arms around my waist and lifts me off the ground, closing the door behind him before stepping over broken glass. When he sets me down and steps back, he reaches out for my hands, his eyes running over me, head to toe. A slow smile spreads across his face, but I can barely see it through my pooling tears.

Pulling me back to his chest, he wraps me in a tight embrace and rests his cheek on my head. "Hey, Evansville."

# Healing

Evan

"Don't take this the wrong way, because you being here is the only bright spot in two months of soul-sucking agony, but where the hell have you been?"

He reaches for the hem of his T-shirt and starts to pull it over his head.

"Hold on there, cowboy, I'm not *that* happy to see you."

He chuckles but continues, baring his torso before turning around. I suck in my breath, and my fingers shake as I reach out and brush them against the angry burns on his back.

"Does it hurt?"

"Hell yeah." I snatch my hand back and he laughs again. "But not as bad as it did."

"Have you seen a doctor?"

"Not yet, but I will. I needed to see you first."

"Bryce, the longer you wait, the harder it'll be to avoid scars."

"You think I'm worried about how I look?" He tugs his shirt back on and moves closer, taking my face in his hands. "I had to know you were okay. That's more important."

I take a step back. "Why?"

He smiles. "You really have to ask?"

I swallow. "Bryce…"

He sighs. "What happened with Cyrus? Your dad said he left."

"You saw Eddie? When?"

"Yesterday, or the day before, I guess. I went to his place as soon as I got back. He filled me in on everything. I stopped by to see my mom, then hopped a train and came straight here."

"Am I the last person to find out you're alive?" I spin away and fling open the mini-fridge to grab a beer. "I can't believe you. Do you have any idea the hell I've been going through?" I yell, twisting off the bottle cap and flinging it at him.

"Hey, hold on." He puts his hands up in surrender. "You're not the last to know. You would have been the first if you'd been at Eddie's, but I didn't want to tell you over the phone."

Fresh tears pool in my eyes, and I turn my back, angrily shoving them away. I shouldn't be mad at him. Shit, an hour ago, I'd have given anything for him to be alive. And he is.

"What happened out there?" I ask.

"Can I have one of those?"

I return to the fridge and grab another beer and hand it to him. Pushing past him, I open the sliding glass door and head out to the balcony, sitting in one of the chairs. Bryce drops into the other and takes a long pull on his bottle.

"Everything went flawlessly at the first two camps. We ran into a little trouble getting out of the third and had to dodge some bullets. At the last camp things were going great. I set the charges and programmed the timers same as before. I was about halfway back to the spot where I was supposed to meet Rainey when it blew. I don't remember much after that."

"She said she searched for you for hours."

"The next thing I can recall was stumbling around, not being able to hear anything except the ringing in my ears. I knew I'd been burned. Not just my back. Both legs are pretty bad, too. I was disoriented but figured out I was outside the camp with no recollection of how I got there."

"Was it dark?"

"No. The sun was up by then. I looked for Rainey, but I couldn't hear, so yelling was pointless. I was pretty sure I had a concussion and knew I needed to stay awake. I wandered around for a while, trying to find the bikes, but I had no idea what direction I was walking. Eventually I couldn't keep my eyes open any longer. I found a place to lie down and closed my eyes for just a few minutes. When I woke, I was in a bed in a small room. A guy and his daughter stumbled upon me when they were out hunting. They took me back to their place and nursed me back to health."

"I still can't believe you're here," I whisper.

He turns toward me, his eyes searching mine for several long moments. To reassure myself I'm not dreaming, I reach out and run my fingers down his unshaven cheek.

He sighs and closes his eyes. "When I went to Eddie's, I only needed to know everyone was okay. I didn't plan to come see you. I mean I wanted to, but I didn't think I should..." He opens his eyes and bites the inside of his bottom lip. "What happened between you and Cyrus?"

My hand returns to my lap and I stare down at it. "I...I didn't handle your death well."

"I need to tell you something, but before I do, there's something I have to ask."

"What's that?" I ask, my voice quaking.

"With Cyrus gone...is there any chance for us? For you and me?"

"What? No!" I stand and move away from him. "We didn't break up. He went out to the Ruins. To check on everyone. They all went back after...after your funeral. Shit, Bryce..."

He drops his head. "I'm sorry. I had to ask." He finishes his beer and sets it on the table before getting up and heading back inside. I follow him, not sure if he's leaving, but he stops at the mini-fridge and grabs another bottle before returning to the patio.

He takes a sip and stares out at the ocean, his elbows resting on the railing.

I take my seat and watch his back for a few moments. "So what did you need to tell me?"

He downs half his bottle and swallows hard, never turning to face at me. "The girl, the one who found me, we slept together."

"Okay…" I find it odd he's sharing this with me mere minutes after asking me if we still have a chance.

He drags his eyes away from the coastline and turns to me. "She's pregnant."

My mouth falls open, and my eyes bug out of my head. "She's what? Is it yours?"

He scowls. "I wouldn't be telling you any of this if it wasn't."

A sudden surge of fury floods my veins. "Wait…you just asked me if we had a chance, knowing you're having a baby with someone else? What part of my fucked up childhood made you think I'd be okay with that?"

"I don't know!"

"So you were going to abandon her and come back to me?"

Anger flashes in his gray eyes. "No. Seriously? You think I'd do that?"

"What am I supposed to think? You ask me if we can be together while some other girl is carrying your baby? Come on, Bryce! Or were you thinking we'd raise the baby?"

"I don't know. I don't know anything." He runs a hand across the top of his head and drops back into his chair. "I just found out. Like the night before I came back."

"She didn't tell you until the night before you left? Are you sure she's pregnant? Because some girls will—"

"Yeah. I'm pretty sure, anyway. She wasn't trying to trap me, if that's what you mean."

"How do you know?"

He turns back toward the darkened coastline. "She seemed more upset about it than I was. I doubt this was her plan either."

"Where did you leave things with her?"

"I told her I had to come home and take care of some stuff, but I'd be back. I'm not in love with her, and she's not in love with me. She's hung up on some other guy." He lets out a cynical laugh. "Story of my life."

My anger begins to dissipate, and I sit back in my chair, putting my feet up on the railing. "You'll be a good dad. You don't have to get married to do that."

"Yeah, I know." He finishes his beer and stands. "I should probably go."

"Where are you going?"

"Get a room or something."

"Bryce…you can stay here tonight. You don't have to leave. I just got you back."

"Are you sure?"

I roll my eyes. "I wouldn't have offered if I wasn't."

He gives me the full-dimpled smile and leans back. We spend the next few hours talking about everything that went down that crazy night two months ago.

Sunlight streams through the hotel window as dawn breaks across the ocean. Rolling over, I bump into Bryce. He lies on his back on top of the comforter in a pair of pajama pants and not much else. The burns wrap around his torso, stopping shy of his belly button. He's so beautiful and so alive and so not dead anymore. My heart feels light for the first time in months. I allow myself to watch him breathing for a few minutes before slipping out of bed and closing the drapes. He might as well sleep for a while.

I head into the bathroom and quickly dress, grabbing my pre-packed bag from the chair by the door. Before sliding out of the room, I write Bryce a quick note, letting him know where I'm going and why. He's got an appointment at the hospital this afternoon and will probably be there for at least a week as they genetically map and print new skin for him.

Hopefully I'll see him again before he goes back out to the Ruins to be with the girl who's having his baby. Hell, if Tony and I can accomplish what I hope we can, he can bring her here. Instead of telling Bryce's story, we can tell *our* story, the story of all of us and how we brought down the Uprising. It's the only way things are going to change, and things *need* to change.

I head to the A-Train station and buy my ticket. While I wait, I pull up my text app and stare at it, trying to figure out what to say to my mom. Simple is best, and I decide on, *Mom, I'm heading back to the Western Province. There's something I have to do. Everything is going to be okay. Really. I'm good, better than I've been. I'll explain everything soon. I love you.*

The train pulls in and I find a seat in an empty row and settle in before typing a short note to Eddie letting him know I'm on my way, and I'll check in with him after I meet with Tony. My last text is to Tony, telling him I'll be there tomorrow afternoon.

I turn my tablet off and stuff it back in my bag. Reaching up into the overhead bins, I grab a pillow and blanket. All cuddled up, my thoughts drift to Cyrus. I wonder where he is. If he's not back by the time Tony and I are finished, I'm going out to the Ruins to find him.

The slowing of the train pulls me from a deep, dreamless sleep, something I haven't experienced in what feels like a lifetime. My shoulder aches from pressing against the side wall. I sit up and stretch my neck, looking around. We're not approaching a station. Why the hell are we stopping?

I peer out the window, trying to figure out what's going on. Maybe the train is malfunctioning, although that almost never happens. A murmur rises through the car as my fellow passengers voice my concerns aloud.

Across the aisle, a guy stares at his tablet, his eyes widening. His head pops up and his horrified gaze locks with mine, sending a chill through me.

"What's wrong?"

"We're being boarded."

"What? Who's boarding us?"

"A bunch of people with guns. They call themselves the Uprising."

The chill becomes ice, freezing my blood in my veins.

Two words repeat in my head: *We failed.*

*The end*

# Dear Reader

Thank you for reading *The Uprising*. As an independent author, gaining exposure relies on readers spreading the word, so if you have the time and are so inclined, please consider leaving a short review on Goodreads, Amazon, or your favorite site for books.

*The Uprising* was originally written only from Evan's point of view. But so much happened when Evan and Cyrus were apart, that they spent far too much telling each other what was going on, it became unsustainable. Over the past two years, I've re-envisioned this as a dual POV story. Getting inside his head was challenging and fun, and started with *Found*, the story of *The Union* from his point of view. I hope he'll grow and develop through the rest of the series as much as Evan does.

To stay up to date on the latest releases and get access to exclusive content, including *Found*, be sure to sign up for my newsletter: http://thhernandez.com/newsletter.

## The Union Series

# Acknowledgements

Thanks, as always, to my wonderful husband, Ernie. He gives me the ugly truth, even when no one else will. Because of him, this story is so different from the earlier draft, and so much better.

Thanks to my parents for giving me everything – love, encouragement, support, and most of all, life.

Thanks to my fabulous children for your ideas, your love, laughter, and morning cuddle time.

Thanks to my fantastic beta readers, Bethel, Carine, Ernie, Ilona, Inês, Jamie, Jen, Jennifer, Judy, Karen, Karole, Kathy, Kayla, Macy, Mattea, Meredith, and Todd.

Thanks once again to my badass cover artist, Mark Sgarbossa, for such an amazing cover, I had to force myself to stop staring at it and get my edits done!

Thanks to my wonderful editor, Barbara Trageser, for polishing my writing to a sparkling shine!

To super talented graphic artist, and one of my BFFs, Suzi Walker, for the wonderful interior graphics.

And, finally to Jen D. for all your support, your honest feedback, for making me laugh, and letting me unload when I need to.

# About the Author

T.H. Hernandez is the author of young adult books. *The Union*, a futuristic dystopian adventure, was a finalist in the 2015 San Diego book awards in the Young Adult Fiction category.

She loves pumpkin spice lattes, Comic-Con, Star Wars, Doctor Who marathons, Bad Lip Reading videos, and all things young adult, especially the three young adults who share her home.

When not visiting the imaginary worlds inside her head, T.H. Hernandez lives in usually sunny San Diego, California with her husband and three children, a couple of cats, and a dog who thinks he's a cat, often referred to as "the puppycat."

You can find her online at:
Website: http://thhernandez.com
Newsletter: http://thhernandez.com/newsletter
Twitter: https://twitter.com/TheresaHernandz
Facebook: https://www.facebook.com/thhernandezSD

To stay up to date on the latest releases and get access to exclusive content, including the story of The Union from Cyrus's point of view, be sure to sign up for my newsletter: http://thhernandez.com/newsletter.